Dancing on Deansgate

FREDA LIGHTFOOT

Dancing on Deansgate

CANELO

First published in the United Kingdom in 2003 by Hodder & Stoughton Ltd

This edition published in the United Kingdom in 2020 by

Canelo Digital Publishing Limited
Third Floor, 20 Mortimer Street
London W1T 3JW
United Kingdom

A CIP catalogue record for this book is available from the British Library.

Print ISBN 978 1 78863 797 8
Ebook ISBN 978 1 78863 666 7

Look for more great books at www.canelo.co

Printed and bound in Great Britain by Clays Ltd, Elcograf S.p.A.

In memory of my dad, who died during the writing of this book, aged eighty-two.

He assisted with the research, which was most helpful of him. When just twenty, he was a new recruit in the Manchester Regiment at the start of the war, and had to dig bodies out of the rubble caused by the Christmas blitz in 1940. Any spare time he was allowed he would spend at local dances as he needed relief and loved the big band sound. His beloved wife, my mum, taught him how to dance, a hobby they enjoyed their entire life together. He is still greatly missed.

For information on the dance halls of Manchester I am grateful to the books of Phil Moss published by Neil Richardson. I recommend them to anyone with happy memories of that time.

Chapter One

Christmas 1940

It was dark in the cellar so the girl felt quite safe in not pulling down the blind, despite blackout restrictions. At least the darkness within helped her to see better what was happening outside in the street, although the light was fading fast on this grey December afternoon.

The gentle brown eyes were just about on a level with the pavement as she peered up through the grimy window set high in the wall. Had anyone taken the trouble to look in, they would have seen how huge they appeared in the pale oval of her face, which bore the marks of her mother's beauty yet with none of its brittleness. These cheeks were round and soft, the chin square and firm, giving an air of strength to the wan features. Even in the semi-darkness, light glimmered in the long strands of shining fair hair. Looking for the world as if it had been cut with a knife and fork, Jess made no attempt to keep it tidy but allowed it to sweep carelessly about her face. Perhaps she believed it offered shelter from the world and hid the fear, which filled her wide, startled eyes.

Her vision was limited through the grille that covered the window, and what little she could see was obscured by booted feet as shoppers dashed along in search of last minute presents, turning the snow underfoot to a grey slush. War or no war, it was still Christmas.

Somewhere, beyond the periphery of her vision, she could hear a band: the Salvation Army playing 'Hark the Herald Angels Sing', and despite her fear that the raids might start again at any moment the sound brought a strange excitement and a quickening of her pulse. The soft, rose-pink lips broke into a wistful smile for, at sixteen, Jess Delaney wanted to be out amongst the crowds listening to the band, to be a part of the festive scene instead of missing all the fun, confined as she was in her own private hell-hole night after night. At first she'd made little complaint, not seeing it as important but simply another of her mother's eccentricities.

Now it was all too serious.

They were calling it the Christmas Blitz. It had started a few nights ago and in no time the whole of Manchester had seemed to be in flames, making everyone fear for their life. Enemy bombers had come again the next night, following the line of the canal system right into the heart of the city, pounding the life out of it for hour upon hour. Amongst others, Piccadilly had been hit, the Victoria Buildings destroyed, as well as damage done to the famous Free Trade Hall. A landmine had even fallen on Victoria Station.

Who would know if one small house were bombed and a young girl lay buried beneath it? Who would bother to come looking for her? Jess would much rather have gone to an air raid shelter along with the rest of Deansgate Village, but her mother wouldn't hear of it.

'Don't lock me in,' she'd protested as she'd watched Lizzie apply the scarlet lipstick to her full mouth, frizz up her hair and generally attempt to make herself as appealing as possible. Lizzie had several weaknesses, but the main ones came, as she herself was fond of saying, either in a glass or a pair of trousers.

'Don't you start your moaning. I've no time to listen, not now. I have to pop out for a while. Anyroad, you'll be safe enough in the cellar. No jerry bombs'll get you here. Solid as a rock is this house.'

She always offered so-called words of comfort in a tone of voice that sounded careless and disinterested. Jess was all too aware that she'd learned from long experience it wasn't wise to trust her. Lizzie never put anyone's needs before her own, not even those of her own daughter. Being a mother wasn't the be-all-and-end-all in her life.

Having children had never been a part of her plan and she'd apparently been shocked to find herself up the duff with Jess. If she hadn't fallen with a baby at the tender age of sixteen, she might never have married Jake Delaney, and claimed she would still have been free to enjoy life. She half blamed Jess for this perceived misfortune, and also Jake for being so quick to march her down the aisle. He'd insisted he was pleased, that he loved her, that he liked kids and wanted three or four, and had been disappointed when no more than Jess had come forth. What he didn't realise was that his wife had taken precautions, determined not to repeat her mistake.

Jess's beloved father, Jake, was now involved in the war. How badly she missed him. Not that her mother did, right now no doubt meeting up with his brother Bernie, whom she clearly adored. They'd had fun together for years, largely because he had a way with him that Lizzie simply couldn't resist, convinced that she'd married the wrong

Delaney brother. Her only disappointment was that he wasn't prepared to leave his wife for her. In Bernie's eyes, Cora was only one step removed from the Virgin Mary herself, which must make Lizzie feel as if she was some sort of Mary Magdalene, or worse.

But then Uncle Bernie was no oil painting; a big bruiser of a man with a beer belly and a bossy nature. His pale grey eyes with their short, stubby eyelashes would often narrow to slits, the fleshy mouth tighten and the flabby jowls shake with fury if Lizzie or members of his family didn't do as he ordered. There was no mistaking these warning signs. Disobeying him could result in a clip round the ear, or worse.

Now, all Jess could do was listen to the street door bang shut and, with a sinking of her heart, watch her mother's feet in their inappropriately high heels trip by the window above. She was no doubt off to meet up with him at the Queens on the corner of Potato Wharf, where he'd buy her glasses of port and lemons.

The liquid notes of the bugles and trumpets were making Jess ache with the need to get out, filling her with a deep longing to be a part of this festive scene. Music always affected her. But although this would be the second Christmas Eve of the war so far, not forgetting the countless other nights she had spent incarcerated in the cellar while her feckless mother went out on the town, Jess didn't feel any more resigned to her fate than she had on all those previous occasions.

She began to scratch and scrabble with her fingertips, desperately trying to prise open the window so that she could breathe the crisp cold air. If she were a butterfly or a bird, instead of a girl with blond hair and long, gawky legs, she could fly out through the grill, spread her wings and be free.

Jess pressed her cheek against the cracked pane wishing that her best friend, Leah, would materialise out of the gloom, yet knowing it to be unlikely. Leah would be fully occupied serving toasted teacakes to pretty ladies in smart hats at Simmons's Tea Room on the corner of Deansgate where she lived with her parents. She frequently complained about the long hours she had to spend serving tea and washing up, though she would at least be warm, as well as certain of a good meal when she was done for the day and climbed up the stairs to the flat above.

There was never any such treat for herself. No doting mother standing smiling at the cooker, ready with a hot plate of home cooked dinner. And no one to listen to her woes.

Jess shivered. She'd tried to provide what comforts she could for the hours she must spend locked in here, a bed of sorts, blankets and a hot water bottle, which quickly went cold. Yet, as always, it felt cold and damp in the cellar as well as dark. But once she lit the lamp, she would have to close the blind and then would feel shut off from the world outside, from the people in the street and the hustle and bustle of Christmas. She'd be quite alone, save for her books and her mouth organ, and one miserable Tilly lamp, at least until Lizzie returned to let her out. She always promised to be no more than an hour, two at most, yet would stagger home in the early hours, roaring drunk and often with a sailor on her arm.

Jess dreaded those occasions when she could hear the distant squeals, gasps and screeches of her mother in the throes of a drunken passion. She didn't care to imagine what went on behind the closed door of her bedroom, but the close proximity of a young daughter never stopped Lizzie making an unholy row about it. Not that Jess lacked too many details on the great mysteries of love and passion. Lizzie had made sure of that, brutally explaining to her daughter how to keep a man happy. And she'd also seen the messy results: the bruises and bites from her mother's more ardent suitors, the furtive applications and doses. It all seemed most unsavoury and not in the least Jess's idea of love and romance.

She realised that the music had stopped, that a hush filled the air. There followed the penetrating wail of the siren, which brought a chill to her spine and set her heart pounding like a drum. When she heard the low drone of enemy aircraft approaching, Jess knew bombing was going to start all over again.

The house shook with the clatter of explosions, the rumble of buildings collapsing all around. The sky turned blood-red as down by the canal basin warehouses were set on fire. Even here in the cellar Jess could smell the burning, see great balls of greasy cotton flying about, spreading the fire at lethal speed. Feet were running by the grill in panic, Christmas shopping forgotten, as survival became the only consideration. There were screams and cries as people fell, or lost track of loved ones.

From her worm's-eye view, Jess could see it all. One elderly woman was knocked flying, bags and basket cata-pulted from her arms, gifts trodden underfoot as others with less patience pushed past. Jess felt sure it must be the end of the world, that any second the roof of her prison would fall upon her head and squash her flat like a fly.

Turning away from the tiny grilled window to cower in the farthest corner, she wrapped her arms tight about her head, blocking out all sensation, save for that of raw terror.

Chapter Two

The all clear sounded when it was growing too dark to see anything. How long had the raid lasted, she wondered? A couple of hours at least, so it must be after seven, maybe eight by now. Not that it made any difference to Jess what time it was. She was still locked in the cellar with no sign of Lizzie who hadn't come rushing home to see if her daughter had survived. Jess uncurled herself from her cramped position in the corner and made her way over to the window.

Outside, there was activity of a different sort, people starting to pick up their lives and go about their business once they were able to. Irwell Street had got off lightly this time, so far as Jess could tell.

Who knew what tomorrow might bring but for now she could hear laughter somewhere, loud chatter, and even a few flippant notes on a bugle. Her neighbours were clearly counting their blessings and resolving to carry on, like the stalwarts they were. Patriotism ran high here in Manchester. Not for a moment did they mean to weaken. It was then that she heard a voice calling her name.

'Jess, is that you? Are you down there?'

'Leah?' Peering up through the gloom and grime she could just make out the pale outline of her friend's face grinning down at her through the pavement grille above the cellar window.

Leah was as dark as Jess was fair, with bright blue eyes and a pretty, heartshaped face. She was a little older and quite sophisticated at seventeen. Nothing ever seemed to get her down as she positively bubbled with fun and laughter. Much as she loved her friend, Jess envied Leah her ability to laugh at life. She'd quite lost the knack of that herself.

'Cheer up, it's Christmas,' Leah said, as if reading her thoughts. 'We need to get you out of there. Where's the key?' She didn't ask why her best friend was spending Christmas Eve locked in the cellar, having seen her in a similar situation too many times before. She understood about Lizzie, and wouldn't dream of intruding on Jess's family affairs unless information was actually volunteered.

'Hanging on the hook behind the kitchen door.'

'Right, hold on a tick.'

Her face vanished from the grille and Jess felt an aching pain somewhere below her ribs. How would Leah get in to the kitchen? Lizzie would surely have locked the door before she left. Or she might have forgotten to put the key back on the hook and taken it with her.

The minutes ticked by, seeming like hours as she waited for rescue. Any last shreds of hope had quite gone when suddenly there came a scratching at the lock and then the cellar door swung open and Leah appeared before her, looking mightily pleased with herself.

'Nearly got caught by old Ma Pickles when I climbed over the back yard gate. Well, don't just stand there. Mother has mince pies for supper and you're invited.'

'Oh, I thought you'd all be staying down in the shelter.'

Leah gave a little spurt of laughter. 'On Christmas Eve? Ma wouldn't allow even Mr Hitler to ruin her Christmas, not when she's spent so many hours preparing for it. We must fly the flag, she says. So come on, shake a leg, we've even got some of Mr Ruggieri's ice cream to go with them.'

As so often with her friend, Jess felt as if a great black cloud had lifted, that the sun had come out and life was worth living again. Carefully closing the cellar door behind them and putting the key safely back on the hook, the two girls slipped out of the house with helpless giggling at their daring and swung, arm in arm, along the street singing loudly to the strains of 'There's a Bluebird on my shoulder'.

–

Jess sat, pink-cheeked, in front of a blazing fire in the crimson and gold living room with its fine mahogany furniture and solid Victorian piano just as if she were a part of this family. She marvelled in silent wonder as they teased and joked with each other, shared amusing stories from their working day and generally seemed to enjoy each other's company. Even the usually stiff and formal Mr Simmons looked surprisingly relaxed, sitting in his wing chair smiling benignly upon his offspring, making jolly remarks as he smoothed his bristly moustache.

She felt as if she was in paradise. Earlier, they'd all listened to the King's College choir on the wireless, and Jess had been utterly enthralled. It had seemed amazing that you could simply turn a knob and hear such beautiful sounds coming out of a box.

Now they all stood around the piano while Leah played a medley of carols for them to sing in loud, happy voices. Mr Simmons with his deep baritone and Mrs Simmons straining slightly at the high notes. At one point, Jess very daringly brought her mouth organ from out of her pocket and accompanied Leah as she played 'Silent Night'.

Mrs Simmons was delighted. 'My dear girl, that was lovely. You see, we shall enjoy Christmas, in spite of Mr Hitler's efforts to the contrary.'

Afterwards, a maid served tea in a white apron, and the mince pies, as with all the Simmons's baking, were utterly delicious. Jess savoured every mouth-watering morsel. How they managed to get the fat to bake such wonderful tarts, let alone the fruit and sugar that went into them, Jess couldn't imagine but instinctively knew that in no respect would Muriel Simmons have broken the law. Unlike the Delaneys, Jess's own family.

Uncle Bernie and his progeny of good-for-nothing, layabout rogues were forever seeking a way to get around regulations, looking for the quick scam and an easy way to make a bit of brass. Aunt Cora did her best to control those sons of hers, with no support from their father. Roughnecks, hooligans, spivs, call them what you will, every last one of them was a Delaney to the core.

Jess missed her own father badly, and not counting her scatter-brained, pathetic, hopelessly inadequate mother who was a huge embarrassment to her, there was really only her aunt who she cared about. A big, jolly woman, she was a bit of a card was Cora, but then she needed a strong sense of humour having married into the Delaneys, who, as the whole of Deansgate was well aware, spelled Trouble with a capital T.

The Simmons's family were famous with the mill hands and dockworkers for their hot pies and currant buns, generously filled and sensibly priced. One step up from the Co-op, many a new bride had enjoyed her wedding reception within the tea room's cream and burgundy surrounds, and any number of people had been 'buried with ham' at moderate cost, served by suitably unobtrusive waitresses.

'And how is your dear mother?' Mrs Simmons politely enquired in her soft, carefully modulated voice. Plump and matronly but supremely elegant with her swept-up hair, pleated skirt and powder blue twin set pinned at the collar with a tasteful brooch, she was the kind of mother Jess would have loved to have, despite Leah loudly complaining about her high expectations and strict rules. She was caring and yet perfectly controlled, and with exquisite taste.

'Very well, thank you.'

'Is she in employment at the moment?'

This was a question to which Jess was accustomed and she answered with smooth, if ambiguous, dexterity. 'She helps Uncle Bernie from time to time.'

'Ah, down at the docks. How useful. And yourself, are you still working on the Market, dear?'

Jess admitted that she did still work at Campfield but was keeping an eye open for something better. It was lively and fun working on the indoor market but Jess was ambitious, keen to better herself, though she wasn't quite sure how.

'Have you thought what you might do next?'

She shook her head. There was something about the kindness of this woman, which often left her tongue-tied. Even the scent of her Lily-of-the-Valley perfume made Jess feel very slightly grubby and unclean, not really fit to be seated on plush velvet cushions in this rarefied atmosphere of gracious living.

Muriel Simmons seemed to understand and merely smiled more sweetly than ever. 'Well, do come and speak to my husband before you make any final decisions, won't you dear? He is sometimes in need of help in the shop since girls come and go with alarming frequency. He may well have a position at some time in the future, for a fine young lady such as yourself.'

'Thank you, I'll remember that.' It troubled Jess that she had no clear vision of what she wanted, how her life might turn out, or where she was heading. Deep down was the fear that she might end up like Lizzie, wasting her life completely by turning into a feckless tart, or drinking herself into a stupor to blunt the reality of failure. Did she even have the brains or the talent to do anything worthwhile? Jess knew that she longed for a bit of lightness and fun, of which she'd enjoyed precious little in her life thus far. Her heart cried out for independence and freedom. Getting away from Irwell Street and that dreadful cellar would be a start, what she most yearned for at the moment.

'Another mince pie, dear?' Mrs Simmons asked, breaking into her thoughts.

'No, thank you, I couldn't eat another thing. Besides, I'd best be off.' Jess glanced at the clock on the mantelshelf, a solid gold piece with a pendulum that swung ponderously to and fro, the fingers pointing to half past nine.

There would be hours yet before Lizzie came home but she didn't like to intrude further on the Simmons's generosity. She got up to go, carefully folding her napkin and placing it by her empty plate.

'As you wish dear. Leah, show your friend out. I expect we'll see you tomorrow. You must pop over after your Christmas lunch and show us your presents.'

Jess almost laughed out loud. Christmas lunch? Presents? That would be the day. No doubt Lizzie would be in Queens pub or The Donkey till closing time. A sharp pain of disappointment stabbed under her ribs at the prospect of the bleak Christmas Day ahead but she ignored it. Where was the point in fretting? Things could be worse. At least they didn't starve. Lizzie always made sure there was food on the table, even if it was basic and Jess the one to cook it. They certainly wouldn't be having goose as the Simmons family were. But why worry, the war would be over soon, everyone said so, then her dad would come home and everything would be different. Lizzie would have to behave then.

Remembering her manners, Jess smiled at her hostess. 'Thanks for inviting me. Those mince pies were delicious.'

'Well, there's still time to buy some for your dear mother. The shop will be open till ten tonight.'

'I'll mention it to her when I get back,' Jess lied, backing to the door. It was never wise to linger too long or Mrs Simmons might start getting curious and asking awkward questions.

More aware of what went on at the house opposite than she let on, Muriel Simmons slipped four of the remaining mince pies into a paper bag and handed them to Jess. 'Perhaps she's working late tonight and won't have time

14

to call in. Give her these from me, with the compliments of the season.'

Jess blushed bright pink but was not so foolish as to refuse this act of kindness, charity though it undoubtedly was. These mince pies might be the closest she got to pleasure this Christmas, and again she expressed her thanks, more fervently this time.

Leah led her down the stairs to let her out through the shop. 'I can't wait for Christmas, can you?' The shop bell clanged when she opened the door but the two girls behind the counter were too busy serving to take much notice. 'See that you pop over before lunch if you can.'

Jess willingly agreed in the hope she just might be asked to stay. She never had been invited to anything other than tea at the Simmons's house in all the years she'd known Leah, but she lived in hope that this might change as she grew older and proved herself to be both polite and well mannered. Jess always paid careful attention to the way Mrs Simmons held her napkin or used a cake fork. Such niceties might well come in useful one day.

She waved goodbye and set off quickly across the now silent, dark street. There'd been no further air raid warnings, no more sirens to send folk scurrying back to the shelters, thank goodness.

The Salvation Army Band had stopped playing and were standing around chatting and drinking hot tea from their flasks, their faces glowing like pale ovals in the soft light from their carefully shaded lanterns, instruments set aside while they took a breather.

Intrigued, and reluctant to return to the confines of the cellar on this night of unusual and precious freedom, Jess wandered over for a closer look. There had been many nights in recent months when the sound of her mouth organ's plaintive notes was the one thing that had kept her sane. She loved music, a passion she shared with her father. This thought brought a sudden vision of him to mind. Jess could smell the fresh scent of the Lifebuoy soap he used, the Woodbine cigarettes he smoked. She could hear the rap made by the toecaps on his clogs as he came up the lobby each evening after work, feel the vibration of his cheerful laughter as he held her in a great bear hug; but most of all she recalled the hours her dad had spent teaching her to play the mouth organ, and even allowing her to try a few tunes on his piano accordion and trumpet, at which he was an expert.

These sweet memories brought a funny tightness to her chest and Jess had to take a few quick breaths in order to ease it before anxiety over his well-being overwhelmed her and she dissolved into tears right there in the street.

As she crept nearer, her toe knocked against something hard, so that it fell over with a clang. Bending down she scrabbled about in the darkness till her fingers closed about an instrument. A bugle, she guessed, by the shiny feel of it.

She glanced about her. The band members were happily gossiping as they made inroads into a huge mound of sandwiches. No doubt they'd be playing for some time yet. Then, as the pubs closed, they'd collect up the worst of the drunks and take them to the mission hall to sleep it off till morning. Jess smoothed the flat of her hand over the instrument, savouring the seductive shape of it, the smoothly polished surface. It was a miracle that such a small, insignificant object could make such marvellous sounds. She put it to her lips and blew. The note rang out, pure and clean and true, echoing along the darkened street, instantly bringing the gossiping band to a stunned silence.

'Who's there? Who's playing that bugle?'

Jess dropped it with a clatter and fled, desperately aware that someone had set off in pursuit after her.

She was in such haste to avoid being grabbed and leathered for her cheek in blowing a Sally Army bugle, that she didn't notice the chink of light creeping out around the blackout blind in her mother's room. She ran around to the back, let herself in and was halfway down the steps to the cellar when she heard the scream. She recognised it instantly as Lizzie's and, coming so soon after the sweetness of the bugle's call, it seemed all the more horrific, making the hairs stand up on the back of her neck, freezing her to the spot and chilling Jess to her very soul. Then without pause for thought, she called out her mother's name, turned and flew back up the stairs.

Chapter Three

Jess stood at the open bedroom door, paralysed with fear, uncertain whether she should intervene or run for help. To her utter shock and dismay she found there wasn't one man but two in the room, each punching hell out of the other. One moment they were clasped together in a macabre dance, the next rolling on the floor, fists flying, pummelling each other like fury. The night-light that usually sat by the bed had got knocked out and little could be seen beyond shapes and shadows. The smell of blood and fear was palpable, the sound of loud grunts, the crack of fist on bone, and over all the echo of Lizzie's screams. Both men seemed oblivious to her desperate efforts to intervene as she flopped between them like a rag doll, at times suffering the brunt of the blows. But then, without warning, one shook himself free, like a dog ridding himself of drops of water, and fled from the room.

Lizzie called out a name that Jess didn't quite catch, probably because the word was cut off by another blow from the remaining assailant, one that sent her mother sprawling.

'You stupid whore! Have you no sense? You don't do nowt without my say-so. Right?'

If Lizzie made any response, Jess couldn't make out what it was. For several more terrifying seconds she remained rooted to the spot, as the man again turned his fists on her mother. She was lying curled up, whimpering on the rug while he slapped her, each crack splitting the air like a thunderclap. It was the force of the blows that finally galvanised Jess into action.

'Stop that! Leave my Mam alone!'

Jess flew at him, punching her own pathetically small fists into his broad back, her fingers desperately trying to get a grip on his jacket to drag him off Lizzie. He rose up on a roar of rage, tossing her aside so that Jess fell back, cracking her head on the floorboards while he thundered down the stairs to vanish into the night.

For some seconds she lay stunned and dazed, before the sound of Lizzie's sobs brought her round, and Jess struggled to her feet to go to help her mother.

Mother and daughter clung together, Lizzie sobbing while Jess attempted to mop up the blood and tears from a face already turning purple with bruises. She had a bust lip and one eye so swollen it was nearly closed and already turning black. Somehow Jess got her into bed but the next twenty-four hours was a nightmare as Lizzie drifted in and out of consciousness. Jess did her best with cold compresses, blankets and hot cups of tea, leaving her mother alone only as long as it took to nip round to Ma Pickles and ask her to send young Josh to fetch the doctor.

Doc Lee finally arrived late in the evening on Christmas Day. He pulled up Lizzie's eyelids, checked her for broken bones, prodded her with his stethoscope and offered little more than two aspirin and a few strong words of advice.

'She'll live, though whether she deserves to is another matter. Do try to keep your mother off the booze, Jess, if you can. It'll kill her if she goes on in this fashion.'

'It wasn't the booze that made those bruises on her face,' Jess hotly protested, unexpectedly feeling the need to defend Lizzie.

Doc Lee already had his hand on the door latch, his mind moving on to his next patient, as if he'd no time to waste on no-hopers without the wherewithal to pay his bills. Jess saw he would offer neither sympathy nor help. She wanted to tell him that Lizzie hadn't always been this way. Couldn't he see that?

'I try my best, but how can I stop her?'

He paused to smile down at her, revealing himself as a kindly man if perhaps somewhat inured to misery by his chosen profession. 'Because you're made of sterner stuff, Jess Delaney, and despite your exasperation with having such a mother foisted upon you, you love the old besom. No, don't deny it, I've seen it in the way you care for her. Have you any idea who did this to her? One of her drinking cronies, I'll be bound.'

Jess had not got a clear view of Lizzie's assailant in the shadows of the gloomy bedroom. She'd been too wobbly on her feet from her own injuries to attempt to chase after him, but in her own mind was quite certain who it was, utterly convinced as to the identity of the culprit. Uncle Bernie was the one who beat Lizzie up, though who the other man had been she couldn't even guess. None of this she had any intention of revealing to the doctor and shrugged her shoulders helplessly. 'I wouldn't know. I didn't see his face.'

Doc Lee frowned at her, as if sensing some prevarication in the dismissal, but then recalling his busy schedule he shrugged and turned to go. 'Get her along to the Mission Hall. The Sally Army are experts at salvation, even if you're not. It might not be too late. Lizzie is her own worst enemy. If you don't put a halt to this hell-bent ride to destruction she's on, then look to yourself. Otherwise you'll sink with her.'

Jess let him out of the back door, thinking that if she hadn't dented one of the Sally Army's bugles, she might well have acted on this advice. What a Christmas this had turned into! So much for the hope of lunch at the Simmons's.

She slid the bolt into place after the doctor had gone, then rested her forehead on her clenched hands and sobbed her heart out. Why did she have to bear such burdens? Why didn't her Mam look after her instead of the other way round? How was it possible to love her mother as a daughter should, when much of the time Jess felt exasperated and infuriated by Lizzie's stupidity?

Oh, why couldn't she be like any normal mother?

When her hiccupping sobs finally quietened, Jess brushed the tears away with the flat of her hand and went to build up the fire so she could brew a pot of tea. She longed, in that moment, for her dad to be here; couldn't seem to stop thinking about him. Why didn't he come home to help, or at least on leave to see them now and then? She hadn't even had a letter this week, or last, come to think of it. So far as she could remember there'd been nothing since that Christmas card in early December.

There'd always been a certain amount of jealousy and rivalry between the two brothers. Jake was the good looking one. He was honest and hard working, having had a good job at a local saw mill. Bernie always claimed his brother would never have done so well had it not been for the care he'd given him when they were growing up, keeping him out of a home for one thing.

In a way that must be true for having lost both their parents in an epidemic of smallpox while still young. Bernie had made himself responsible for his younger brother and fed them both, largely by living off his wits. Family legend had it that he'd tried everything from running errands, cleaning windows and washing up, to packing and loading down at the docks as well as scrubbing decks. Jess was only too aware that this honest endeavour hadn't lasted long before his true nature had asserted itself and Uncle Bernie had found easier ways of making a living – by nicking stuff.

But although Jake appreciated Bernie's efforts on his behalf, he strongly disapproved of his brother's behaviour once he'd grown up. He took great pride in saying so, a fact that always irritated Bernie.

Lizzie had once explained to Jess that one of the greatest sources of rivalry between them came over their choice of wife. Bernie had opted for the easy-going Cora Garnet, a homely, anxious-to-please type. Making no claims to beauty, Cora was simply grateful that someone as lively and go-ahead as Bernie Delaney had ever looked her way. Lizzie, on the other hand, had been far more attractive with long, curling hair and a shapely figure, eager to enjoy life to the full. Her flirtatious, grey-green eyes had once positively sparkled with mischief, showing an eagerness to taste life, which Jake quite liked. And despite her robust refusal not to be taken for granted, she'd been a loving, caring mother, at least in the early days.

Then Bernie Delaney had pushed his oar in and everything had changed. Jess could pinpoint the date exactly. The last Christmas before the outbreak of war. The two families had made a point of always spending Christmas together and, apart from a few minor squabbles over who was to cook the turkey or provide the pudding, it had always passed off pleasantly enough. Until that day!

Her mother had been wearing a new dress, a rose pink satin rather shorter than her usual style, and with it a pair of black, silk stockings, which showed off her long shapely legs to perfection. Bernie made one or two ribald remarks about her new saucy look, and then quite out of the blue said, 'Come on, why not show off those glamorous pins of yours, so we can all admire them.'

Jake was livid that Lizzie had been prepared to lift her frock to show off her legs and silk stockings, saying she was deliberately encouraging Bernie to fancy her. Lizzie accused Jake of overreacting and provoking Bernie into a row. Jess was packed off to bed but she could hear them arguing furiously long into the night.

Thus had ended family Christmas's forever. Sadly, what had also ended that day was the trust between husband and wife. From that moment on their marriage slid steadily downhill. Jake began to watch his wife more closely, to question her every move: why she was late home from the market, who she'd seen or talked to that day, where she was going of an evening; even if it was only for a bit of a crack in a neighbour's house. Lizzie would scream and yell that he was finding her guilty without even a trial, believing the worst because of Bernie's uncouth behaviour.

Then Jake would be full of apologies and beg her to forgive him. In defiance, Lizzie went out all the more. Suspicion that there was something going on between his brother and his wife, began to fester within him. By the time Jake went off to war, his accusations, blame and misery, had done their worst. Since Lizzie was indeed guilty of flirting with his brother, a coldness, and an increasing distance had chipped away at whatever affection she had once felt for the man she'd hastily married.

Finding herself alone once he'd left, she'd let Bernie into her bed and apparently revelled in the excitement of it, happily accepting the large amount of drink he offered her. She consumed it to blot out a few pangs of guilt, which gradually robbed her of every last shred of self-esteem and remnants of common sense.

Bernie still said that she was no good. Jess feared that he had destroyed her.

Now Jess lifted the spluttering kettle from the hob, poured a drop into the teapot, swirled it about to warm it then emptied the water down the sink before brewing the tea. Next, she fetched Mrs Simmons's mince pies from the tin in the larder where she'd put them for safekeeping on Christmas Eve, and laid them carefully on a plate. She set this with the two mugs on a tin tray. If ever they'd both been in need of something tasty, this was the moment. They'd had nothing to eat all day save for a slice of toast and dripping, and Lizzie had hardly touched hers. If Jess had the time and energy to think about it, she'd probably find that she was very hungry indeed. She didn't dare to imagine how wonderful roast goose might taste, never mind the homemade Christmas pudding Mrs Simmons might also have provided her with.

'Here you are, Mam. Can you sit up? Do you want me to hold the cup for you?'

Lizzie looked upon her daughter with brimming eyes. 'Eeh lass, what would I do without you? I'd be like a bobbin with no thread. I'm not fit to be a mother. Nor to kiss the ground you walk on.'

'Don't start getting maudlin, Mam. You're stone cold sober, remember? Buck up and see what Mrs Simmons has sent you, with the compliments of the season.'

Lizzie looked at the mince tarts in wonder, then her mouth went square and she began to cry in earnest, her nose running and words spluttering out between gasps of tearful self pity.

'Look at me, forced to take handouts. What a failure I am! I'm no use as a mother. I could never manage to bake such delicious pies myself were I to live to be a hundred.'

'You don't have to when the Simmonses can do it for you. Come on Mam, eat one at least.'

With great patience and diplomacy, Jess calmed her down sufficiently to persuade her to eat half of one of the tarts. Lizzie loudly protested that her face ached too much to manage any more, so Jess finished off every last crumb of the remaining three without a trace of guilt. After that, she settled her mother down for the night, refilling her hot water bottle, bringing her a glass of water and another aspirin, tucking in the bed clothes before finally falling into bed herself, utterly exhausted.

Chapter Four

A day or two later Bernie came round, clearly on his way back from The Donkey, and, having acquired a skin full, was even more full of himself than usual. He deposited himself with a bump in the only decent chair and let out a great burp, patting himself on the chest as if he'd achieved something momentous.

'So what's wrong with you?' The expression on his brutish face was one of carefully composed innocence. 'The holidays are as good as over, so it's time to get up and do a bit of business.'

He was dressed even more flashily than usual in a loud, green checked suit with a white silk muffler about his neck in place of a tie, which exactly matched the handkerchief that flopped, dandy-fashion, from his breast pocket.

Jess instantly protested. 'What sort of business? She's not well enough to go out.'

He hooked his thumbs in his waistcoat pockets and glowered at her from beneath bushy brows, his spiteful eyes taking darting glances to capture a quick inventory of every item in the room before settling reflectively upon Jess herself. A smile crooked the corner of his moist mouth, causing a dribble of spittle to trickle down onto his chin. 'Are you suggesting that I don't have your mother's best interests at heart?'

Jess wanted to throw up whenever she looked at him, and wouldn't have been in the least surprised had a snake's forked tongue flickered out from between those thick, blubber-like lips. His skin always appeared shiny and slick with sweat, and he was fond of combing thin strands of brown hair that curved over his baldpate with short, stubby fingers. He was doing it now as he waited for her reply.

'Well, do you?' Jess challenged him. 'You never think of anyone but yourself.'

'What did you say?' he mildly enquired, cupping one hand behind his ear. 'You'll have to say it again. I'm not sure I heard right.'

'You heard right enough.' Jess could feel her heart pounding behind her rib cage. She really didn't know where she was finding the courage to stand up to him. She must be mad, or maybe her brain was turning to mush. And then she recalled how it had been this man's great, podgy fists that had battered poor Lizzie to a pulp.

Perhaps this was as good a moment as any to tell him to leave her mother alone; to follow Doc Lee's advice and warn Uncle Bernie that if her Mam continued drinking and carrying on in this fashion, she'd be a goner. Surely then he'd see sense and let her alone.

Unfortunately, Lizzie chose precisely that moment to make an appearance. She'd no doubt heard Bernie's voice and thought it best to come down. She'd put on her best frock, but her face and hair still looked as if she'd gone ten rounds in a boxing ring with her hands tied behind her back.

Her brother-in-law glanced up at her and raised bushy brows in an affectation of surprise. 'By heck, that's a proper shiner. Which of your lover boys gave you that then?'

Lizzie judiciously made no comment. Jess moved at once to the hob and poured boiling water into the teapot. It was a poor solution to their troubles, but tea was all they had. That and a stale half loaf fit only for toast.

Bernie wasn't in the mood for such niceties. 'Get your coat on,' he ordered, jerking his chin in the direction of the understairs cupboard where it hung behind the door. 'Don't pour one for either of us, we're off out. Like I say, there's a bit of business I want your mam to do for me.'

Lizzie put a hand to her face. 'But what'll folk say about my bruises?'

'They know to keep their noses out of my business. Put some pan-stick on, it'll be right enough.' So saying, he picked up her handbag from the table and tossed it to her. Lizzie did as she was bid. By the time she'd caked her face with the orange tinted powder and daubed her lips with scarlet lipstick, she looked like a sad and garish circus clown. But her glance warned Jess to say and do nothing, as she meekly followed Bernie from the house.

He led Lizzie up Dolefield and along Bridge Street towards Deansgate so that he could avoid passing his own house on Cumberland Street, where he might be spotted by Cora. He kept a firm grip on her wrist, as a reminder on who was in charge. Not too sure what events from the other evening Lizzie could remember, he'd decided to make no further comment about that. Least said, soonest mended, wasn't that what folk said? She'd probably been too drunk to realise who had hit her, though there was still one small matter to be cleared up.

'I reckon you've stepped a bit out of line, Lizzie girl. And need a nudge back. Wouldn't you say?'

'You know I meant no harm, Bernie love. I was only having a bit of fun.'

'Course you were. But we can't have you pleasing yourself when and where you have it, now can we? You seem to forget who's in charge here. This chap what you've been seeing, Jimmy somebody or other? Quite a generous sort is he?'

Lizzie cast him a sideways glance through spiky lashes gummy with sleep and the Vaseline she'd quickly put on to tart herself up, and waited to see what he would say next. She feared Bernie when he sounded at his most reasonable.

'He brought you presents, I shouldn't wonder. Paid for your tricks, eh?'

'Only the odd packet of fags, Bernie, nowt special.'

Bernie gave her a fierce shake, making her teeth rattle, shoving her down a back alley where they wouldn't be disturbed. His grip on her arm was tenacious and Lizzie whimpered with fear. 'If you don't want any more bruises to add to the ones you already have, you'll let me be the judge of what's special, right? He could've been useful to me, had you shown the sense to introduce us. These sailors pick stuff up from foreign ports. But you kept him to yourself, which disappoints me greatly. I thought I could rely on you better than that, girl.'

'Oh, you can Bernie, you can. Like I say, we were just—'

'Having a bit of fun. Aye, so you said. Like I say, I'll decide when you can trip the light fantastic, assuming you deserve to. It comes to something when I'm forced to follow you to find out what you're up to. That's not good, Lizzie, not good at all. I don't like it, you know what I mean?'

'Oh, I'm sorry, Bernie. I really am. I meant no offence. I would have seen you all right, you know I would, if he'd given me owt worth sharing.'

'Would you indeed? That's a laugh.'

'You'll not hurt me again, will you Bernie, love?'

'We'll have to see how sorry you are, won't we? Whether you're going to be a good girl from now on.' Well lubricated with beer, he was feeling a bit randy so after a quick glance to make sure they weren't about to be interrupted, Bernie unbuttoned his flies, pushed up her skirt and thrust himself into her, giving her a good pounding.

'Stop whining,' he growled, when she complained he was banging her head against the brick wall.

It was over very quickly. It gave him great satisfaction to see his brother's once gloriously attractive wife do as he pleased with her skinny, worn out body. How it would enrage Jake if and when he ever found out what he was up to. Loyal as Bernie was to Cora, he resented the fact that it was his wimp of a brother who had nabbed this beauty. He was the one who should've had the best looking girl, just as he should have the most money and the best of everything, being the eldest and the one who had suffered the most. He deserved it.

While Lizzie fussed about making herself presentable, Bernie lit up a cigarette, drawing the smoke deep into his lungs as he considered the situation. It had been hard graft for years keeping body and soul together. Mind, he'd soon recognised that working for others was a mug's game and had started siphoning off a bit extra into his back pocket, though he'd been careful not to overdo it so that he didn't get caught.

But what did Jake know about that? He could barely remember the hard days before his parents had taken sick. Being only six at the time, ten years younger than himself, Jake could barely remember the beatings their dad had given them, the days when they'd lived on scraps from other folks's dustbins because there was no work to be had, or the times Mam had taken the two boys out begging on the streets. Bernie had wept very few tears when they'd died, and had managed to survive due entirely to his clever skills. Not that Jake had shown proper gratitude, simply taking his efforts for granted, even daring to criticise his style of operation.

Since then, everything had seemed to fall neatly into his young brother's lap. He'd done well at school, was liked by all his teachers and never got the strap. What's more, he had a stunning musical talent, which won him any number of friends and applause, then he'd landed himself a good job before marrying the best-looking bird around. Serve him right if she turned out to be troublesome. Now he'd turned himself into a tin pot hero by volunteering to join up, and was apparently in line to be made sergeant.

Bernie watched with interest as Lizzie bent over to adjust her stocking tops and suspenders for she still had a nice pair of pins on her, even if the rest of her did look a bit well used. He licked his lips in anticipation at what lay ahead at the end of the evening. He'd have her again later, at a more leisurely pace this time. Lizzie was always more accommodating after she'd been knocked about a bit. Women needed to be sharpened up, which did them a world of good. In the meantime, he dragged his attention back to the business in hand. 'Now then, this Jimmy, he frequents the Top Hamer on Byrom Street, did you say?'

Lizzie smoothed down her skirt and nodded.

'And he's worth a bob or two. He does usually carry a wad, right?'

'I don't know. Why d'you ask, Bernie, love? What is it you're going to do?'

Bernie shook her again and this time his grip on her wrist was so tight Lizzie thought it might cut off the blood supply to her fingers. 'When it's your turn to ask questions, I'll let you know. All right?'

'Yes, Bernie.' She wondered if she dare tell him he had a smudge of her scarlet lipstick on his cheek, but decided against it.

'It's time this Jimmy character paid for the bother he's caused. I hope you've learned your lesson to do as you're told, girl.'

–

He took her straight to the pub and there was Jimmy, sitting with his chums as usual. Lizzie heartily wished that for once he'd stayed on board his ship and got on with the maintenance work or whatever it was they were berthed here for.

'Now all you have to do is get him on his own and persuade him to buy you a drink. Bernie slid a small packet into her hand. While he's getting it, you slip this into his. It should quieten him down nicely. Got it?' He tapped the side of his nose with a nicotinestained stubby finger and winked at her. 'You can leave the rest to me.'

Lizzie wanted to ask what effect this would have on her lovely Jimmy, and what Bernie intended to do after that, but she didn't dare. One glance into his frosty, pale eyes and she could only silently nod. It'd be a broken cheekbone next time if she disobeyed him. She knew that for certain.

'Put on your best smile, girl. We don't want him to suspect owt, now do we?'

It all worked with terrible predictability. Jimmy was delighted to see her, instantly offered to buy her a drink and didn't notice as she slipped the powder into his beer while he was away at the bar. He drank his 'Mickey Finn' without a trace of suspicion, too occupied in showing his concern for the state of her face, and explaining why he'd thought it best that he made a run for it the other night in the hope of saving her further suffering before the police were called and things turned nasty.

Lizzie smiled and nodded, thinking how weak men were and feeling a nudge of regret that Jimmy should be as much of a let down as all the rest. It didn't take long for him to lose the thread of the conversation. Bernie came in just as he slid into unconsciousness.

The pair of them half carried him out the door, laughing and joking as if he were simply the worse for booze. Once safely around the corner in a back alley, Bernie propped him against a wall and stripped his pockets bare. He was indeed carrying a thick wad of notes, along with a gold watch and a cigarette lighter. Bernie stowed them all in his own pockets, then as Lizzie bent to check if Jimmy was all right, he grabbed her arm and pulled her away.

'That'll teach him not to interfere in my affairs. Now we need to put as much distance as possible between us.'

Lizzie made no protest as he dragged her along the street; glancing back only once at the figure still slumped on the cobbles. But not for a moment did she imagine that Bernie had done this out of a fit of jealousy. It was the fact she'd not shared her winnings with him, nor given him his cut that had got his dander up. She realised what she should have known all along: that he didn't give a toss about her, that all his sweet talk about fancying her was just so much flannel. And didn't she have the bruises to prove it?

'Can I go home now, Bernie? I've a bad head on me tonight.'

But he wasn't done with her yet. 'No, you flipping well can't. Just one last trip around the shops then you can have your Christmas, even if it is a bit late.'

'What d'you want me to do next? Have I not done enough?'

'There you go again, always asking stupid questions. You owe me money, Lizzie Delaney, right? So get cracking.'

She tried to object, saying how she thought it was too risky. 'Bernie love, what with the Christmas sales there are too many people about.' She didn't say 'I'd stand out like a sore thumb with this face on me,' though that's what she thought.

Bernie took no notice of her protests. 'Button your lip and do as I say without any argument.'

He led her from shop to shop, methodically working his way along Deansgate, down King's Street to St Anne's Square and the routine was always the same. He kept the assistant occupied with his chat up lines, while Lizzie filled her pockets with whatever little items took her fancy. Sometimes he told her exactly what to take and she mutely obeyed. In Lewis's she tucked two pairs of leather gloves into the inside pockets of her coat, and slid some nice costume jewellery into her bag. From Taylor's, she purloined a few packets of Passing Cloud cigarettes. Last but not least, she grabbed several tins of salmon from a stack tucked neatly behind the counter in a small grocer's shop near Shudehill while Bernie waited outside.

Lizzie had almost begun to enjoy herself by this time, savouring the excitement and relishing the thrill of the risks, as she always did. She hurried out of the shop, about to suggest they nipped back to Kendals as she was in need of some new shoes, but could see no sign of Bernie anywhere. It was at this point that she came face to face with the policeman.

Chapter Five

'Woman gets three months for stealing six cans of salmon,' it stated in the local papers, followed by some caustic comments on the failure of the government to stamp out black market profiteering. Jess was appalled to read this and discover that her mother had been arrested for theft. Heaven knows what stuff she'd nicked. She'd apparently been nabbed the minute she stepped outside a shop, the manager was sharp enough to notice her and had quickly sent a young lad off to call the police.

Coming to visit her in Strangeways, Lizzie told her how she'd had to stand in line before the prison warder and patiently wait to be divested of her last remaining dignity. 'Not that I had much of that left anyroad. I lost the voluptuousness of my youth years ago.'

All evidence of her mother's former glory had clearly gone, leaving in its wake a thin, string bean of a woman with a pale fragility about her. Her cheeks were flattened and sunken, making her nose too prominent and bony. Her once richly coloured, wavy curls hung in greasy strands on her shoulder, all straggly and unkempt, badly in need of a wash. Even her eyes seemed to have lost their grey-green sparkle, looking pale and lifeless as a washed out dishrag. Where was the glamorous allure, the flashy bravado she'd once been famous for? What a stupid woman she was.

'Why were you so foolish as to do such a crime, and how long will you be locked up here?'

'Three months.' Lizzie's eyes filled with a sudden gush of tears. 'I was stripped and thoroughly investigated in every orifice, given a bath with a large dollop of disinfectant in the water and more dumped on my hair till I stank to high heaven.'

'Accept your lot, Mam, then come home and never do such a stupid thing again.'

'Stop nagging, and don't feel the need to visit me. Not good for you to be anywhere around this prison.'

Watching her daughter march off in a huff, Lizzie recalled how she'd tentatively scraped the rough bristles of the bath brush over the bruises Bernie had given her that covered her back and skinny ribs. Even the warders had asked a few awkward questions about these but had quickly lost interest. No doubt they were used to such sights. It was sad that she'd lost all her hopes and dreams. Lizzie had once imagined that she'd fallen on her feet proper in marrying Jake Delaney, but then it had all gone wrong. He'd accused her of being flirtatious with all and sundry and abandoned her as a consequence. She'd been relieved when he'd joined up in the war, as that put an end to the constant bickering between them.

When they were first married Lizzie had worked at Gatrix's, but once she'd had Jess, she'd never fancied getting a proper job again, and flogging herself to death doing war work wasn't her idea of fun either. After Jake left, his brother had taken over her life. No Delaney worth their salt believed in wasting unnecessary effort unless it was absolutely necessary, not if there was an easier way to make money, so why should she object to Bernie's demands? Save for his tosspot of a wife, the saintly Cora, she'd be chortling with glee to be close to him.

But what would happen to Jess now?

Admittedly the girl was bright, sensible and practical, so much so that there were times when Lizzie had felt herself to be the encumbrance. Now having a convict for a mother wouldn't help her to get any good job she'd hoped for, let alone pay the rent on their home. So far as Lizzie could see, there'd be no hope for either of them after this time in jail.

In complete silence the warden handed Lizzie a night-shirt and toothbrush. Dressed in regulation cotton dress, woollen stockings and flannelette underwear, she was led up a metal staircase, along a landing to where a door stood open. Lizzie was ushered inside the cell.

'Not quite the Ritz, is it?' she drily remarked, but turning to check if the officer would give her an answering smile, she only found the door banged shut in her face. Lizzie thought she would never forget the sound of it closing, or the rattle of the key in the lock as it turned, no matter how long she lived.

–

Jess had been living with Uncle Bernie and Aunt Cora for a whole month and, despite her aunt's efforts to make her feel wanted, absolutely hated it. Every morning she would prepare breakfast for her three cousins, Harry, Bert and Tommy before they went off to work down at the docks, as well as for Sandra who was nine and went to Atherton Street School. This must be the first honest work the three lads had ever done in their lives. The older two were only doing it in preference to serving in the forces for which at twenty-two and twenty they were eligible. Strangely, it was skinny little Tommy who, at seventeen, was itching to be called up, much to his mother's dismay.

'You couldn't push an 'ole in an echo,' she'd say, 'let alone fight Germans.'

Poor Tommy would flush and protest. 'I might not have put on much weight, Ma, but I'm fair strong.'

'Eat your breakfast then and shurrup. You've legs on you that a linnet would be proud of.'

It was proving handy for Bernie to have his sons involved in loading and unloading at the docks where they could keep an eye open for broken crates and other goods that chanced to go astray.

'One never knows what might fall off the back of a lorry,' he'd say.

It was also easy to overload a van with more meat or other rationed goods than had been accounted for, and send it off on a slight detour. Bernie had a growing list of shopkeepers glad enough of anything they could get not to ask too many questions.

While Jess was seeing to the older boys, Aunt Cora would slop about in her carpet slippers and tatty old blue dressing gown, happily chivvying her family.

'Look sharp. No dilly-dallying allowed here.'

Most of her attention was given to attending to the five year old twins who had just started school and were referred to by Bernie as the result of pilot error, which Jess didn't think was very polite. She liked the twins, again both boys: Seb and Sam, and would much rather have made breakfast for them rather than those hulking great lumps. If she ever spoke to nine-year-old Sandra, the girl would glower at her and sulk or make spiteful little comments.

'We don't want you here. Who said you could come and live with us?'

'Your dad, actually.'

'Well, don't think he can be *your* dad too. He's mine.'

'Don't worry, you're welcome to him. My Dad is in the war, yours isn't.' And Sandra flounced off in a huff.

Harry, the oldest, greediest and biggest show-off of the brothers, would shovel porridge into his mouth at record speed along with several slices of bread and whatever else was going, washed down by copious amounts of tea. He also complained loudly if Jess didn't have his snap tin and brew can ready the minute he was ready for off.

'And put more sugar in it this time,' he instructed, making a double decker sandwich comprising of a cream cracker plastered with syrup wedged between two thick slices of bread. Jess watched in horrified fascination as he took a huge bite and managed to talk as he chewed, dribbles of butter and syrup running over the stubble on his unshaven chin.

'We haven't enough points for more sugar. You get what we can spare.'

'Don't talk to me about points and ration books,' he said, spitting cracker crumbs all over the tatty oil cloth that covered the kitchen table. 'Me dad always has plenty.'

Bert chipped in, 'Don't be so mean, our Jess. I like it sweet too. Ladle it in, we can get some more,' Taking the spoon from her, he scattered sugar everywhere, knocking over the milk bottle in the process. It made her wonder, not for the first time, how the Delaney family managed always to have so much food in their larder and be so care-less with it, when everyone else was making do with a dab of marg or an ounce of corned beef. She wasn't so inno-cent as to put it all down to Cora's skilful housekeeping. No wonder poor Lizzie had ended up the way she had, having been dragged into Bernie's nefarious schemes.

There was never any sign of Bernie at breakfast. Cora always made him a bit of a fry-up later, once she'd got everyone out of the house and he had time to eat in peace. Lucky Bernie, Jess thought, as she managed no more than a few spoonfuls of the porridge and a quick slurp of tea before dashing off to work at the last minute, gritting her teeth and slapping tears of self-pity from her eyes.

It might well be true that her uncle's life had been hard. Not that that was unusual on the streets of Manchester, particularly during the Depression years, yet not everyone turned into a petty criminal. He was fond of reminding them how he'd acquired his skills at the school of hard knocks, bragging about how the amount he earned in his wage packet had only been half the story and a quarter of the profit. None of that excused the way he'd treated Lizzie.

This shoplifting episode was simply the latest in a long history of abuse, and the worst to date. Coming away from the magistrate's court after seeing her sent down and visiting her in Strangeways, Jess had felt aggrieved and concerned for her mother.

'She'd never be in Strangeways if it weren't for you. She should've been home with me that night, safe in her own bed, not picking pockets and shoplifting. It's a wonder you have the gall to look me in the eye after what you've done.'

'I didn't teach her to nick stuff. She learned that trick all by herself. Makes her feel good.'

'I assume you encouraged her and took your cut.' Jess had felt all hot and bothered, terrified about what was going to happen next. To Lizzie, and to herself.

Bernie had simply smirked. 'Eeh, I do like a lass with a bit of spunk who knows how to speak her mind. I admire you for sticking up for your mam but the problem with our Lizzie is that she doesn't think big. She's not clever enough, bless her. She's like a magpie lifting a few pretty trinkets and knick-knacks here and there. Complete waste of time, as she's bound to get nicked in the end. Where would you be today, little lady, without me? You'd have no home for a start. Come to think of it, you can't stop in Irwell Street on your own, not a young girl like you. Not now your mam's in t'clink,' he'd said, filling her with shock and anguish.

'I'll be all right on my own, ta very much. I'm sixteen, nearly seventeen. I can manage to look after myself well enough, as I have been doing for years.'

'Nay, I'll not be accused of child cruelty on top of everything else, so I'll have no more lip from you, miss. Get your bags packed. You'll come round to ours.'

And so the worst period of her life had begun. Bernie had let out their old house and she'd moved into their overcrowded little house on Cumberland Street. Jess had made up her mind that this was only temporary. Once her Mam was released, they'd find another house, or a room to rent somewhere. Then they could make a fresh start. She meant to take much better care of Lizzie in future, keep her out of pubs and well away from sailors. And Jess would make absolutely certain that her mother had nothing whatsoever to do with Uncle Bernie and his nasty schemes. How she would achieve this miracle, she'd no idea, but she'd certainly try. Hadn't he done enough damage already?

–

As the weeks slipped by Jess came to resent the fact that everyone seemed to go out of their way to keep Bernie happy. What was so special about her uncle that he had to be given such treatment, so that his entire family tiptoed around him as if he were some sort of god?

One afternoon, when she and Aunt Cora were enjoying a warming cuppa after she'd got back from the market half frozen, Jess risked asking her why she'd married him.

'Because he was a real bobby-dazzler in them days, and I wasn't. Truth is love, I were bullied by my school mates something shocking for being a bit on the plump side like. One day two girls tied me up with their skipping rope and sold ink pellets at 'appenny a time for the other girls to throw at me.'

'Oh, that's dreadful!'

'It wasn't very nice, no. My mam gave me gyp when I got home, I don't mind telling you. Anyroad, Bernie spotted what was going on and he went for them. You should have seen them girls run.' Her plump jowls shook with laughter as she recalled the moment. 'He made it clear that if anyone had a go at me in future, they'd have him to deal with.'

'I see.' Jess understood perfectly, even if she did think it dreadfully sad that Cora had been fooled into seeing Bernie Delaney as some sort of hero. Ever since then Cora had been his adoring slave, accepting all he told her as gospel, content to devote her entire life to waiting upon him, hand, foot and finger, without complaint.

But what about his sons? What caused them to be so meek and mild?

Leah was mystified when Jess explained it all to her as they sat together by the Irwell near the old Botany warehouse.

'Bernie is always given the largest share of pie or portion of meat and them big lads of his never say a word despite the fact they're both working at hard, physical jobs down at the docks.'

She explained about Cora, how she buttered his bread for him, tied his tie, fetched his *News of the World* or *Manchester Guardian* whenever he wanted it.

'Heavens!' Leah giggled. 'Does she scrub his back for him on a Friday night as well, do you think?'

Jess nodded and her eyes twinkled. 'Not that we're allowed to witness it, mind. She shoos everybody out while Bernie does his ablutions, so who knows what they get up to. Happen she gets in the bath with him.' Both girls fell into fits of giggles at the very idea.

'I don't think women that old can have sex, can they?' Leah wondered out loud, and Jess laughed.

'Lizzie seems to manage it without any difficulty.' And then she slapped her hand over her mouth as she realised what she'd said.

'It's all right, Jess. I won't say anything wrong about your mam. I don't believe half what they say about her anyway. Go on with telling me about your uncle, and these cousins of yours. What are they like?'

Jess knew only too well that more than half of the rumours about her mother were indeed true. Leah might be a year older than herself but she was years younger and a sight more naïve than herself in that department. Muriel had protected her daughter, perhaps too well. Not wishing to consider Lizzie's current situation Jess gladly continued with her tale.

'You'd like Tommy. He's grand, about your age and desperate to join up, unlike the rest of them Delaney lads, dozy cowards that they are. There's big and boastful Harry, and daft Bert. I suppose there's more to them both than that, but it about sums them up. Cora's twins, Sam and Seb, are lovely, but Sandra seems to have a permanent scowl on her face. I don't think she likes me being there. She sulks a lot and rarely speaks to me, not even to pass the time of day. She doesn't say much to anyone, come to think of it, but then she's not expected to, being only a girl.'

'You could try setting her an example of what a thinking woman can achieve in life when she sets her mind to it.'

Jess laughed, which Leah often made her do with her fancy, middle class way of looking at things. 'Fat chance. She's spoiled rotten by her dad, whom she worships. Even Aunt Cora will do anything to stop her going into one of her moods. But I still can't understand why no one ever disagrees with Uncle Bernie, not even his sons, so far as I can see. You'd think they'd want to challenge him now and then, wouldn't you?'

'Perhaps they're a bit afraid of him, so pretend to do as he says and yet quietly go their own way,' Leah shrewdly suggested. 'We can't let chaps have things all their own way. No matter what his family does, *you* at least, must stand up for yourself.'

'Oh, I do, don't you fear.' And they grinned at each other in perfect accord.

'Are you very unhappy living with your aunt and uncle, Jess? I could always ask Mother if you could stay with us for a while.'

Jess looked at her friend askance. 'What, me being the daughter of a jailbird bunking up with you? Oh, I can't see Mrs Simmons approving of that.'

Leah vigorously protested. 'Mother isn't at all snooty or toffee-nosed, though admittedly she does fuss at times. She understands about Lizzie and her... problems. I could ask her about the possibility of a job for you after Easter. Would that help?'

Jess gave a keen nod, flushing with shame in the face of such generosity. 'That'd be grand.'

'Consider it done. I know what's wrong with you,' Leah said. 'You need cheering up. Isn't it your birthday soon, that should liven you up. You'll be having a party, I expect?'

'Don't be daft. They've no plan for that.'

'Oh Jess, that's awful. You don't turn seventeen every day of the week.' Leah fell silent for a moment, stunned that any family could choose to ignore such a significant event. Then she brightened. 'I know, we'll celebrate on our own, and what better way than to go dancing.'

'Dancing?' Jess gazed at her friend wide-eyed, as a flicker of excitement burst within her. She'd never been to a dance before, nor even listened to a dance band, but loved music so Leah's suggestion was a good one. Turning seventeen was something special, which should indeed be celebrated. 'I'd love that, but I've no idea how to dance.'

'I know a few steps. I'll teach you.'

Chapter Six

They practised their dance steps night after night in Leah's bedroom over the teashop on Deansgate, with only a very old wind-up gramophone playing a cracked record of indeterminate vintage that had belonged to Muriel in her younger days. Neither girl was particularly adept, although what they lacked in style they more than made up for in enthusiasm. They were quite certain it would be much easier with an actual dance band.

With her usual thoroughness Mrs Simmons stepped in to arrange for the two girls to have proper lessons at Winters Dance Academy. Mr Simmons stoically agreed to act as dance partner each evening to help them practise the basic steps while his wife offered endless instructions on the etiquette of the ballroom: such as how a girl was not obliged to accept an invitation but must sit out a dance completely if she should refuse a prospective partner for any reason.

Leah and Jess listened most attentively, for all they were desperate to laugh, knowing that Mrs Simmons's real motive was that she believed this to be an excellent opportunity for her daughter to find an attractive husband, preferably a rich one.

As the big day drew near, Leah announced her decision. 'We'll go to the Plaza on Oxford Street.'

Jess gasped. 'But isn't that a very grown-up sort of place?'

'So what? With a bit of lipstick on and a ribbon tied round that wild hair of yours, you'd pass for eighteen any day. You could be a real stunner, Jess Delaney, make no mistake.'

Jess giggled. 'You sound just like Mam. She's always saying I don't make enough of myself.'

Mrs Simmons gave her blessing to the idea, together with her carefully considered opinion that the Plaza was most respectable. If all went well, perhaps next time she might allow the girls to try the Ritz. 'You'd meet a much better class of partner there. But do watch your posture, my dears, and always listen most attentively when a young man talks to you.'

'What if there's a raid?'

Leah shrugged. 'So what? How do you reckon everyone else is getting through this bloomin' war? Largely by ignoring it. We'll be safe enough. Why shouldn't we have a bit of fun? What's the problem anyway?'

'Uncle Bernie,' Jess ruefully admitted. 'He'll never let me go.'

'Oh, leave him to me. I'll fix your Uncle Bernie.'

And she did that too. Once all the arrangements had been made, Leah gazed up at him with those entrancingly blue, innocent eyes and asked if it would be all right for Jess to stay at her house the following Saturday night.

'Mother's invited her to supper, to celebrate her birthday, and doesn't feel it would be safe for Jess to be going home in the dark afterwards, with the blackout and all.' Leah lied without a flicker of guilt, but Jess was quite

49

certain he'd refuse to allow her to go. He might even offer to come and fetch her home himself but Leah's charm held good, and to her delight, he grudgingly agreed.

–

On the night of the dance, Leah's brother Robert acted as escort, faithfully promising his parents that he would keep an eye on the two girls and bring them safely home. They caught the bus, collecting Robert's fiancée on the way, each of them carrying silver dance slippers. In Jess's case an old pair of Leah's, wrapped in a brown paper bag. Once inside, they slipped them on, depositing their outdoor shoes in the cloakroom together with their coats, scarves and handbags.

As anticipated, Robert was more interested in spending the evening with his one true love than supervising his sister, and left them to it, agreeing to meet up again at the door at half past ten on the dot.

The band was playing 'Run, Rabbit, Run' and the two girls were standing by the door, optimistically hoping someone might ask them to dance.

They'd done their best to make themselves suitably alluring. Leah was dressed in a peacock blue satin frock, which reached right down to her ankles and shimmered as she walked, clinging to every curve of her slender figure. With scarlet lipstick, fair hair piled high and those brilliant blue eyes, she looked as if she'd stepped straight out of the silver screen. Jess saw it as a proper, grown-up ball gown rather than the knee skimming day dress style she herself was wearing, yet felt not a trace of envy for her friend.

Leah had delved into her wardrobe and found a pale blue crêpe frock for Jess. It had a lacy collar and covered buttons all down the bodice, fastening at the waist with a neat little belt that had a gold buckle. Since Jess had point blank refused to wear a ribbon, Leah had pinned up her hair into fashionable coils all about her head, then applied not only a soft pink lipstick but also powdered her nose, put rouge on her cheeks and smoothed Vaseline on her eyelashes to make them shine.

Mrs Simmons had declared herself enchanted by the result, and had generously dabbed a touch of her favourite Lily-of-the-Valley perfume behind each of Jess's ears, proclaiming she'd be the belle of the ball, as Leah would be too.

Jess had never felt so glamorous in her life. It was all so exciting.

'I do hope I don't make a fool of myself,' she said, a note of anxiety in her voice. 'What if I forget the steps and everything we've learned?'

'You'll be fine. Look at you, jigging to the beat already. How could someone as musical as you not be able to dance?'

They'd hardly been standing there for five seconds before a sailor claimed a delighted Leah for a dance, spinning her away into a fancy quickstep. Now Jess stood alone and she flattened herself back into the shadows of the entrance, heartily wishing that the ground would open up and swallow her. In the corner by the stage she could see a number of professional dancers, of both sexes, who were there to partner people like herself who had no one to dance with. Except that she couldn't afford to pay sixpence for a ticket, so she would have to remain a wallflower, probably for the entire evening while every man in the room would no doubt snap up her more glamorous friend.

She could feel her cheeks starting to burn with shame; longing now to escape or creep to a chair in a corner, were she able to find one. The only seats available were placed around the small tables, which circled the dance floor, generally occupied by what were obviously courting couples. Just watching them kissing and cuddling made Jess feel even more the odd one out; a reject, a failure, unwanted by anyone. She noticed that Leah was now dancing with a soldier and was waving to her over his shoulder.

What on earth had possessed her to come? Mrs Simmons had given her a lovely birthday tea, wasn't that enough?

'May I have the pleasure of this dance?'

Jess almost jumped out of her skin. Someone was actually asking her to dance. He was quite skinny with ears that stuck-out, a bulbous nose, and dressed in an air-force uniform that looked three sizes too big. Nevertheless she graciously accepted, not feeling any right to be choosy.

From then on her luck changed, or perhaps she just looked more relaxed and smiley but she was soon inundated with other offers, never short of a partner for a single dance.

There were admittedly one or two near disasters, though not through any fault of hers. There above the soldier who was so much shorter than Jess that his face came perilously close to her bosom while she could barely see more than the top of his head. The plump man who kept treading on her toes as he tried to steer her around the crowded floor, runnels of sweat steaming down his flushed face, evidently due to the concentration involved. Then there was the one who gripped her so hard she was flattened against his chest in an iron hold, while she strained to turn her face away from his tainted breath, which stank strongly of pickled onions.

There was always an element of tension as a possible partner approached and each of them would wonder who he had his eye on. Their response could be either relief or resignation but they were never anything less than polite. Mrs Simmons would have been proud of them.

--

No alcohol was allowed in the dance hall but during the interval the two girls bought a glass of lemonade each and slipped outside for a breath of fresh air. The room might be hot and overcrowded but Jess found the atmosphere magical, the crush of people intoxicating. The band was superb, and the singer seemed to float across the stage in her long, white evening gown, her voice filling the room with achingly sweet love songs like 'A Nightingale Sang in Berkeley Square' followed by rousing numbers such as 'We're Gonna Hang Out the Washing on the Siegfried Line'.

'It's fun, isn't it?' Leah said, giggling. 'I reckon I clicked with that last sailor I was dancing with. He offered to marry me on the spot. I told him I had every intention of staying fancy free, thank you very much. No quick wartime wedding for me. Not my scene, I said.'

Jess laughed. 'What do you think of the band? I love the sound of them. Three trumpets, two trombones and five saxophones. Brilliant!'

Leah raised her eyes in despair at the fact Jess had troubled to count the instruments. 'I was more interested in their looks. The drummer's rather dishy, don't you think? Maybe we should go and chat him up while he's on his break.'

When they returned, the band was already back on stage playing 'The Blackout Stroll' and for the next hour they scarcely saw each other as they were kept busy on the dance floor.

'I don't think my feet will ever recover, not to mention these silver shoes of yours,' Jess groaned. 'They've been trodden on so much.'

Next came the 'Ladies Excuse-Me'.

'Come on,' said Leah. 'Now's our chance. I fancy the dishy airman dancing with that fat girl with the spotty chin. I'm sure he'd much rather have his arms about me. Which one have you got your eye on? Make your mind up quickly, then we can dance round together.'

Jess glanced about, wondering if she had the courage to actually walk up to some perfect stranger and ask him to dance, or even more daring, interrupt a dance in progress and drag him away from someone else who he might very well prefer. She could feel her cheeks burning with embarrassment at the very thought. 'I'm not sure that I can. You go. Don't worry about me.'

'Grumpy. You're turning into a real old misery boots.' But Leah didn't hang around to argue, as she was intent on grabbing her airman who seemed delighted to be relieved of trying to make conversation with his more ample partner.

For a moment Jess felt utterly bereft, again standing alone on the perimeter of the dance floor while everyone else seemed to be laughing and dancing, changing partners with dizzying frequency and clearly having a marvellous time. Was Leah right? Was she turning into an old misery boots? This was a whole new experience for her. She felt rather dazed by it, overwhelmed by the reckless determination of everyone wanting to have a good time, no matter what tomorrow might bring.

Some of these young men could be flying planes straight to their own deaths next week. Innocent young girls might be bombed in the factories where they slaved away every day making parachutes or nuts and bolts for aeroplanes, or even in their own homes while they hid under the stairs. Yet here at the Plaza it seemed impossible to imagine that there was a war on at all. How could there be, when everyone was so happy?

Jess had just decided that she'd sit this one out when she saw a young man.

Her gaze homed in on him, perhaps because he was not in uniform as almost everyone else was, or because he sat huddled in a corner beside the stage, a rapt expression on his face as he concentrated entirely upon the band. He seemed so alone, apart from the colourful swirl of dancers, the only sign of movement being the tapping of one foot, and fingers beating in time to the music. Perhaps he was deliberately hiding himself away, as if not for a minute did he expect a gorgeous girl to ask him to dance. Jess felt a rush of sympathy for him. Hadn't she experienced the very same emotions herself, a resolve to appear disinterested and unavailable. Without even pausing to consider her action, she set off across the floor.

'Hello, you look like you're enjoying the music and since this is a ladies's choice, may I have the pleasure?'

Jess really didn't know where she had found the words, or the courage to ask. She nearly turned and fled as he lifted his gaze to frown up at her. In the long silence that followed, she felt quite certain that he would refuse and she would have to creep away, rejected and humiliated. Jess could feel her heart beating wildly against her breastbone. Why was he studying her so intently? The next instant his frown melted away and he smiled at her, unbelievably. 'I don't do fancy steps.'

'Neither do I.'

'That's okay then.'

He had a thatch of tousled, red-brown hair, which looked in dire need of cutting, and the kind of face that was surely made for smiling, round and open with a seemingly permanent upward tilt to the wide mouth. And hazel green eyes that sparkled with ready mischief from beneath halfclosed lids as he continued to consider her with quiet scrutiny. The next instant he took her in his arms and swung her effortlessly on to the dance floor. He proved to be a far better dancer than he'd claimed. Without any apparent effort, he managed to steer her amongst the throng of couples without bumping into any of them, pulling her close should there appear to be any danger of someone crashing into them. Jess rather enjoyed the sensation, feeling cherished and protected, perfectly at ease in his arms.

When he talked, he looked directly into her eyes, giving the impression that he truly cared what she thought, that he was interested in her opinion. Jess smiled up at him, utterly enthralled.

'My name's Steve Wyman,' he told her. 'I work at A.V. Roe as an aircraft engineer, a reserved occupation. And yes, I like music so much I play in a band most evenings. Tonight is my night off.'

'So what are you doing here then?'

'I was told I might be needed. Hal, the band leader, thought there was a risk some of the lads might not show up and asked me to hang around, just in case. Waste of time, as you can see, except it isn't since I'm now dancing with you.'

The dance ended and he asked if she'd like a coffee.

Jess flushed and shook her head. 'No thanks, we've just had a lemonade.' He looked disappointed and she was too naïve to realise that the offer had simply been a ruse, to keep her to himself for a while longer.

The music changed, a foxtrot this time and breathlessly Jess strived to keep up with his expert steps while she asked what instrument he played.

'Saxophone, trumpet, cornet, comb and paper, and whatever I'm paid to play.'

'It must be marvellous to be in a band.'

He chuckled softly, negotiated a reverse, a half turn and then slowed his step so they could talk more easily. 'It's unbelievable. Hot, sweaty and tiring work, but good fun.'

'It always seems so glamorous. Don't tell me all the girls aren't desperate to get to know you.' She remembered her own boldness in asking him to dance. No wonder he was laughing.

'You haven't told me your name, or anything about yourself. What do you do?'

Before she could answer, Jess found herself elbowed out of the way by a very determined girl in a WAAF uniform. 'Excuse me,' the girl said, casting Jess a bright smile of triumph. Jess caught a glimpse of regret in his hazel-eyed gaze as the pair whirled away and she could only smile ruefully before turning and going in search of Leah. It was ten-twenty, very nearly time to go home. But at least she could tell Leah that she'd clicked well. Almost.

Chapter Seven

Going dancing with Jess became a regular part of her routine for Leah, although not always to somewhere as grand as the Plaza. Sometimes they would go to the Co-operative rooms, to various church halls, or take the bus to the ballroom at High Street Baths. Robert and his fiancée nearly always accompanied them.

Her mother, however, was growing dissatisfied over the length of time it was taking for a suitable candidate to step forward and claim her daughter's hand in love and marriage, at least one young man she approved of. Leah had spent almost an hour explaining why it was she didn't care for Ambrose Gregg: that he was boring and spotty and she had no intention of accepting his invitation to go to the pictures, have supper with him, go for a walk or any other ploy he could think of to get her on his own.

Unimpressed by her protest, her mother said, 'How do you know he's boring if you've never spent any time with him? Ambrose might have a fascinating hobby, or wonderful plans for the future, and the poor boy will grow out of his spots in time. He's eighteen, about to start work in his father's printing business, quiet and well-mannered, and he comes from a good family.'

'Mother!'

'Oh, I know darling, you don't like me saying such things but I'm not being snobby, merely sensible. The Greggs are business people, like ourselves, and believe in hard work and endeavour. Coming from a similar sort of background to your own is so important.'

Leah knew that her lovely, charming mother was extremely practical. She was the kind of woman who made lists of everything. She knew to the last pickled onion what she had in her larder, the price butter was last year, when the loft had last been cleared out and the dining room dusted and when they would require attention again. She sent her husband's suits regularly to the dry cleaners, kept his humidor well stocked with his favourite cigars, and woe betide the tobacconist if he'd sold out just when dear Clifford needed fresh supplies.

Worse than this concern over domestic minutiae was her obsession with commanding her children. She had always kept a close record of their progress: first tooth, when they started walking, the dates when they'd suffered from measles, chickenpox and so on. It was now a habit that she was quite unable to break. She continued to keep a careful note of their school reports, lists and addresses of all their friends annotated with her opinion on their suitability, as well as a diary with dates such as when Robert or Leah were next due to visit the dentist, even though they were both perfectly capable of organising these matters for themselves now that they were grown up.

'Why is it important to come from similar backgrounds?' Leah grumbled.

'I beg your pardon, dear?'

'For what purpose does it matter?' Leah wondered why she bothered asking. Perhaps in a bid to secure her independence.

'Because you'd get along perfectly.'

'You mean were we to marry?' Leah challenged. 'Why can't you be honest with me Mother, and admit that you're picking him out as a likely candidate for a husband? For goodness sake, I'm still only seventeen!'

'And nearly eighteen, so pay him attention.'

Time and again they'd had this conversation, which nearly always concerned some young man her mother currently favoured. Always at this point, Leah would feel trapped and thoroughly exasperated. Her brother had likewise found this sort of manipulative behaviour on the part of his beloved mother particularly galling. Having failed his medical for the army because of poor eyesight and flat feet of all things, he'd been driven to working for the family firm, much against his will.

Muriel had been delighted to keep her son safe at home and had taken advantage of the situation by introducing him to Sophie Winstock, the daughter of a friend from her local bridge club. She'd engineered various social functions between the two families in order to bring the young couple together. A wedding was now planned for two years hence, and a new house had been built for the happy pair. Always supposing the war was over and done with by then, of course.

Robert gave every appearance of being content with his situation, but occasionally would rebel about some-thing or other, not being allowed to join the ARP for instance. Leah sometimes wondered if her brother still yearned for a different sort of life. Now she feared her mother was embarking upon a similar campaign with her. Leah adored her parents and in her heart had believed they would never force her into a marriage she didn't want. Nevertheless, their immensely reasonable arguments, persistent persuasion, and intense sense of logic, felt at times like psychological bullying. What Leah feared most was that one day she might be at such a low ebb that she would agree to go out with one of these dull young men her mother procured for her, if only for the sake of peace.

Perhaps this was why her tone had been sharper than she intended.

Her mother sounded greatly offended. 'Please don't be rude, darling. It isn't polite. I only want what's best for you, as every good mother should. What is so wrong in that?'

'I need to grow up and please myself, find myself a job, have fun, and live a little before making long term decisions I don't yet feel ready for.'

Muriel clicked her tongue with impatience, shaking her head in despair at her daughter while adopting the tone of voice she might have used on a six year old. 'I don't expect you to marry for a while yet, darling. How very silly of you to suggest it, but we must plan ahead. You can't simply allow life to happen, as if by accident.'

'Why can't I?'

'Because that isn't sensible.'

'Or practical. As you say, one must be seen to mingle with the right people,' she caustically commented.

'Absolutely, darling,' her mother said, not recognising the irony in her daughter's tone of voice, believing this meant that she finally understood and agreed.

Leah sighed and gave up, knowing she'd completely failed to make her point.

–

After every raid, the streets of Manchester would look increasingly battered as huge areas of the city were wiped out and the numbers of bombed-out buildings grew week by week. There were sandbags everywhere and not a place name in sight. Much of the centre had gone, although here and there an historic building could still be seen protruding out of the heaps of rubble. The Old Wellington Inn stood proud next to the ruins that were once the Old Shambles. The elegant circular building that was the Central Library looked as fine as ever, though the Gaiety Theatre nearby was on the verge of collapse. Tragically, even Salford Royal Infirmary was bombed, a number of the nurses killed.

Unfazed, Mancunians soldiered on, knowing their city inside out and resolving to defend it. Roads might often be blocked and ambulances face long detours in order to reach the wounded; the local buses might look dented and very much the worse for wear from their efforts to get through, yet it didn't prevent them from trying. And as the list of casualties and fatalities grew, many were equipped with stretchers and doubled up as first aid vehicles, or to transfer patients away from danger. The Salvation Army too somehow managed to be there at the right moment with their mobile canteens.

'Where there's a will, there's a way,' became the oft-heard cry.

Everyone was determined to do their bit. Except for one or two notable exceptions. Harry Delaney never for a moment thought of offering his services to the community. He'd avoided call-up by sending his mate George Macintyre to have the medical meant for him. Since George had a dodgy ticker and carried Harry's identity papers, that had got him off the hook. When it came to Bert's call-up a year later, George had gone again, this time wearing spectacles as a disguise, but it had been a different doctor so nobody had recognised him. It cost thirty quid each time but Bernie had gladly paid, considering it worth every penny. George had done well too out of the deal, now with a little business going.

Harry, of course, was much cleverer than George and as well as being naturally concerned with saving his own skin, he was keen to make a profit out of the war, as was his father. He certainly meant to use his natural skills of subterfuge to great advantage.

Now he took one look at the loaded van standing in the yard, checked it against the docket and came to a snap decision. The driver had parked it up the night before to wait for its load, but this morning had sent his wife with a note to say he was sick. More likely hungover. Harry could quite easily have found another driver to move it, but why should he? What was one small vanload of sugar? Who'd miss it? And even if they did, so long as he made sure the paperwork was up to scratch, no blame could be attached to himself. They'd assume some bugger had nipped into the yard overnight and nicked it. Such things happened all the time in a war.

He turned to Bert. 'We're a driver short so we'll just take this van over to t'depot. Gerrin.'

'What, me an' all? Why d'you need me? You'll be back in a jiffy.'

'Shut your noise and don't argue. Can't you spot an opportunity when you see one?'

Harry admired his father and had always been eager to follow his lead. But he was twenty-two for God's sake and had no intention of playing second fiddle. He wanted to become a big shot in his own right. There'd come a day, not too far off, when folks would have the same tone of respect in their voice with him, as they used whenever they spoke of Bernie Delaney. Harry knew he could achieve even greater heights than his father, if he put his mind to it.

He was not so cautious, being a bit of a gambler and not afraid to take risks. He enjoyed the right to be in charge and make decisions, and had far more sense than his brother Bert, which wasn't difficult. There was no reason why one day he shouldn't be a man to be reckoned with. Generally speaking, folk thought him a sociable, easy-going sort of bloke. Women certainly did, seeing him as quite good looking with his square-jaw and closely cropped fair hair. He'd never had any trouble in that department, and Harry knew how to keep a woman happy as well as in her place. Indeed he did!

All he needed was a lucky break to make his mark. Perhaps this could be it. He climbed up into the cab. 'Come on dummel-head. Shape theeself.' Seconds later they were driving out of the loading bay. 'Couldn't be easier. Sweet as pie.'

'Or sugar,' Bert sniggered, fidgeting up and down in his seat as he swung this way and that to check they weren't being followed. 'Who needs coupons? So what now, Harry? Where we taking it?'

'Home to Mam, plank-head, where else? She'll be made up with this lot.'

–

Cora stood with her fists firmly clenched against her substantial waistline and looked at her two sons as if they'd run mad. 'You've fetched me what, a lorry load of sugar? And what the hell am I supposed to do with that lot?'

'Don't worry Ma, Dad'll see to it. We just need somewhere to store it while we take the van back. We have to look sharp or we'll be missed.' Harry had the doors open and was already starting to unload, arms full of large blue bags.

'Heaven help me, you can't fit a lorry load of sugar in my pantry.'

'It's a small van, Ma, not a lorry.'

Bert stopped juggling bags of sugar and frowned. 'She's right though, our Harry. There's not enough room in the pantry for all this lot.'

'Shurrup, muzzle-head. I know that, don't I? I were only going to give you a few bags, Mam. To stock up like. We'll sell the rest.'

'Where? When?' Bert wanted to know, hopping from one foot to the other and sounding agitated. 'There must be tons of the stuff here. Where can we keep it all, our Harry?'

'Stop asking so many questions.'

Storage was a complication Harry hadn't properly considered. Acting on impulse to take the van had seemed like a golden opportunity but perhaps, in retrospect, he'd been a touch reckless.

When Bernie arrived minutes later, having been dragged from his favourite watering hole by a frantic Cora, it was to find a van blocking the back street. His pantry, kitchen table, even the Anderson Shelter in the backyard was full to the brim with blue bags of sugar.

'Where are your brains, you great gobbin?' he yelled at Harry.

'I thought you'd be pleased, Dad. This sugar's worth a fortune.'

'It's worth several months in Strangeways, if not life imprisonment. How could you take such a risk in broad daylight? D'you want to get nicked? Your mam's right for once, where are we supposed to store it? It'll take us months to shift this lot, a few bags at a time.'

And so it proved, but at least the Delaney family could pander to their sweet tooth without a care in the world. Though what would happen at the next air raid when they needed to use the Anderson Shelter, no one cared to consider. The moment arrived sooner than expected, by which time they'd only managed to shift a fraction of the sugar, which meant there was room for only Cora, Jess and the three younger children to sit with any safety in the air raid shelter.

'We could always use them as sandbags,' Cora suggested, but since Bernie didn't find this the least bit amusing, nobody else dared laugh, although young Tommy went very red in the face for a while as he desperately held his mirth in check.

The boys and Bernie took refuge in the cellar with several bottles of beer to keep them company. As enemy aircraft droned overhead, dropping their weapons of destruction upon the city of Manchester, Cora said, 'Aren't we the lucky ones?'

In a way Jess had to agree. She'd had enough of cellars to last her a lifetime. But young Sam and Seb clung to Cora as if to their own personal lifeline, pushing their little faces into her big, fat belly for comfort, desperately blocking their ears against the dreaded drone of aircraft and whine of falling bombs. Sandra, wearing her usual scowl, said, 'Mam, I'm hungry, can I have a sugar butty?'

–

There followed a number of raids in quick succession and Harry and Bert soon grew bored with being confined in the cellar and announced their intention of going down to the shelter on Dolefield. They felt in need of a bit of company, they explained. In truth they intended to do some scavenging in the bombed-out ruins. A bit of salvage work, as you might say. Where was the harm in that?

The backyard was already a clutter of junk: bits of old bicycles with wheels or chains missing, car tyres, lengths of timber which might come in useful one day, unused gas masks, rolls of chicken wire they'd picked up for a song. It did no harm to add to the collection. You could make a tidy profit out of selling anything these days, particularly if you hadn't paid for the stuff in the first place.

'I thought you didn't like the municipal shelter,' Bernie mildly enquired.

The two lads exchanged a quick glance, having no wish to divulge their plans at this stage. Harry was worried his brother might blurt it out, and Bert was half convinced his father could read his mind anyway, so they both looked guilty.

'We don't like it much but it must be safer than our cellar, and the main thing the Anderson is protecting is that blasted sugar.'

'I don't like the communal shelter. Can I stop at home, Bernie?' Cora asked, glancing nervously at her husband. He'd not objected before but you never could tell with Bernie.

'Course you can love. You can keep an eye on our investment.'

Cora went happily off as usual with her brood to settle in among the heap of blue bags and Jess went along with her. It didn't seem fair to leave her aunt to cope with three children on her own.

Bernie said no more as his sons swaggered off, but his eyes narrowed with suspicion. He'd need to keep a close watch on those two. They were getting too big for their boots. Happen he should have encouraged them to join up after all. A bit of square bashing might have done them both a world of good. Harry in particular might like to give the impression he was obeying instructions but half the time Bernie suspected he was doing exactly as he pleased.

As for young Tommy, he wasn't even here this evening as he'd taken it into his head to volunteer his services as a firewatcher. He'd gone along a few weeks ago with his pal Frank Roebottom to the nearest warden post where they were each given a steel helmet and an axe and told to stay awake and use their common sense. At first they'd thought it all a great adventure, a bit of a lark, messing about in the dark, sleeping in odd corners of factories and pretending they were heroes while they waited for action. But when it came, it had been a different story.

They'd found themselves kicking incendiaries off the roofs of buildings, suddenly realising that war was a very serious business indeed.

–

When the siren sounded, Leah welcomed it with heartfelt relief because it put an end to yet one more long and fruitless discussion with her mother about what she must do with her life. To most people going to the shelter felt like a restriction to their freedom, for Leah it represented an escape. She reached for her coat and the latest romance she'd borrowed from Boot's library. 'Here we go again, Mother. Grab your knitting bag. Let's go.'

Mrs Simmons disliked going down into the communal shelter. She told herself that it wasn't because of any snobby tendencies on her part, but a perfectly natural desire to be clean. The smell of those places was quite nauseating and the sight of so much human suffering always depressed her. But knowing there was no help for it, she pressed her lips together with firm resolve, picked up her bag and followed her daughter down the back stairs and out into the street.

One glance along the lobby told Leah that the girls in the shop had already gone, no doubt quickly locking up and taking the cash box with them, as instructed. Her father, who was this evening doing his stint as an ARP Warden, had set rigid rules which he was most insistent they follow most precisely. Leah quickly closed the interior lobby door and led her mother out the back way. It was as she turned the key in the lock that her mother remembered she'd left her spectacles behind and began to fluster, wanting to go back for them.

'You can surely manage without them for once, Mam,' Leah protested. Manchester was a prime target. It didn't do to hang around dithering.

'No, dear, you know how bad my eyesight is these days. A night spent in a shelter is miserable enough without being deprived of my knitting. I simply won't be able to read the pattern.'

Leah sighed. 'You stay here, I'll go and find them.'

She unlocked the back door and shot upstairs, running from room to room in a frantic search, finally unearthing the spectacles from under a cushion where her mother had tucked them. Leah pounded back downstairs, banging the door to behind her. 'Got them. Come on, we must hurry.' Grabbing her mother's arm she propelled her along the back street.

'Did you remember to lock the door, darling?'

Leah hadn't the first idea whether she had or not. She was out of breath, hot and bothered and desperately anxious to get off the street before the raid started. Already she could hear the dreaded drone of enemy planes getting ever nearer, a sound that softened her bones to water and blotted every sensation but fear from her mind. She knew the shop door would be locked, so what did it matter about the one at the back? Most folk didn't bother to lock any doors at all on the grounds that there were far more important considerations to think of, like saving their lives.

Even as she hesitated, considering this question, there came the all too familiar whine, cut off into an ominous silence, followed seconds later by a blast that blew them both off their feet, although it must have come from a couple of streets away. The air was thick with dust, the smell of cordite choking their lungs and making them cough. Winded but still in one piece, Leah dragged herself and her mother to their feet, and even retrieved the tangle of knitting. 'I'm certainly not going back again to check. Quick, run for it.'

Chapter Eight

The Delaney boys ambled from street to street, about their usual scavenging. As always Bert found it impossible to walk in a straight line and, whistling tunelessly, dashed to and fro peering in windows, trying doors, generally prying into every nook and cranny. They'd discovered how very careless folk were with their goods, and chattels once they heard the air raid warning. Exactly as they'd hoped!

Passing The Globe, they noticed the door standing wide open and not a soul inside. 'Hey up, someone'll be in bother,' Bert remarked. 'They've up and made a dash for it without bothering to lock up.'

'How fortuitous,' Harry commented. 'I don't know about you but these raids always leave me fair parched.' And giving a little swagger, he wandered into the pub, calling out hello, just in case. But as Bert had rightly suspected, the place was deserted.

They helped themselves to a couple of pints each, followed by several shots of whisky as a chaser, leaning contentedly on the bar counter and drinking at their leisure, as if the war would be happy to wait until they were done. 'We'd best lock up when we go,' Harry said. 'Make sure it's safe like.'

'Aye,' Bert smirked. 'Wouldn't be right for the poor barman if owt got nicked.' After stuffing their pockets with a few packets of Woodbine and Craven A, the pair left, carefully locking up behind them and posting the key through the letterbox.

Several streets later they were back on Deansgate, and once again Bert took the lead, suggesting they take a shifty look round the back of Simmons's Tea Rooms, just in case. They couldn't believe their good fortune to find the back door unlocked, and didn't hesitate to go inside. First they went along the lobby and into the confectioner's shop. Ignoring the door, which led into the tea room, they went straight to the counter, looking for the till. They couldn't find it anywhere but the silver trays of cakes arrayed in the glass display counter looked tantalisingly delicious.

'By heck, see that custard slice. It must be three inches thick.' Bert stretched out his grubby fingers and took one, barely wiping the custard from his mouth before reaching for another, and a third after that. Harry helped himself to a wedge or two of apple pie, to which he was partial, before finally coming to his senses.

'Here, what we wasting time on this muck for. If there's no till, where's the cash box then?' To their great disappointment they couldn't find that either. Someone had judiciously taken it with them to the shelter, so they went upstairs instead. Here they had better luck, discovering the Simmons's identity cards and ration books in the kitchen drawer, and a wallet full of notes in the dresser.

'The best of it is there's no fear of being interrupted during an air raid. I knew it would be profitable to go out and about doing a bit of business while everyone else cowers in the shelter,' Harry bragged.

'So long as we don't get bombed,' Bert said, his thin face creasing into a worried frown.

'No chance of tha! We're indestructible.' Stuffing all of these precious treasures into their pockets, along with a cameo brooch and a pretty blue necklace that might be sapphires, which they'd found in the dressing table drawer of the front bedroom, then they let themselves out and went on their way, happily whistling.

–

'Would you like a scone dear and a refill of tea?' Jess glanced up at a kindly face framed by a blue bonnet, and smiled.

'Don't mind if I do.'

Just to see the Sally Army roll up and start serving tea, soup and sandwiches had lifted everyone's spirit. There were some who said the smile alone was worth a tanner, but no money ever changed hands as they gave their services free. They might try to sell a few copies of their magazine: *The War Cry*, later. They never enquired what denomination people were, or even if they believed in God, but simply offered to 'serve and to succour', providing what they called 'the human touch'. If the answer to a person's spiritual needs were discovered, so much the better although not in any way compulsory.

Jess wasn't sure what she believed in. Certainly Lizzie had made no effort to instil any sense of the spiritual in her, and she never set foot in a church herself, let alone take her daughter to one. At times Jess's hopes for a good future was so clouded by her mother's lack of tact, she felt a dreadful sense of bitterness, a feeling she struggled to

75

resist. She smiled again at the girl in the blue bonnet and asked if she'd made the delicious scones herself.

'Goodness no, we get them cheap from Simmons's because they're a bit stale. But still good, don't you think?' she said, with a gurgle of laughter.

'Delicious. But then they would be if Mr Simmons or Robert made them.' How generous kind and thoughtful that family was. Jess couldn't imagine Uncle Bernie doing anything that didn't bring in a decent profit for himself.

Cora and the children were certainly glad of the scones, slightly stale or not, as well as the hot tea. She'd been in a dreadful state by the time the ARP Wardens had pulled them from the rubble of their bombed house, anxious to find her children and check all their limbs were in good working order. Miraculously they were, but Cora had only just stopped shaking. She looked pale and vulnerable drinking the tea with her children gathered close to her side, as if she had shrunk within her comfortable layer of fat. Her usually rosy face was the colour of parchment, her wire wool hair still in curling pins and her swollen ankles spilling out over the top of the inevitable carpet slippers. As always, there was about her person an underlying, acrid scent of sweat, on this occasion mixed with plaster dust and cordite.

The house was badly damaged, with the odd door and window blown out and the back scullery flattened completely, but it could be repaired and parts of it were still habitable, or would be when the smell of smoke had gone and the water from the fire hoses had dried up. Even more amazingly, the Anderson Shelter had withstood the blast intact, if with sugar spilled everywhere from the burst bags.

Bernie wasn't too pleased about this. 'There'll be little hope of selling the stuff now its full of muck and plaster.'

'Never mind love, that sugar has saved our lives,' Cora told him. 'I'll never hear another word against our Harry.'

Fortunately, Bernie had managed to close the door on this damning evidence of black marketeering before the rescue party arrived, who fortunately didn't investigate too closely. They accepted, without protest, his decision not to leave the house or be checked over by the first aid people. They warned him of possible gas leaks, and the further risk of fire but Bernie insisted he must look for a few personal possessions, then board the house up, so they left him to it. They had far more to worry about than folk who wanted to poke through the rubble to find family pictures or stay to guard their precious belongings.

Jess ate the second scone and drank a third mug of tea. By this time Sam and Seb were curled up on their mother's knee like a pair of puppies, fast asleep with thumbs in their mouths. Sandra was snuffling and complaining about wanting to go home while Cora patted and soothed her, urging her to close her eyes and try to get some sleep. Feeling at a loose end, as if she didn't quite belong in this moment of family togetherness, Jess volunteered to help serve tea. Besides the young girl in the bonnet with the pretty face and bright eyes who said her name was Harriet, there was one other girl, a qualified nurse in her main job, and a man, all in Salvation Army uniform. Another batch of bombed-out victims had arrived and the three of them seemed to be run off their feet.

'You could brew a fresh pot,' Harriet readily agreed. 'This one is getting low.'

'Right you are.' Jess refilled the big urn and lit the gas beneath it. The next hour or so flew by as she refilled the big brown teapots with scalding hot, fresh tea, time after time. Sometimes, she poured it out into tin mugs, seeing bowed heads lift, smiles appear and faces lined with grime and despair light up with pleasure and gratitude. At one point she took the mouth organ from her pocket and played 'A Nightingale Sang in Berkley Square', and everyone joined in for a bit of a singsong.

'Eeh love, that was grand,' one old woman said, wiping tears from her eyes.

There were a few others blowing noses or wiping away surreptitious tears, so she played a rousing version of 'She's a Lassie from Lancashire' to cheer them up. To Jess, it felt a worthwhile thing to do. Better than cowering in a cellar, or even a sugar-bagged Anderson shelter. She wondered how Lizzie was faring. Was she having a singsong and a mug of tea? Did they take the prisoners down to the shelter, she wondered? Feckless as her ma was, she really didn't deserve to be in that awful place, let alone with all this going on. If only she could find somewhere better for them to live when she came out.

'It's Jess Delaney, isn't it?'

Startled by this sudden interruption to her thoughts, Jess turned to find herself being closely scrutinised by an officer in Salvation Army uniform. He was a tall, thin man with a waxy moustache. He wore a peaked hat square upon his head, beneath which a pair of large ears protruded. There was a gleaming badge pinned just above the hat band, plain strips of navy braid in horizontal lines across the front of his jacket, as well as a brighter variety on the shoulder epaulettes. He looked vaguely familiar to

Jess, but she couldn't put a name to him or know why he recognised her.

'I'm Sergeant Buxton, or just plain Ted if you like. I knew your dad. How is the old codger?'

Jess flushed with pleasure. It wasn't often she met anyone who knew her father, Jake, not since they'd moved out of Salford to be nearer the rest of the family after he'd gone off to war. 'He's overseas with the army.'

'So I heard. I enjoyed your playing of the mouth organ, which isn't as easy as it looks. Nice tone you got out of it. But then your dad was always musical. Good trumpet player, he was.'

'I think he did play a trumpet occasionally, but mainly his accordion.'

The sergeant's eyes seemed to take on a challenging twinkle. 'He could play pretty well any instrument he fancied, and I reckon you've inherited his talent. You're no doubt a dab hand at the trumpet yourself.'

Jess laughingly shook her head. 'I've never tried to learn that, so I very much doubt it. All I can manage is this mouth organ.'

Sergeant Buxton frowned. 'It wasn't you then who blew that bugle on Christmas Eve?'

Jess gazed up into what had now become an alarming scrutiny and found herself at a complete loss for words. After all this time she'd thought she'd got away with it. Apparently not. Swallowing painfully, Jess knew there was no help for it but to own up. 'I'm sorry, and that I dropped it. I was a bit startled by the noise it made. Was it badly dented? I've no money to pay for a new one just now but I'm hoping to get a better job soon, so I could save up. Pay a bit each week towards a new one for the band. Would that do?'

The sergeant heard her out in silence, listening to every breathless utterance. When she finally stopped talking, he started to chuckle, then put back his head and laughed so loud and for so long that his hat fell off and he had to pick it up before it rolled away and got trodden on. 'Eeh lass, if I'd known you were worrying so much over that, I'd have tried harder to find you. The bugle came to no harm at all, well not much, anyroad. The odd dent won't matter.'

'Oh, I am glad!' Relief swept through her. Jess really didn't see how she could ever have earned enough to buy a new one, but felt the need to make that offer.

'I did try to find you afterwards, as a matter of fact, but you'd left the house on Irwell Street and I didn't know where you'd gone. I'm glad to run into you again, though sorry about the circumstances, particularly since you've been worrying about that bugle all this time. Daft ha'porth.'

Jess smiled ruefully. She found she quite liked Sergeant Buxton, and as she poured him some tea and made him a sandwich because he was ravenous having worked half the night, they continued to chat as if they were old friends. 'Was it you that chased after me?'

'Aye, not to tell you off though, love. I was a bit shaken when I heard you play that note. I'd never heard one so true, not played by a novice.'

If this surprised her, Jess was even more startled by his next words.

'And if you really don't know how to play the trumpet then you should learn. You have a natural gift.'

'Natural gift? I don't know what you mean.'

'To put it simply, woodwind instruments have a reed in the mouthpiece that vibrates when you blow. With brass instruments it is the shape and position of the lips you make, which produces the note. But the important thing is not to strain or push the breath, which you didn't. Being relaxed is vital so that when you come to a high note you can deal with it sweetly. Course, there's still a lot to learn. Scales and such like, which usually takes a lot of practice, but I could teach you. If you were interested.'

Jess gasped. 'If I were *interested*?' She couldn't imagine anyone not wanting to make music. 'Oh, I'd love to, but I don't have an instrument. Or the money to pay for lessons.'

Sergeant Buxton shrugged, as if these were minor matters. 'We can always borrow one from the band. As for payment, look at what you're doing now?'

'What, pouring tea?' She handed him his potted beef sandwich and he bit into it with gratitude.

'You could pay for your lessons by working with us in the mobile canteens. We need all the help we can get. How about it? Is that a fair exchange?'

Jess could hardly believe what she was hearing. It seemed too good to be true. 'You mean in return for making tea and sandwiches I get to play the trumpet any time I like?'

'Oh no, any time *I* like. Whenever I can find the time in between everything else I have to do. And you'll have to learn to play the bugle as well, so that instead of using your hard-earned brass to pay for the dents in the one you dropped, you can play a bugle in the band instead.'

Jess was laughing by now, because it was all so amazing. 'Are you serious?'

'Never more so.' He held out a hand. 'Is it a deal?'

Without hesitation, she firmly shook on their agreement.

—

Bernie stood at the corner of Irwell Street with a group of his cronies looking very much as if he was waiting for The Globe to open and watched his two elder sons swagger off along Cumberland Street, hands in pockets, whistling tunelessly. They looked so innocent they must be up to something. As if he didn't have enough on his plate with that niece of his, obstinate little baggage, not forgetting Lizzie who was likely to be let out before too long. With a growing family to support, as well as an appetite for the odd each-way bet and a pint or two at The Globe here, he needed to think of some way to improve his income. Money was getting worryingly tight.

What's more, it'd be a living nightmare soon with two women in the same house. He could see it coming. Right now there wasn't a damn thing he could do about that. He certainly couldn't afford to keep two houses going.

Cora wasn't going to be the least bit happy to have Lizzie around the place, mainly because she had a suspicion that Jess wasn't his niece at all; that she was in fact Bernie's own child. He'd wondered the same himself, till he'd heard her play that mouth organ, then he'd known it was all a figment of his imagination. He'd had a bit of a fling with Lizzie even before she married his brother. She hadn't ever been the loyal sort. Not like Cora.

His missus didn't have a bad bone in her flabby body, which was why he'd married her. He couldn't be doing with strident women, the kind who thought they were as good as any bloke. Cora knew her place and had always shown proper respect and gratitude for the fact he'd chosen her above more glamorous possibilities. Oh aye, he'd never considered himself to be a faithful husband, but he'd always been discreet. He felt he owed that to Cora, at least. So who would help Lizzie if she was daft enough to flaunt their liaison too brazenly when she came to live with them in Cumberland Street. The fat would really be in the fire then.

Poor old Jake, what a shame things had turned out so miserable for him. They'd got word that he was a PoW, being held in a camp some place. Bernie smirked with pleasure at the thought of his more fortunate brother suffering for once in his life. The smile quickly faded as he watched his sons sidle out of an alley, obviously up to no good. What a pair of tosspots they were. He'd skelp the pair of them if they messed things up for him. Jake had got one over on him too, by breeding the most intelligent and decent child of the whole Delaney bunch. Perhaps that was why Cora didn't hold it against Jess personally. She'd quite warmed to the lass. But then that was Cora, generous and open hearted to a fault.

He called after his sons. 'Here, where are you two off to?'

They turned, hesitated a moment before ambling reluctantly over. 'Just having a nose around. See what's doing.'

'Well, keep me informed.'

'Aye, course we will, Dad, don't we always?'

Bernie edged them away from the growing crowd outside the pub, lowering his voice to a whisper. 'And fetch back something I can shift this time, as well as store. Not a van load of flipping sugar.'

'Right!' Both lads grinned amiably and nodded.

Bernie caught their shifty look and inwardly groaned. Life was growing ever more complicated with these lads of his starting to flex their wings. Pickings on the black market weren't so easy as they'd once been. One or two deals had fallen through lately, let alone that blasted sugar. The authorities were growing ever more suspicious and tended to make spot raids on shops, demanding to see receipts and examine stock rooms, checking out their sources of supply. So far Bernie had been lucky and not suffered such an inspection himself, although he'd had one or two close shaves.

'Have they had any problems here with air raids?' Harry was asking, intruding on his thoughts and nodding in the direction of the pub doors, still fast shut.

Bernie frowned, struggling to concentrate on the implication behind the question. 'Not that I know of! What sort of problems would that be exactly?'

Bert shuffled his feet while his cheeks fired beetroot red, 'Oh you know, things going missing like. Doors not shut proper.'

Harry gave his brother a hefty kick on the ankle and daft Bert yelled out loud in protest. 'Hey, what did you do that for, our Harry?'

'Do what?'

Bert caught the glower on his brother's face and realisation dawned. 'Oh, right. Nowt.'

Bernie glowered. 'What are you rattling on about Bert?'

'Nowt, Dad! Right, we'll be off then, shall we? And we'll remember what you said like.'

'Aye, think on. Mind what you get up to. I don't want any problems that I can't handle.'

Harry snorted, the faintest note of irony in his voice. 'There's not much you can't handle, Dad. See you.' And giving a cheery wave, he thrust his hands back into his pockets, nudged his brother with one broad shoulder to make him get a move on, and the pair ambled off.

Eyes narrowing to slits, Bernie watched them vanish around the corner into Deansgate. His sons weren't turning out to be the bonus he'd hoped for and sadly he knew why that was. Drive and ambition they might have, but they lacked imagination and any degree of common sense. They went at things like the proverbial bull in a china shop and weren't even very good at following orders. He sensed a definite note of rebellion in the way they avoided answering his questions. Dumb insolence, you could call it. What was most curious about their behaviour was that they went out on these expeditions during an air raid. Despite being afraid of getting hit, they didn't seem to use the communal shelter on Dolefield. So what exactly were they up to? Damned if he'd be bested by his sons, Bernie turned up his coat collar, shoved his hands deep in his pockets and loped off, deep in thought.

Chapter Nine

Bernie came home early from his football match one Saturday afternoon instead of going for his usual pint at The Globe, mainly because he had a bit of business to do later and had decided to have an early tea. He found no sign of any food on the kitchen table, only Ma Pickles chatting with his wife. How women loved to gossip! He expected her to up-tail and run at sight of him but, engrossed with a story she was evidently enjoying telling, she made no move to go. The whole family seemed to be riveted by her tale. Jess was sitting enthralled, a look of horror on her face. Cora leaned forward in her chair so as not to miss a word, with Sandra clinging to her mother's arm. Even Harry and Bert appeared eager for every juicy detail.

'What's all this then?' Bernie asked, unable to help himself.

'Go on,' Cora said. 'Tell him.'

Ma Pickles was more than happy to provide a résumé, relishing running through her gory tale yet again. 'It's Cissie Armitage, her what works at the Co-op. She was bombed-out the other night, and didn't get off lightly. Her Jack lost both his legs in the blast.'

Cora began to look faintly green and Bernie realised the old woman was almost enjoying her story. 'Get on with it, you old bag.'

Ma Pickles sniffed loudly, unfazed by his scorn. 'One of her childer were killed outright in his cot when the roof fell in and poor Cissie's a bag of nerves as a result. They took her and the other two kids down the shelter to give them first aid. They're right enough, bless 'em, but she'll never be the same again. As if she hadn't suffered enough with all of that lot, when she got back home there was a load of stuff missing. There's something fishy going on, I says to her. It's a funny sort of bomb what leaves your handbag intact and blasts all the shillings from your purse. And you know where she kept her rent book, same as everyone else, on the corner of the mantelshelf?'

Cora nodded gravely.

'Well, it was still where it should be, right next to the spills what she uses to light the fire. But the ration books and identity cards what should have been with it, were gone. Now what sort of clever bomb is that, d'you reckon, what can pick and choose the bits of paper it destroys? And clever enough to pick a few bits and bobs of trinkets out of Cissie's little box in her top drawer. She was right cut up about them, I can tell you. Even her mother's wedding ring were taken.'

Fascinated, despite himself, by this sordid tale, Bernie slid his gaze in the direction of his two sons and realisation slowly dawned. He could see by the twin spots of colour on Harry's ghost pale cheeks, and the way Bert was fidgeting with the buttons on his overalls, just exactly what they'd been up to. He should've known, the morbid little scavengers. What kind of sons had he raised? Where were the skill, the wit and the canny judgement in picking over folks's belongings while they were in an air raid shelter? Yet it was cunning. He did admit that. Pity he hadn't thought of it himself. But then he'd have chosen a better target than Cissie Armitage.

–

The moment Ma Pickles had gone, he jerked his head in the direction of the back door. 'A word, outside.'

The two lads sidled out into the yard without protest, Cora and Jess watching with some trepidation as Bernie lifted the strap from the hook behind the back door.

'What's wrong now?'

'Never you mind.'

'Don't do anything you might regret, Bernie,' wailed Cora, wringing her hands together.

'Don't worry, there won't be any regrets.'

Once upon a time, when they were young lads, he might have instructed them to drop their britches. Now he flexed the strap and told them to hold out their hands. Bert meekly obeyed but had Bernie not been so arrogantly certain of his power, he might have noticed that at twenty-two, going on twenty-three, this was one step too far for Harry. He was inwardly steaming with anger. It came as something of a shock when his eldest son point blank refused.

'Like hell I will,' he muttered, half under his breath.

Hand still outstretched though trembling with antici-pation of the blows to come, Bert said. 'What did we do, Dad?'

'You know damn well what you did. Without any by your leave.'

Harry gave a snort of derisive laughter. 'I'll tell you what we did wrong, Bert; we left him out of it. We didn't give the great Bernie Delaney, our clever dad here, his cut. And why didn't we? Because he's past it.'

Without pausing to consider the wisdom of his action, Bernie aimed a punch deep into his son's belly. Harry doubled over, giving a surprised grunt, yet was barely winded. When the second one came, an open-handed clout across the side of his head, he staggered but quickly righted himself. His son might consider himself too old to be beaten, but Bernie paid no attention to how his eyes narrowed. When he swung the next punch at the lad's jaw, not only did it fail to connect, but he also found his hand caught in mid-air by Harry's huge fist, held in a crushing grip.

'You great clot-head, I'll wallop you one,' Bernie gasped.

'Just try it.'

'Choose your window and I'll throw you through it.'

'You and who's flaming army?'

Bernie realised he'd run out of threats and was very nearly out of puff as father and son glared furiously at each other almost nose to nose, their eyes revealing all their pent-up frustration and anger. After several long seconds, Harry finally released his hand, knowing that he'd made his point. Bernie flexed his bruised fingers, shocked to the core but desperately trying not to reveal it. When did these lads of his grow so strong? 'It's a challenge you want then, is that it?'

'It might be.'

'What, an arm wrestle, to see who's top dog?' If he couldn't control these lads with his fists any more, he'd have to find some other way.

Unable to resist this offer to flaunt his impressive skill in arm wrestling, Harry grinned and began to roll up his sleeve. While his attention was thus distracted, Bernie lunged at him, grabbed hold of Harry's collar and flattened him against the back yard wall, nearly cracking his skull against the stone. He managed to restrain himself and not cause his son too much damage. His reprimand was mild by past standards, but happen he had been a mite careless. Nevertheless, he was determined not to give in. 'Don't you dare challenge me, you no good, useless lump of lard! And next time you go scavenging, don't do it anywhere near my home. Pick a better target. It's carelessness like that that could get you caught, and me along with you, once the polis start poking their flaming noses in our business. Right?'

Surprise registered briefly on Harry's face, looking capable of throwing his father off. 'How could I get caught? Everyone was in the shelter, including the police.'

'Open your ears and I'll say it one more time so there's no mistaking you understand what I'm saying. Stay away from bombed-out houses in this locality. Go where you're not so well known, and where *you* don't know who you're nicking from. Not a friend. Is that clear? Have I drummed it into your thick skull? That way we're less likely to suffer repercussions, either by folk like Ma Pickles poking her beak in where it's not wanted, or the polis. Right?'

Bert was dancing around, almost wetting his pants with anxiety. 'Don't thump our Harry again but we can't do that, Dad. We're demolition men and must go where we're told.'

With a show of reluctance, Bernie released his hold on his son. 'Demolition? What rubbish is this?'

Shaking himself free and dusting down the new jacket he'd bought, Harry said, 'Aye, it pays better than the docks, and there are many opportunities. Nobody asks questions of demolition workers poking about a bomb site.'

Bernie was stunned by this new information, appreciating this might well be true. Yet it rankled him that his sons should show such enterprise without consulting him. They were getting even more canny than he'd given them credit for. It strengthened his suspicion that they believed they could please themselves with what they did, which wasn't the case at all. He was still the boss, still in charge.

'So you thought you'd cut me out of the deal, is that the way of it? Well, don't ever try to pull a fast one like that on me again, right? Anyroad, what did you collar? Money? Coupons? Whatever it is, hand it over. I'm still the boss round here and don't you two ever forget that.'

With grudging ill will, Harry pulled a few trinkets out of various pockets. A couple of watches, a ring, and two fivepound notes. Bert handed over a wad of petrol coupons.

'That's more like it. Right, we'll say no more on the subject. Just see that you keep me informed in future.'

It was only after Bernie had gone back inside, certain he'd re-established his position as head of the hierarchy that Harry muttered, 'Just like I told you, Bert. He's lost his nerve. And if you ever tell him we didn't give him everything, I'll wring your flaming neck.'

Jess buttoned up her best navy blue coat against a cold north wind that was rattling the kitchen window and tugged on warm woolly gloves. The coat was too short and a bit tight about the chest since she'd grown quite a bit recently, sprouting breasts, which were a great embarrassment to her. But the coat would have to be adequate, much as she hated it. Jess felt prickly with nerves; all jittery inside, not that worrying about how she was dressed would help one bit. True to her word, Leah had asked her father about a job and Jess had been granted an interview. She'd brushed her blonde hair till it shone, scrubbed her nails, which seemed to be important in the circumstances, and put on her only decent navy skirt and a clean white blouse. Now she could only hope and pray that she didn't look as awful as she felt.

Cora, who had come to know the girl well in these last weeks recognised the problem instantly. 'Nay, don't get in a fret you look a right champion. Remember it's only Mr Simmons and you know him well enough. Besides, grand girl like you he'd be daft not to give you a job, assuming you want one, of course.'

Much as Cora admired her niece, she was a bit nonplussed by her capacity for hard work. As well as helping her with the childer, she spent most evenings working with the Sally Army on their mobile canteens. And she was still looking for a better job, as she called it, 'a step up from the market stall.'

'Course I do.' Working in a confectioner's shop might not have been her first choice or in any way glamorous, but at least it would put her on the road to independence, and there was always the chance of being asked to work in the tea rooms where there was the possibility of tips. If she saved hard, she'd hopefully have enough money to move away from her uncle and make a home of their own for herself and Lizzie, even if not in time for her release in a few weeks time. But she couldn't say any of this to Aunt Cora, who'd shown her nothing but kindness.

'It's important that I make a good impression. Mr Simmons has a reputation for being a bit of a stickler for what's proper and correct. Good manners, rules, stuff like that. Deep down, Leah says, he's a fair man and a good employer, if not exactly generous, but he likes things to be done just so. He calls it "running a tight ship".'

'Aye, bosses are like that,' Cora said with feeling, and wound a scarf about the girl's neck. 'See you don't hang about in the wet. We don't want you sickening for something.'

'I won't. I promise.' She'd been invited on several occasions to stay for supper at the Simmons's in recent months, despite her mother being in jail. No mention was ever made of Lizzie, and there were no more offerings of mince pies or similar items of home baking, but either out of pity, charity, or sheer good nature, the family had raised no objection to her continuing friendship with Leah, for which Jess was immensely grateful.

Leah's friendship was important to her. She loved going to the dances with her friend and although she'd found herself looking out for him, she'd never again spotted Steve Wyman, which often left her feeling low and disappointed. Not that you could feel down for too long, not with Leah chivvying her to dance with every sailor, soldier or airman who asked.

Cora said, 'Don't forget to call at the butchers on your way back. Ask him if he has some of them nice sausages. And if you see any interesting queues, tag on behind just in case. Who knows what might be going.' She thrust a ration book into her hand and Jess stared at the unfamiliar name on the front cover.

'It's my cousin. He's planning to stop with us for a few days,' Cora said. Even if her plump cheeks hadn't been flushed, Jess guessed this to be a lie. There'd been a few too many strange happenings during the weeks of her stay. For one thing, both Cora and Bernie seemed to have two sets of identity papers, each bearing different names, which meant they also had two different sets of ration books that they used in different shops. It was becoming increasingly difficult to remember the details when Cora sent her out shopping.

Leah had complained recently about the Simmons's identity cards and some money having gone missing while they'd been in the shelter. She'd been outraged to hear Ma Pickles's story the other day. It was hard to imagine anyone so heartless as to steal while an air raid was in progress. They'd even taken a few trinkets from her mother's jewellery case on her dressing table.

Jess had sympathised but now a small fear kindled in the pit of her stomach. That theft couldn't have anything to do with the Delaneys, could it? Was that why Uncle Bernie had taken both lads out in the yard for a skelping? Lord, she hoped not. She wanted Mrs Simmons to go on issuing invitations so that she could continue to taste a little of normal family life, even if it wasn't her own. Visiting the Simmons's house was her main sanctuary, besides the Sally Army. Leah's mother had once or twice allowed her to practise her trumpet and accompanied her on the piano. Jess couldn't bear it if the Delaneys messed that up for her as well.

'Isn't it wrong for Uncle Bernie to have so many spare coupons, Aunt Cora?' Jess blurted out the question with the innocence of a young girl who still believed in the ideal that everyone should pull together, particularly during wartime.

Cora, wiser by a mile, let out a heavy sigh. 'Rationing is a blight on the poor. You don't think the rich are hidebound by it, do you? They have the money to get round such things.'

'But how could they? I mean, however much money you might have, you can't buy a new frock unless you have enough clothing coupons, can you?'

'Has anyone ever told you girl, if you'd any more mouth, you'd have no face to wash?'

'Meaning?' Jess looked puzzled.

'You talk too much.'

'But where does Bernie get them all from? I found a whole box of coupons when I was cleaning your bedroom yesterday.'

Now Cora looked alarmed and distressed, glancing fearfully about as if she half expected her husband to appear before them. 'Nay, don't let on to Bernie you've been snooping when cleaning our bedroom. Whatever next? He won't like that, not one little bit. He's a very private man, with his own way of going about things.'

'Don't you worry about him?'

Cora's tone grew sharp, with a bitter ring to it. 'Course I worry, but I know how to keep my lip buttoned and not ask too many questions, a skill you'd do well to learn.'

Softening her voice, she stroked Jess's pale cheek. 'You have to be careful, lass. He might seem generous to a fault, always fetching us good things to eat and bringing the kids new clothes and such, but underneath he'd take skin off your rice pudding if he had a greater need for it. So don't go poking your nose in where you shouldn't. Leave all his cupboards and drawers firmly shut tight, particularly under the stairs. Got it?' And nodding meaningfully, she ladled an extra spoonful of sugar into Jess's mug of tea.

Not that Jess wanted it, she was growing to dislike sugar. Besides, Cora might be happy to sit hour after hour sipping tea and gossiping with her neighbours, but Jess preferred to be out and about, living life to the full. And this morning she was particularly anxious to be on her way.

'I reckon I'd best be going. I don't want to be late.'

'Aye, all right love, but remember what I said. You're a grand lass, and Simmons's Tea Rooms will be the loser if they don't sign you up on the spot.'

Cora was marching her niece briskly to the door as she said all of this, smoothing the collar of her navy blue coat, tucking in the scarf and checking Jess had her bag and the ration book.

'I don't think it's in the tea rooms, Aunt Cora. I think it's just serving bread and cakes in the shop.'

'Well, that's a start, I suppose.' Cora looked doubtful but then a thought struck her and her face brightened. 'Here, you might be given the odd stale loaf, you never know, or some muffins, or Eccles cakes. Eeh, I do love them so think on that. Chin up and best foot forward.'

Jess suddenly felt a wealth of compassion for this over-sized, big-hearted woman in her wrap-over pinny and carpet slippers and gave her a hug. How could such a caring, warm person endure living with her loathsome uncle? Poor Cora had gone from being bullied at school as a girl, to being equally bullied by her husband. Was that how it was? Once a victim, always a victim? Jess had never actually seen any physical evidence that Bernie beat his wife, but she knew for a fact he was capable of such violence, had witnessed his temper when he'd attacked Lizzie. He might well be clever enough to inflict bruises upon his wife where they didn't show. Cora was certainly afraid of him. 'Thanks. What would I have done without you these last weeks?'

'What are families for? Have you thought what you'll do when your mam comes home?'

'I mean to look after her.'

'Course you do love, and you're welcome to stop on here, both of you. You know that, being family like.'

Jess felt tears block her throat for although Cora didn't sound over-enthusiastic she knew the offer was a generous gesture since the two women didn't get on.

'Maybe we won't need to bother you. Uncle Bernie might be able to find us a place of our own to live.' Jess was anxious about what was going to happen when her mother was released. Nothing had been said about that. No plans made.

'He always did put himself out for your mam,' Cora said, a wealth of cold in her tone, which Jess thought best not to comment upon. Then she kissed Jess's cheek and gave her a little hug. 'Right then, off you go chuck, and remember to be proud of yourself, or nobody else will be. Oh, and don't forget them sausages.'

Chapter Ten

Lizzie came home at the end of March, by which time Jess had already started work in Simmons's cake shop to help with the Easter rush. She soon learned the names of all the cakes and different types of bread, found little difficulty in adding up and giving change, and the other girls she worked with seemed friendly enough. She liked serving in the shop, enjoyed chatting to the customers who came in and out all day long; loved the long mahogany and glass counter, which was so shiny and beautiful. The cakes displayed on the glass stands in the window looked and smelled so wonderful she could hardly resist them.

'Go on, have one if you want one,' Leah would say. 'You'll soon grow tired of them when you've had a few.'

Jess was shocked by the suggestion. She would never have dreamed of taking anything without asking. That would be tantamount to stealing, although the smell of the meat and potato pies and pasties, and in particular the heady aroma of a newlybaked loaf hot from the oven were so tantalising they made her juices run.

Only on a Friday did the shop girls treat themselves to a cake each, at trade price of course, to celebrate the end of another week. Jess looked forward to it and would debate with herself the choice that she would make for days beforehand. Would it be a custard slice, an Eccles cake or a slice of battenburg, which they called church windows? Or even a cream horn, though perhaps it should more rightly be called a mock cream horn, rationing being what it was. Whatever the choice, the cake was a special treat and always delicious.

The best part of working in the shop was that she got to see her friend every day. Leah worked in the tea rooms full time, despite complaining bitterly that she really wanted to be an actress or a newspaper reporter. She longed for a job that had some excitement and zest to it and didn't involve being under her parents's gaze all day long.

'It's so boring! Half the time the tea room is empty because there aren't any customers, or else we don't have the ingredients to make enough scones and cakes. How Robert can stand working in that hot bakery day and night, juggling recipes to make something out of nothing, I really can't imagine. And I have to stand about in a frilly apron and silly cap looking like a proper Charlie, being polite to fat old ladies who shouldn't be eating cake anyway.

'And would you believe, despite having finally escaped school and my horrible teachers, Mother still makes me do my piano practice every night, just as if I were still a child. I wouldn't mind so much if she allowed me to play anything interesting, but it's always scales and boring exercise pieces. It's so unfair. Oh, why doesn't something good ever happen to us? Our lives ruined by Mr Hitler?'

Her friend's vehemence always set Jess off into fits of giggles. She certainly didn't take her complaints at all seriously. It was perfectly plain that Leah's parents adored her, and everyone knew that Ambrose Gregg was absolutely potty about her. So what did she have to worry about?

'You could always marry Ambrose, if you want to escape your parents's clutches,' Jess suggested as they sat relishing their Friday treat together. This week Jess had chosen a cream horn and Leah a Cornish split.

'What? I'd rather *die*! He's so dreary, and always looks half asleep with those droopy eyelids of his, droopy everything in fact, there's so much blubber on him.'

Jess chuckled. 'You're exaggerating, he's just well built, that's all.'

'I know. Like a tank, but I shudder to think what he'd be like in bed. I bet he couldn't raise the energy to fire his guns.' And both girls burst into a fit of helpless giggles, Jess getting a blob of mock cream on her nose as a result. To hear Leah talk in such a ribald fashion always set her off because her friend had known absolutely nothing about sex until Jess had explained it all to her. Leah's mother had made only a vague mention about a wife's duty, gave her daughter a sanitary towel and belt, then left it at that.

'Where did you learn all this stuff?' Leah had asked, listening goggle-eyed to the sordid details of procreation.

'Don't ask, I get a running commentary every breakfast, and sound effects every night but take it from me, men are all out for what they can get. Romance doesn't come into it.'

'How heartless and cold you sound! I don't believe you for a minute. I mean to fall hopelessly in love with someone dark and handsome, and have lots of beautiful children one day. Don't you? Wouldn't you find that the most romantic, exciting thing in the world?'

'Not unless a man could give me what I most need.'

'Which is?'

'I'm not sure.' Jess licked the cream from her horn while she reflected upon this for a moment and then realised that she didn't need to think at all. What she wanted most of all was to play music. She'd started lessons with Sergeant Ted and absolutely loved it. He called her a natural. Not that she was, of course, since Jess practised for hours at home. Cora never minded, but her uncle was another matter, always complaining.

It was too much to hope for a normal, happy family life. Jess longed to be free of Uncle Bernie and the Delaneys to have a home of her own, freedom for herself and safety for her mother. What she needed most of all was someone to help her achieve that. 'Maybe *I* should marry Ambrose. His parents are well off and it would at least get me away from Cumberland Street and Uncle Bernie.'

'Don't even consider that. Bernie might be a rat, but Ambrose is just a big fat mouse. And who'd care to be squeaked to death? So boring!'

–

The joy of starting work was muted slightly for Jess by her worry over Lizzie. Her mother seemed listless and frail, so unlike her usual self. Jess couldn't even persuade her to get up in a morning. She'd lie in bed half the day, and then spend the rest of it flopped in a chair, getting on Cora's nerves simply by being there. Jess could tell by the way her aunt compressed her lips and sniffed disapprovingly whenever Lizzie didn't appear for breakfast, or slopped about all day not lifting a finger to help that if something didn't change soon, her patience would explode.

She'd make excuses, explaining how Lizzie was finding it difficult adapting to life after her time in prison, and couldn't get a job now that she had a record. Cora would simply mumble something to the effect that Lizzie never did like work at the best of times. But even worse than the sullen silence which was the normal state of affairs between these two women, as the weeks slipped by there developed a cut-throat battle for attention from the man of the house.

If Lizzie ever did stir from her chair it would be to make Bernie a cup of tea, to fetch his slippers and fuss over him, fold his evening paper or butter his bread just how he liked it; all the tasks which were normally Cora's province. She would offer to make him toad-in-the-hole, tune in his favourite programme on the wireless. Bernie wasn't interested in the news, or the state of the war, but he did enjoy 'stinker' Murdoch in 'Band Wagon' and 'big-hearted' Arthur. Lizzie always insisted on waiting up for him to come home at night, no matter how late it was, which annoyed Cora more than anything else.

'I never wait up for him, so why should she?'

'She means well,' Jess would say, stuck for a better answer.

'Like hecky thump she does. She means to get her feet under my table, preferably when I'm no longer sitting at it.'

One night as Lizzie settled herself in the battered old fireside chair to wait for Bernie, Cora pulled up a stool opposite, folded her ham-sized arms and made it clear she didn't intend to budge. 'You can go to bed, I'll see to him.'

Lizzie looked confused by this show of stubbornness on Cora's part, being somewhat out of character. Wasn't her sister-in-law supposed to be meek and mild, a victim who'd been bullied and should be grateful for any consideration at all? Not be sitting there with her hair in curlers and her tatty old dressing gown on, with an 'I'm-not-shifting' expression on her round red face.

'I would've thought you had enough on your plate during the day with all them kids of yours to see to, without having the energy to stop up late. I'll look after him for you, Cora. Don't you fret.'

'He's *my* husband. *I'll* be the one to do whatever he needs doing. You get off up them apples and pears to your bed. Happen you'll be needing to conserve your own strength for when you start looking for work.'

This was a prospect that had never entered Lizzie's head. Thankful to at last be out of prison and safely ensconced in Bernie's house, she had not the least intention of doing anything so reckless. 'Bernie'll look after me,' she said, pulling her lipstick from her pocket where she kept it handy so she could always look her best for him. Using the spotted mirror over the mantelpiece, she carefully applied another layer to her already thickly coated lips. 'He's said a dozen times how he likes having me around.'

'He does heck-as-like. He's only making use of you, as he does everybody that crosses his path. More fool you for doing his bidding. Would you jump in the canal if he told you to? He thinks you're a flaming nuisance, a thorn in his side. A dummel-head.'

'That's not true!' Lizzie had gone quite white, turning in spitting fury upon Cora and lashing out with nails like scarlet talons. The stool went flying but Cora, light on her feet despite her bulk, neatly ducked and evaded the blow. Wrapping her arms about Lizzie's waist, she grappled her to the dusty, clippy rug in a style of which any rugby player would have been proud. As Lizzie screamed and kicked and attempted to rip the curlers out of her sister-in-law's hair, Cora, with the benefit of size, pinned her easily to the floor. With five sausage-like fingers circling Lizzie's scrawny neck, she was sorely tempted to put an end to her opponent there and then.

'I could wring your flaming neck like the old boiler hen you are.'

'If you hurt me, Bernie will part your hair with a meat cleaver. It's me he thinks the world of, not you! That's why you're jealous. You know I can pinch him from under your nose any time I like.'

Lizzie might have been safer putting a match to an incendiary bomb.

Enraged by this threat to her position as wife and helpmeet, Cora picked Lizzie up as easily as if she were a scrawny chicken and might well have wrung the life out of her, or tarred and feathered her, had not Sam and Seb chosen that precise moment to come downstairs to see what all the pandemonium was about. Seeing her beloved children standing there in their pyjamas crying for their mam, brought a rush of tears to her eyes and a shaft of common sense into her brain. She gave Lizzie one final shake and reluctantly dropped her back in the chair. 'Flaming tart, see what you've made me do. Shown myself up before me childer. Gerroff to bed afore I finish t'job proper. Make yourself scarce.'

Wisely, Lizzie did just that. Viewing it as a necessary survival tactic in order to return and fight another day.

'He's a right lummock, your dad,' Cora told her two precious darlings as she gathered them into her brawny arms. One who, despite being the champion of her youth, had proved to be less attentive as a husband than she'd hoped. She never knew a moment's peace with him, always wondering what trouble each day might bring, jumping at every knock on the door, fearing the polis would come at any moment and cart him off to the clink. But he was her property and nobody else's. He certainly didn't belong to her sister-in-law.

–

'Can't we have our old place back?' Jess begged her uncle. When Lizzie had related this episode to her, in full graphic detail, she'd realised that the matter was far more serious than she'd appreciated. Not that she made any mention of the scrap to her uncle. That wouldn't do at all, not for any of them, least of all Cora, who really had all her sympathy. But something had to be done, and quickly. They couldn't go on living together in this tiny little house, not if blue murder was to be avoided. 'We don't fit in here any more. We need our own place, maybe a room somewhere?'

Bernie looked sceptical. 'Oh aye, and who would pay for it? You couldn't, not with what you're earning.'

'I'm doing better now I've got a new job, and I'll keep working hard. I'll manage to pay the rent, I promise. Besides, Aunt Cora has enough to do looking after her own family.'

Fond as Jess was of her aunt, nobody could ever accuse Cora of being the best housekeeper in the world. She'd sit with her feet propped up on a stool reading the paper, or have a crack with her friends for hours at a time, ignoring a sink full of dirty dishes and a table littered with the remains of breakfast. She wouldn't stir a muscle to sweep or mop the filthy kitchen floor, or think to peel a potato until the very last minute before her brood started to arrive home. She would bully sullen Sandra into doing various chores the minute the poor girl walked through the door.

Jess did most of the washing and ironing, which she was quite certain wouldn't get done otherwise. Even so, Cora didn't change the beds often enough to suit her, and never thought to make one.

'What's the point when you'll be getting back into them in a few hours?' she'd say, and laugh at what she called Jess's 'pickiness'.

Jess now persisted with her plea. 'If Mam had her own kitchen, she'd pay more attention to what's going on around her. She'd maybe want to get up of a morning to make breakfast, light the fire and stuff. Better than sitting about all day with nothing to do except get under my aunt's feet.'

'Cora's never said owt to me,' Bernie grumbled and Jess didn't dare claim that his wife was too afraid to object to anything, for fear of unleashing his nasty temper.

'I'm sure it would be good for my mam. It'd liven her up no end to have her own place.'

'I can find her something useful to do if she's bored,' Bernie snapped. 'Everyone has to pull their weight round here. I'll have a word with her, make her pull herself together.' Fearful that she might have made things worse for her mother, Jess wished she'd kept her trap shut and not said anything at all.

–

Jess took to eating her meagre breakfast in peace and quiet on the bakery doorstep until Mr Simmons came down to open up. He never seemed surprised to see her sitting there, even when it was cold and raining, believing her to be diligent and keen.

'Morning Jess,' he would say.

'Morning, Mr Simmons.'

'You'll sweep and mop the shop and tea room through for me?'

'Glad to, Mr Simmons.' And he'd nod and go off to the bakery to see if his son had the morning loaves ready.

Jess would happily do these tasks because it was warm in the tea room, situated as it was next to the bakery, and blissfully silent until the other girls arrived. Apart from the bakery, her other main avenue of escape was the Salvation Army. Ever since the night they were bombed, she'd helped out regularly in the mobile canteen. Jess thoroughly enjoyed helping and felt she was paying something back for the regular lessons she was having with Sergeant Ted. He'd taught her the rudiments of playing the trumpet: how she must keep her lips fairly slack to produce the low notes. She could make them lower still by pressing down the valves that opened the extra lengths of tubing. Tightening her lips, Jess pushed the air in the tube onwards before it had too much time to vibrate, which made for a higher note. Thus she learned to regulate the sounds. Oh and didn't she love playing that trumpet. She never missed a lesson. She'd also started playing in the Bugle Band, and six months on had been given a uniform to wear, which made Harry and Bert laugh like drains.

'You're a Junior Soldier now, eh? Have you been saved just because you play that flipping trumpet?' Harry teased.

'I think she looks proper fetching in that bonnet,' Bert sniggered.

Young Tommy answered for her. 'Leave the poor lass alone, you big bullies. She's doing a good job. More than some I might mention. We should all try to do our bit.'

'Says who?'

'What've you lot ever done for the war? Go on, impress me with your patriotic fervour.'

'We bring money into the house, a deal of money, if you want to know.'

'And how did you come by it? Not with honesty, I'll warrant.'

'Hey, who you calling dishonest?'

Jess grew tired of their simmering threat, fearing fire and brimstone might explode at any moment in the shape of her uncle coming roaring down the stairs demanding to know what all this row was about, whacking Tommy or Bert across the backs of their heads simply to make his presence felt. He never touched Harry these days, strangely enough. But then Harry himself was not averse to flinging a punch at poor Bert if he'd helped himself to one too many of the sausages that he'd twisted the butcher's arm to supply.

Leaving the brothers to their bickering, who seemed to be a sad fact of life here in Cumberland Street, Jess hastily walked away with a sigh. Thank goodness Cora and Lizzie were not going at it hammer and tongs. Goodness knows what her mother got up to during the day while she was at work, but it was vitally important that she keep her job and save every penny. With or without her uncle's help she meant to get them a place of their own and gain their independence once and for all.

Chapter Eleven

1941

The war was getting worse, with more bombing and air raids having occurred since the Christmas Blitz, and many buildings destroyed here on Deansgate. Women were now being called upon to work in place of all the men who had joined up. To her delight, Mr Simmons called Jess into his office and told her that he'd decided to give her a try as a waitress in the tea room. Jess was thrilled. Not only could she now work directly alongside Leah, but it was better pay and with the possibility of tips, which would top up her savings. Her friend was thrilled too, even though Jess and Leah hadn't seen much of each other lately.

Their trips out dancing had been curtailed somewhat. Jess had been busy with the mobile canteen and her trumpet practise, while Leah's social life seemed to be more closely regulated than ever. There was always some function or other that her mother, Mrs Simmons, had arranged, a seemingly endless parade of coffee mornings and rummage sales, a Weapons Week Fundraising Dance where Leah spent most of the evening in the cloakroom rather than on the dance floor; not to mention collecting newspapers, jam jars, old woollens, and all manner of other goods in need of recycling.

Leah would wrinkle her nose in protest, and Jess would suggest that she make an excuse to get out of it. Or perhaps one of Muriel's friends might be persuaded to go along instead, although this never quite seemed to work for some unknown reason. If Muriel ever found anyone, they always mysteriously backed out at the last moment, leaving Leah again as the only available option to accompany her.

Consequently, she'd feel sorry for her mother and succumb. 'Ma likes to do her bit for the war effort. If she needs help, how can I refuse? I can't leave her to struggle alone, can I?' Afterwards, she'd roll her eyes and admit that Ambrose Gregg had again been there, as suspected. 'It was clearly a ploy for us to get together. It won't work, no matter what she does. I can't stand him.'

Jess would smile, knowing that much as Leah might object to her mother's match-making and being dragged along to her charity functions, in reality she adored and admired her. She was, in Jess's opinion, an ideal mother; the kind anyone would be pleased to have. She too would happily have volunteered to help Mrs Simmons, were she not busy with the Sally Army. 'One day you might agree to marry him just to please her, or because it's a sensible, practical thing to do.'

'Never! I'd elope with the milkman's horse before I'd do that.'

Jess giggled at her loud protestations, unable to imagine a situation that would induce anyone with sense, herself included, to marry someone they didn't love. 'At least now we'll both be working together and can chat during the day.'

'Ooh goody, in between serving tea and scones to fat old ladies who shouldn't be eating them at all,' Leah irreverently added. 'I do wish something exciting could happen, don't you?'

So far as Jess was concerned, it already had. If she worked in the tea rooms she might get tips, and if she added these to the savings in the tin box she kept under her mattress, she might soon have enough to find her and Lizzie a place of their own.

–

Jess had become a great favourite with the Salvation Army band. She loved everything about it, not simply the performances, sometimes held at the citadel for a service, or at the Mission, as well as on street corners where they would collect a crowd and attract donations. She enjoyed the comradeship, the easy laughter and happy teasing, the feeling of being part of a group and doing something worthwhile, a sensation she'd never experienced before. Nor did she mind the rehearsals, or the endless hours of practise. She didn't even object when Sergeant Ted shouted at her for playing a wrong note. She would practise all the harder to get it right.

However much fun performing for a lively crowd might be, what she really loved most of all was the feel of the instrument in her hands. She loved the pressure of the valves beneath her fingers, the wonderful sensation that flowed through her veins like liquid gold whenever she put her lips against the mouthpiece and the most marvellous sounds came out. Ted told her that she played the bugle like a dream and the trumpet with a warm, mellow sound. Jess could hear only her own imperfections and glaring mistakes. Oh, but she meant to play better one day, she really did. She must just keep practising.

Sergeant Ted insisted that she do at least an hour every day, preferably two. She must go through the fundamentals, starting with the middle register and working through to the higher. Jess then ran through the scales and practised chord changes, striving to improve the flexibility of her lips and make sure she blew straight out and not down. Eager to achieve the right degree of tension, she worked hard on the exercises and pieces of music set for her. Much later, Jess would allow herself to play whatever she liked, attempting to improvise, since she possessed no written music of her own.

No matter what hurdles Uncle Bernie might put in her path, however much he might shout and complain about 'having that din in my house' which often meant that she was forced to practise in the back yard, or out on a stretch of waste land down by the River Irwell, she would never give up. To Jess, it didn't matter where she was, nothing and no one would prevent her from doing what she loved most: playing the trumpet. Were he to clout or beat her black and blue all over as he had Lizzie, it wouldn't make any difference, she'd keep on playing.

Sometimes she was allowed to play for the bombed-out victims, fed on tea and sympathy at the mobile canteen. Jess started to attend the citadel on a regular basis, though to her shame it was again more as a means of escape than genuine belief, at least initially. To her surprise, she found that she enjoyed it. She would regale them with 'We'll Meet Again', 'Mareseatoats', and her current favourite: 'A Nightingale Sang in Berkeley Square'. The people were warm and friendly and made her welcome, particularly liking the way music was a major part of the service. She would sing at the top of her voice before finally accompanying them on her trusty trumpet while Harriet would bash her tambourine.

Ted declared himself proud of his success in teaching her to play well, and that she should be pleased to be blessed with such a rare talent. He said that folk often made out they were in trouble when really they just wanted to listen to the liquid notes of her music. People round about only had to hear the trumpet start up and the canteen would be full in minutes. 'We'll have to start charging,' he joked, 'or we'll have nothing left for the genuine needy.'

'They're all genuinely needy,' Jess would protest. 'Look at the state of their lives, ruined by the war.'

'Aye well, whether that's the case or not, you pull your weight in other ways, lass.'

It was certainly true that whenever Harriet or Ted went out selling *The War Cry*, or taking round their collecting boxes to get donations to fund the work they did, they'd ask her to go along with them. Playing 'Lili Marlene' in the pubs would be sure to bring a rattle of coins into the collecting tin and Harriet had been known to sell out of *The War Cry* if Jess should play 'Danny Boy', there not being a dry eye in the house. That way they made twice as much money. Jess enjoyed going, not only because she loved playing her trumpet but because it got her out and about, escaping the misery of Cumberland Street for yet another evening. And she met a good many interesting characters along the way.

Sadly, it wasn't *her* trumpet at all. It belonged to the Sally Army Bugle Band. Jess longed for an instrument of her own. How to get one was beyond belief. She certainly didn't have any money to spare at the moment. Every penny she earned went towards paying for their keep, both for herself and Lizzie, and saving towards a better future for them. If there ever was anything left over, which was rare as Bernie was always claiming extra expenses for this, that and the other, it went into the savings tin, which she kept tucked under her mattress. This represented her one hope of escape from the tyranny of her uncle.

–

Over supper one evening, Jess happened to casually mention how Mr Simmons had put new locks on his doors since the break-in, and bought a new till, which she believed would be safer than the old cash box. 'It feels odd having to ring things up. It gives receipts and everything, but we had a queue a mile long at dinnertime because we kept getting in a muddle over it. People were shouting that they'd die of starvation if we didn't hurry up,' she related with a giggle.

This had been meant simply as an amusing story but proved to be a bad mistake. Bernie lowered his paper to listen, showing an unhealthy interest in the tale, wanting to know how the till operated, where it was kept and who locked it up. It suddenly dawned upon Jess that he was asking far too many pertinent questions and she quickly changed the subject, talking instead about a new bread recipe the shop was trying out, which didn't use as much yeast. 'I use some of the old dough to get the new batch going. It's quite clever really, and very economical.'

Bernie wasn't interested in making bread rise. Folding up his paper he quietly slipped out, presumably in search of his usual evening pint.

A day or two later, hurrying to get ready to go to the mobile canteen, as she usually did after work, Jess couldn't find her trumpet anywhere. There were occasions when she'd gone for a walk during her dinner break so that she could practise down a back street or by the railway sidings, any opportunity she could find since Bernie made such a fuss whenever he heard her practising in the house. But she didn't like to trespass too much on Mrs Simmons generosity, so had stopped bringing it to work. But where the heck was it?

Frantically searching to no avail, she became alarmingly aware that Bernie was watching her closely, almost smiling with satisfaction as he sat in his chair by the fire, smoking his Craven A cigarettes. Cora cast an anxious glance in her direction as she ran up and down the stairs, pointedly saying nothing. Jess dragged open drawers and cupboards, banging them shut again. Lizzie, prostrate in the chair opposite, with her eyes half closed was taking no interest.

At her wits's end, Jess finally said, 'Where did I put that trumpet, Cora? Did I take it to the shop with me this morning? Have I left it at work?'

It was Bernie who answered. 'No, I've pawned it.'

Jess stared at her uncle in stunned disbelief. 'You've what?'

'We've suffered enough of that row night after night. It's doing my head in. I've put it in hock where it'll do nobody's nerves any harm.'

Jess wanted to fly at him, to beat his brains out. Only the pained anxiety in her aunt's face, and the tremor of her plump jowls held her back. Cora silently mee-mawed at Jess, making a pantomime of gestures with her eyes and mouth in an effort to indicate to her niece that she shouldn't worry, that they'd get it back in due course. Bernie spotted the performance and lashing out one hand, gave his wife a clout across the back of her head. Her curlers flew everywhere and Cora's cheeks went bright red but she made scarcely a sound by way of protest.

Jess was instantly enraged on her aunt's behalf and leapt in front of him, as if to protect her from further reprisals, hands clenched into tight little fists. 'Don't you dare hit my aunt, you big bully. I don't care if you have nicked the trumpet, but don't take it out on Cora.'

This only made him laugh. 'Oh aye, you do care about that trumpet. You never stop blasting our eardrums with it. Drove me crackers.'

'Well then *you* can explain to the Sally Army where it's gone, not *me*.'

Bernie got lazily to his feet, flexing and swelling out his ample flesh so that Jess was forced to take a quick step backwards or she could be knocked over as he moved threateningly towards her. 'I don't think so, girl. If you fetch it into this house again, I'll hammer it flat so that it'll be no more use to you than a squashed tin of beans.'

'You can't do that! You've no *right*. That trumpet belongs to the Salvation Army. What will Sergeant Ted say when I tell him? How can I ever repay them for losing one of their best instruments?' Tears were blocking her throat, a swell of pain in her chest. She should never have brought it home. But how could she not, considering all the practising she needed to do?

Even Lizzie was looking anxious, her befuddled gaze flicking from one to other, clearly trying to understand what was going on. 'Don't you talk to our Bernie like that, girl. Show some gratitude for what he's done for us.'

Determined not to dissolve into tears, Jess turned on her mother. 'Gratitude? Huh! You must be joking! We owe him nothing. He's ruined you already, and will do the same to me if I let him, the mean old—'

'Shurrup Jess, you owe him everything, and don't you forget it. Where would we be if he'd refused to put a roof over our heads?'

'We wouldn't have lost the roof we did have, if he hadn't taken you shoplifting that Christmas.'

Lizzie was on her feet in a second, swaying slightly as if she'd been drinking, although she'd promised Jess faithfully that she'd never touch another drop as long as she lived. Some hope. Her eyes were flashing and her voice filled with spite. 'If I'd never had you in the first place, I wouldn't have needed to pinch stuff. I'd've been in clover with nothing to worry about.'

Jess felt as if she'd been punched in the face, but why did Lizzie always turn nasty? Why couldn't she defend her own daughter instead of her brother-in-law? But then Jess knew why, only too well. Her mother lacked that normal part of human nature known as nurturing, which parents were supposed to exhibit towards their young. She didn't have it because Bernie had corrupted her with his own brand of greed and self-interest. Instead, Lizzie was the one needing to be cared for, and protected from his evil influence.

Cora was wringing her hands, trying to put in the odd soothing word in a frantic attempt to cool growing tempers. 'Don't fret about it, love. We'll get that trumpet back somehow.'

Jess was beyond comfort. She'd done her best not to be a nuisance, worked hard to pay for their keep while her mother lay about half the day, or prowled around shops running the risk of being arrested for shoplifting yet again. She felt filled with guilt and remorse for having brought the instrument home in the first place, frightened of admitting to her new friends at the Sally Army what had happened to it. And most dreadful of all, how on earth could she ever afford to replace it when she was saving so hard for a place of their own. Would she never be free?

Jess felt such hatred for her uncle that she simply couldn't contain her emotion. Tears were brimming over, rolling unchecked down her cheeks, and it felt as if a great weight were pressing down on her chest, threatening to crush her. 'This is all *your* fault,' she yelled at him. 'You've ruined all our lives.'

Bernie hitched up his trousers with the thick elastic of his braces and ambled over to her. Everyone in the small, overheated room seemed to hold their breath. Although it was plain what was going to happen next, Jess stood transfixed as she watched his fist come towards her in what seemed like slow motion. It hit her full in the chest, sending her flying so that she fell so hard against the chair upon which Lizzie had previously been sitting, that it tipped over backwards. Jess cracked her head on the sideboard and fell in a crumpled heap, one foot twisted awkwardly beneath her. Pain shot through her, but she wasn't blessed with oblivion as the room spun dizzily about her. There was something wet and sticky on her face, which she took to be blood and she could hear Cora crying.

The next instant her uncle was standing over her, a smile on his face that could only have come from the devil himself. For the first time Jess experienced real fear as she felt her own helplessness.

'Don't cross me girl. I don't like it.' Then he hunkered down beside her, pushing his face so close she could smell his stinking breath, the result of too much tobacco and whisky, and days of unscrubbed teeth. His voice was soft, but rich with menace. 'When I ask for details, I expect to get them. Understand? This evening you'll fetch me the details of the location of the new till Mr Simmons has thoughtfully provided, and where he keeps the key for it. Also, the likely day when there'll be most money in it. That is not on payday or when he goes to the bank. Is that clear?'

Chapter Twelve

After a largely sleepless night worrying over the loss of her trumpet, and trying not to think too much about the implications of Bernie's latest threat, Jess set off for work the next morning without bothering to collect herself a breakfast. She was far too anxious to escape. But despite leaving especially early, she didn't succeed.

Bernie jumped out in front of her just as she was walking along Cumberland Street, which shocked her. Jess stopped in her tracks, hand pressed to her chest and breathing hard. Nervous of inflaming her uncle's temper, she remembered Cora's advice and kept silent, waiting to see what he wanted this time, though she could guess.

'I wanted to catch you before you went off to work because I don't think you understand what it is I want from you. I thought it best if I explain it again, calm like, with no tantrums or tears. All right by you, poppet?'

Jess felt a chill run down her spine. Never had he used endearments towards her before, and nothing good could be meant by it. If he thought she would be cowed by his bullying, he'd another think coming. Nothing would induce her to betray the Simmonses. 'I understand perfectly what you want, but I've already told you I can't provide any information at all about the new till. There's nothing more to be said on the matter.' She made to move past him but he blocked her way.

'Tha's behaving la-di-dah. Fact is, you don't appreciate how things have been a bit tight lately, what with the war and your mam not being fit to work. The fact is, I need you to contribute more towards your keep.'

Jess was appalled. She already paid him a pound a week for herself and her mother, plus extras towards rent and other household bills that Cora never quite seemed able to manage. 'I pay my whack, and can't afford any more. Anyway, it's as much your responsibility as mine that Mam is in the state she is. You owe it to her, and to me, to help get her back on her feet.'

His face was as hard and cold as polished steel but his tone remained soft, barely above a whisper. 'That's what I'm saying, girl. Do me a favour and I'll see what I can do to help you.' He rested one massive hand on the wall above her head as he leaned closer, thus bringing the stink of his breath to her nostrils yet again. Jess almost threw up when he started to scratch his crotch right there in front of her. What an unpleasant, despicable man he was, surely the very worst uncle a girl could possibly have.

'A young lass like you should be able to think of some way to please a chap.'

Terror pierced her. 'I don't know what you mean, but if you don't let me go soon I'll be late for work. I wouldn't be able to pay you anything if I then got the sack.'

His smile was chilling. 'I just need a minute to talk about this reluctance of yours to give me information on that new till at Simmons's. Folk struggling to get the hang of it could prove useful. Instead of ringing up the exact sum, you could 'appen ring up less and pocket the difference.'

Jess thought she must not have heard him right, but apparently she had. 'Never! You must think I'm soft in the head.'

His lips curled upward in a most unpleasant parody of a smile. 'It's easy. If the customer spends half a crown, you only ring up two bob and put the rest in your pocket. A few extra shillings and sixpences here and there'll add up to a tidy sum by the end of the month. Don't overdo it, mind, just be canny.'

Jess was aghast by this suggestion. 'That's stealing!'

'Nay, think of it as a bonus on your wages, and one you deserve for working hard.'

'It's not a bonus it's theft! And why on earth would I steal from Mr Simmons? He's never done me any harm. In fact he's been kindness itself.' She didn't say how he'd started unlocking the door even earlier in a morning now that summer was changing into autumn and it was often cold or wet. How he let her warm herself in the bakery before giving her any jobs to do and, having one morning noticed the poor size of her breakfast, had insisted Robert give her a buttered bap from the bakery, sometimes with a bit of fried Spam to go with it. 'What do you think I am?'

'A chip off the old block.'

Jess went hot with fury. How dare he presume such a thing? 'Just because my mother was stupid enough to do everything you told her and landed herself in jail as a result, doesn't mean that I'm as daft as she is. Anyroad, even she only stole that one time you made her.'

Bernie laughed. 'One time, is that what you think? Shows how little you know your mam.'

Some instinct warned Jess he could be right. Maybe Lizzie might have gone in for more petty thieving than she'd admitted to so she shifted to another tack. 'Mr Simmons would soon spot that the money in the till didn't match what had gone off the shelves.'

'He wouldn't suspect a thing, not if you do as I say and don't ring up the full amount. He'd put it down to problems with you numbskulls still learning how to operate the new machine. There's no danger of anyone suspecting you of doing summat criminal, not with that angelic face of yours and those big brown innocent eyes. And if you think Lizzie has mended her ways, then you must indeed be soft in the head. She's still at it, even now. If you don't want her back inside, it's up to you to stop her. Who knows what might happen, otherwise?'

'Is that a threat?'

'Let's call it a timely warning.'

Jess felt a small panic within her. Had Lizzie really started her shoplifting again? Surely even her trollop of a mother wouldn't be so stupid? 'You know I don't want her back in jail. Nor do I have any intention of ending up in prison myself, ta very much.'

He stroked a finger down her cheek, making Jess shudder with revulsion. 'You're a bonny lass and, as well as being prettier than your ma, you're more intelligent, so you've the sense not to get caught. Just remember, I can't afford to bankroll the pair of you any longer. You'll have to pay her whack as well as your own, one way or the other.'

Jess was shaking in every limb, trembling with fear yet determined not to become a victim, like her mam. 'I'll not do it. One thief in my family, thanks to you, is enough.'

He flipped out a hand and clouted her across the side of her head, sending her staggering with the weight of the blow. 'Watch that glib mouth of yours, girl.'

'And you watch that fist of yours,' Jess shouted, her eyes filling with hot tears. 'Don't think you can bully me. I'm not my stupid mother!'

He grabbed her by the shoulders and shook her violently, making her head rock backwards and forwards on her slender neck. Jess could smell the sweet-sour stink of stale sweat on him and, screwing up her nose in distaste, she tried to pull away but he had too firm a grip. The pressure of his bloated stomach trapping her against the wall made her cringe with loathing. Fear was overwhelming her and her senses were reeling.

'We need to come to a mutually beneficial arrangement, then your trumpet might magically reappear. Fetch a few sixpences, or better still, pound notes, home from that shop and I'll get that blasted instrument out of hock for you, so long as you play it outside and not in the bleedin' house. I can't say fairer than that, now can I?'

'I'll *never* do that!' Jess firmly stated.

His face darkened. 'You're our Jake all over again. He tended to argue the whole damned time. Never would do as he was told.'

'If you mean that I speak my mind and stand up for what's right, I always will. I intend to remain honest, like my dad. I'd rather replace a hundred trumpets you steal from the Salvation Army than give in to your nasty threats.'

Placing his mouth close against her ear, his voice dropped to a hoarse whisper, 'Look at it this way, girl, it's your mam who would benefit. If you want to keep her safe then do as I say or you'll live to regret it. If you refuse, I'll make you sorrier than you can imagine. I'm a patient man, but I wouldn't recommend you push me too far. Who knows what I might be forced to do then.'

If she'd felt a prick of fear before, now she was drained of all energy, limp and helpless in his massive hands. Aware of her fragile vulnerability, Jess felt as impotent as a fly caught in a giant's fist. He could snuff her out without a second thought. As he said himself, Lizzie was useless, and Jess sensed in Harry and Bert the start of a quiet rebellion. They were tired of dancing to his tune and wanted to make their own way in the world. Besides, if she let Bernie get away with bullying her, as he had Lizzie and Cora, then she would be forever in his power. In the few seconds it took to think this through, Jess resolved she would never allow that to happen.

Lifting her chin she looked him straight in the eye, somehow managing to dampen down her fear sufficiently to say her piece. 'Do your worst, great bully that you are. I'm saving for a decent future for Mam and me, so don't think you can force me to do anything wrong or against the law, because you can't. I'll never do that. *Never!*'

Momentarily startled, either by her bravery or her cheek, his hands went loose, which gave Jess the chance to wrench herself free of his grasp. She swung away from him to march away up the street, her head held high. Then the sound of his raucous laughter followed her every step of the way.

'Buy your own trumpet and keep it well hidden from your uncle.' Leah urged Jess, as if the solution were simple.

'Do you know how much trumpets cost? And where could I possibly put it to keep it safely away from his grasping fingers?' Jess had made no mention to her friend about the real reason for her uncle pawning the trumpet: his insistence that she should steal from Leah's own father. It didn't seem appropriate, and if Mr Simmons ever got wind of it, might well result in Jess losing her job.

They were sitting on a couple of chairs in a corner of the dance hall sipping lemonade as they exchanged confidences. On this occasion they were at the Harpurhey Baths Ballroom on Rochdale Road with strict instructions not to miss the bus and to be home by ten. Jess was now staying over at the Simmons's house on the nights they went dancing. Such a relief.

There were a lot of air force trainees around tonight who were stationed at Heaton Park, so neither of them had been short of partners. At that moment an airman asked Jess for a dance and, remembering Mrs Simmons's advice, she politely accepted despite being far more concerned about what to do about the loss of her trumpet. She had to concentrate hard to give the young man her full attention. It was a quickstep and he didn't start off too well as he immediately trod on her foot, then let his hand slide down to her bottom as he pretended to lose his balance.

'Sorry about that! Quite a crush in here tonight.'

'That's all right,' Jess said, placing his hand back on her waist.

As they danced, she scoured every face in the band as always, and was disappointed not to see anyone that she recognised. There were two trumpets, one bass, three saxophones and a trombone, plus a pianist and drummer. They were good, putting lots of energy into the music, but Steve Wyman was not amongst them. She became absorbed watching the trumpet players, checking their finger work as they played her favourite, 'Don't Sit Under the Apple Tree'.

'Am I boring you?' her partner asked, rather rudely.

Her cheeks coloured with shame over her inattention to him. His hand felt hot and sweaty on her back, in fact it was edging around to the front, creeping up her rib cage and Jess began to feel acutely uncomfortable. He was pushing her round in a dizzying whirl, and had again trodden on her feet a couple of times. He must be the clumsiest dancer on the floor. She couldn't help but compare him with Steve's skill, wondering where he was playing these days.

Leah shimmied past in the arms of a sailor. 'You could always store it at our place.'

'What? Oh, I don't think so.'

'Accept charity. What are friends for?'

'Excuse me,' said the airman, his probing fingers now squeezing the curve of her breast. 'Are you with her or me?'

'Her,' Jess said, and walked away.

Jess decided that she really wasn't in the mood for dancing tonight and spent the remainder of the evening hiding away in the cloakroom, chewing over her problem. What could she do? She didn't want to give up her trumpet lessons, nor her work with the Sally Army. But she was going to have to explain to Sergeant Ted that she'd lost the instrument, hopefully without creating more problems. The last thing she wanted was for the sergeant to come and tackle Uncle Bernie, aware who would come off the worst as a result of such a confrontation. Why did he have to spoil everything for her?

Later, as they changed their shoes and collected their coats and bags, Leah noticed that Jess still looked troubled and tried to offer some comfort. 'He'll have taken it to Mr Yoffey's pawn shop. Why don't we go and talk to him? We may be able to negotiate a deal. The dear man has a heart of gold and may let you have the trumpet back without paying a penny.'

Jess didn't believe this to be a possibility, but eagerly agreed with the plan anyway. What did she have to lose?

Chapter Thirteen

Abe Yoffey considered the two girls very seriously from behind his owlish spectacles for a long time in contemplative silence. He liked young people, having served as Treasurer for some years in the Manchester Young Zionist Society, now sadly in abeyance. On the other hand, he was of the opinion that the role of the female of the species was best confined to the home front, to nurturing, and to providing refreshments for functions at the synagogue or, in this case, the citadel. Playing the piano, as Miss Leah was known to do, was one thing, wanting to play a trumpet seemed to be quite another entirely. What was the world coming to? Dear, dear, dear. Girls were even driving trams these days. Yet he liked to think of himself as having a generous nature, not the narrow-minded breed that so blighted every religion, including his own. Prejudice against women was equally bad. He had no wish to be guilty of such a thing.

He woke each morning in a cold sweat, waiting for the knock on his door, which would bring incarceration. Early in the war, May 1940 to be exact, most of his friends had been taken away to be interned as aliens for the duration simply because they were Jews. For some reason, perhaps because of his age, eighty-nine next birthday, and the fact that he was well liked, he had been saved. Abe suffered the occasional brick thrown through his window but he could live with that. He desperately longed to stay in his own home and, for now at least, a blind eye had been turned and he remained unmolested. But he had little hope of it lasting. It would be his turn next. Being a Jew anywhere, even in Britain, wasn't a good thing to be in this war.

He gave an expressive shrug. 'You want for me to give you a trumpet? I'm so old and foolish I would give something away for nothing?'

'It would only sit in the back of your shop otherwise, wouldn't it, dear Mr Yoffey?' Leah artfully pointed out.

'Forever, I should think. Don't I get better ones through my doors every day of the week?'

'Then I'm sure you wouldn't mind letting it go.'

'You have no money?' He flapped his hands up in a helpless gesture.

Leah wasn't for giving up. 'You could think of this offer as a loan.'

'A lending library for instruments, is that what I have to be? You would take advantage of an old man, a fine young girl like you from a good home? Am I not so poor that I live on Bismark Herrings morning, noon and night? Worn out with too much work and this endless war. Do I not deserve a rest already?'

Jess giggled. Even as the old man was complaining and flourishing his hands about with an air of disapproval, the eyes behind the spectacles were glimmering with laughter and mischief. It was as if he was saying he'd have sharp fun with them before he gave them what they wanted. 'My uncle had no right to hock it. It didn't belong to me, only to the Salvation Army whom I work for. If I got it back, I would take better care of it,' she promised in a neat, small voice.

Abe Yoffey frowned. He liked these two young girls, and had no quarrel at all with the Salvation Army. Sadly though, on this occasion he carefully explained how he'd refused to accept the trumpet from her uncle, not believing his reassurance that it was honestly come by. 'Is it my fault that people underestimate my intelligence? I told him to put it back wherever he found it. He was not pleased.'

'I can see that he wouldn't be.'

Seeing the bleak expression of pain in her soft brown eyes, he almost wished that on this occasion he'd been less particular. There was something about the way she tipped down her head and allowed that wild mane of shining hair to shield her disappointment from pity that cut to the heart of him. He knew instinctively how she had suffered, and could sense her courage in every line of her too slender, young body. 'I suppose it's a musician you think you are?'

Jess gave a little shrug, still not meeting his gaze as she addressed the tattered linoleum beneath her feet. 'I'm trying to learn. It isn't easy.'

'Play for him,' Leah suggested, suddenly seeing a way of winning the old man over. 'Go on, give him a tune.'

'He's just told us, Leah, that he doesn't have the trumpet. Weren't you listening?'

Leah put her arm about her friend's shoulders to give her a little squeeze, as if assuring her to have faith before rewarding the old pawnbroker with her most dazzling, blue-eyed smile. 'I'll bet he doesn't know half what he's got in that cavern behind his shop. There could well be any number of trumpets back there, if he looked hard enough.'

Mr Yoffey blinked, meeting their conjoined gaze for several long seconds without saying a word. Then turning on his heel, he disappeared into the dark recesses of his shop. He was gone for some time, so long that the two girls grew curious and edged further into its depths, examining the weird and wonderful treasures within: a moth-eaten stuffed fox, a tarnished silver tea pot, a Victorian pianoforte complete with candelabra. There were the usual collection of clogs, boots and shoes; hats, coats and dresses by the score and any number of boxes all bearing carefully printed labels to identify their contents.

Finally, he emerged out of the gloom, trumpet in hand: a shiny, graceful instrument, which had clearly been properly cared for over the years, and well loved by its previous owner. Jess wondered if it had hurt very much to be forced to pawn such a wonderful item, but then forgot to worry about this unknown stranger, whoever he might be, as the pawn shop owner put the instrument into her hands. The reverence in this simple act seemed to indicate he was anxious to hear her play, if only she could be persuaded.

Jess gave the trumpet a quick check of all its working parts: the valves, the mouthpiece, testing the feel of it in her hands. When she felt comfortable with it, she put it to her lips and began to play. She chose 'Goodnight Sweetheart' and could hear Leah humming softly beside her, see Mr Yoffey nodding his head in time to the beat. Jess found herself lost in the music.

When she was done, the old man took off his spectacles and dabbed at his eyes with his polishing cloth, before giving his spectacles a furious wipe and setting them back on the bridge of his nose. 'So I am a fool to myself. It has cluttered up my shop for long enough. You take it, and do what you can with it.'

Jess stared at the instrument in her hand in a daze of disbelief. 'I honestly don't have any money to pay for it.'

He lifted his two hands in a gesture of defeat. 'I'll live till I'm ninety, you can pay me by then. I'll be hearing plenty of trumpets after that. See that you make good music, and don't let that uncle of yours anywhere near it.' Then he flapped his hand for her to take it away quickly before he changed his mind.

–

Jess called again on Mr Yoffey and the old man was delighted to see her. 'Ah, so you like coming to my shop? Ay, ay, ay, normally I have to coax people in off the street by dragging them in by the scruffs of their collar.'

Jess giggled. 'I don't believe you have to do that at all.'

He gave one of his expressive shrugs and chuckled. 'Folk come to me because they must. They wish to eat more than their need for fancy suits, as do we all.'

'I wanted to tell you how I was getting along with the trumpet you lent me. I'm taking great care of it, and keeping it in good condition.' Pushing back a tangle of blonde hair, Jess cast him a sidelong glance. 'I will try to pay you a little each week. I think I can manage that, now that I'm making good money in tips. Then it truly would be mine one day.' Her big brown eyes looked so beseeching that, utterly captivated by her charm, he instantly agreed.

'How can I resist such limpid beauty when you use such powerful blackmail?'

On impulse, Jess gave the old man a hug. 'You are wonderful and it isn't blackmail at all. I just want to do the right thing, to pay you what the trumpet is worth.'

'It is worth nothing at the back of my shop. Besides, a shnorrer you are not.'

'What on earth is a shnorrer?'

Abe waved his hands about and made a little poofing noise by blowing out his cheeks. 'She does not know what is a shnorrer? It is a beggar, or as you Lancashire folk say, someone always on the scrounge. A cadger. I think you are not one of those, little one. You are pure gold, and when you play that trumpet it too turns from base metal into something magical. Besides, am I a selfish old man? I should be the one to deny the world the benefit of your talent?'

'Then you'll agree to let me pay for the trumpet?'

His eyes were twinkling. 'I agree only because you will have to call in my shop every week to make the payment and I can enjoy your company. Perhaps you would do me the honour of taking tea with me.'

'I would be delighted.'

He bowed in gratitude, like the gentleman he was. 'I shall look forward to it with pleasure.'

Taking tea with Mr Yoffey became a regular feature of her week. Jess would call every Friday evening after she'd got paid and hand over a shilling, sometimes a florin or a half crown if her tips had been good ones, which he would enter with meticulous care into a large ledger. After that, he would brew a pot of tea and they would sit in the back of the shop. Mr Yoffey would have his cat on his knee, nodding wisely, interrupting only rarely as she told him about the kind of customers who came into the tea room.

'There are the ones who send back the toasted teacake because they say it is too dry or too cold when really it's perfectly acceptable. Or they ask for a teapot for two and extra hot water, so that it doesn't cost as much, even though there are four persons. They eat several cakes off the stand and then expect these to be included in the price of the standard afternoon tea they've also consumed.'

How Mr Yoffey loved to listen to her gossip. 'People are an endless source of entertainment,' he agreed.

When she finally stopped talking long enough to draw breath, she would accept the bagel he offered, and listen enthralled while the old man told his own tales.

One particular evening Mr Yoffey said to her, 'Your trumpet practice, it is going well? You have the instrument with you? I know you wouldn't think to play it for a weary old man?'

'Of course I would.' Jess slid it out of its case, put it to her lips and began to play 'Joy, Freedom, Peace and Ceaseless Blessing' to the tune of 'Swanee River'. It was a haunting melody and one she played often in the Citadel.

She'd barely played a couple of bars when the door burst open and a young man strode in. He stood stock still in the middle of the shop, glaring at her with red-hot fury in his eyes.

'What the hell do you think you're doing with my trumpet?'

–

Unable to believe her eyes, Jess stared in dawning horror at Steve Wyman. After all this time, she'd found him at last! She'd always dreamed he might ask her to dance and hold her close once more. She would picture them slowly dancing the last waltz together to the tune of 'Dancing in the Dark' with the lights in the ballroom spinning around them. Naturally, in those dreams, Jess made up exciting conversations between them where he found her absolutely fascinating and asked to see her again. Now she needed to tell him her name, and a carefully edited version of her life and situation. Before she could gather her thoughts, Mr Yoffey stepped in front of her, redirecting the intruder's attention away from his young protégé.

'Young man, you cannot charge into my shop like a bull in the proverbial china shop and claim ownership of my property.'

'That trumpet is *my* property and I've come to redeem it.'

'Too late. Too late.' Mr Yoffey said, tutting sadly and shaking his head. 'More than a year it has sat collecting dust on my shelves. Am I supposed to give it house room forever, till you decide you might like it back?'

'Yes, dammit, that's the whole point of pawning something, isn't it?'

The old man shook his head with vigour. 'Ay, ay, ay, you think I run a charity? You leave your trumpet. You take my money. You should come back within the time it states on the ticket to pay the full amount, plus interest, you understand? Then you get it back. Are you able to show me your ticket, within the time permitted?'

Jess had listened to all of this in stunned silence, uncertain what to say. Now she finally found her voice. 'Are you saying this is your trumpet? I thought...'

Ignoring her completely, he suddenly began searching his pockets, pulling out a fistful of coins and notes and slamming them on the counter. 'I don't have your damned ticket, nor a clue how long you allowed me to redeem it, but here's my cash. Every penny I possess. Take it all. Just give me my trumpet.'

'It belongs to this young lady now. She has paid for it.'

He cast scarcely a glance in Jess's direction. 'Don't talk rubbish. It's mine and I want it back this minute.'

A part of her was thrilled to have found him again, while her heart was sinking over the circumstances that had brought them together. Had that young man not been scowling so disagreeably, Jess might well have reminded him that they'd met before. She dismissed this notion as a dangerous folly. His mouth was compressed into a tight line of fury and his green eyes were blazing. Perhaps her memory had played tricks, or she'd been mistaken to think him attractive on that first occasion. It must have been the magical atmosphere of the ballroom that had gone to her head for she really couldn't find anything to like about him at all right now. The collar of his blue shirt was white and the necktie all askew. Neither matched the brown suit he wore, which was shabby to the point of threadbare.

When he'd first entered the shop he'd been carrying a small brown suitcase fastened with a leather strap, together with the sort of case, which would hold a musical instrument, surely something larger than a trumpet. Jess wondered what it might be. He'd placed them both on the floor and dropped a shabby trilby hat on top that had also seen better days.

This precious instrument, which she'd hoped would replace the one Bernie had stolen from her and disposed of, was clearly his. She felt devastated, never having experienced in her life such embarrassment. What on earth should she do? She certainly couldn't keep it, not if it still rightfully belonged to Steve Wyman. Yet she'd already made several payments on it, and endured a long and uncomfortable half hour explaining the whole sorry tale to Sergeant Ted, who, finally, and very generously, had agreed to let the matter lie. He said the missing trumpet might well turn up one day, when her uncle was in a more generous mood. Was it any wonder if a part of her had no wish to meekly hand over this instrument, particularly since its original owner was being so objectionable towards poor Mr Yoffey.

The old man was gathering up all the loose change, collecting and folding the notes. Putting them safely in an old brown envelope, he handed it solemnly back. 'I am sorry, but the trumpet is no longer available. You are too late. As I have already explained, this young lady has made several payments for it, and is now legally the new owner.'

This young man swung around, at last fixing his penetrating green-eyed glare exclusively upon Jess. 'I'm sure you think you've won,' he growled. 'I'm damned if I'll let you get away with it.' Upon these words, he swung on his heel and stormed out of the shop.

Jess found herself trembling so badly that she had to sit down. Won what, the trumpet? 'What did he mean, Mr Yoffey, by saying he would not allow me to get away with it? I really don't want any trouble or unpleasantness.'

'Tut, tut, unpleasant that young man certainly is. Too big for his britches, he does not deserve so remarkable an instrument. Drink your tea, little one. Will we worry about him? No, I do not think so.' To her astonishment, Mr Yoffey stoutly defended her.

–

Jess couldn't believe her bad luck. It seemed sadly ironic that for some time she'd been hoping against hope that she'd find Steve Wyman again, perhaps playing in a band at some dance hall or other. To come across him in such circumstances was truly heartbreaking. All she could do now was practise harder than ever with the trumpet, trying to justify depriving him of his precious instrument. 'I'll Be Seeing You' became one of her favourite tunes. Tears would roll down her cheeks as she played, 'I'll be looking at the moon, but I'll be seeing you'.

Jess had been relieved when he wasn't waiting for her when she'd left Mr Yoffey's shop that day. Yet at the same time oddly disappointed. He must not have recognised her, which showed what a poor impression she'd made on him when they first met. The reality was that they'd simply enjoyed one dance. Nothing more. That was several weeks ago, so no wonder he'd forgotten all about her. Nor was he at the shop the following week when again she called with payment, although Mr Yoffey admitted he had spotted a young man hovering outside the previous day.

'You won't tell him my name, will you?' she begged, suddenly concerned that Steve might still be angry with her. 'Or where I live?'

'I look like a man with no brains? Would I do such a harebrained thing?'

Strangely, Jess felt disappointed by his vehemence when really she should be relieved. 'I've been thinking about that trumpet. Perhaps I should return it, since it was important for him to hand over all the money he possessed to get it back.'

'Poof, that young man simply likes to have his own way, I am thinking. That is how he saw it, as a competition to be won. He couldn't bear someone getting one over on him. I know the sort. You keep the instrument, little one. It is yours now.'

Remembering how difficult Steve had been, and how he had threatened her before walking out, Jess tucked the trumpet under her arm, deciding that Mr Yoffey was probably right for her to keep it. But she couldn't stop thinking about Steve Wyman. Despite their meeting going wrong, she couldn't stop thinking about him, longing to find him around some street corner. The only solution seemed to be to continue attending the dances, as if nothing untoward had happened, even though all hope of their friendship had vanished.

Chapter Fourteen

1942

The first weeks of 1942 still seemed to be in a mood of bleak austerity. After a long period of quiet the day finally dawned when the skies were again filled with enemy bombers. Bernie viewed this as a chance to make some much-needed money. He saw himself as indestructible, almost revelling in the excitement of the massive explosions, like giant fireworks, and the walls tumbling before his eyes. He didn't feel in any great danger out in the open. Even the screams that came from the less fortunate made him feel brave and powerful. It was common knowledge that plenty had been killed outright in their own cellars, so nowhere was truly safe, not in this war.

But he still had his bit of business to attend to. Not wishing to have his disguise tested, he slipped quietly away down a back alley. Nobody saw him go. The air was thick with dust; the smell and taste of fear and death almost tangible. The streets seemed to be piled high with stuff: abandoned bicycles, chairs, tables, clocks and clothing spilling out of rooms ripped open to the four winds, like doll's houses with the fronts lifted off. He even found a fur coat in one garden, a bit moth-eaten but likely to fetch a few quid. Bernie helped himself, filling the handcart he'd brought with him and trundled his booty back to Cumberland Street. This would be the easiest money he'd ever made.

'Here, what am I supposed to do with this lot?' Cora wanted to know. 'Haven't we got enough lumber?' She indicated the accumulated pile of junk that already took up half the back yard.

'Throw a tarpaulin over it and put it in the Anderson shelter. Whatever you think best, only keep it safe till I have time to dispose of stuff at the right price. It'll only arouse suspicion if I do it too quickly.'

'Oh aye, everything must be kept safe, except your wife.'

He flung out one hand and smacked her across the face. 'Shut your mouth, woman. When I want your opinion, I'll ask for it.' Seb and Sam, seeing their mother abused, opened their twin mouths and let out a loud wail of protest. 'And shut them brats up an' all.'

He stormed off in a rage, banging the back door after him so hard, it rocked on its hinges. Cora took what satisfaction she could from how daft he looked in the tin helmet and ARP overalls, both of them several sizes too small for his substantial girth. Happen Jess was right and she was daft to put up with such treatment. Surely she deserved better? Then she bent to comfort her children.

'It's all right, yer Mam's not really hurt. Come on, my little loves, how about a chip butty?' And gathering her children to her bosom she gave them a cuddle.

When Jess came home she did a double take the minute she clapped eyes on her aunt. 'What have you done to your face, Cora?'

'I walked into t' pantry door. Never look where I'm going, me.'

Jess opened her mouth to express her disbelief at this tale, then spotted the wide, frightened eyes of the twins and thought better of it. 'Put your feet up, I'll make a brew.'

'Eeh, yer a good lass.'

When Jess handed her aunt the cup of tea, she said in low voice that the twins wouldn't hear. 'You don't have to put up with this. Tell Bernie you'll leave him if he ever hits you again. Tell him you'll not be used as a punch bag.'

Cora gave her a blank look. 'I don't know what yer talking about love. Eeh, is that an Eccles cake you've fetched me?'

She then went out to sort salvage into four different buckets, which she kept safely in the back yard: scrap metal, paper, waste food, though there was never much of that left, and one for old bones to make glue, of all things. She seemed to imagine she could build a warplane single handed with the stuff, and constantly nagged her family to switch off the light. She also spent a lot of time listening to *The Radio Doctor*, learning which foods were good for them, and how to cook lentil roast and the dreaded Woolton Pie. Rationing, queues, make-do-and-mend had become common practice, and she had to do her best to protect her husband.

Bernie reckoned nothing to such tasteless fare. He liked his meat, his bacon and eggs, and his potatoes fried, making sure he had the wherewithal of extra points, to provide these necessities for his comfort. Nor did he subscribe to the theory that folk should be limited to one complete set of new clothing a year. The government could devise whatever schemes they liked, using poorer materials, cutting down on turn-ups and pockets, telling folk to buy a size larger so it'll last longer. Utility they called it. Bernie didn't care for that scheme either. He agreed with Churchill that 'stripping the people to the buff' was not a good thing to do. A man of substance, such as himself, deserved a touch of style. He was going up in the world, come what may, war or no war.

Even petrol coupons were losing their value. The government insisted you couldn't use a car unless it was for essential war purposes. With a tin box stuffed full of petrol coupons, Bernie's profits had consequently taken a nosedive. Yet another blow to his economy. Some folk cheated and pretended to be on essential business when they weren't, but most abided by the rules much to his disgust. It was downright inconsiderate of them to be so honest, and for the powers-that-be to keep changing the rules. How could a chap hope to make a decent living under such conditions?

Fortunately it wasn't Bernie's policy to follow orders, or meekly do as the government ordered. Nor did he feel inclined to stand by and do nothing while his sons took over. In no time at all they could be the ones ruling the roost. He had to hand it to them lads of his for sowing the seeds of an idea. However, he required more money to turn his life around completely. He'd show them who was the top dog.

Even that niece of his was puffing herself up above her station, earning more money than any young woman had a right to. That girl needed bringing into line. And she still hadn't brought him any cash home from that blasted tea room. She went off dancing twice a week and did her bit with the Sally Army. He thought he'd spiked her over that flipping trumpet but damned if she hadn't got herself another, which she kept hidden some place he couldn't fathom. Once he was nicely placed with a little nest egg stowed away, then he'd tackle that little madam once and for all. But first he had to get his hands on a bit more brass, not just a few trinkets here and there or the odd ration book.

–

It was with some relief when one night at the Plaza, Jess spotted her favourite cousin, Tommy. His presence was like a breath of fresh air and she quickly introduced him to Leah, her best friend, then chatted about family.

'I know what you mean, our Jess. It's fairly true that few can find my brothers Harry and Bert lovable. That's hard to reckon, but they're each walking out with a girl.'

Jess was all ears. 'Are they really? Good heavens. No wonder I haven't seen much of them lately, and what a relief that has been. They must be saints, these girls, whoever they are.'

'Or hard up,' Tommy laughed.

As Jess saw Tommy casting shy, sidelong glances at her friend, she turned to Leah to explain. 'Tommy is the only Delaney who believes in doing his bit for the war effort. Harry and Bert are both bone idle and only out for themselves, while Tommy here is a fire-watcher.'

Tommy grinned. 'Aye, I'm the only one daft enough to put myself in the firing line, although I'm hoping to join the army by the end of the year. Can't be worse than sleeping on a camp bed in some freezing warehouse or other, waiting to play football with incendiaries.' Then he regaled them with a funny story of trying to get water up from a bucket with a stirrup pump to put out a fire. 'It would have been quicker to chuck the bucket of water on it.'

Leah was roaring with laughter. 'Why didn't you then?'

'Regulations. Anyroad, we didn't have any water left.'

'What a war!' They were all laughing, then seeing his bright, adoring gaze Leah gave him one of her soft, enticing smiles. 'You can dance with me, if you like.'

'Oh, I want to all right.'

'You have to ask properly.'

Tommy grinned. 'Can I dance with you properly then?' He took the laughing Leah on to the dance floor and Jess never clapped eyes on her again for the rest of the evening, which left her feeling more depressed than ever.

The dance with Tommy lasted no more than a few moments before they were rudely interrupted. 'Hello, Tommy lad, who's this little chick you've picked up? Does she know that you're only just out of short trousers?'

'Leave off. Don't push your nose in where it's not wanted.'

'I reckon we should let your lovely partner here be the best judge of that.'

Leah found herself looking into a roguishly handsome face with a square cut jaw, grey laughing eyes and close cropped, almost black hair with just the hint of a curl. Broad shoulders and a powerful chest gave way to slim hips and long, interesting legs. Hanging on to his arm with feverish tenacity and clawing red fingernails, was a girl with bleached blonde hair and a sulky expression on her thin, pale face. And no wonder. There surely wasn't a girl in the room who wouldn't be delighted to dance with him, and the way he was eyeing her up made Leah's stomach clench in a thrill of excitement. He was, to her mind, utterly gorgeous!

'Perhaps you should introduce us, Tommy.'

She could sense his reluctance as he swiftly and carelessly introduced the newcomer as his eldest brother. 'This is our Harry.'

So this was the devilish Delaney who Jess was constantly going on about? Leah found herself utterly entranced and put up a hand to tidy a wayward strand of her hair, wishing to improve her appearance. Drat it, why hadn't she worn her new blue silk with the dazzlingly low cut neckline instead of this old green linen number. But then that might have been too daring and frightened him off. He clearly found her attractive, judging by the way his gaze was devouring her. The butterflies in her stomach started up a clog dance in pure ecstasy. Maybe Harry was exactly what she'd been waiting for, someone to put some zest and passion into her life, and bring an edge of excitement to it.

Gripping her firmly around the waist, Tommy attempted to steer Leah back into the melee of the other dancers. Harry, however, had obviously taken a fancy to her and had no intention of letting her go.

'Why don't we exchange partners for this one, eh Tommy lad? You take Dotty here, and I'll give – Leah is it? What a pretty name. I'll take her on a merry little spin around the dance floor.'

Yes, Leah thought with wry amusement. I bet you've led many a girl a merry spin. At eighteen Leah was longing to be more grown up, to try out some of these adventures she heard the other shop girls whispering about, some of them younger than herself. 'Sounds good to me,' she said, somewhat breathlessly, trying not to feel guilty at the shaft of disappointment that flared in Tommy's eyes. Why the hell shouldn't she swap partners? Harry looked infinitely more interesting.

Once in his arms she could feel his magnetism, sense other girls eyeing him up and envying her. He was, in Leah's opinion, one of the handsomest men in the room. Why had Jess never mentioned that simple fact? Was she blind to his masculine charms? Obviously she didn't appreciate his potent sex appeal, since he was her cousin. Leah suddenly felt all girlish and shy, unlike her normal self and absolutely lost for words.

'So you're our Jess's friend, from the tea room, eh?'

Leah nodded, wanting to kick herself for her own silent inadequacy. Why should a man have this effect upon her just because he was good looking? Admittedly, he was a few years older than her and very full of himself. But then she liked a man with an air of self-assurance; one with authority who knew where he was going in life. Clearly the bottle blonde he'd abandoned was less than pleased at being dumped on his younger brother. Leah couldn't help but think that she'd got the best of the bargain.

'Cat got your tongue?' The charcoal grey eyes were laughing at her, even as he pulled her closer in his arms, smoothing a hand up and down her spine which sent little shivers of excitement pulsating through her.

'No, of course not. I was just thinking that I ought to be finding Jess. She'll be wondering where I've got to.'

He gave a deep, throaty chuckle. 'Nay, you weren't thinking anything of the sort. You were wondering how quickly we could get out of this place so we could get to know each other a bit better.' Harry was thinking that if he played his cards right he'd have her up a back alley with her knickers off in no time. He imagined them as white, lacy, and very French.

'Heavens, you are full of yourself, aren't you? Why would I want to go anywhere with you when I'm quite happy dancing?'

'Because you fancy me rotten, just as I fancy you, so what about a breath of fresh air? No harm in that, as we could go for a walk and see where it takes us.'

Leah felt a tightening in her chest. 'What are you suggesting? I'm not that kind of girl.'

'Course you're not. That's why I intrigue you, being the right kind of chap.'

Oh, she was indeed intrigued by the way he regarded her through the speculative glint of narrowed eyes; the wicked twist to his wide, laughing mouth. She found herself trying to imagine what it might feel like to have him kiss her. The prospect set her pulses racing. For all she knew, Simmons's Tea rooms could be bombed to smithereens tomorrow and she might die without discovering what the greatest mystery in life was all about. And what a tragedy that would be, never knowing the true meaning of passion. Time suddenly seemed to be running out for her, as if she must experience everything before it was too late and she'd lost the opportunity forever.

Besides, once again this morning, she'd had words with her mother over plans for the weekend. Muriel had arranged for the Greggs to come for tea on Sunday, and Leah was naturally expected to entertain Ambrose. She couldn't get it across to her mother that she found him dull as ditch water and had no intention of agreeing to walk out with him, let alone marry him, however suitable his family background may be. But her mother assumed her daughter would welcome his attention. The best way to stop this plan was to find herself a different boyfriend. Harry looked a likely candidate. Leah very much doubted she could ever accuse a Delaney of being dull. Coming to a swift decision, she rewarded Harry with a brilliant smile so that he appreciated what a very fortunate chap he was. 'Why not?' she agreed. 'A walk would be lovely, so long as we're back by nine-thirty, in time to meet up with Jess and go home.'

'No problem.' That would give him the better part of an hour. If he hadn't made his mark by then, he wasn't the man he thought he was.

–

Leah was pressed up hard against a brick wall down by the Irwell with dust in her hair, lipstick gone, and all she could think of was what a good kisser he was. She'd never spent such an exciting half hour in all her life.

'Where have you been all my life?' Harry said, rubbing his hand over her breast.

Dazed by his passion, with his hands going everywhere and aware the situation was rapidly running out of control, Leah felt reluctant to stop him. She didn't want to offend him, was, in fact, anxious that he saw her as some silly weed of a shop girl who'd go running home if he touched her where he shouldn't.

And she wanted him to ask to see her again.

Even as she masqueraded sophistication, as she was so fond of doing, Leah felt confused. Harry Delaney was the most exciting bloke she'd ever met in her entire young life.

He was making her head spin so that she couldn't seem to think straight. She could feel him edging up her skirt as he pushed one knee between her legs. His fingers slid beneath her stocking top and she experienced a burst of panic. Was she ready for this? Did she really want to do it? Not yet, surely. He'd think her cheap. When she did risk this, she'd want to be sure that he took proper precautions. She was no dummy.

She pulled his hand away and pushed down the hem of her skirt. 'What kind of girl do you reckon I am, Harry Delaney? I think that's enough, don't you?'

'Not for me it isn't, nor you neither, sweetheart, from the look on your lovely face. I can tell when a girl's begging for it. But mebbe not right now. I'll retire gracefully and admit defeat.' He gave her waist a little squeeze and said, 'Come on, Cinderella, time I was taking you back to our Jess.'

An odd disappointment warred with a sense of relief that he'd given in so easily. Leah knew in her heart that it would take very little persuasion on his part to make her change her mind. 'You do like me though?' she softly enquired, accepting his caution as respect, instead of the canny manoeuvre it actually was.

Harry's instincts with women were much sharper than his level of intelligence might signify, and he prided himself on knowing when to draw back, and when to push a little bit more. This one needed to be hooked first. 'Course I do, love, but I don't want our Jess nagging. She'd never let me hear the last of it if you missed your bus.'

He abandoned Leah the moment they went back inside the dance hall, just as if the half hour of intense passion between them had never taken place, or he'd wiped it completely from his mind. 'See you're around then,' he said, and loped away with a sly grin on his face. Aware he left her quivering with uncertainty, looking desperate for him to see her again or ask her out. Oh, he was an expert on women. Next time, she'd be eating out of his hand, panting for it, and more than willing to let him do whatever he wanted with her.

Chapter Fifteen

Feeling guilty at having missed their regular tea time meetings for quite a few weeks, not simply because she'd been working hard, but she'd been nervous of meeting up with Steve again, Jess went to Mr Yoffey's little shop to make her apologies. She intended to hand over a final payment for the trumpet, having borrowed money from her store of savings under the mattress. She arrived to find the door locked and the blinds drawn. The dusty closed sign hung in the window gathering cobwebs.

Jess clanged the bell that hung by the door, rattled the letterbox and hammered on the window. There was no sign of the old man and nothing for it but to go away. She returned the next day to find exactly the same situation. The shop was locked up and barred, wearing a lost, sad sort of air. Jess felt a sickness start up deep inside. Where was he? What had happened to the old man?

'They've taken him away.' The answer seemed to come out of nowhere but, turning, she found the very person who had kept her away from his door had spoken the words. Steve Wyman was frowning at her in the way she remembered only too well.

'Taken him where?' Her heart was pounding, more out of fear for poor Mr Yoffey. Nothing else seemed important.

'He's no doubt been interned in the Alien's camp on the Isle of Man.'

'But why?'

'Who knows! Perhaps he's considered to be a serious threat to peace,' said Steve drily.

Rage bubbled through her veins. 'That's ridiculous. An absolute scandal! He's an old man, not a threat to anyone. Who would do such a thing? The City Council or the mayor? Where would I find them? I shall give them a piece of my mind.'

She set off at a brisk pace down the road, as if about to march that very minute into the Council offices and take them all on: the mayor, the corporation and the city fathers, while her blood was boiling. Steve caught up with her and grabbed her elbow.

'Jess, hold on. You're wasting your time. This has nothing to do with the local council who tried to protect him, but in the end had no say. This is a government thing.'

'Oh, but how can the government imagine Mr Yoffey, a dear old man, to be a threat to anyone? It's so wrong!'

'I agree. Oh, don't cry Jess. Please, I can't bear to see you upset.'

She wiped the tears from her cheeks. 'How do you know my name? I never got around to telling you that time, not at the dance, nor in the shop. And Mr Yoffey promised that he'd not tell you either.'

'For once he broke his word. Look it's my fault so don't blame the old man. Will you let me buy you a cup of tea, then I can explain?'

He took her to the Ritz, to the afternoon tea dance. The stage was brightly lit, the place heaving with people, many in uniform and all bent on having a good time. People were laughing and talking to each other as they jigged about to the music with varying degrees of skill. The band was playing 'The Jersey Bounce' and it was all Jess could do to resist tapping her feet. Instead, she folded her arms and put on her most disapproving expression.

Steve was looking shame-faced. 'I thought this would be a convenient place for us to talk. I have to go to work in a minute, or would you rather dance first?'

Jess couldn't wait to get on to the dance floor, to be held in his arms as she'd long dreamed of doing, and feel the power of his body pressed close against hers. Not wishing to admit this, she frowned. 'Work where, at the aircraft factory?'

'Nope, up there, on stage. My spare time job.'

For a moment she was impressed by this unexpected piece of information, but obstinately didn't show it. 'You're lucky to have any spare time at all. Most of us are too busy working at a proper job, as well as doing our bit for the war effort.' However unkind such a remark was, some devil had got inside her and she couldn't stop these hurtful words from pouring out of her mouth.

'Mr Yoffey told me that you spend your spare time helping the Salvation Army. A worthy cause. Or is that how you pay for your trumpet lessons?'

'I do need to contribute and like helping them. It sounds like you and Mr Yoffey had quite a chat. It's a wonder my ears weren't burning.'

'Sorry, but I admit to applying pressure by explaining that we were already acquainted. He was quite moved by the tale of how we were whisked apart before properly getting through the basic introductions. I assume you do remember how well we danced together on that first occasion? Which is why I thought you might wish to repeat the experience. However, I'm not the sort of chap to push myself forward where I'm not wanted.'

Jess felt flustered, her traitorous cheeks starting to burn and decided it was far safer to go on the attack. 'I take it you don't approve of women trumpet players?'

He grinned at her. 'I don't recall saying any such thing. I do remember commenting that you had purloined my trumpet.'

Jess glanced down at the instrument case clasped in her hand, then hugged it defensively close to her chest. 'Purloined?'

He saw the gesture and chuckled. 'Borrowed then, yet you refused to return it. It's all right. I'm not going to steal it back. I've accepted defeat, for now, anyway. Let's check it safely into the cloakroom, shall we? Neutral territory.'

Jess reluctantly handed over the case to the smiling girl, took a ticket in return and, as always, stuffed this inside her shoe so that she wouldn't lose it. Breathing deeply, she struggled to decide how to handle what could turn into a tricky situation. 'I didn't steal it. That's not how it was at all.'

'Well, you certainly weren't for handing it back, were you? Even though I'd brought every penny I possessed to pay for it. How would you feel if you'd been forced to hock your favourite instrument and then some idiot who thought they could play, nicked it from you?'

Jess gasped. 'I've told you I didn't nick it! I'm not an idiot and I can play.'

He had the gall to give her a dismissive laugh. 'Who told you that? Some tin pot do-gooding Salvation Army chap, I suppose. What would he know about real music?'

'A great deal, as a matter of fact! What's more if you think I'm—'

The wind was knocked out of their argument as an airman grabbed hold of Jess to whisk her on to the dance floor. The band had struck up 'Boomps-a-Daisy' and soon she was bumping backsides with a perfect stranger while Steve, she couldn't help noticing, was rocking with laughter as a very fetching strawberry blonde in WRNS uniform wiggled her bottom at him.

This was followed by 'The Hokey-Cokey', with a good deal of shaking of arms and legs, then feet stamping in the 'St Bernard's Waltz', followed by the 'Gay Gordons', where Jess thought her head might never stop spinning again. Oh, how could she resist when she was having the time of her life. It was all great fun.

Finally, as the music changed to the 'Progressive Barn Dance' she found herself back with Steve, held firmly in his arms going round in circles. For some moments Jess glared furiously at him, then recognised a mischievous challenge in his gold-flecked hazel eyes and began to giggle. They both laughed so much that tears ran down her cheeks and she had to hold on to his arm to prevent herself from toppling over.

When he led her off the dance floor, he said, 'Jess, that was the most fun I've had in a long time. Thank you.' And, without warning, he gathered her into his arms and kissed her. She didn't protest, she couldn't possibly have done so. Jess felt herself melt against him, aware of the soft warmth of his lips, the powerful strength of his body against hers and the magic of the moment.

–

Jess had discovered an enormous appetite. She consumed Steve's slice of cake that came with the tea, along with her own. They talked, oblivious of time, right up until the moment he went on stage to play his saxophone. Jess retrieved her own instrument from the cloakroom but instead of dashing off to catch her bus, couldn't resist lingering to listen. He played 'The Way You Look Tonight'. She felt utterly entranced, not least by the fact that his eyes rarely left her throughout. It was as if they were alone in the ballroom and he was playing only for her. Jess felt privileged to be singled out amongst all the other girls crowding around the stage.

He finished to rapturous applause from his adoring audience but then after whispering something to the bandleader, approached the microphone and spoke softly into it.

'Folks, we have a special treat for you today. We have with us this afternoon a young girl with a very special gift. A dear old friend of mine reliably informed me that she has no mean skill with a trumpet. Let me introduce to you, Jess Delaney. Come on, Jess. Step up on stage and enchant us all.' Holding out his hand, everyone turned to look in the direction he pointed.

Jess felt as if she might die on the spot. She knew her cheeks were burning like fire and wanted nothing more than for the floor to open and swallow her up. She could feel the music case holding Steve's very own trumpet scalding her hand. Was this his revenge for her appropriating it? She could see his eyes twinkling and realised that he was issuing a challenge. This was his way of saying, so go on then, prove to me that you're worthy of owning my trumpet. Play it well or hand it back. Drat the man, if he expected her to turn and run, he'd mistaken his opponent.

Hardly able to believe that her feet were actually taking her, Jess made her way up the steps on to the stage. People were standing back to let her through, smiling and clapping, looking her over with open curiosity.

Was she quite mad? Did she want to make a complete fool of herself in front of this crowd, some of them professional dancers? Her hands were shaking as she lifted the trumpet from its case, Jess fearful she might drop or dent it as she had the Salvation Army bugle. Then Steve's hands were on her shoulders, as he turned her gently to face the audience.

'Keep smiling and tell me what you want to play.'

Jess swallowed and looked about her. The bright lights were so dazzling she could scarcely see the blur of faces, which seemed to spin before her eyes in an eerie, disembodied sort of way.

His voice in her ear said, 'Don't look at them too closely, they'll only make you nervous.'

Then he was smiling down at her and perhaps it was just as well that his gaze was the only one she could truly register. For a long moment Jess felt as if she were losing all grip on reality, and yet seemed to be filled with a new strength and courage. Finally, she answered his question.

'I'll Be Seeing You.' She didn't know where this idea had come from, somewhere from the deep recesses of her mind.

Steve spoke to the bandleader then nodded at her, smiling his encouragement. 'Go on then, knock 'em dead.'

Jess lifted the trumpet, adjusted the tension of her lips, and blew. It was a hesitant start, shy and tremulous but confidence grew in her. She put all her heart and soul into the number and long before she was halfway through, her audience were holding on to each other, swaying as they sang along with the music. Jess didn't need Steve, or the bandleader, to tell her that she was playing well. When she was done the room erupted, the audience cheering and calling for an encore. Jess couldn't move a muscle, feeling drained, exhausted and yet exhilarated. All she could do was smile in a bemused, astonished sort of way, laughing with relief as she took her bows to rapturous applause.

'Pity you're not a man,' said Hal, the bandleader, shaking her vigorously by the hand. 'Or I'd offer you a job on the spot.'

Steve, she noticed, had suspiciously bright eyes as he led her from the stage, then once more she was in his arms, his cheek nestled close against hers as he held her tight.

'I take back every word, Jess Delaney. My trumpet is yours. Keep it. Mr Yoffey was right to lend it you. You can make that instrument sing.'

–

Following that afternoon at the Ritz, life became more exciting. Jess couldn't believe she'd been so daring as to actually go on stage. Those few magical moments had changed her life, and she knew that the sound of the applause would live with her forever. What was even more thrilling, Steve took to often waiting for her outside of Simmons's Tea Room whenever she was on late shift and he was free. He'd take her out to supper before dashing off to some dance hall or other where he was due to play that evening. Jess would gladly go with him and in the interval when some other band took the stage, he would hold her close in his arms and it was even better than all her dreams. He would sing the words softly in her ear, 'I dream of you' and her heart would melt with happiness.

Sometimes, because of the distance, or Jess's commitments with the Salvation Army, it wasn't possible for her to go with him and they'd linger in the bus shelter kissing and cuddling, promising to meet the next day or the one after that. But the two of them were rarely apart. Every moment they could, they spent together. Jess guessed that she was falling in love with him, but strove to remain sensible and practical, as she always had. This wasn't really the time for dreams or romance. Not with a war on.

Jess was sorely troubled that something odd was going on. Lizzie had suddenly taken to going out during the day, not coming back till quite late in the afternoon. Sometimes she wouldn't be there when Jess got home from the shop. Cora was naturally delighted to be free of her sister-in-law for a few hours. But Jess was desperate to investigate exactly where it was she went, what Lizzie got up to, and if she was drinking again. She considered following her, and might have done so if only she'd had more time. Jess rarely saw Leah either these days, who she assumed was walking out with Tommy. She thought it best not to enquire into her friend's life, being engrossed with her own.

Working as she did for long hours in the tea rooms and bakery, her days were pretty well filled, and whenever she wasn't helping out at the Salvation Army mobile canteen, she simply couldn't resist spending more time with Steve. Jess had finally admitted to Steve why she'd wanted that trumpet, Uncle Bernie having robbed her of the one she'd been granted by the Sally Army. Fortunately she was able to persuade him of the fruitlessness of taking any action.

'I want to protect you, and make you happy,' Steve said.

'Oh, but you couldn't believe how much you have already.' For the first time in her life, Jess felt truly cherished. No doubt about it. She was in love.

Chapter Sixteen

Cora was avid for details about Jess's young man and today, as on so many occasions recently, she was trying to persuade her to bring him home so that she could meet him. 'Fetch him, why don't you? Let's have a shufty at him.'

Lizzie lazily lifted her head to light a fresh cigarette from the one she'd smoked down to the butt before callously remarking, 'Don't imagine it'll last. Who'd want to marry Saint Jessica? Stifle any man's lust.'

The remark stung and Jess could think of no satisfactory reply. But perhaps Lizzie was right in a way. It was certainly true that she'd always had a tendency to be somewhat naïve and moral, despite her colourful upbringing, or perhaps because of it. With a mother like Lizzie she was bound to be, and having been involved with the Salvation Army had made her more so. At every meeting in the citadel they were urged to resist the temptations of sin and Jess agreed with the sentiment. If you didn't stick to the stony path of righteousness, you landed up in Strangeways, like her mam.

'I have boundaries over which I'm not prepared to cross. What's so wrong with that? Better than having none at all.'

Lizzie snorted in derision. 'If that's a dig at me, it won't wash. You always think you're so much better than everyone else, a stuck up little madam.'

'I'm not! I just have morals, which you seem to have lost sight of.'

'Ooh, hark at her,' Lizzie mocked. 'Has an answer for everything. Spoil anyone's fun, she would.' She was annoyed that Jess was stubbornly arguing, but then the lass was forever telling her what to do these days, keenly watching her every move. Fortunately, Lizzie had managed to sneak a few swift shots of whisky this morning, though that had been before breakfast and now was desperate for another. She'd got into the habit of taking a nip or two whenever Jess wasn't looking, or when she was out for the evening with her chap. Bernie kept her well supplied with the stuff. He was such a treasure.

'Nay Lizzie, that's no way to talk to your daughter. The lass hasn't got a mean bone in her body.' Cora sounded weary of fending off her sister-in-law's insults, once again attempting to intervene between mother and daughter as she'd frequently been called upon to do over these last weeks. 'Where's the harm in a bit of hand holding, or a kiss and a cuddle?'

'Shurrup and mind your own business,' Lizzie snapped. Turning to her daughter, she hiccupped loudly and, swaying back into her seat, gave a nasty smirk. 'You're a hoity-toity madam, Jess. So lah-di-dah and full of yourself! Always looking down your nose at other folk. Let's have a gander at this fella of yours. Fetch him home, why don't you? See if he's got one head or two. Or are you ashamed of him?'

'Of course I'm not. Have you been drinking again, Mam? Is that why you're in such a foul mood?' The prospect of allowing Steve to meet her family made Jess feel sick to her stomach. What would he think of them? Would his feelings for her change, once he'd seen her as part of such a nefarious crew? 'I hope you haven't got another bottle tucked away some place?'

'As if I would have.' Lizzie pushed the half bottle of whisky further under the cushion behind her. 'Anyroad, it's none o' your business. I'm over twenty-one and can do as I please.'

As Lizzie reached for yet another cigarette, Jess snatched away the cushion and whipped out the whisky bottle in a flourish of exasperation. Ignoring her mother's pitiful wail, she poured the contents down the sink, then gave her a lecture on how she must behave for the sake of her health and respectability. It was vitally important that her mother should make a good impression. 'We don't want none of your caustic comments Mam, so watch that waspish tongue of yours. And don't you dare mention Strangeways. It should be a quiet family tea, right?'

Lizzie affected innocence, claiming not to understand her daughter's concerns, even manufactured a few tears to win sympathy. In desperation, Jess resorted to bribery. 'Just keep your trap shut and I'll bring you a lovely cream cake home from work by way of a thank you, right?'

'Agreed,' she said with a wry smile.

–

Jess brought Steve to tea the following Sunday afternoon, with a sense of trepidation.

Lizzie said, 'By heck, no wonder she's been keeping you to herself. I wouldn't mind if you warmed my bed.'

Steve laughed, as Jess blushed to the roots of her hair. Trust her mother to make such a crude remark. Bernie walked in at precisely that moment and stood stock still in the doorway, startled to find a stranger on his territory. Being a man who guarded his privacy, he didn't care for unexpected callers. 'Who's this then?'

Introductions were made, Bernie barely interested, scowling and complaining he'd had to spend half his Sunday down at the docks trying to get a shipment of merchandise released.

'You have my sympathy, Mr Delaney. Red tape is tying us all in knots these days, issuing endless lists of instructions, which I'm sure wastes far more paper than we actually salvage.'

'You've put your finger right on the nail there, lad.' This seemed to thaw the ice between them and in no time at all they'd launched into a mutual condemnation of the evils of bureaucracy, seeming to hit it off surprisingly well. Jess put this miracle down to Steve's supreme tact and good manners.

Cora was her usual, warm, caring self, fussing like a mother hen as she brought out a plate of tinned salmon, saved for such a special occasion. There were a few slices of cucumber to go with it, as well as lettuce and tomato. Steve tucked in with gusto as if he'd never seen such a feast.

'This is grand, Mrs Delaney. Can't remember the last time I tasted a nice bit of salmon. Living in digs as I do, I rarely get anything half so good. You must be an excellent manager. It's not easy to get hold of these days.'

Cora preened herself at his compliment. 'I've made a nice trifle to follow. I've always been well known for them.'

'I can't wait.' Steve even succeeded in eliciting a smile from Sandra by admiring the pretty colour of the ribbon in her hair, and had Sam and Seb giggling in no time as he plaited his handkerchief into the shape of a rabbit. Fortunately, Harry and Bert were out today, though no one was quite sure what they were up to. Jess was simply relieved not to have them around, stirring up mischief. Tommy had done what he'd been threatening for so long and accepted his call-up without protest, unlike his cowardly brothers. He'd gone off the previous week to join the Manchester Regiment. Jess had noticed with interest that Leah had been moping about with a face like a wet fortnight for ages. Tommy's sudden departure was unlikely to improve her mood.

Conversation at the table was slow and rather stilted, occupied mainly upon the disaster of war, how buildings had been ruined in and around Deansgate village and what improvements would be needed when it was finally over. 'Which it will be soon enough,' Bernie announced, as if Churchill had assured him personally of that fact.

Cora's mind was not on the future, but firmly set in the past. She was entertaining her visitor by reminiscing over going to Smithfield market on Shudehill to buy fish and vegetables when she was a young girl, and seeing the barrow boys selling cherries.

'Two-pence a pound they were, though I had to be a good lass to get even a farthing's worth.' Cora went on to say how she thought it was nothing short of a miracle that Barton Arcade had survived the Blitz when all the rest were tragically little more than a memory, buried beneath a heap of rubble. 'Not that I have time to do much shopping these days as I leave all that to Bernie, don't I dear?'

Bernie cleared his throat, a warning sound that caused Cora to cast a nervous glance in his direction. 'Eeh, hark at me, rabbiting on. I'll fetch the trifle, shall I?' And leaping from the table Cora hastily began to clear and stack plates, Jess jumping up to help. Lizzie patted her pockets for a cigarette, then remembering how Jess had deprived her of these too, she sank into a deep sulk.

Bernie closely examined their visitor, wondering whether this relationship could be turned to his advantage. He hated to miss an opportunity of using somebody who might prove useful and, judging by this young man's comments earlier, he clearly possessed certain views. 'So what line are you in then? How come you aren't in uniform?'

'Aircraft building! Can't say too much about that, sorry. Pretty hush-hush.'

Cora placed a dish of trifle before him with a small flourish of triumph. 'Course it is. Let the lad enjoy his tea in peace.'

'Thank you, that looks grand, Mrs Delaney.' Steve tucked in with relish, having been previously warned by Jess not to ask how Cora got hold of the coupons, despite all the fruit and cream.

Bernie's interest perked up at mention of an aircraft factory, as he wondered whether he could get his hand on a load of screws or bolts. 'I suppose security must be pretty tight at them places?' he blithely enquired.

'I'll say. Tight as a drum. We're searched going in and coming out. The pressure is immense but I let off steam by spending my evenings playing in a dance band.'

'A dance band?' Bernie said the word with utter contempt since he could think of no possible benefit from working in a dance band. What was there to trade from there? Sheet music was useless, and he'd not got any more than a few quid for that blasted trumpet when he'd finally found someone to take it off his hands. 'Why would you do that? Does it make you much money?'

Steve laughed, shaking his head. 'Wish it did. The pay can vary, depending on the booking but no, that isn't the main reason I do it. I love music, and being a part of that band is a joy.'

Bernie gave a disparaging growl deep in his throat. 'Our Jess took a notion into her head to play a flamin' trumpet with the Sally Army of all people. I soon put a stop to it, making it plain she shouldn't waste time playing it any more. Daft as a brush she is, and useless. I wouldn't mind if she was any good, but she's like a troop of tomcats on the prowl.'

There was a short silence. Sam and Seb looked about them, bemused, as if expecting a troop of tomcats to appear out of nowhere that very minute. Sandra giggled and Lizzie gave a snort of laughter, which turned into a loud hiccup as a result of the snifter of gin she'd just downed in place of water.

Cora said, 'Now Bernie love, don't start on that, not when we have a visitor.'

'Start on what? I'm simply stating a plain fact. Having my eardrums blasted day and night with that caterwauling, wasn't my idea of domestic bliss. I put a stop to it, quite rightly.'

'I think Jess is a good player,' Steve said, smiling proudly at her.

Bernie's mouth dropped open. He was not accustomed to anyone daring to challenge his word, certainly not at his own table. 'What did you say?'

Ignoring his host's nasty scowl, Steve turned to Lizzie and blithely smiled. 'You must be so proud of your daughter's musical talent, Mrs Delaney.'

Lizzie, unable to resist masculine charm and feeling very slightly woozy, gave a weak smile. 'She takes after her father who is quite gifted in that direction.'

Jess felt the need to intervene and prevent what could be coming next, but Steve grasped the hand she was flapping at him and held it firmly in his own. 'She played at the Ritz the other afternoon and stunned her listeners. What a talent she has. Pity we can't bottle it and sell it to the troops, we'd win this war in no time then. Vera Lynn had better watch out, or they might adopt a very different sort of force's sweetheart.'

Bernie was staring at his niece, dumbfounded. 'You played at the Ritz? How did you manage that? Didn't I get rid of that flaming trumpet to make damned sure you never played it again?'

Jess hung her head, for whatever she said would be wrong. She should've known this visit would turn into a disaster. Steve had unwittingly dropped her right in it. Uncle Bernie would never let her hear the last of this.

Steve, perhaps realising her state of anguish, said quickly. 'Oh, it was my trumpet, not hers. She borrowed the instrument from me.'

The glance of gratitude she sent him was intercepted by her uncle and all too accurately interpreted. 'Do you reckon I was born yesterday? I know a barefaced lie when I hear one. Where is it lass? Upstairs? Go and fetch it.'

'I can explain…'

'Go and fetch it this minute.' Bernie was on his feet now, his voice raised in temper as he slammed his fist down upon the table and glared furiously at the pair of them. 'I'll not be bested in my own home.' He jerked one thumb in the direction of the door. 'And you, young man, can fling your hook. Jess is underage and I say where she goes and what she does. If I put a stop to summat, it stays stopped. Got that? I'll have no bloody trumpet playing in this house. I had enough of that poncey, arty-farty rubbish with her dad. If this little madam has time on her hands, I can find a better use for it, see if I can't. Do I make myself clear?'

Steve, looking deathly pale and deeply concerned, had half risen to his feet. Jess squeezed his hand by way of reassurance. 'It's all right. You go. I can handle this.'

'Like hell you can. I'm not leaving you to cope with this on your own.'

'I can manage, really. It won't help, your being here. It'll only make matters worse.' She was almost in tears, urging him to go, wishing this whole scene had never taken place. Oh, why did her uncle always have to spoil everything?

Looking Bernie straight in the eye, Steve said, 'The trumpet she has is most definitely mine, and if anything – unfortunate – should happen to it, I would be very, very angry! Even more important, if any harm should come to Jess, simply for having possession of it, the fact she played at the Ritz, or for any other reason, I will take action on her behalf. Do *I* make myself clear?' Then turning to Jess he continued more quietly, 'I'll go now since you insist that I do, but I'll be back later to check you're all right.' And politely thanking Cora once more for entertaining him so royally, he collected his hat and made for the door.

Tears filled Jess's eyes. Nobody had ever stood up to Bernie like this before, not so steadfastly, nor on her behalf.

'No, wait Steve. I'm coming with you.' At the door she paused to look back at her uncle, who was sitting frozen in his seat with a face like thunder, and took a deep breath. 'I'll be back when you've calmed down, but I'll not give my music up for anyone. I thought I'd already made that clear. You'd do well to remember that I'm not a kid any longer and I'll do as I please.'

'Like bleedin' hell you will.' But the words went unheard as Jess and Steve escaped into the street, hand in hand.

'I fear you've done that lass no favours,' Cora quietly said.

Bernie flung out a hand to give his wife a thump, then threw the remains of the trifle to the floor, trod through the resulting mess and stormed out of the house, yelling, 'My brother Jake's pesky daughter might have won the opening skirmish, but I shall win the flaming battle. See if I don't.'

Chapter Seventeen

'Hello, Harry,' Leah said, trying to sound casual. She'd been coming out of the shop door and there he was, large as life and twice as handsome as she remembered. It made her knees go all wobbly just to see him. 'Thought you'd forgotten all about me.'

'Now how could I forget a smashing bird like you? The best looking chick around. I did mean to get in touch before now, but I've been a bit tied up with business lately. Feel like coming with me to the flicks tonight?'

'Oh yes,' Leah breathed. He'd asked her out. At last! She felt made up. That was one in the eye for Mother and all her clever machinations. Leah knew she was treading on dangerous ground but she really didn't care. Harry Delaney was much more fun than flabby Ambrose would ever be.

They went to see Jane Russell in *Outlaw*, and Leah felt almost jealous as Harry was clearly slavering over the Hollywood actress, his eyes nearly popping out of his head in the stable scene when she was showing off her considerable assets in that low-cut blouse. Perhaps that was the reason why she let him go a bit further than she'd intended, allowing him to fondle her between her legs which Leah was ashamed to find got her all excited, and even more curious about what might happen next. Maybe she would let him tonight, or was it too soon? Once she'd given in there was no going back and, deep down, Leah still had her doubts.

Harry was filled with optimism that he'd be quids in tonight and on their way home, took her down a suitably dark alley and got going on the kissing and cuddling. He found this part boring but girls expected it and he was willing to oblige. It paid to humour them, to grease the wheels as it were, and this lass was certainly responsive; gave every impression of wanting him to go all the way. But the minute he slid his hand up her legs she shoved him off, as if he were a bit of muck she needed to shake away from her. Irritation flared within him over her lack of response.

'I've told you, Harry. I'm not that sort of girl.'

He longed to mock her silly, complaining voice, but managed to remain calm and resolutely single-minded. 'Don't pretend you aren't interested, chuck. Come on, what're you afraid of?' And then light dawned within him. 'Blooming heck, you're still a virgin. Is that it?'

Leah could feel her cheeks start to burn and knew she was blushing. Thankful now for the blackout, and the privacy of the alley. 'So what if I am? Not a crime, is it?'

'It's bloody marvellous! Sorry sweetheart, shouldn't swear in front of a lady. It's just that a chap like me doesn't come across a girl like you very often, not in a month of Sundays.'

'I don't suppose you do in today's world. Though I'm sure you've any number of girls panting for you to have your wicked way with them.'

Harry saw that he'd made a big mistake. She was backing off and he was so eager to satisfy his desire, the pain was excruciating. 'I should be so lucky. Nay, it's the war. Everyone wants their oats before it's too late.'

But he wasn't going to get any oats, not tonight, leastways not from this silly little bitch. She was busy tidying her hair, tucking her mouth in all prim and proper, insisting they must dash to the bus stop this very minute. 'Mother will go spare if I'm not home soon. She gets very anxious whenever I'm late.'

By heck, so she called her 'mother' not 'mam'. So full of herself she used fancy words all the time. 'How about next week then? Or have I put you off?'

Leah almost cried with relief. She'd been afraid that she had indeed put him off, by being prissy. She really must stop being so nervous. What was there to be afraid of? Everyone was entitled to a bit of fun. There was a war on, after all. And hadn't she craved some excitement in her life? If anyone could provide that, Harry Delaney certainly could. 'That'd be lovely,' she said, casting him a speculative, sidelong glance to make sure he was still genuinely interested and not just asking her out of pity. She really fancied him like crazy, so what was holding her back? Probably the fact that he was Jess's cousin, and her friend would not approve as the two of them didn't get on for some reason.

Harry rewarded her with his most charming smile in a valiant attempt to disguise his irritation. Daft cow! She obviously liked playing hard to get. She'd better be worth the wait, or he wouldn't be best pleased. 'Right, you are then. Same time, same place.'

'I could meet you inside, if you like. I don't mind paying for myself.'

He puffed out his chest as if she'd greatly offended him. 'When Harry Delaney takes his girl out, he expects to pay the full whack. Got to keep you sweet, haven't I? And you are my girl, aren't you, Leah?' Harry wheedled, dropping his voice to a soft, husky note. He often played this card because, generally speaking, it worked like a charm. Tonight proved to be no exception.

Leah had heard only those two simple words. My girl! She could hardly believe he meant it, and couldn't resist making sure. 'Is that what I am, Harry? Your girl?'

'Course you are, sweetheart. Would I say it if it weren't true? At least you can be, should you play your cards right. It's up to you, chuck. Hey up, here's your bus. You'll be all right now. I can walk from here, after I've seen to a bit of business with a mate of mine.' God, he thought, I'm starting to sound like my old man.

Leah gave him a kiss on the cheek before happily climbing on to the bus, and waving a cheery good night as it trundled away. The moment it turned the corner, he went straight into the nearest pub and ordered himself a pint of bitter. What a waste of a night that had been, not to mention the one shilling and sixpence each for the flicks. Flaming scandal! There was Jane Russell getting him all fired up and nowhere to run his engine. What a let down.

Virgins, in Harry's world, were as rare as hen's teeth. Maybe she never would cut the mustard, though she didn't seem the frigid sort. If she didn't make him so blasted randy, he'd not bother with her again.

There was the added attraction that everyone knew old Cliff Simmons was bow-legged with brass. When Harry had broken into the shop that day – walked in since the back door had been unlocked – he'd almost been able to smell money. There surely must be a safe in there some place, where the old chap stashed his takings. If so, Harry meant to find it. At the very least he could happen squeeze a few more interesting details out of Simmons's daughter than his dad had out of Jess. Like when the wages were made up for a start, and if there were any more interesting pieces of jewellery than the odd bits of trinkets he'd already picked up off that dressing table. A cameo brooch and a blue necklace that had turned out to be glass with no value.

As he staggered home later than night, he bumped into Thirza Shaw, who used to be in his class at Atherton Street School and was very nearly as inebriated as himself. Harry took her up a back alley off Tonman Street and found her much more amenable. He'd barely unbuttoned his flies before she was ready for him. If only all girls could be so accommodating.

–

It was a week or two later that Bernie announced his decision to find them a place of their own to live. Jess was so startled by this change of heart that she was instantly suspicious and asked what he was up to. He adopted a wounded expression, as if she'd mortally wounded him.

'I can surely do something for my own kith and kin. I decided that you and Lizzie do need your own home. Why would I put up with your daft interest in playing music?'

Jess frowned at her uncle and said, 'I thought you said you couldn't afford to help us. Anyroad, if the money isn't honestly come by, I'm not sure I want anything to do with it.'

'There's no pleasing you, even though I'd be doing you a favour. The war can't last forever so we have to start thinking of the future. You and that chap of yours will happen want to settle down and get wed one day.'

Jess flushed bright crimson and, as always, when embarrassed, instantly went on the attack. 'Nothing of the sort has been suggested. In any case, it's none of your business what we decide to do. I can't believe you're doing this out of the kindness of your heart because you haven't got one. You must have some ulterior motive.'

'That's a mite dodgy, Jess lass.' Bernie felt he could afford to be generous since he'd recently enjoyed a stroke of good luck. Some weeks ago on one of his scavenging missions in a classier area on Stretford Road out Hulme way, he'd enjoyed a most profitable expedition. He'd picked up a velvet bag, from the hand of its former owner who was still holding on to it having lost her life, so would never have the opportunity to use it again. She'd obviously copped it when her house came down in ruins around her ears while dressing for some fancy do. Inside the bag was a box, and in the box he'd found a ring. The fact it was so neatly stowed away within the velvet jewellery bag convinced him that it must be valuable. Perhaps she'd been about to put it on before going out gallivanting.

'I'll give it a good home love,' he'd promised, shoving the ring in his pocket, together with a strand of pearls, a diamante brooch and a couple of pairs of earrings. Then hiding her velvet bag with a few cheaper items in the rubble to avoid harbouring incriminating evidence, he'd quickly scurried away.

His old friend, Bodger Smith, had identified the stone as a diamond and handed over a fair sum for it. Admittedly that was nowhere near its true value but then, as Bodger explained, he had his own expenses to account for, and needed to find a buyer for the ring before he himself made any money out of it. Bernie was more than happy with the deal. The pearls and brooch had fetched a tidy sum, though the earrings weren't worth much and so Bernie decided to hang on to those. Happen he'd give a pair to Cora for her birthday, or to a more exciting woman should one 'appen along. He could afford to be a bit more choosy in that department if he had a bit of brass in his pocket. Lizzie didn't satisfy him any more. She was as besotted with him as ever and all he had to do was to keep her supplied with the booze and she'd stay that way, but whatever sparkling titillation she'd once provided had long since fizzled out.

He believed that the end of all his troubles were at last in sight. He'd got enough money to settle his debts, with plenty left over to expand his enterprises. With this bit of spare cash in his pocket, he was seeking an opportunity not only to rid himself of a tricky situation of having three women in one house, but also to manipulate matters to his own advantage. He felt this was his moment to branch out, stop being a small time crook and slide smoothly up a notch into a bigger league.

'I've never neglected you, always seen you well provided for, even when your mam were in t' clink. Your wellbeing is my chief consideration and ever will be,' he said, stroking the strands of greasy hair across his baldpate and smiling at her in that sickening way he had.

He was up to something, Jess decided, but what? She'd have to take extra care till she found out exactly what it was.

–

Ever since that afternoon at the Ritz when she'd played her trumpet in front of all those people, Jess's attitude towards her music changed, aided and abetted by Steve championing her in front of Bernie at the Sunday tea. She was used to entertaining bombed-out victims at the mobile canteen but saw that not only could she bring pleasure and comfort with her trumpet but also make it serve a very different purpose.

It occurred to her that, were she to be part of a band, she could play at dances, as Steve did, with the added benefit of earning money. She might be able to buy the Salvation Army a new trumpet to replace the one her uncle had so cruelly disposed of. Although Ted had very kindly held no grudges over the loss of the instrument, Jess knew well enough that the band could ill afford to suffer such a blow. Yet she held little hope of persuading Uncle Bernie to return it. She'd already visited every pawnbroker in Manchester searching for it, and now with Mr Yoffey gone, could think of nowhere else it might be.

Besides all of this, it would be another way of escaping the claustrophobic four walls of the house on Cumberland Street, her miserable, complaining mother and Uncle Bernie's tyranny.

The very next day after finishing work at the tea room, Jess screwed up all her courage and went to the Ritz to ask Hal, the bandleader, for a job.

'Sorry love, you're good, I'll give you that. But my chaps would never accept a chick in the band.'

No matter how much she protested about there being a war on and women doing all kinds of different jobs they'd never done before, he refused to budge. Disappointment bit deep and the ambition to play in a dance band, now she'd been given a taste for it, simply wouldn't go away. Being rejected brought all Jess's stubbornness to the fore and she became more determined than ever. She could play as well as any of the lads, even if she was only a girl. And so another idea was born. She didn't talk to Steve about this in case he tried to put her off. Besides, who better to share the idea with than her very best friend?

On hearing her plan, Leah laughed. 'You're going to start what a dance band? Have you gone soft in the head?'

'No, I'm perfectly serious. Just a small one to start with and all female! We'll need a saxophone player, clarinet, maybe a cello or double bass, most certainly a drummer, which might be the most difficult to find. You could play the piano and I would play the trumpet.' Then with an anxious frown, she said, 'You don't look too well, are you sickening for something?'

'Whatever makes you think so?'

'You look a bit pale, and green about the gills.'

Leah was struggling to drag her attention away from her distracting thoughts. Ever since that day when she and Harry had finally 'gone the whole way' and put the seal on their growing romance, she'd been in a lather of concern. She really couldn't recall him taking any precautions, and she'd been in such a mad, reckless mood herself that day she'd never thought to ask. She'd counted on her fingers and deduced that in a couple of weeks she'd know for certain if she was safe or not. In the meantime, she was glad of anything that took her mind off the terrifying possibility she might be pregnant, and her safe, comfortable world might collapse about her ears.

And what if it did?

She felt far too young to think of anything so grown-up as matrimony. She just wanted a good time, to put some fun and excitement into her boring, sheltered life. Besides which, would Harry even consider marrying her? Leah very much doubted it. So where would that leave her? Unable to cope with her worries she put them resolutely from her mind. 'I'm fine, thanks. Where would we play with this band?'

'At dances of course! So, are you with me on this, or not?'

'Too right, I am. Anything is better than playing Beethoven to Ambrose flipping Gregg.'

Chapter Eighteen

Weeks earlier, Leah had been at home on Deansgate, making every effort to resist her mother's insistence that she play a little Beethoven to entertain the Greggs. Muriel had invited them to tea, along with their beloved son, the ubiquitous Ambrose, and Leah was having great difficulty in maintaining the expected level of politeness one should adopt for guests. Perhaps her mother had been right in one respect, he no longer resembled a suet pudding, all fat and squashy with red currants pitted into his skin. He looked more like a pink slice of Spam in a sandwich as he sat on the sofa between his even more substantial parents. Leah could hardly bear to look at him without feeling a huge urge to laugh.

His mother had spent the last hour or more listing his virtues and attributes, explaining at length how her precious son would soon be going to university to train as a doctor, and she was hoping this would be considered suitable war work in place of active service.

Ambrose looked as miserable as Leah felt as he stared at the floor in gloomy silence.

'The war can't last for ever,' Mr Simmons assured her, clearly wishing to draw a line under this fruitless and seemingly endless discussion. 'Even if Ambrose is called up, I doubt he'd be in any real danger. Genuine advances are being made, we're hitting factories in France, our convoys are reaching Russian waters and with the help of American armoured divisions, it won't be long now before Hitler throws in the towel.'

'Ah, but you can afford to take such a relaxed view since you don't have a son likely to be sent into active service.'

Cliff Simmons looked momentarily stunned, as if Robert's bravery and not his poor eyesight had been called into question. 'We are all affected by the war in some way or other, dear lady.'

Muriel stepped quickly to her husband's aid by dragging Leah up from the chair where she'd been skulking for the entire evening. 'I think, darling, we'd all appreciate being lifted out of our war gloom, perhaps with a little Beethoven?'

Leah thought this might be much more likely to depress them still further. Hadn't she suffered from years of being coerced to play whatever her mother thought suitable? But seeing how her father's brow had darkened ominously, she obediently made her way over to the pianoforte. No point in making a fuss, as there'd be confrontation enough later when she'd tell them all about Harry. She'd been out with him a few times more since that first date, enjoying a marvellous time together so what did it matter if their backgrounds were slightly different? They lived only a few streets apart in Deansgate village. Their respective families were both working class folk. There surely wasn't that much to choose between them? Except that her parents would not see it that way. To Muriel, the Delaneys were the lowest of low. Once her mother discovered she'd been dating a Delaney she'd have a heart attack for sure. How could she convince her that the same brush of his father should not tar this son?

Leah placed her fingers on the keys preparatory to launching into Muriel's favourite piece, the 'Moonlight Sonata', when her mother artlessly suggested that Ambrose could turn the pages for her, almost as if this were a spontaneous thought that had occurred to her on the spur of the moment, probably planned in detail hours earlier.

Mrs Gregg gave her son a gentle nudge. 'Go along dear! I'm sure Leah would appreciate your assistance.'

Finding Ambrose at her side, ready to behave as the obedient son he undoubtedly was, Leah's nerves seemed to fizz with suppressed fury. Why would he imagine that she needed or wanted his assistance? Men were so arrogant, always believing themselves to be indispensable. Leah had largely ignored him all evening, which she fully intended to continued doing. Why would he behave like a damned puppet, allowing his mother to pull the strings?

But was she more resistant with her own mother who had insisted she must stay in this Sunday, not asking whether she wished to do so. She'd gone on to inform Leah how she'd invited the Greggs and she would be expected to entertain them on the pianoforte. Consequently, she was now ordering her to play Beethoven, despite knowing he was a composer she had no interest in. Leah felt rather like some nineteenth century young miss being asked to perform at a musical soiree. Perhaps she should be wearing a pretty empire line gown instead of pale blue slacks and sweater. Yet despite her resentment, here she was seated at the piano, about to do exactly as she was bid. What next? Jump in the lake? Marry Ambrose?

Leah recklessly decided that if she had a choice in the matter, she'd choose the former.

Leah glanced up at Ambrose ready to tell him, in a fit of rebellion, that she didn't require his help but for the first time recognised a similar fury in him. For a moment Leah was so stunned that she met his gaze unflinching, instead of avoiding it as she usually did. He didn't look like a loyal son at all, more like a rabbit caught in a trap. He was definitely not enjoying these parental machinations, any more than she was.

While chairs were being moved in preparation for the anticipated recital, lamps lit and blinds drawn, Leah politely enquired if he read music, feeling the need to say something in this awkward moment.

Ambrose shook his head. 'Not really my thing.'

'What is your thing?' She felt a spurt of curiosity about this young man who had so little to say for himself.

'I like rugby and other sports, most of all fishing on the quiet canal bank.'

'Ah.' Leah nodded, struggling to understand anyone who preferred silence rather than filling their head with beautiful sounds. She lowered her voice while riffling through sheet music. 'What I mean is, I know what your mother wants for you, but what do *you* want? Do you wish to go to university and train to be a doctor, or else become a printer like your father?'

He leaned closer so that he wouldn't be overheard, and there was almost a smile on his round face. 'Neither. I've always intended to join up the minute they'll have me. In fact, I've already been in touch. I'll be going any day now and I've every intention of staying in the army, war or no war. I want to become a regular soldier.'

Leah's eyes widened, stunned by this remark. She could actually feel her mouth slacken and drop open. Never, in all her life, would she have imagined him wanting this, and being so brave as to go ahead and do it. How amazing.

'You haven't told your parents?' she whispered in awed tones.

He shook his head.

'Because your mother won't like it?'

'Neither will yours.' He grinned and Leah gave a spurt of laughter, which she quickly smothered with the flat of her hand. 'No, indeed she won't. Okay, let's give them something to think about, shall we?'

She played the opening bars of the 'Moonlight Sonata', as directed, developing the mood of the piece, aware of the hush of appreciation from the assembled company, of Ambrose seated beside her, following the notes and patiently waiting to turn the page at her signal. But then with her left hand, she placed her finger and thumb together on the lowest note she could reach and drew them swiftly up the length of the keyboard, running one note into the next in a rising crescendo of sound, before lapsing into 'Tiger Rag'.

Leah had always been more of an instinctive musician than one who followed notes, played chromatic scales or studied appropriate exercises. Now she let rip, putting all her heart and soul into the music. Jazz and swing were her thing, not Beethoven. Out of the corner of her eye she could see Ambrose grinning, his square fingers happily tapping out the rhythm on his knee. When she was done and the music ended in an abrupt and startled silence, he burst into lavish applause. No one else moved a muscle.

Later that afternoon when the Greggs had gone home in a flurry of excuses, Leah made her apologies to her tight-lipped parents. Wishing to escape their frosty silence, she declared herself in sore need of fresh air. Taking a walk by the canal, to her delight she met Harry, and quickly told him what she'd suffered.

'Was that lad your intended?' he asked.

Leah gave a grunt of disdain. 'He would be, were my mother to have any say on the matter.'

'Which she doesn't?'

'None at all.'

'I'm glad to hear it. Feel like a stroll?'

'Can't think of anything I'd like better.'

He grinned. 'I can think of something far more exciting than walking.'

With practised ease Harry kissed her, probing her soft mouth with his tongue. Within moments he'd slid open the buttons of her dress to peel it off her shoulders. And judging by the way she moved closer to him, she wasn't complaining. Removing her brassiere was soon dealt with and, before she'd thought to protest, he ripped off her knickers, which were white, lacy and very French, his excitement at such a fever pitch that he thrust his way into her in seconds.

She made a small startled cry as he entered her, which served only to inflame his passion further. Perhaps, because of her inexperience, Leah wasn't as excited as he'd hoped, although taking a virgin always had its own kick of satisfaction. In no time at all it was over, and Harry felt completely vindicated by his patience. No other bloke could ever have what he'd just taken. By heck, but he was a clever chap. Wasn't he just?

Jess was excited when she received permission from Sergeant Ted to hold the auditions at the back of the mission hall, where there was an ancient but welltuned piano. Fortunately, he was most helpful with advice and assistance and had become quite interested in their little enterprise, as had many of the regulars who came in for soup or a bed for the night. They would tap their feet in time to the music, or bang on the wall to complain if they hit too many wrong notes, which they frequently did at first.

She'd spent quite a few weeks circularising all the local ballrooms and dance halls to tell them of their plan. Then next had placed an advert in the small ads of the *Manchester Guardian* mentioning their expertise, although sadly had received fewer replies than she'd hoped for. Now she and Leah settled down one Saturday afternoon at the Mission, after the tea room had closed, to wait for the hopefuls to arrive.

'Do we have any expertise?' Leah asked with a giggle. 'I mean, so far there's only you and me.'

'We can only pray that there might be one or two last minute entries to give us some sort of choice. So far we have possibilities: a Mary, Flossie and Lulu.'

'Lord, the names alone put me off.'

Mary turned out to be tall and elegant and absolutely refused to play jazz. Her instrument was the violin and she'd only ever played Beethoven. She was willing to lower her standards a little, she informed them, in order to do her bit to entertain the soldiers, but there were limits. Leah thanked her politely for coming and Jess said that perhaps the advert had misled her, knowing full well that the wording had plainly stated they were forming a dance band. Who, in their right minds, would choose to dance to Beethoven, worthy as that great composer was.

Flossie, as her name might suggest, was plump and overdressed in a pink floral frock with an amazing array of frills about the hem and neck. She breathlessly agreed that she'd play absolutely anything they wanted. She really had no particular preferences herself, absolutely loved music and dancing, and was simply desperate to be a part of their band. The only problem was that she couldn't truly play. If she hit a right note on her brand new, shining clarinet, Jess freely admitted afterwards to having missed it. Leah could scarcely accompany her on the piano for giggling.

'Thank you so much! Have you been playing long?' she asked.

Flossie confessed that this was a recent hobby, taken up when her husband was sent overseas at Easter and he'd bought her the instrument as a going-away present to keep her company.

'Come and see us again when you've had a bit more practice and experience.'

Flossie went away quite happy, vowing to work harder at her music lessons, now that she had a goal in mind. Lulu breezed into the room all fire and energy and boundless enthusiasm, her sleek and shiny blond hair cut in a stylish bob bounced upon slender shoulders seemingly with a life of its own. With lips painted a bright fuchsia and nails to match, she would clearly be a wow with soldiers. She was also clearly gifted on the tenor sax. Reduced to tears by the skill with which she played 'As Time Goes By', her chosen piece, Jess offered her a job without a moment's hesitation.

'You do realise that it's on the understanding I can't pay you any money until we start earning some. This is all a bit of a gamble. I intend to make a start by advertising ourselves in the local rag, visiting ballroom managers to actively seek work, and maybe organise a dance of our own, just to get us launched.'

Lulu agreed this all sounded perfectly fair. 'Hell, why not? Life's short, let's experiment and have fun.'

'Hear, hear,' echoed Leah.

Jess cast her a sideways glance, the fleeting thought crossing her mind that her friend looked a little pale and hadn't been quite her usual smiling self recently, despite a show of bounce and superficial good humour. There being no further candidates that day, Jess locked up and the two girls celebrated the start of their dream with fish and chips on their way home.

–

Over the following days, Jess optimistically got on with making preparations for the dance. She arranged to hire Atherton Street School Hall and had posters printed, which she and Leah stuck up a few days later all over Deansgate village. These gave full details of the dance and announced the introduction of Delaney's All Girls Band, tickets being available at the Co-op. But Jess was still trying to find other band members. One trumpet, a saxophone and a piano was nowhere near enough. She and Leah trawled through all the dance halls, asking around, hoping that word would spread.

'What if we don't find anyone else?' Leah dared ask one day as yet another week slid by with no further response to a second ad in the *Manchester Guardian*, or to their many enquiries.

Jess brushed her concern aside. 'Don't worry, and we've still got three weeks before the date of the dance. Plenty of time.' Privately, she felt nowhere near as confident as she sounded.

On the plus side, Steve too was proving to be entirely supportive, as she should have appreciated he would be from the start, in particular by helping them to find suitable tunes to play, and providing some sheet music to rehearse with. He'd even offered to fill the gaps in the band with some of the lads, if necessary. Jess expressed her gratitude but refused point-blank. She simply wouldn't hear of it.

'Absolutely not! I intend to create this as an all girls band. I so want to show that women are every bit as good with music as men. But I'll cancel the dance if I have to admit defeat.'

'Independent to a fault,' he teased, shaking his head in mock despair while approving of her determination to make the plan work.

Then just as Jess had almost given up hope, a young girl walked in on their somewhat half-hearted rehearsal one evening, saying she'd heard they were looking for a clarinettist. Adele was small with shining black hair, ruby lips and flashing dark eyes, appearing to pulsate with optimism and energy. 'I smoke, drink, have never managed to hold down a decent job in my life because I have itchy feet, and hate to be in one place for more than five minutes. Oh, and I'm never on time.'

'You are, at least, honest,' Jess said with a wry smile. 'But you would need to be on time for rehearsals with us, and never miss a performance. Right?'

'I'll do my best. Hey, and I also have a weakness for sherbet dabs. Playing this thing is all I'm any good at.' And lifting it to her lips, she started to play 'I Got Rhythm'. Jess was so impressed by this performance she hired her on the spot, and would work on her punctuality problem later.

Chapter Nineteen

1943

What would Bernie say if he knew that 'this daft music business', as he called it, was practically taking over her life? Every evening when she wasn't working at the mobile canteen, Jess, together with Leah and the other two girls practised hard in the back room of the mission hall. She was still on the look out for more band members. All in all, matters were proceeding very smoothly. There'd been little interest from the ballroom managers thus far, but Jess had hopes that after they'd run a dance of their own, they might sit up and take notice. The word would soon get about if they played well.

Adel announced one day that she'd been talking to her old music teacher, who played the cello like an angel apparently, and was interested in joining the band. Miss Mona, as she liked to be called, proved to be a quiet, dignified lady of mature years with white hair and spectacles perched precariously on the bridge of her sharply pointed nose. The idea of hiring someone's music teacher sounded rather daunting to Jess. However, it was such a huge relief to have another band member signed up and, with the day of the dance drawing ever nearer, she was beginning to panic just a little.

'All we need now is a drummer.'

The lack of a drummer proved to be the least of their worries. Cissie Armitage, an old neighbour who, having been bombed out, was now working at the Co-op in order to keep a sick husband and her two remaining children, had been happy to help with selling tickets. But days before it was due to take place, she apologised to Jess and informed her that she'd sold very few. 'I did my best, love. Most folk are in need of a bit of a laugh these days, but few had even heard the dance was taking place and had already made other arrangements. Others said they wouldn't touch it with the proverbial barge pole.'

'But why hadn't they heard of it? We put up posters everywhere. People love to dance, and I thought it would cheer everyone up in the middle of winter.'

Cissie went to the shop door, opened it and glanced up and down the cold, empty street to check they weren't being overheard. There was little that she ever missed in this close-knit community, but she wasn't keen on other folk knowing her business.

'It's nearly dinner time, you can go off early,' she told the young boy who helped her behind the counter. He grabbed his coat and wasted no time in dashing off. A wind whistled bitingly in and she shut the door again with a bang, pulled down the blind and slid the bolt across. She nodded at Jess. 'Come through to t'back.'

Once she was satisfied that they were quite alone, Cissie continued, 'I reckon you should have asked that uncle of yours what puts folk off. If you ask me, he's been using threats left, right and flipping centre, telling people to stay away if they know what's good for them; that he'll make sure there'll be trouble at the dance. He warned me that I'd live to regret it if I sold a single ticket over this counter. I told him to fling his hook. Having lost my baby, and what with an injured husband, I don't give a two-penny damn. I've no proof but I reckon it were those two cousins of yours who nicked my stuff that night we were bombed and my husband lost his legs, so I've no wish for Delaney to bully me. Anyroad, folk should enjoy themselves while they can, in my opinion.'

Jess listened to all of this in stunned silence. How dare her uncle try to spike her plans? What right did he have? First he stole her trumpet, now he was trying to ruin her future by destroying her dreams. Presumably because she refused to steal what he demanded from the tea room. What a nasty piece of rubbish he was. Oh, but she wouldn't let him ruin her life.

Undeterred, Jess asked Mr Simmons for a day off work and spent the entire day calling on friends and neighbours to tell them that the dance was going ahead regardless, and would they spread the word that tickets were available at the door.

When the day finally arrived, Jess and her fellow band members, including Adele, all turned up on time at Atherton Street School Hall, and started to tune up. Seven o'clock approached and, apart from Cissie with one or two of her mates, Ma Pickles and her son Josh, there were only a few regulars from the mobile canteen and two little boys all goggle-eyed, asking if they could get in for half price. No one else turned up. It proved to be a complete disaster. Delaney's All Girls Band waited in vain for three quarters of an hour, then packed up their instruments and went home.

Further investigation revealed that every one of their expensively printed posters had been ripped down, so was it any wonder if few people had seen details about the dance. And none knew better than Jess how Bernie could bully those who did know of it, to stay away. Wasn't he an expert in that department?

'We're done for,' Leah said, her eyes bright but almost feverish.

Jess considered her friend more closely, surprised and a little hurt by this negative attitude. 'Nonsense, it's not the end of the world. I, for one, am not at all eager to hang up my trumpet, not after all the trouble I had getting hold of one in the first place, let alone learning how to play the dratted thing. Didn't we always say that women were the stronger sex, that we aren't going to rush into marriage but live life to the full, war or no war? Hey, do you have a boyfriend?'

'No,' she said, quickly shaking her head. 'Do you?'

Jess laughed. 'Course not. How would I ever have time, being obsessed with my work and music. You still don't look too bright, so I reckon you're missing Tommy, is that it? Don't fret. He's like a cat is our Tommy, blessed with nine lives. Nothing dreadful will happen to him.'

The colour in Leah's pretty face paled even further. 'Why would I be worried about him?' She still hadn't owned up to the fact that it was Tommy's brother Harry she was dating. Jess had put two and two together and made five, all because of once meeting Tommy that time at a dance.

'I expect we're all just a bit strained and tired. It was a distressing evening and I didn't sleep well afterwards, did you?'

Leah could scarcely think straight but Jess's artless comments made her feel worse than ever. She'd got away with it last month and the one before, but her period this time was two days late and the disappointment over the band was the least of her worries. It seemed as if her greatest fear could be about to come true. She was terrified. What would her mother say? Muriel would crucify her for sure; throw her out of the house and tell her not to darken her doorstep ever again. Leah couldn't begin to imagine how she would manage to bring up a child on her own, homeless and without a father, and with the shame of illegitimacy attached. Not for one moment did she expect Harry to do the decent thing. He was far too self-centred and had never uttered any protestations of undying love. They'd just been having fun, nothing more.

She'd done her best to avoid him during these last couple of weeks, and on one occasion when they met up, she'd been more than a little frosty towards him, much to his irritation. When she'd slapped his fumbling caresses away as he'd walked her home after the pictures, he'd stormed off and left her all alone in the middle of Albert Square. Afterwards, Leah had regretted being so abrupt and, to her shame, had cried herself to sleep that night. It had been their first quarrel.

What a mess! It would never do for Jess to suspect the truth. Didn't she have enough on her plate? Her uncle was being particularly difficult, and her mother sliding back into her old bad habits. Her dear friend was desperately striving to find a solution to all of this by risking her meagre savings in order to fulfil her musical ambitions, and provide a more secure future for her family. Right now it was better for Jess to continue to think she was simply worried about Tommy.

–

The moment Jess heard Lizzie's warbling snores tune up, she dug out the old toffee tin from under her mattress and counted every carefully hoarded shilling. She knew she was asking too much of herself. She couldn't repay Sergeant Ted for the trumpet Uncle Bernie had nicked, as well as save enough to set up a place of their own, let alone organise a dance. Nor could she allow her uncle to control her life and get the better of her. Jess felt she had to somehow break free to fulfil her own ambitions, not become obsessed with family problems, dire though they may be.

She supposed that a part of her had snatched at the idea of starting a band in the hope that it would prove to be a good investment, and help her not only to replace the money she'd withdrawn from her savings, but also add to it. What she hadn't bargained for was this disaster. Still, in for a penny...

With this in mind, she resolutely determined to start from scratch all over again. Only this time she sought Cora's advice, in the hope that her aunt might give her some tips. Jess was beginning to understand that Uncle Bernie's family avoided direct confrontation with his bad temper by careful manipulation, not pure chance. That's why no one ever disagreed with him. They kept what they were up to as secret as possible, in order to avoid trouble. Cora's reaction proved her to be correct.

'Don't tell our Bernie you're going to hold another dance, nor owt about what you're up to, love, then he won't have the chance to spoil it.'

'How can I keep quiet when I need to advertise the dance in order to get people to come to it?'

Cora slid a fried egg next to the chips on Jess's dinner plate as a special treat to compensate for her disappointment, and conceded that this might indeed create a difficulty.

'Well then, you'll just have to put your posters a long way from Deansgate where folk aren't scared of our Bernie.'

'But why would perfect strangers, people from another parts of Manchester come to our little dance when they can go to the Ritz or somewhere nearer to home?'

Stumped for an answer to this one, Cora picked up a chip and absent-mindedly dipped it into the yolk of Jess's egg. 'Well, that's true, love! Here, look what I'm doing. Eat your dinner lass, before I pinch the food off your plate. Eeh, that's it. That's the answer.'

'What is?' Taking her at her word, Jess began wolfing down her dinner at record rate. A fried egg was too rare a treat to share, though she didn't begrudge her aunt the odd taste.

'What is it folk crave more than anything in these austere times? Good food, that's the ticket, of which we are never short, praise be.' Cora pulled up a chair and sat down beside Jess at the table, her plump jowls quivering with excitement. 'We could make a pie and pea supper. Folk would come in droves for that.'

'But we'd need pastry, meat for the pies, and fat. How could we find any?'

'I've enough dripping saved to get us going, and Bernie could provide the coupons for the pork meat and any future fat we'll need. Not that we'll tell him what it's for, eh? How about it? I don't mind making pies. No bother at all. I dare say Cissie would give me a hand.' They both knew Lizzie would be no use at all.

New posters were done, hand written this time since money was scarce, advertising a pie and pea supper, which would be included in the admission charge of one shilling, as well as the thrill of introducing the new Delaney's All Girls Band. Tickets available on the door or from the Co-op. The dance was to be held in a local school hall. Neighbours and friends became very excited at the prospect, and word spread quickly. Cissie was soon asking for more tickets, having sold her initial bundle. Everything seemed to be progressing smoothly.

They even found a drummer. Ena Price certainly had rhythm, even if she was a Catholic who nursed a secret ambition to be a nun. 'Except that I can't quite bring myself to give up sex, to which I'm quite partial, being still in my prime. You might as well know that I've got two boyfriends, not that either of them is aware they aren't my one and only. Jeff is in the fusiliers, and Pete on a boat somewhere in the Med. I've no intention of giving up either one of them. Not yet.'

'Suit yourself,' Leah said, with open admiration at the difficulties that must be involved in juggling two relationships, when she couldn't even manage one properly.

She was feeling quite perky this morning, having started her period at last, overflowing with relief and happiness that her fears had been groundless. She'd also wisely decided not to trust Harry to take the necessary precautions in future, and had visited the birth control clinic and got herself set up with proper protection. Not that the doctor had approved of the fact that she was unmarried, and had delivered a long lecture on why she should marry her boyfriend forthwith, before she sank too low. Let him make an honest woman of you, had been his unyielding advice.

Leah had smilingly agreed. But of one thing she was quite certain. She didn't know if marriage was a possibility, but she couldn't possibly give Harry up. He was far too gorgeous, making her tummy wobble just to think of him. But she was not prepared to go through this agony month after month. She knew that her friend Jess had put her poor mood down to a sense of boredom, now believing it to have livened up due to the success of their new venture, an assumption Leah was happy with.

Jess didn't volunteer to help with making the pies. She devoted every moment of her time to rehearsing her new band, which was enough of a worry.

Cora and her team, which comprised of Cissie Armitage and Ma Pickles, gladly brought their rolling pins round to help so they wouldn't miss out on all the fun and maybe gain a bit of free food along the way. They worked hard at cooking. Between them they made half a dozen large meat and potato pies in huge basins, borrowing half their neighbours's ovens in order to cook them all. Even Sandra agreed to help by making sure the mushy peas didn't boil over. She sliced and pickled lots of onions and red cabbage, weeping copious tears as she did so.

Lizzie was given the job of potato peeling and some washing up, not being interested in cooking. 'Why do I always get the rotten jobs?' she moaned, and frequently nipped out to the back yard for a quick smoke, as she was forbidden to do so in the kitchen near the pies. Jess hoped she didn't have a bottle hidden out there, but accepted that her mam was doing her best to help, in her own way.

Adele excelled herself and wasn't late to rehearsal once, although Lulu was nearly always half asleep since she worked in a munitions factory and her days were long and tiring.

'I need my sleep, darling, eight hours a night as this is the first time I've done any real work in my life. Allow me that small indulgence and I'll be fine and dandy, crackling with renewed vigour, ready and willing to work hard and do whatever is asked of me.'

'Well, do make sure you get plenty of sleep the night before the dance.'

'I will, dear.'

Miss Mona was calm and upbeat. Her vast experience included having once played in the Manchester Youth Orchestra many years ago, a spell in Vienna, and several more years playing at the opera house in Prague. She now confessed to Leah that she'd actually had an affair with the conductor and got thrown out. At this stage in her life, she admitted to boredom with the classical scene and the need for something more lively. 'Before it's too late.'

'You'll certainly get that with us,' Jess told her. 'So long as my nerves can hold up.'

Chapter Twenty

When the night of the dance finally arrived, Jess turned up early to find a queue stretching right around the block. She could hardly believe her eyes. Could they at last be ignoring Bernie, or did he have some other card up his sleeve, to play later when she was least expecting it? She'd just have to hope for the best and not lose her nerve. Oh, but that wasn't easy! Jess felt sick, the butterflies in her stomach doing a frantic clog dance.

'Lord, will you look at that. How will I face all these people without you beside me to whisper sweet words of confidence in my ear?' she said to Steve, hanging on to his arm for support.

'You'll be fine once you get up there,' he told her with a grin. 'I know you can perform well.'

It did indeed prove to be a riotous success, packed to the doors with everyone having a marvellous time. The girls in the band did their part to add a touch of glamour by wearing evening dresses they'd made themselves from fabric donated by Cora. Jess didn't dare ask how she'd come by it. Taken off the 'back of a lorry' by her husband or sons at some point, no doubt. They all looked so elegant and glamorous, and played as they never had before in this small school hall.

Steve did his bit by agreeing to act as Master of Ceremonies, introducing each flow of dances by announcing their style or name. He also watched out for any irregularities, checking that the code of etiquette on the dance floor was properly followed. Jess had at first been concerned to have a man around in case of trouble, but thanks to his charm there was none at all. And everyone was having far too good a time. They absolutely loved the music, applauded every number, whistled and shouted and showed their appreciation to the full. Performance proved to be great fun. Delaney's All Girls Band started with 'Jukebox Saturday Night', followed by a couple of Glen Miller numbers, and more to follow.

Even though Jess had loved every moment of being on stage, of thrilling people with her music, at that moment she almost regretted not being able to take part in the dancing herself. She ached to be held in Steve's arms, and to have him kiss her as all these other lovers were doing. She couldn't even see him with the lights down so low, although she was keenly aware of him standing close by, and could sense his pride in her success.

What's more, there was nothing but praise for the pie and peas. Cora glowed from the praise and became a different woman for days afterwards, far removed from her usual born-to-please, down-at-heel old self. At one point she even told Bernie to make his own sandwich if he was hungry, since she was busy planning the supper for the next dance Jess had booked for the following Friday. Life had taken a huge leap forward for Cora, and she wasn't for stepping back into the dark ages, not if she could help it.

Bernie, having realised that he'd failed to put a stop to Jess's daft music business, sat and glowered then stormed off in a huff. She'd thwarted him this time, but he'd have the last laugh, see if he didn't.

–

It wasn't as easy to get the band underway as Jess had hoped. Band leaders and ballroom managers sucked in their breath, puffed out their cheeks and accused them of not being able to withstand the physical hardship of long hours of playing.

'Women don't have the stamina that men have,' said one.

'Limited scope,' said another.

'Women are fine on looks but short on talent.'

This attitude incensed Jess and she would tell them in no uncertain terms that her girls could play 'In the Mood' every bit as well as they could play 'Greensleeves'. 'We aren't in the business of employing young ladies who think it might be fun to show off on stage, however charming and genteel they might be.'

One manager had the gall to say that women had no real sense of rhythm in a jam session, as they were hopeless at improvising. Another, trying to be conciliatory, remarked, 'I see why you ladies are offering to step in, with all the men having been conscripted for service and bands desperate for decent musicians. But we're looking for professionals, not amateurs. We need the best.'

Outraged, Jess's response was sharp. 'We are the best, and how can we ever get to be professional if we're never given the chance.'

He gave a shake of his head. 'Women aren't expected to sit on stage and blow their brains out.'

'We could blow the men right off it.'

No bookings were forthcoming at the top ballrooms such as the Ritz, the Plaza, or any number of others in and around the Manchester area. They spread their net wider, checking out more modest venues, and finally their first professional booking came. It was at a Lads's Club in Bury. Jess thought the manager took them on out of pity. He didn't, however, bill them as professional musicians, but as 'Patriotic Angels with a Big Talent.'

Adele said, 'I suppose we'll have to settle for that, grit our teeth and bear it. What choice do we have, girls, except to hope that maybe it'll lead to better things, and attitudes might change, in time, when they hear us play.'

'Borrow my nail varnish,' Lulu offered. 'We'll knock their eyeballs out.'

'Then we'll hit them with our music,' Miss Mona quietly added.

'We certainly will,' Jess agreed. 'Bet your sweet life.'

The lads and their sweethearts, not to mention the rest of the folk who attended the dance, thankfully did not share the manager's view. To them, it didn't seem in the least incongruous that the band was comprised entirely of girls. After all, if women could build ships, work in factories and buses, why not in a band? They saw them as the patriotic 'Rosie the riveter' types, who were freeing men to fight. They cheered and applauded and declared the girls played every bit as well as men.

'I wish they'd say we played like musicians,' Ena grumbled, after one of her ear shattering drum solos.

'I want to make a career out of this,' Adele said. 'I haven't spent years learning to play the tenor sax just to be thought of as a temporary replacement for men in the war. Nor am I just a pretty wench with no talent and a good body.'

'Folk like glamour,' Lulu reminded her. 'Go on, try the varnish. Fuchsia is just your colour, sweetie.'

'Look, I'm not tarting myself up just to get bookings,' Adele protested. 'I'm a serious musician. Don't you agree Miss Mona? Aren't I right?'

'Well, dear, we have to please the customers.'

Jess listened to all their worries and concerns then tried to steer them on, gently pointing out that they could be both. 'We do need to look attractive, be feminine *and* prove that we are skilled musicians.'

Playing at the Lads's Club became a regular booking and, following this success, Jess persuaded a few more managers to give them a try. Their glamour was applauded and became very much an attention-grabbing part of the gig, making it clear that the public greatly admired them. The girls grew convinced that they were required to look good in order to attract the custom.

'These military boys on leave like to see a pretty girl. It reminds them what they're fighting for,' said one manager, and since he'd just booked them for every Friday over the next six weeks, the girls smiled and charmingly agreed.

The next day Jess went to Kendals department store and bought a bolt of blue taffeta for new gowns. They were about to turn into glamour Queens. She could but hope that wouldn't create problems for them.

–

Whether it was their new glamorous look or the skill of their playing, their popularity increased with every new booking. The girls wore halter-tops and swirling taffeta skirts, or a slinky number with a thigh-high slit, which made it a little harder to play. As Adele pointed out, playing a tenor sax and trying to do battle with a strapless bra at the same time wasn't easy. The halter strap cut into a bare neck, and high heels were so uncomfortable to wear for any length of time that the girls would quietly slip them off once they were safely ensconced behind their music stands. Then they could feel free to wiggle their toes and stretch their aching feet, although Ena had a pair of comfy flatties handy so she could operate her drum pedal.

They did have one sticky moment when a ballroom manager took Jess to one side and suggested she drop Miss Mona. 'She's too old, dear. No one wants to look at her tired old face, or that white hair.'

Jess took a deep breath, crossed her fingers and said, 'If Miss Mona goes, we all go. I'd never find a replacement half as good.'

A long pause, and then a sigh. 'All right, sweetheart, but get her to do something to improve herself, a bit of lipstick might help. Or dye her hair. Something! And tell her to take those spectacles off. They make her look like a schoolmarm.'

Fortunately, Miss Mona was not averse to Lulu 'dolling her up a bit' as she put it, and the girls spent a riotous evening giving her a blue rinse and trying out different lipsticks and eye shadows. She was even persuaded to remove her specs, though she insisted on hanging them on a velvet string around her neck, just in case she forgot the music and needed to take a peep now and then.

This glamorous allure did help to bring in the book-ings, but sometimes worked to their detriment as they would find men hanging around outside the stage door as they left. 'They must see us as easy meat,' Adele complained, flashing her dark eyes and pouting ruby lips. 'Not like little wifey waiting at home! Perhaps they consider it our patriotic duty to entertain them backstage as well.'

'I might consider taking up the odd offer,' Ena said, 'were I not already double-booked with my fellows, Jeff and Pete. Two's enough I suppose.'

'I should think it is,' Jess giggled, and neatly sidestepped one goggle-eyed sailor who seemed determined to persuade her to come for a little stroll with him down by the canal.

'And you could kiss goodbye to your virginity on that little walk, assuming you've still got it,' Leah said with a sly wink.

'Fully intact as is yours, cheeky madam,' Jess countered, laughing, and fortunately turned away to watch Adele sign her autograph for a soldier, so didn't notice her friend's blush.

–

'I don't know what you're worrying about,' Steve said, as they walked along the canal bank on their usual Sunday afternoon stroll.

His arm was around her waist, her head tucked into his shoulder. Just being with him made Jess feel supremely content. Were it not for problems over her mother and Uncle Bernie niggling away and threatening to spoil everything, her life would be perfect. But it was difficult to explain all of this, even to Steve. 'I don't trust him.'

'I understand how you feel, love, and your uncle might be a bit of a chancer, but you've got to admire his ambition. He's thinking ahead for when the war ends. There'll be money to be made then, one way or another.'

'Yes, but how does he intend to make it? There surely won't be enough to be made out of selling a bit of beer, not for Bernie Delaney. What is this property he's bought going to be exactly? I've no idea. He won't say.'

'Does it matter so long as you and your mam can get away from Cumberland Street and from being at his beck and call all day. You'll be able to play your trumpet to your heart's content then. Perhaps for the customers, or even hold one of your dances there.'

'If he'll let me, which I very much doubt.'

'True, I could easily have clocked him one that Sunday when he insulted you over your music. What has he got against you?'

'Don't ask. It has a long history, all concerned over being jealous of my dad. Utterly stupid! As a result, he'll make life difficult for me any way he can.'

Following that Sunday tea when Steve had so valiantly stood up to her uncle, she'd tried once more playing the trumpet in the house, stuffing the horn with a large handkerchief to mute the sound. Cora had listened enthralled as Jess had played Gershwin's 'The Man I Love', dreamily saying how wonderful it sounded.

'Eeh love, that fair brought tears to my eyes. You have a gift, you really do.'

Bubbling with happiness, Jess had hugged the older woman, pressing close against the apple softness of her cheeks and singing in her ear, '"Someday he'll come along, the man I love",' and they'd both laughed.

'Eeh, happen he has already, love. Play some more. Go on, I could listen all day.'

And she did. They'd enjoyed a wonderful afternoon together with Jess playing tune after tune, including 'But Not For Me' from the musical *Girl Crazy*. Cora had been happily singing 'A lucky star's above, but not for me' when Bernie had burst in from the backyard where he'd apparently been sorting his spoils.

'Stop that racket at once.'

Had it not been for Cora's intervention, Jess might once more have been deprived of her instrument. It would certainly be good to get away from Bernie's volatile temper, no matter what the truth about his new scheme. But Jess had no intention of leaving a good job at the tea room to work for her uncle behind the bar in this public house, as she'd already made clear. She felt well able to stand up to his bullying, at least aware that Mr Simmons would be loath to lose her.

Her concern for Lizzie was another matter, a public house being the last place her drunken mother should be living. She remained vulnerable and if too much was expected of her could very easily slip back into her old habits. Jess was aware of her secret drinking but at a loss to know how to prevent it. Keeping Lizzie on the straight and narrow was a full time occupation, demanding constant vigilance. How could she do that and work as well?

Explaining none of this to the man she loved, Jess leaned into his shoulder as she smiled ruefully up at Steve. 'I suppose you're right and I should stop worrying. I'd just like to know what Bernie's up to. I've asked him point blank and he simply won't say.'

'Oh that's easy to explain. Keeping his plans secret is all about power. Why should he tell you anything? Being a woman, you wouldn't understand his business matters.'

She stopped walking to stand and stare at him. 'What has being a woman got to do with that? I've a brain in my head, same as him, same as you, same as any man in fact.'

Steve held up his hands by way of defence. 'I didn't say that was my opinion. It's the way *he* thinks, that men and women are different.'

'So you don't believe men are more intelligent than women?'

'Course they are,' he quipped, ducking as she took a swing at him, then catching her in his arms, he laughed at her show of temper. 'No, of course I don't think they're more intelligent. Except in the case of present company.'

'Drat you, Steve Wyman, I'll...'

'What will you do?'

'I shall – er – kiss you to death if you say one more word against women.'

'Oh well, in that case, I think they're all stupid, save for you, darling, so go ahead and kiss me to death' he joked.

Jess laughed, pushing out of her mind whatever nonsense it was they'd been sparring over, including worries over her mother, and Uncle Bernie's entrepreneurial mysteries. Nothing else seemed to matter except she and Steve should share and explore the deep feelings they had for each other, in the only way possible. She felt exhilarated, filled with optimism for the future. The world was her oyster, and she was in control of her own life now, not Uncle Bernie, hoping to make a success of her band. Best of all, there were far more interesting elements of importance between herself and

Steve. Whenever he kissed her, as he was doing now with strong passion, she relished the intoxicating sensation that pulsed within her.

The exploration of their desire for each other killed all sense of polite resistance, and it was there, deep in the long grasses among the heady scent of bluebells, that they finally made love. He paused only once to ask, 'Are you sure?'

Dazed with emotion, Jess was too choked to speak and could do no more than pull him closer and help him to undo her bra. She then gave herself willingly to him. It seemed entirely right for her to do so. She loved him, and deep inside knew that he felt the same way about her, even though he'd never actually said as much. But he would. She was sure of that. Happiness and love were being offered to her at last, after all her troubles and disappointments in life. And wasn't this man the one she'd always longed for?

Chapter Twenty-One

Having made his plans, the details of which he largely meant to keep to himself at this stage, Bernie announced to Jess that he'd found them a property he thought would be just the ticket. 'It suffered considerable damage in the blitz but has great potential.'

Jess's first instinct was to refuse but she bit back her protest. Money was still tight and much as she longed for complete independence, she couldn't afford to be too stubborn. She decided to play for time. 'Where is it, this house?'

'It's a commercial property on Deansgate. I mean to open it up as a public house-cum-club for servicemen. But you and Lizzie can be the ones to live on the premises, to act as caretakers like. It'll make a nice home for the pair of you, and useful for me to have someone living in. It'll be rent-free of course. I can't say fairer than that, now can I?'

Surprised though she was by this sudden show of generosity, Jess desperately longed for independence, so she damped down any lingering doubts about still being obliged to live on premises her uncle owned. What did it matter who supplied the roof over their heads, so long as it was separate from his own?

'I'll look it over,' she agreed, trying not to be concerned when her uncle gave one of his sly grins.

'Rightio,' Bernie cheerily remarked, and went off whistling.

He'd almost decided against involving his sons in the scheme but common sense had prevailed. Tommy was an honest lad and had bravely gone off to join the war, but Harry and Bert surely had more sense. The pair quickly volunteered for the job of barmen, and to find a supply of booze, which was useful. You couldn't run a pub without beer.

Harry suggested they employ girls to wait on and act as hostesses. 'I know one or two who might be interested. Thirza Shaw for one. Quite a looker, she is. And amenable, you know what I mean? I could check a few more out, ask around her friends like.'

'They'd need to be tasty, high class lasses,' Bernie warned. 'Fresh and young. No old scrubbers. We need to provide the right sort of tone for the place. I'm not running a knocking shop.'

Harry widened his eyes in mock innocence. 'Never thought you were, Dad. Though what these girls get up to after they've served the drinks, is up to them, right?'

Bernie smirked. 'So long as I get my cut.'

'Goes without saying.'

Bernie was more than happy to leave this little matter in Harry's capable hands, and father and son did seem to be on the same wavelength for once. He couldn't wait to see his name over the door, proudly proclaiming that he'd well and truly arrived. One up from a common-or-garden pub, Delaney's of Deansgate would be a classy sort of place where a bloke could buy a drink, enjoy a game of cards and place the odd bet (discreetly of course, since it wouldn't be strictly legal), as well as the more usual dominoes and darts. And what with all these Yanks pouring into the city, business should be good.

'A bit of flash and razzmatazz won't come amiss.' Bernie felt he needed to make his mark, and Harry and Bert would make certain that no one else would try to move in on his patch. Oh aye, they were handy lads to have around.

–

Jess's first viewing of the property did not exactly fill her with unmitigated optimism. It was situated close to the junction of Tonman Street, near Campfield Market. A busy thoroughfare and not one she would have chosen to be a place to live. The building itself looked half derelict, as clearly at some point it had been hit by a high explosive bomb. Surprisingly, the walls remained intact, for all it lacked doors and windows. Part of the roof was missing, and here and there were huge gaps in the flooring. When Bernie asked her what she thought, Jess was hard put to know how to reply.

'It's very large and in a sorry state.'

'There you go again, never showing a morsel of gratitude.'

'I only said it was in need of attention, which is plain to see. I didn't say I wasn't grateful, but why this particular property? Wouldn't you get a better clientele at the other end of Deansgate, further away from the railway and the docks?'

'Hark at her. La-di-dah,' Lizzie said, fluffing out her stringy, hennaed hair.

'Shut your trap, Lizzie, for God's sake.' Bernie turned to Jess with a sickly smile. 'I got it cheap some months back, off a mate of mine. It'll be right as ninepence when I've done it up a bit. I've organised some chaps to start work tomorrow. You won't recognise it in a week or two.'

Despite her misgivings, Jess soon became quite interested in the whole project. The upper floors and roof were repaired, doors and windows put back, the entire place cleared of the heaps of old brick, plaster and rubble. Its rebirth seemed to herald the promise of a new beginning, a world that one day wouldn't be dominated by war, where people would be able to dust themselves off and start to live again.

Everyone was saying that now the Americans were involved, the war was all over bar the shouting. However optimistic this might be, Jess could only hope that they weren't too far wrong. Perhaps when it was finally over and her dad came home, they would at least have a decent place for him to live, and hopefully a job waiting for him. Jess thought that if things had been better between her and Uncle Bernie, she might have offered to help improve it. But no one could claim them to be on good terms, for all his protestations of family loyalty.

By the time the work was only halfway finished, Jess was awestruck. The property seemed to grow bigger every time she saw it. There were eight bedrooms plus living room, kitchen and bathrooms on the two upper floors, while the ground floor boasted two bar lounges and a snug. On the first floor there was also one long room that ran the full length of the building. Jess couldn't help but visualise that as a possible venue for a dance, and wondered if she dared approach Uncle Bernie with the suggestion, whenever she could summon up the courage.

But she couldn't resist calling in every evening on her way home from the tea room to watch in disbelief as richly patterned carpets were carried in and fitted in each and every room, save for the long one in question. Here, the wooden floors were stained and polished, as indeed were the rooms on the ground floor where a bar counter was also installed together with a brass foot rail around its perimeter.

Next came the furniture, carried in by Harry and Bert: large beds, ornate wardrobes and dressing tables. Sofas and comfy chairs followed; together with tables of every size and shape, both for the upstairs rooms and for the ground floor, none of it utility stuff. Jess didn't care to ask how Bernie had acquired it. It must have cost him a small fortune, or had he borrowed the money? It was all becoming rather garish and brash, and Jess began to feel decidedly uneasy about the project.

–

'You've decided to be friendly again, have you?' Harry said, when he found Leah waiting for him one afternoon, full of apologies for their quarrel and with the suggestion that he might like to come dancing, as a change from the flicks. He'd been so annoyed when she'd turned up her nose and refused to see him for a while that he'd told himself he'd have nothing more to do with her. But one glimpse of her shapely little body and his mouth was watering. 'Am I supposed to be grateful that you've suddenly remembered me?'

'I just thought you might still be interested. Sorry if I've neglected you but I've been a bit busy lately with the band. We're settling into a routine now so I could manage to find time to squeeze you in.' She said this with an air of indifference, as if it really were of no interest whether he agreed or not, yet inside she was quaking with nerves that he might refuse.

He gave a crude, lopsided smile. 'Why not, I like a bit of a squeeze,' he smirked, making Leah blush.

In that instant she saw him for what he was: a crude, rough bloke out for what he could get. What am I doing making myself look cheap chasing Harry Delaney, she asked herself. But then as he and Bert manhandled a piano into the new pub his father was setting up, she watched with trembling fascination and knew why. She simply couldn't resist him. To her eyes, he was gorgeous and so alluring. The rippling muscles beneath the grubby vest, the way his lazy, deep-lidded gaze slid over her, as if stripping every stitch off her, set her pulses racing even while she was filled with guilt over her own shameless behaviour. He excited her and felt she must have him, no matter what the risks involved.

Harry only had to look at her to feel randy and he glanced up and down the street, irritated suddenly by all the shoppers on Deansgate, the traffic and even the sight of a rozzer not too far off. Inside this property, however, was another matter entirely. 'Bert, go and get yourself a pint.'

'I'm not thirsty, Harry.'

'Aye you are. Be off with you.'

Bert looked from one to other, got the message and skedaddled. Harry grabbed Leah by the arm and took her up to one of the bedrooms, empty save for a large, comfortable bed.

'It's not made up and probably damp,' Leah protested, her mother's training suddenly coming to the fore.

'Who needs sheets and pillows? Let's just test the merchandise, shall we? Try it for size, like.' And in no time at all, he'd pulled them fancy French knickers off and was satisfying his lust.

–

'Where are you getting all this stuff from?' Jess challenged Harry a day or two later, but he only laughed and tapped the side of his nose in a fair imitation of his father.

Bert said, 'Don't worry, there's plenty more where that came from,' which did nothing to ease her concerns. And that wasn't the only puzzle.

By the time she and Lizzie had finally moved in, setting out their few meagre possessions in the cavernous wardrobes and chests of drawers, her curiosity had reached mammoth proportions. Jess tried to express these concerns to her mother. 'Since there's only the two of us, who are all these bedrooms for? Is it meant to be a boarding house as well as a pub, do you reckon? He hasn't asked you to provide bed and breakfast for commercial travellers, or the armed forces, has he? Because you can't cook to save your life, and I already have more than enough work, ta very much.'

Lizzie shook her head in bemused ignorance. 'He hasn't said anything of the sort to me. But then I was quite happy in the old place, despite Cora, and would still be there if you hadn't moaned so much.'

Jess didn't trouble to answer this accusation, knowing it would be a waste of time to attempt to explain to Lizzie the value of privacy and independence. All her mother wanted was to be near her beloved Bernie. Cora, on the other hand, had been delighted to see her sister-in-law depart, and had gladly helped her to pack.

'You know where we are Lizzie, if you feel like a natter.'

'I wouldn't set foot back in this house again if you paid me,' Lizzie had perversely responded.

When Jess returned for the last load of their belongings, she'd had a private word with her aunt over a quick cuppa. 'What are Bernie's plans for this place, do you know? Is it to be a club, a pub, a boarding house or all three?'

Cora said, 'Nay, don't ask me. He does as he pleases does our Bernie.' And as Jess knew from past experience, Cora would never question her husband, not directly. Yet something was going on that Jess didn't understand and for some time she'd felt the urge to ask her uncle a few questions.

She found him with the builders, sleeves rolled up, collar undone, a flat cap still in place on his head, perhaps to keep the dust out of his precious few strands of hair. He seemed to be happily putting up glass shelves, which would presumably hold the liquor, while an electrician nearby was fixing wall lights in a lovely rose tinted hue. 'I'm curious to know why this place is so big. What were you thinking of doing with that long room on the first floor?' she asked. 'I don't suppose you'd consider letting us hold a dance there?'

He tapped the side of his nose, revealing chipped, tobacco stained teeth, a sour expression on his face. 'I'm not playing silly kids's games! I mean to make real money.'

Jess rightly guessed this room might well involve gambling and asked no further questions. This property seemed to increase in grandeur every time she saw it, now having sprouted chandeliers, but she was still filled with curiosity. 'And what do you intend to do with all the other bedrooms?' To her intense disappointment, though not in any way a surprise, Bernie refused to answer a single one of her questions.

'You'll be told what's what, all in good time. Let's just say we have our living to make and you'll be no exception.'

'I hope you appreciate that Mam can't cook and has never managed to keep a house clean in her entire life. As for me, I have jobs I'm not prepared to leave in order to work here for whatever business you intend to run.'

'You sound more like your dratted father every day,' Bernie said, a nasty gleam in his eye that should have warned her against such a comment. 'You always like to argue, and look what happened to him. He went off to fight for King and country, to be a hero, and where is he now? God knows. So keep your nose out of my business. You'll be kept informed, as and when.' And refusing to say another word on the subject, he hitched his trousers up by the braces, and chuckling softly to himself he lumbered off, screwdriver in hand, in search of another shelf.

Jess watched him go with deep sense of despair. When Uncle Bernie spoke in his usual foul-mouthed voice, there was bound to be something he wasn't telling her. She was beginning to regret accepting his offer of accommodation here, not at all the kind of home she'd planned for herself and Lizzie. She'd wanted a two up and two down, similar to the one they'd occupied in Irwell Street. This one was sumptuous to the point of grandeur, but very much a public house. So why was that?

Chapter Twenty-Two

Delaney's All Girls Band went from strength to strength. They liked to think that because they were women they were able to express more emotion in the music. Certainly men watching might fall in love with them on sight. But as well as keeping up their new glamorous image they also impressed with their musical skills, and the number of bookings proliferated. The band was becoming hugely popular and proving to be a serious rival to their male counterparts.

Not that you would have thought so from the reports available in the press. Photographs would be taken of them in their gorgeous gowns, smiling and holding their shining horns aloft, Leah perched provocatively on the lid of her piano, Ena with her drums. It all seemed like harmless fun even if it rankled slightly when the photographer called out for them to 'Flash a bit of leg, darling.'

Jess was always at pains to explain their passion for the music, and how they trained hard. But the reporter would be more concerned with asking for their favourite recipes, how they did their hair and what beauty tips they could give to the lonely wives stuck at home. When the piece appeared in the paper, it would say what fun it was for them, as if it took no serious musical effort at all. It stated how Jess had learned to play in the Salvation Army Bugle

Band and spoke of her 'fresh beauty', describing how she worked in a cake shop, thus implying that she was just a fluffy little woman, with no brains or talent at all.

The band didn't go on tour, largely because they all had jobs during the day which must be kept up, but they did love to play for locals as well as troops at an army base or hospital. They would always allow time for comforting those young soldiers who seemed in need of it, smiling, teasing and flirting with them to ease their fears.

The military were sometimes favoured with famous names such as George Formby, Joe Loss, Gracie Fields or Charlie Chester. But more often, unknowns, like themselves, entertained them. And Delaney's All Girls's Band could bring the house down. At first they'd felt somewhat overwhelmed to be faced by a room full of soldiers, as the troops would go wild, whistling and cheering, stamping their feet and yelling, loving every minute of their performance.

They always started a gig in the same way, with Leah and her classical piano trailing a few opening bars of some quite serious melody or other. The audience would listen in respectful silence. Then there would be a roll from the drums, a fanfare on the trumpet, the drums would answer back, cymbals crash and they'd be away, swinging into action playing 'Bugle Call Rag' or 'St Louis Blues'.

Jess might do a trumpet solo or Leah improvise something on the piano, and of course everyone loved it when Ena became the focus of attraction on her drums. One night Miss Mona got so carried away she tossed aside her bow and started plucking the strings of her cello with her fingers. The troops went wild and she never used it again after that.

Once, at a function for naval officers on board a destroyer, Jess felt able to soothe the girls's nerves by reminding them that these were a class above the ordinary enlisted men so there would surely be a bit more decorum. She was delighted when not only did they play terrific music that night, but looked pretty good too in new slinky gowns of gold sateen. Perhaps too good, for afterwards the Chief Petty Officer came round and invited them to 'come and mingle' so they could have 'a drink with the boys'.

'I'm not sure that's such a good idea,' Jess said, glancing around at the others to make sure they agreed with her. She could see at once that they did, perhaps with the exception of Ena, who was already giving the Chief Petty Officer the glad eye. How that girl ever imagined she could survive in a nunnery, Jess couldn't imagine.

'Come on now girls, be fair. You've got to be kind to the lads. They enjoy spending time with a pretty woman. A bit of fraternising does no harm at all. They deserve it.'

'What, exactly are you suggesting?' Adele asked, her dark eyes narrowing to a dangerous slit.

'Why do you think we invited *you* and not a men's band? Some of these guys might not see a woman again for months, if at all. Do them a favour, girls and be generous. You know that's what is expected. Why else would you have accepted the invitation?'

Lulu poked him in the chest with her sharply pointed, fuchsia tipped finger and pushed him backwards out the door. 'Sod off, you nasty little man. We're musicians, not tarts!'

They were most careful thereafter on which bookings they accepted. Enlisted men, they discovered, were in fact far more respectful than the officers, certainly in their experience.

–

Jess arrived home late one evening to find the bar full to bursting with people and a party in full swing, one that had obviously degenerated into what was generally known as a knees-up. The sound of their raucous laughter and singing met her at the door. Half opened boxes stood about on the floor, on tables and the bar counter itself, spilling their contents over every surface. That was all she needed. She'd just had a wonderful evening with the band, playing at the Tramways Club for the conductors and drivers, and had come away happy and glowing with success. Now she came tumbling down to earth when she viewed the reality of her life.

'What's going on?' she asked, of no one in particular, which was just as well since nobody was listening. Only Cissie Armitage, always ready to drown her sorrows at someone else's expense, bothered to answer.

'Your cousins, Harry and Bert, have taken a new delivery. Not that anyone's asking too many questions about which lorry it dropped off the back of.'

Jess certainly knew better than to ask such a question. Bernie could lay his hands on anything, once he'd set his mind to it. He'd put out feelers with his particular contacts, then would send Harry and Bert to chance upon a few cases that had accidentally lost their way. As a result, folk had poured in, the place now humming. Jess made a quick check that all the blackout curtains were safely drawn then went in search of Bernie. It was nearly midnight and if the police came by he'd be in dead trouble, likely lose his licence, assuming he possessed such a thing.

He saw her coming and got to his feet, swaying slightly, whisky bottle in one hand and a large glass in the other. 'Now don't start your fretting again,' he warned when she relayed this possible cause for concern. 'Just enjoy yourself. Gin, vodka, whisky, we've got it all here.'

'So I see.'

'You don't change, Miss Lah–di–dah, do you? Always so flipping self-righteous. Well, I'm going up in the world with my own club, eh?'

From the look of him, Jess rather thought he was on his way down, not up, but didn't risk saying so. It would be far too dangerous to quarrel with Bernie when he was in this state. Before anything more could be said, he'd lurched away and vanished in a fug of smoke, lost in the crowd at the bar.

With its dim lighting and general mêlée, Jess could barely see who was who. She spotted Ma Pickles, or rather could hear her laughing loudly after having swiftly drained her glass of milk stout. Seated obediently by her side, Josh, her devoted son, was neither drinking nor adding a word to the lively conversation going on around him. What a sad little life that poor man led. Would she ever allow him to grow up?

Someone started singing Roll out the Barrel', and George Macintyre, who clearly wasn't allowing a dodgy ticker to prevent him from enjoying his whisky, joined in at the top of his voice. As did Frank Roebottom, Tommy's old firewatcher mate. Cousin Tommy himself was in Italy, not allowed much in the way of leave. He'd written with his congratulations over the new club, and Jess's success with the band.

Aunt Cora was fast asleep in a corner, the children cuddled up beside her, as usual. There were a few other vaguely familiar faces including Sandra, full of her own importance and flirting outrageously with a young sailor. She was fluttering her eyelashes and behaving as if she were eighteen not just turned thirteen. Jess went over and gently suggested that she really ought to be in bed, as should the twins.

'Would you help me gather them up and take them home? Your mam looks worn out and it's near midnight.'

Sandra gave her a scornful glance. 'Push off, you.' Then wrapping her arms around the sailor's neck, captured him in a long and passionate kiss. Jess panicked and fled, deciding she was probably making matters worse as Sandra would do anything to shock her, so any interference would only make matters worse.

There were other servicemen, well gone on Bernie's booze, and a number of girls making up to them. The place seemed mainly to be full of strangers and Jess couldn't help wondering whether, in the fug of cigarette smoke and the excitement of having so much alcohol to drink, anyone was keeping a proper watch on who was paying for it. Still, it was none of her business whether Bernie made a profit or not, or what those girls were up to. It was then that she saw Lizzie, who, like Bernie, was rip-roaring drunk.

The all too familiar sense of disappointment kicked in. Ever since her mother had been released from prison, Jess had dreamed of saving Lizzie from her own stupidity. Creating a home of their own so they could be a proper family, hoping it would be the making of her, had been her main hope. Instead, this move looked like it could be her ruination. Oh, but Jess knew who to blame, and felt a flare of anger towards her uncle who had driven her mother into such a state. Only this wasn't the moment to make such a fuss. Her priority must be to sober her up.

'For goodness sake, Mam, what have you done to yourself? Or rather, what has Bernie done to you?'

Lizzie got up from the table at which she'd been slumped and staggered over to her daughter to wag a finger in her face. Close up, the fumes from her breath nearly knocked Jess out.

'Don't start on one of your lectures, girl. I'm having a good time, so shurrup.' Unable to curb her own propulsion, Lizzie continued across the room and collapsed in a state of semi-consciousness on the floor.

Heaving a resigned sigh, Jess marched over and tried to drag her to her feet. 'Come on, let's get you upstairs. What were you thinking of to let yourself get into this dreadful condition?'

'There you go again with your flippin' lectures. I were having a bit of fun. What's wrong wi' that? That Sally Army lot hash done you no good at all. Why can't you let your hair down onesh in a while and enjoy yourself like the rest of us?'

'Because someone has to maintain some degree of common sense and decorum, and don't insult my friends. The Salvation Army have supported me more than you ever have over the years.'

'Ooh, hark at her. La-di-dah!'

Anger seared through her, blurring her mother's face inches from her own to a sickly oval, and the effort required not to slap it was almost overwhelming. Why had she even bothered to try and help the silly woman? Lizzie was quite beyond redemption.

How Jess had longed all her life for a normal upbringing, for a mother who cared for her, who would make sacrifices as Mrs Simmons did for Leah by saving up to pay for music lessons. Admittedly, Leah didn't always approve of being introduced by her mother to possible husbands, but maybe she didn't appreciate how she was well off. Jess tried not to feel any envy for her friend but, deep inside, she couldn't help it because Leah had everything that Jess wanted. Security, and a loving family! A good job and interesting prospects planned for her future, everything that Jess was desperately attempting to provide for herself.

'I'm only eighteen, Mam. Why have you never looked after me? Tell me that? Why couldn't you manage to do such a basically simple thing? No, don't sit on the floor, I'm not leaving you to loll about, halfcut.'

Lizzie opened her mouth to protest but instead vomited the contents of her stomach all down the front of her daughter's clean skirt and blouse. Jess experienced a strange kind of detachment and all her anger drained away, dissipating in a familiar wave of weariness and resignation.

'Want a hand?' Woken from her slumbers by the noise, or else the stink of vomit, Cora waddled over. Jess accepted her aunt's help with gratitude.

'Best if we take her round to mine. You can't manage her on your own in this state. Much as I hate the silly old besom, I'll not see her choke on her own vomit. And I wouldn't care to imagine what's going on upstairs. Now then, Lizzie, be a good woman and come home wi' me, chuck.'

Making no comment on this decision, Jess took hold of Lizzie's arm and the two of them began to steer her towards the door, Sam and Seb trailing behind, clinging to their mother's skirts.

Lizzie shook Cora off with a violence and strength that was astonishing. 'Gerroff! You keep your flaming nose out of my business.'

'For goodness sake, Mam, Cora's only trying to help.'

'I don't need no help, not from her anyroad. Nor you telling me what I should and shouldn't do the whole time neither. You can both shove off and leave me alone. If I want a bit of fun, I'll have it, and neither you – nor po-faced Cora, is going to stop me.'

Bernie came up behind them to see what all the hubbub was about, slurring his words, 'Aye, leave your mam alone. It's nowt to do with anyone what we does of a night! If we want to get well-bevvied, why the bleedin' hell should we not?'

Jess turned on him with fury in her eyes. 'Because you'll destroy her, that's why. When I said I wanted a place of our own, I meant a little house, one of peace and quiet, not a drinker's paradise. This whole idea was a bad one. I can see that now, and we'll be moving out first thing in the morning.'

'Where to?' Cora asked, her round face creasing with a new anxiety. 'I'd have you back any time Jess love, but not yer mam. Just tonight, and no more! I've had enough of Lizzie, more than I can rightly stand.'

Jess didn't wonder at that, feeling very much the same. 'We'll find somewhere to live, don't you worry. We won't be bothering you or Uncle Bernie, ever again. I'd live in Camp Street air raid shelter sooner than here.'

'Nay lass,' Cora's eyes filled with tears. 'Don't say such terrible things. It tears the heart out of me to see you so cut up.'

But she didn't retract a word of her declaration, Jess noticed. Instead, she half turned and shouted over her shoulder in a voice, which cut through the din like a knife through butter. 'Sandra, put that sailor down and get over here this minute.'

How they managed to get Lizzie home that night, Jess could never afterwards remember. For all there were three of them, it took every scrap of strength and Cora's powerful arms to drag her through the dark streets and fight off her flailing fists. Jess quickly changed out of her stinking clothes then hurried to help Cora wash Lizzie's face, undress her and get her into bed. Sandra was delegated the task of putting the twins to bed while the two women dealt with Lizzie.

'Never mind her nightie,' Cora told Jess. 'Let her sleep in her slip. That's as much of a battle as I've strength for tonight.'

Usually, Jess and Lizzie shared a bed but the stink of vomit that still lingered in the small room made Jess gag. She certainly wasn't prepared to climb in beside her mother tonight. Not in her present condition. Cora seemed to be of the same opinion.

'Sleep on the settle in the front parlour. Don't you worry about his lordship. I'll wait up for him for once, so the drunken fool doesn't bring everything crashing around his ears when he tries to get up them apples and pears. You've nowt to fear from him, being too drunk.'

Chapter Twenty-Three

It was cold in the parlour, filled with dark shadows and creeping mould up the walls. Jess doubted a fire had been lit in here since last winter, and even then probably only on Christmas Day itself. Seeing her start to shiver, Cora shovelled up a bit of coal from the kitchen range and set it in the empty grate. Instantly the room seemed less forbidding. 'That'll not last long but it'll help you get off to sleep.'

'What did you mean when you said you didn't care to imagine what was going on upstairs?'

'My mind was happen wandering.'

'I don't think so, Cora. Bernie's not told me everything, has he? I can tell by the gleeful expression in his nasty little eyes. I'd like to know what it is he's keeping to himself.'

'I wouldn't know, love, but I'll have a word with our Harry and Bert when they get in. They'll happen know something. In the meantime, you get some sleep.' Cora covered her with a blanket, tucked back a strand of hair and kissed her cheek. Jess suddenly caught her hand.

'You've been a better mother to me this last year or two than my own has been throughout my entire lifetime.'

Cora's eyes filled with a rush of tears. 'Eeh lass, what a thing to say.'

'It's true.'

'All I know is that it's been a pleasure to have you around. I think of you as one of me own. There now, you'll have me crying in a minute.' And dabbing at her tears with her apron, Cora shuffled off, her carpet slippers making a shushing sound on the lino.

After she'd gone, Jess lay on the prickly horse hair sofa, covered with the single blanket and wished she was anywhere in the world but here, in this cold, mouldy parlour. Perhaps she wasn't in control of her own life at all. What exactly was Bernie up to? What did the future hold? Jess felt tired and dispirited, disappointed in her mother, and filled with all her old insecurities.

She gazed into the flickering flames of the small fire and thought about her father.

'Where are you Dad? Are you safe and well? Oh, how I miss you.' All she knew was that he was a PoW somewhere, but what was the camp like? Could it be as bad as Strangeways, or worse even?

Sergeant Ted said PoWs got regular Red Cross parcels, and the Salvation Army helped by putting families in touch with each other, so her letters should be getting through. If only he'd reply. Why didn't Dad write? And why did he have to be locked away? What a family they were. Why couldn't everything be simple, a normal life with parents who cared about her; with no war and nobody fighting one another? How marvellous that would be.

She must have fallen asleep while the tears were still wet on her cheeks because some time later Jess woke with a start to the sound of shouting. Pandemonium had broken out in the kitchen. She could hear Bernie's deep booming voice shouting that he could do what he flaming well pleased and didn't need anyone's say so. Cora was screaming her fury at him. Then there came a loud thud and a crash, which sounded like something, or someone, falling amongst the fire irons behind the fender. This was followed by complete silence, which, in a way, seemed all the more ominous.

Jess sat up and rubbed the sleep from her eyes. Should she go in? Was her aunt hurt, or had it been her uncle falling in a drunken stupor? It was a wonder that Sam and Seb, or Sandra at least, hadn't come down to see what all the fresh commotion was about. Perhaps they were used to it and knew when to keep their own counsel. While Jess was debating the wisdom of intervening between husband and wife, she heard someone fiddling with the door latch. Swiftly, she lay down again, pulling the blanket over her ears, desperately trying to keep still and quieten her breathing.

She heard the parlour door click open, footsteps approach, and there was no doubt in her mind who they belonged to, as Bernie weaved an unsteady course towards the old sofa where she lay. After a moment the squeak of his shoes stopped and Jess could hear the sound of laboured breathing, smell the reek of whisky on his breath. She was keenly aware that he must be standing quite close by, watching her. It was as if his gaze was searing into her soul and she had the urge to get up and run, could hardly bear to keep still beneath his silent scrutiny.

After the longest moment of her life, he spoke. 'I know you're not asleep, so listen to what I have to say. Tomorrow morning, first thing, you'll come back to the club and start being nice to my customers. Neither your mam, nor Cora, and certainly not an interfering little whipper-snapper like you, is going to tell me what's what. I've had enough of your lip, madam. Is that clear?'

Jess longed to argue, to speak up and defend herself but decided it was wiser to maintain her silence and persist in the pretence of being asleep. She could but trust that he would soon give up, go off to bed and leave her and Cora in peace. These hopes were instantly dashed as the blanket was suddenly stripped away and a great weight fell upon her, knocking all the breath from her body.

Her eyes flew open as she realised, to her utter shock and horror that he was lying on top of her, fumbling with her clothing. Vapours of sour beer were overwhelming her and Jess almost vomited. She felt suffocated, trapped beneath the malodorous bulk of her uncle, becoming all too horribly aware that the more she shoved and pushed at him, the more aroused he became.

'Get off me, you drunken fool!'

But he only hiccupped loudly in her ear and made a grab for her breast.

Dry mouthed with fear, his tongue cleaving to the roof of her mouth, Jess could barely manage to utter anything more than tiny, frightened mewing noises as she fought desperately to free herself.

'Give us a kiss, you miserable bitch. Come on, don't be so mean.'

His great, wet mouth fastened over hers and now Jess was sure that she would indeed vomit, so revolted was she by the sucking sensation. She freed one hand and scratched him right across his cheek, making him howl in protest.

'You little bugger, I'll fix you.' His fat face was streaked with blood yet he held her down easily with one hand while sausage-like fingers worked away at her nightdress, dragging it up her legs, poking beneath it he pulled down the knickers she'd left on to keep herself warm. As she squirmed and wriggled, desperately struggling to be free she heard his breathing quicken as excitement mounted. Then his fingers probed her groin and entered her, the pain excruciating as he thrust them inside her, but as she opened her mouth to scream, she found another hand the size of a trap door clamped down tight across her mouth.

'Stop playing the coy little maid, drat you! You let that Steve touch you up, I'll warrant. You're a filthy little whore, just like your mam. Stop fighting and open your flaming legs, blast you.'

Panicking and sick with fear, Jess could almost smell his arousal, feel the erect hardness of his penis pressing against her most private parts. She could hear him grunting with pleasure, a kind of animal satisfaction while her screams went unheard of behind the barrier of his filthy hand. With her mouth squeezed tight shut; her kicking limbs as useless as matchsticks against the thrusting violation, Jess suddenly felt a quiver ripple through him, like the rumble of an earthquake.

'That'll teach you, you dirty old man,' Cora yelled, as she struck him over the head with her rolling pin. And giving a loud, piteous groan, Bernie slid heavily to the floor.

–

It took Jess some time to recover from her hysterics. Cora washed her bruised and sore body and settled her into her own bed. Even then, she was afraid her uncle might come upstairs and attack her again.

'Nay, he's out cold till morning. Drunk as the proverbial. He'll not bother you again tonight, or any night after this, mark my words.'

'How will you stop him? He thinks he can bully us all: Lizzie, you, and now me. I can't stand it, Cora, I really can't. He's turned me into a victim, completely in his power.' And she began to sob, utterly losing control.

'Nay, don't take on. You're nothing of the sort. Trust me, there'll be no more victims in this house. He'll not lay another finger on you, I swear. Nor on me neither. He'll have learnt his lesson after this, I can tell you. So come on love, drink this hot milk, it'll help you sleep. I've put a nip of brandy in it, for the shock. I'm sure the Sally Army will forgive you a little snifter for once. You'll feel better after a good night's sleep.'

In a voice barely above a whisper, Jess murmured, 'How do I ever get over something like this?'

Cora tut tutted, not quite knowing how to answer. Then, coming to a decision, she gently said, 'I got him with the rolling pin quickly enough, right? He hadn't gone all the way, had he, love? We certainly don't want any repercussions.'

For a moment Jess felt bemused, and then understanding slowly dawned. Cora was talking about a possible rape and pregnancy – of Jess having her own uncle's child. All the colour drained from her face and bile rose in her throat. 'Dear God, don't let that happen. I'll kill myself sooner.'

'Take it easy love! Don't believe the worst, and you won't look half so bad come morning.'

Jess swallowed painfully then shook her head. 'I did feel his fingers, and then...' She choked in anguish. 'I don't remember what happened after that. One minute he was pushing and shoving at me, the next he'd gone. It's all a bit of a blur.'

Cora looked anxious for a moment, then briskly attempted to console her. 'He were probably too drunk to finish what he started. I was there fairly soon, so I'm sure he can't have got very far, love.'

Jess was shaking, shock taking its effect upon her. 'How can I be certain of that? I've little experience of such things. Although me and Steve... we did once...' Remembering the magic of their first love-making brought fresh tears springing to her eyes, to run unchecked down her cheeks. How could it be the same for them ever again?

Cora muttered under her breath what sounded very like a curse. 'Like I say, best way is to put it out of your mind, like it never happened. You'll get over it, in time. Your Steve will never know, if you don't tell him.'

In her confusion and fear, Jess couldn't be certain of anything. Nor could she simply sweep it aside, as Cora urged her to do. That was quite beyond her. Her nasty uncle had attempted to force himself upon her, and Jess felt soiled by his brutal assault, made dirty by the violation she'd suffered. If he'd actually raped her, she shuddered at the memory. How could she tell Steve what Bernie had done to her? And how could she ever let him touch her after this? Her gentle weeping turned to tearing, heart-broken sobs.

For a long while Cora rocked her in her arms, tears rolling down her own plump cheeks. If she hadn't already done so, she'd lay him out cold, to be sure. She'd done no more than slap a bit of iodine on to her own cuts and bruises. Now she gave a smile, which looked more like a lopsided grimace. One eye was half closed and becoming strange shades of black and purple by the second. Her lip was split, a tooth missing, and blood spilled over her plump chin to drip on to her ample bosom where it made a pool of scarlet on her floral pinny. She ineffectually swiped at it with the back of her hand.

Jess kissed Cora's soft flushed cheek before sipping the hot milk, as instructed. It was sweet and soothing, and did indeed calm her. 'What was it you were arguing with him about?'

'This public house of his, or club, whatever it is.' Cora heaved a sigh. 'Do you know what sort of club it's going to be? A house of ill repute, no less. It will be a place for service men to have a drink, enjoy prostitutes and generally have a good time. Up in that big, first floor room he's put tables for gambling, entirely illegal, where he means to deprive the punters of their hard-earned brass. After they get acquainted with them girls they can slip upstairs to avail themselves of their charms in those fancy bedrooms next to your little flat.' At this point Cora looked her straight in the eye. 'Lizzie was supposed to see to them, assuming she could manage not to get legless in the process. And you were to be the star attraction.'

'What? Playing in the band?'

'Aye, happen he might have agreed to that in the end. If you were a good girl and did as you were told. But he had other tricks in mind for you.'

A short pause, and then, 'Oh, my God!'

'Don't worry, love. I wouldn't let it ever happen. So don't feel any guilt over me whopping him one. Serve the old bugger right for thumping me. You've been spared that at least.'

Once Jess was asleep, Cora went back into the parlour to examine the prostrate form of her husband. She could feel a heat building up inside her, the muscles of her stomach bunching with a new fear. He was strangely silent. Not like him to stay still for so long, drunk or no. She gave him a sharp kick in the ribs, and shook him by the shoulder.

'Come on you lazy tyke. Gerrup! I can't lift you up onto this sofa, not on me own. Not that you're coming upstairs tonight. Happen not any night, after what you've done to young Jess. I've put up with your temper long enough. D'you hear me?' She kicked him again and the heavy body rolled over, his beady eyes staring blankly up at the ceiling.

–

Cora sat by the dying fire for some time, struggling to deal with how to cope with this disaster. Even as she put the final plans into place in her head, she heard stumbling footsteps at the back door. She could but hope those lads of hers weren't too far gone in drink.

Harry and Bert tumbled into the room, arms around each other's shoulders, surprised to see their mother sitting there. She'd never been one to wait up, preach to them about their drinking habits, or any other bad habits, come to that. They were looking smart enough in their best suits, Harry's a dark navy check, while Bert's was a smooth brown, both lifted from the wardrobe of a house near

Philips Park. Over these they wore beige raincoats, casually unbuttoned, again from the same address. Only the trilby hats had been legitimately paid for, which they always wore to the club in their new role as entrepreneurs. It had been worth the sacrifice of a few quid as the hats provided status, and also paid good dividends when trying to impress a woman.

'Hey up Ma, you look like you've lost a shilling and found a tanner.'

'Harry, Bert, am I glad to see you two. No, don't take your coats off, I've a little job that I want you to do for me. I was wondering if you knew of any bomb sites that haven't been properly searched or cleared yet.'

'Aye, any number! Why Mam, what you up to?' Harry dug his brother in the ribs with one elbow and gave a guffaw of inebriated laughter. 'Don't tell me you're going to take up scavenging an' all.'

'I was thinking of burying something in the muddle and muck like.'

Harry took off the trilby hat and scratched his thatch of greasy hair. 'Have you gone off your head, Mam? Why would you want to bury something on a bomb site?'

'There's been what you might call an accident here tonight. Your dad got a bit above himself and did something nasty to our Jess. Oh, she's all right. Don't look so alarmed, Bert. Not that she was unhurt – but she'll live. Your dad, however, didn't do right at all. I did for him good and proper with my rolling pin. I had to get him off her, d'you see?'

Cora met their startled expressions with a calm, if rueful expression. 'He's out cold in the parlour, and I'd say we'll be needing that big handcart what you use when

244

you go out on your demolition work, Harry. And happen you'd best change. You don't want to mess up them smart new clothes.'

Chapter Twenty-Four

Losing a body, even one as substantial as Bernie Delaney, amidst the bombed out ruins some safe distance from Deansgate proved to be surprisingly easy. Removing his gold watch, cufflinks, wallet and anything else that might identify their father, Harry and Bert buried him deep amongst the rubble. They hoped that, if and when he was finally unearthed, no one would recognise him or know who he was. They'd simply assume he'd copped it when the building got hit and had subsequently been overlooked by any rescue parties.

Back at the house, they quaffed a much-needed glass of Guinness each, as they watched the sun rise. Having heard the full, unexpurgated tale from their mother, they'd packed her off to bed and gone off to deal with this unsavoury business. Now they were contemplating the implications.

'You don't reckon Mam will be arrested, do you, Harry? Taken off to Strangeways and hanged.'

'If you've nowt intelligent to say, shut your trap. What d'you reckon we've been up to this last hour or two, if not making sure nobody suspects what took place here tonight. What we have to do now is forget all about it, right? If you open your daft mouth and spill the beans we'll all be in the soup. The only way to keep Mam, and us, safe, is to tie that loose tongue of yours in a knot. Understand?'

'Oh aye, Harry. I'll not say a word. You can rely on me.'

Harry gave his brother a withering look. 'That's what I'm afraid of. We've no choice but to rely on you.' He took a swallow of the rich black liquid, letting it slide down his dusty throat, wiping the froth from his mouth with the back of one hand. Then he eased off his boots and propped his feet in their sweat and dirt encrusted socks on the warm brass fender. 'You know who's really to blame, don't you?'

'Who's that, Harry?'

'Our beloved cousin. If it weren't for her flaunting herself, Dad would never have been tempted to try his luck, and Mam wouldn't have needed to clout him with the rolling pin.'

'I don't think it's quite fair to say it was our Jess's fault.'

'I've just said so, haven't I?' Harry snapped.

'Oh right, well it must be then, if you say so, Harry. I was only thinking that Dad were always one to get in a paddy over nowt.'

'Well it wasn't over nowt this time. It was because she wouldn't do as she was told. She wouldn't agree to help out at the club. Jess defied him, as always.'

Bert was frowning. 'But we've never done what Dad told us neither, Harry. Not properly. We've made out that we were willing, but in reality we always do as we please.'

Harry heaved a sigh of exasperation over Bert's slow-ness at catching on but then allowed himself a small smile as a new thought took root. He got up from the hard chair on which he'd been sitting and took what he considered to be his rightful place in the battered old fireside chair where his father had sat night after night, reading his Sporting Chronicle and issuing orders. Harry settled into its dusty depths with a satisfied sigh. 'That's as maybe, but we won't need to use subterfuge any more, will we? I'm in charge now, not Dad. He's history.'

He was top dog now, the one who would move up in the world, as he rightly deserved. He glanced about the shabby kitchen, at the milk jug turning sour on the battered deal table, the old Lancashire range, which his mother black-leaded week after week. The tiny scullery where he could just catch sight of the old brown slop-stone sink where she did the washing every Monday, half hidden behind a strung-up curtain. She deserved better, as they all did. And it was up to him to provide it. He'd find them a better place to live, though not at the club where the spare bedrooms were needed for a more lucrative purpose. He'd maybe take a wife to give him that much needed air of respectability. Harry puffed out his chest, quite liking the idea. He reminded himself how he'd reached this exalted position, partly by his own skill, but also because of what had happened tonight. He'd never forget that.

'Is there any more ale in that jug? Top us up then, there's a good lad.'

And as Bert rushed to do his bidding, Harry blithely remarked, 'We'll make her pay for this mess, see if we don't. That lass'll be sorry she ever upset a Delaney and put our mam's life in jeopardy. She'll wish this night's business had never taken place.'

–

Jess wished, with heartfelt agony, that last night's events hadn't taken place. She knew deep in her heart that she could never see Steve again. She was no longer fit to be his girlfriend, not after what had happened. Where was her hope for the future now? How could she bear to have any man touch her, even Steve, without bringing back a painful memory that was rapidly turning into a nightmare. Jess doubted she would ever feel clean again. Cora had bathed her afterwards, and this morning at first light Jess had crept down to the kitchen and washed herself again from head to foot, striving to cleanse the filth, which had penetrated her body. A feeling she couldn't eradicate.

Cora brought her breakfast in bed, telling her to stay where she was, that everything was at sixes and sevens. She said Harry and Bert were having a lie-in and the twins were being particularly fractious but she'd have them on their way in no time. Jess was not to worry as she'd sent a note with Sandra to Mr Simmons to say she was a bit poorly and wouldn't be in today. 'A day in bed and you'll be right as rain tomorrow, soon your old self.'

Jess knew she would never be her old self ever again. Despite her determination over the years never to become one of her uncle's victims, the horror of what he'd done to her would be lodged forever in her soul. She'd have to go away, anywhere so long as it was as far from Uncle Bernie as possible. But for today, Cora was right. She needed to hide under the covers; once she'd washed herself yet again in the big basin of hot water her aunt had brought up.

When Jess finally did emerge downstairs later in the day, it was only because Cora had convinced her that he was nowhere around. Lizzie was sitting in her usual chair crying through a haze of cigarette smoke. Cora took

Jess's hand and led her to a stool by the fire, which blazed halfway up the chimney despite it being a warm, sunny day, making the kitchen stiflingly hot.

'Come on love, sit yourself down and have a nice cuppa. Take no notice of your mam. She's a bit upset over Bernie doing a moonlight flit.'

'He's left me,' Lizzie wailed, as if she were the wife and not Cora. 'Without so much as saying goodbye.'

'What? You mean…?' Jess could scarcely take in the import of these words. Ignoring Lizzie's wails, she turned to Cora, 'Is she saying he's gone?'

Cora's tone was bitter. She'd been putting on an act for most of her married life, making out she was happy when only her childer had brought her any comfort. It would be a relief to tell the truth about her marriage at last, although a few more lies would be needed to bring the matter to a satisfactory end. But if it made this lass feel better, it was all to the good.

'Aye, he's up and done a runner, as he always does when things get sticky. Good riddance to bad rubbish, that's what I say. Who needs him? We can make a do without him, see if we don't. There you are love, I've put two sugars in, since we have plenty and you need to keep your strength up.'

'But why has he gone? And where to?'

'Nay, I wouldn't know and don't want to. He's slung his hook, that's all that matters. He left a note on t'mantelshelf to say he'd seen the error of his ways. I'd show it to you, only I flung it on the fire in a temper. He apologised for having crossed a line he shouldn't have and thought it best if he took himself off to pastures new.' Her lies were coming thick and fast, smooth as butter. This was the best explanation Cora's feeble imagination could find. Aware it didn't sound convincing, because when had Bernie ever troubled himself about crossing lines or caring what folk thought? She kept well away from Jess while she told her tale, busying herself by giving the twins their daily dose of cod liver oil. 'Keep still will you,' she complained as they deftly evaded the spoon. 'You're like a pair of wriggling worms.'

This sent Sam and Seb flat on the floor, wriggling about on their stomachs, giggling uproariously. Cora slapped down the spoon and shook a fist at them, a grin on her round face. 'I'll batter you two when I catch you,' she teased them, making them laugh all the more. After chasing the two wriggling worms around the room, Cora finally captured her quarry by the scruff of their collars and placed both children at the kitchen table, rewarding them with a stack of thickly cut wedges of bread and dripping for their afternoon tea. 'There's good little lambs,' Cora indulgently remarked.

Then she opened the back door and yelled in a voice that would carry not only to the bottom of the back yard where Sandra was sitting on the wall talking to her mates, but very likely to Salford docks as well, '*Sandra*, get inside this minute. I'll not tell you again.'

Plonking herself back in her chair, rasping for breath, she urged Jess not to worry. 'You've had a bad shock, lass. Best to take it easy for a while, and be glad we're shot of him. I certainly am.'

'But I thought you adored him, Aunt Cora. Worshipped the ground he walked on.'

'He looked after me well enough once, but he soon gave up on that, the bossy man. Happen we'll get a bit of peace round here now.'

'Bernie wasn't bossy to me,' Lizzie shouted.

'Aye, he was, shurrup talking rubbish.' Growing desperate to change the subject, Cora was almost willing for her twins to be naughty. 'Now then you two, don't eat all that bread and dripping, leave some for your mam. Nay, look at the state of you!' Jumping to her feet, she began to scrub the hands and faces of the terrible twosome with carbolic soap, eager to put an end to this difficult conversation.

–

Having slept for much of the day in a state of shock, Jess had trouble getting off to sleep that night. She huddled under the covers listening to the intermittent sobs and snores of her mother beside her, perhaps still mourning for her lost love. She'd now lost hers. This budding romance between herself and Steve might well have developed, if life had continued as smoothly as she'd hoped. Tears rolled down her cheeks, wetting her pillow and draining her of energy. Could she tell him about this terrible thing that had been done to her? Never!

If she'd known him better, if they'd been engaged, or if he'd told her that he loved her, she might have been more confident of his reaction. But their friendship was too new, too fragile, and she didn't feel able to inflict this news on him. Jess became so depressed that she even convinced herself that he might not believe in her innocence, that he'd assume she'd encouraged Bernie and brought it on herself. Men were always eager to be seduced. Hadn't her mam said as much a thousand times? Lizzie could be right.

And yet she didn't want to lose Steve. Oh, what should she do?

The next morning, aching with tiredness and red-eyed through lack of sleep, Jess went to the tea room as usual, pretending she'd had a touch of flu but was now recovered. The other girls told her she still looked ill and should be in bed, which was true in a way. Jess felt very much below par, almost as if she had indeed suffered a bad dose of influenza. Her limbs felt weak and trembling, one minute all hot and prickly, the next ice cold. She felt quite unable to show interest in anything or anyone, could scarcely concentrate on anything, being too haunted by the image of life without Steve. How could she possibly survive now that she'd fallen so hopelessly in love with him?

She spent much of that day and the next, constantly sneaking off to the bakery kitchens to get warm, while Leah's brother Robert would very kindly give her a warm scone or a mug of hot cocoa. One afternoon towards the end of that dreadful week, Leah found her cuddled up in the airing cupboard, squeezed in beside the tea towels.

'So this is where you've got to. I thought you might have gone off home, feeling sick again. You came back to work too soon and haven't been well all week.'

Jess shook her head. It had developed into a dull ache, wishing for once that her friend would leave her alone. 'I'm fine,' she said, even though most nights she spent sobbing quietly into her pillow, worrying over what she could do to keep Steve? Her friend went on to speak of the hilarious tale of the piano recital, which Jess had already heard *ad nauseum* so didn't trouble to listen. She still felt strangely detached from reality, only vaguely aware of Leah's voice droning on. It was as if the world had tilted and everything was slightly out of focus.

Something must have caught her attention because she tuned in again to hear Leah saying, 'I haven't told Mother yet,' rolling her eyes heavenwards in mock despair. 'God knows what she'll say. Harry is a darling, thrilling and very romantic, don't you think? He brought me roses and went down on one knee. I could hardly believe my eyes or how he said I'll be the making of him. Isn't that wonderful? Sadly, the fact he's a Delaney will count against him, I'm afraid, so far as my mother is concerned. She will not be pleased, bless her. Oh dear, and she had such hopes for me. Too high for my taste, I'm afraid. I wondered if you'd be with me when I tell her. It would help so much if you explained how he isn't at all like his dreadful father. Who else could I wish for?

Jess was staring at her in blank disbelief. 'Sorry, I think I've missed hearing what you were saying. I thought for a minute you said Harry.'

Leah flushed, carefully avoiding eye contact with Jess, knowing that in these past few weeks while she'd been seeing Harry, she'd deliberately misled her by letting her think it was Tommy she was pining over.

'Of course I said Harry. Who else would I mean? Aren't you listening to a word I said? Here's me talking about going against my better judgement and tying the knot with your delicious cousin and you aren't paying the slightest attention.'

'Delicious cousin? Tying the knot?' Jess regarded her friend with wide, astonished eyes, not quite able to believe she'd heard correctly. 'That *is* what you said, right? But you can't mean *our* Harry! I thought it was Tommy who—'

'No, I said Harry because I mean Harry. Isn't Tommy in Italy? We've been walking out for a while, two or three months in fact. I thought you knew,' she airily remarked, regarding Jess with a studied innocence.

Jess was not fooled. She knew her friend far too well. 'You deliberately didn't tell me who you were involved with. You didn't want me to know, did you? I can't quite take this in. Harry isn't sweet and decent like our Tommy. Harry is... Harry.' Lost for words, and appalled by the idea of her dear friend doing such a reckless, crazy thing she hotly protested, 'You can't possibly agree to marry *Harry*!'

'Why not? I can marry anyone I choose. *I* being the operative word, not my mother. He's explained to me how he's taken over the club on Deansgate, has sown his wild oats in the past but now has a great future before him as a businessman. I do love him, you see. We have had great fun together. He's a bit... well, "wild" perhaps is the word, but he excites me Jess. He believes in living life to the full, even if that involves taking risks, as do I. You know how terribly boring I found Ambrose, and every other man I've ever met. And working at the tea room nearly drove me demented at times. I was always longing for something amazing to happen in my life. Well, now it has! I've never been bored with Harry. He's the man for me.'

'You aren't...? He hasn't put you up the duff, has he?'

'Heavens, no, what do you think I am?' The bright crimson that suddenly stained her cheeks, revealed the lie to this cry of innocence.

'Oh Leah, are you telling me a fib and really are pregnant?'

Leah shook her head. 'No, it's all right. I did think I might be for a while, but it was a false alarm. For heaven's sake, be happy for me. No doubt you and Steve will be doing the same soon, so come down off your high horse and start thinking about what you're going to wear for my wedding. It will take place soon, so you'll have to get your skates on. Oh lord, listen to me, I'm growing hysterical. Come to tea on Sunday, please! I shall tell Daddy before he goes off to his ARP duties after lunch. He might not react too badly, but I feel the need to have you there when I tell my mother.'

'What have you done?'

'I thought, as my friend, you would understand. It will mean that we'll be sisters – or is it cousins-in-law? Related anyway.'

Jess put her arms about Leah and held her tight, her mind a turmoil of emotion. Life seemed to be hitting her with one shock after another. 'You realise you're quite mad, to consider joining the Delaney family.'

'I hope not, but I understood it to be a requirement.'

Chapter Twenty-Five

Jess's presence when Leah announced her wedding plans to her mother did not seem to help in any way, not at all as she'd hoped. Jess felt very much a spare part, an intruder between mother and daughter as, ashen faced and tight-lipped, Muriel made her feelings on the subject very plain. She did not approve of the match and never would, had no intention whatsoever of attending the forthcoming wedding and foresaw nothing but misery and disaster for the happy couple in the years ahead.

Deep down, Jess agreed with her; she had already tried to say as much but Leah hadn't approved of a word she'd said either.

'I would remind you, dear, that you are still underage.'

Leah, glassy eyed with fury, swiftly responded. 'Fine, but don't think you can stop me. Harry and I love each other and if you won't give us permission then I'll simply go and live with him. Cora would have me, wouldn't she?' Leah asked, defiantly turning to Jess.

'I – I'm not certain about that. Little fazes Cora, it's true, but the house is a bit overcrowded, what with her family and us. Mam and I decided to stay with Cora to keep her company, now Uncle Bernie, the cause of their friction, has done a bunk. Though we can only stay so long as the pair of them manage not to do blue murder to each other. They can't resist letting fly at the least provocation. Mam flung her porridge at Cora the other morning, so there's no guarantee they'll get on.'

From out the corner of her eye, Jess caught the look of absolute horror on Muriel's face. Seeing a shudder run through her, she quickly strove to adopt a more positive note. 'However, I did hear Harry saying the other day that you and him could move into the little flat over the club. Bert and his girlfriend, Maisie, have found a place on Quay Street, so it should all work out.' Jess ground to a halt in some confusion, not sure whether such comments made matters better or worse.

'You and Steve will be getting married soon too, won't you?' Leah said, almost as if this would make her own decision seem perfectly reasonable.

'Oh, I'm not convinced of that.'

'Why ever not? I thought you were itching to wed Steve Wyman.'

Jess didn't know what to say, or how to explain her doubts. 'For one thing, he hasn't asked me. For another, I'm far too young to even consider such a thing yet.'

Muriel stoutly agreed and turned to her daughter with a nod. 'There you are, you see. Even dear Jess isn't so stupid as to rush into matrimony. I maintain that you are far too young.'

'How can you say that, when you've been trying to talk me into it for years?'

'But that was with a charming young man, one with the right sort of background from a decent family who could offer you security and happiness, not a *Delaney*. I can only pray that you'll have second thoughts. Please give yourself time to think and don't do anything stupid.'

Leah cast a furious glance at her mother. 'What a big help you've been,' she starkly retorted, then stormed out of the house.

Left alone with Mrs Simmons, Jess for some reason felt obliged to apologise. 'I'm so sorry. Our family isn't all bad. Cora is lovely and her son Tommy is honest and clearly adores Leah. Unfortunately she has shown no interest in him. Bert's harmless enough, being too thick to be otherwise. Harry is very go-ahead, and he certainly has good looks but is not an easy man. What with Uncle Bernie having done a runner and Leah now by his side, Harry might well settle down to become an honest and upright businessman. We can but hope this will be the making of him.'

Having now said the wrong thing and reminded Mrs Simmons that her daughter was about to marry the one Delaney who most resembled his disreputable, bullying father, Jess thought it time to quickly take her leave. As she crept down the stairs she heard Muriel start to weep.

Back home in Cumberland Street while her mother sat up in bed smoking her last fag, Jess paused only briefly in the application of smoothing cold cream over her face when Lizzie drily remarked, 'That chap of yours came round this evening looking for you.'

'What chap?' Though the rapid beat of Jess's heart was telling her that she knew only too well.

'That musician bloke, Steve, or whatever he's called.'

'What did you tell him?'

'That you were out with the God lot.'

Jess bit back the urge to take issue with this comment and simply said, 'Thanks.'

'What'll I tell him if he comes again?'

'Tell him the same. That I'm busy working for the Sally Army.'

'Hey up, love's young dream died the death has it?'

'What's it to you?'

'Nowt, only if you don't want him, happen you wouldn't mind if I had a crack at him meself. He's a good looking lad.'

Jess switched off the light and slid into bed, keeping as far away from her mother as she possibly could, paying no heed to her rasping, dry-throated laugh.

—

Strangely enough, Bernie's sudden and unexpected departure seemed to benefit the entire family, including herself. Jess felt certain that she would never be able to erase the memory of what had taken place that night. Steve hadn't called again, in fact hadn't seen him for some days. He'd sent her a note to say that he was working long hours in an important operation on some hush-hush project, in a place he wasn't allowed to name. 'I'll contact you when I return, but have no idea when that will be.' Against all reason, because of that part of her brain obsessed by the assault, she welcomed his absence with a sense of relief. It would give her the time she needed to think and to recover.

Jess had considered writing him a reply, to say that it was all over between them but that had seemed too cruel and stark. Who knew what danger Steve was now facing, so best to wait till this project, whatever it might be, was over and done with. By which time she should have acquired the necessary strength to confront him with what she'd suffered. She had no idea whether Cora had confided in Harry and Bert about the attack. If she did, they might mention it to their mates at the club after a pint or two. It made Jess a bit jumpy to think of gossip spreading behind her back, as it so easily seemed to do round here.

When two more weeks slid by without the usual appearance of her period, she realised that her troubles had gone worse, as she had feared. Leah had got away with a false alarm but she might not be so fortunate.

Should she ever find the courage to tell Steve what Bernie had done to her, and its result? She couldn't bear to imagine the revulsion in his face. Even if he stuck by her, how would she know that it wasn't simply out of pity. Aware how very much in love they'd been, she'd readily allowed Steve to make love to her, but had felt quite safe with him as he'd surely taken proper precaution? She certainly had no desire to blame him, instinctively assuming this possible baby could not be his. How could she expect him to accept it when it had been forced upon her in such a revolting manner? Best to make a clean break before her situation got any worse. She could but pray that a solution might present itself.

And as Steve was away, she was surely free to organise her own life. She of course had her music. Jess wished she could convince herself this was sufficient, and that she didn't need any love in her life, nor respectability. Both of which she'd craved for all her young life. But even if she was doomed to spend her future as an outcast, she would survive somehow by pouring all her energy into playing with the girls band. Nothing would stop her from doing that. Not even if she was truly having a child. Just making this decision to dismiss Steve chilled her to the bone. And how could she feel any love for a baby foisted upon her in such an evil way?

Jess almost blamed herself for what had happened, oddly fearing she'd made matters worse by provoking her uncle into such a rage that he'd revelled in assaulting her.

She shuddered, slapping the tears of self-pity from her face, telling herself not to mope. If she couldn't rid herself of her uncle's child, Jess knew she must find the courage to face whatever lay ahead. What couldn't be cured must be endured. Isn't that what Cora was fond of stating in life?

'There is no escape,' she told herself sternly. 'I shall simply have to learn to live with reality, dealing with matters one day at a time.'

Despite a genuine sense of unease over Leah's impulsive decision to marry Harry, the worst of the Delaney bunch in Jess's opinion, she nevertheless felt a spurt of envy for her dear friend. Leah, having been cherished and over-protected by her doting parents, had come up smiling as she'd fortunately been spared the shame and dishonour of an illegitimate child. She would soon be celebrating a wedding, free to enjoy life and love without fear.

Jess stared at her own reflection in the spotted mirror on the wall of the bedroom, exclusively hers now that Lizzie had moved into the two boys's old room, and watched tears of despair slide slowly down her pale cheeks. She knew in her heart that there would be no hope of a wedding for herself, any love or blissful contentment. All such possibilities had gone forever. It hurt more than she could describe that, never having enjoyed an easy life, she was at a lower point, with a sharp raw pain in her breast, as her hope for a joyful future lay in ruins at her feet.

Leah looked lovely in a blue velvet gown with pink bud roses and lilies-of-the-valley in her bouquet and on the circlet she wore in her lovely dark hair. Her bright blue eyes shone with happiness, only occasionally clouding over when she remembered the pressure she'd had to apply in order to get permission for this wedding to take place. Neither parent attended and there was no reception afterwards at Simmons's Tea Room. Not even her father was present to give her away, that role being carried out by her brother Robert. Jess was maid of honour in a pretty, strawberries and cream two-piece, while Bert acted as best man to his beaming brother Harry, who looked particularly pleased with himself.

'Your parents will come round eventually,' he kept saying, whenever Leah glanced anxiously and hopefully towards the door. 'Even if it takes a month or two, and anyroad, they'll come round fast enough when their first grandchild appears.'

'Don't be crude, Harry,' Cora scolded him. At least she'd come up trumps by providing them with a substantial tea of potted meat sandwiches, home-made scones with jam, and of course, one of her famous trifles since she still hadn't run short of sugar.

Harry and Bert had made sure there was a plentiful supply of booze for friends and family to enjoy. By the time the groom staggered to the marital bed at four in the morning, he scarcely even noticed that his new wife already occupied it. Leah lay listening to his drunken snores until every tear had been shed and exhaustion finally claimed her.

Jess was thankful for the distraction of her work at the mobile canteen, which was as hectic as ever. Manchester had taken a battering, much of Deansgate near to the Cathedral in ruins. Closer to home, parts of Duke Street and Camp Street were also badly damaged among countless others, including Gatrix's warehouse on Quay Street where her mother had once worked in the days when she'd taken more care of herself. Her mind firmly on the task in hand, Jess put a scraping of marg on another slice of bread and agreed with Ma Pickles, who'd just popped in, that they might be lucky and escape a raid tonight.

'Your uncle, Bernie not yet back from his travels?' she blithely asked, narrowing her deceptively mild gaze as she edged closer to focus upon Jess.

'No doubt he'll turn up again one day, like a bad penny,' Jess tartly responded, not anxious to discuss family business with anyone, let alone the likes of Ma Pickles. 'You'll have to excuse me, since we're a bit busy tonight.'

Despite there being no raids on now, the Salvation Army canteen was packed with people, all apparently in need of assistance. Sergeant Ted was busily occupied taking down details of someone in need of accommodation. He kept a list of anyone prepared to offer temporary bed and board but a permanent arrangement was always more difficult as so many buildings had been damaged and rooms were in short supply. Some families were stretched to breaking point with overcrowding.

Many of their regulars popped in simply because they sought solace from the desperate conditions they were enduring at home, thankful to be free of a night spent in the air raid shelter and while they slurped hot soup or gulped down great mugs of tea, conversation revolved around the war, as always. Everyone agreed that there was a general feeling that a corner had been turned and they were surely now on the home straight.

'We have the planes and the brave chaps to fly them. Bomber Harris has made a big difference,' one man said. 'Not least through a sustained assault on German Industry.'

'Aye, but them lads had the stuffing knocked out of them a few times,' said another, and went on to claim that it was the Russians capturing Stalingrad and pushing the Germans back further, that had finally done the trick.

Italy had apparently sunk into political chaos and largely given up altogether, which made Jess worry about young Tommy. And it was generally agreed that the North Africa campaign had ended in total victory. Finally, since the attacks on Hamburg in July where more people had lost their lives than in the London blitz, everyone believed that the enemy was all but beaten. Yet it hardly seemed appropriate to celebrate, and Jess's heart went out to those German families caught up in this terrible war with the Nazis through no fault of their own, just as folk were here in England.

Was her Dad surviving? Jess had got one postcard with various printed sentences upon it, many crossed out, others with ticks beside them. It told her little more than that he was alive and well taken care of. She didn't believe that for a minute, fearing he was being held as a prisoner.

'Nay, we're getting a bit maudlin. Play us a tune, girl,' one of these old men urged.

Jess readily agreed. Anxious to take her mind off these problems, she played Kenny Baker's 'Always in my Heart', sentimental enough to bring the tears to anyone's eyes, but it was too much for her so she changed to 'We'll Meet Again; the White Cliffs of Dover' and all the usual favourites in order to get everyone singing. But when someone called for 'I'll Be Seeing You' she shook her head and hurried into the kitchen to do the washing up instead.

'Are you all right, Jess?' Sergeant Ted asked, his kind eyes soft and enquiring.

'Yes, I'm fine. Only I'm a bit pushed this week at work, do you mind if I skip my lesson for once? Mam's not been too well.'

'Course love! Whatever you like.'

She smiled, all her heart in the gaze she bestowed upon him. 'It was a lucky day for me when I dropped that bugle. Where would I have been without the Sally Army all these years? You've kept me sane.'

He patted her shoulder, only too aware of her personal difficulties at home. 'Things will buck up for you soon, love. The war won't last for ever and you'll soon be free to make your own way in life.'

Jess turned away to plunge her hands into the hot soapy water, not able to bear his sympathy. 'I'll get this lot done,' she said in her brightest voice, and wisely Ted left her to it so that he wouldn't see her tears fall. He didn't rightly know what was wrong and didn't like to enquire too closely, but something was.

Resolutely dry-eyed, Jess strove to get her emotions back under control. There was too much suffering in this world, people who'd lost loved ones, those who'd been maimed and injured by the bombing, far worse than she had to deal with so where was the point in her self pity? She felt proud to wear the red shield, worn by Salvationists involved in social and emergency services since the early days in the First World War. Soldiers then had been glad to see the 'Doughnut Girls' bringing sustenance and a cheerful smile. Jess knew that many had also been gifted musicians, boosting the morale of the front line troops, singing, praying and leaving wild flowers at the gravesides. The canteens thought of themselves now as a flying squad, ready to move at a moment's notice on the home battle-front.

Sometimes, Jess worked all night long, not getting to bed until the early hours. There'd been times when she'd found this hard going, having to work at the tea room the next day. But in the weeks following her assault, sleep seemed beyond her, therefore a state of exhaustion was a requirement to stop her thinking too much.

Jess had seen little of Leah since her wedding, her not having shown up at a couple of functions that the band had been involved with, which had left them short of a pianist. Not that Jess blamed her for that, being newly married and obsessed with her husband. Leah still worked at the tea room and had been anxious to apologise, swearing that wouldn't happen again. But there had been little time for them to chat recently. It was as if neither of them felt quite in the mood to exchange confidences as easily as they once had. Perhaps now they were growing up they were losing interest in each other. Leah and Harry had moved into a little flat above the pub, or Delaney's Club, as it was now known, where they were settling happily into married life. Her dear friend obviously wished to keep her life private and Jess felt too conscious of her own shameful secret, of which she couldn't bear to think about, let alone speak of it.

Steve was still away on war duty, wherever that was. Somehow, she must find the strength to finish with him once he returned. And goodness knows if she could ever make her life worth living without him. Thank goodness she was involved with the girls band.

On the night in question
through the streets in th...
with their instruments
round a bev...
...r a gr...
not a...

Chapter 1.

Jess's desire to concentrate on he.   in
an unexpected way. To their aston   delight,
Delaney's All Girls Band were asked t   on the wireless. Some producer or other had seen them perform and
he wanted them for a late night show, which featured new
bands.

'It's on a Monday night so nobody will be listening,'
Adele said, puffing frantically on the third cigarette she'd
started since she'd heard the news just moments before.

Jess smiled, knowing that the thought of playing to so
many people had given her an attack of nerves. That's
why she was sometimes late for a rehearsal, although she'd
never yet missed the start of a performance. Her stage
fright was crippling and she would often be found sitting
backstage sucking sherbet dabs. Once out there in front
of an audience she instantly recovered and would play her
heart out, loving every minute of it.

Lulu was very excited. 'This could be a big thing for
us. Lift us on to a whole new level.'

'Too right,' Ena said. 'Today the wireless, tomorrow
the Ritz.'

'Oh, hecky-pecky thump,' Adele groaned, and Miss
Mona silently handed her another sherbet dab.

they fumbled their way blackout, then into the studio ...ts and gas masks at the ready, creeping ...dering array of screens and curtains so that ...immer of light would escape. They didn't speak, ...t even to console the shivering Adele as they were all a little nervous, wishing they were simply doing a gig at a factory or hospital.

But once inside, the atmosphere changed. They entered a brightly lit room full of jolly people all happy to see them and anxious to make them feel relaxed and comfortable. The session went like a dream. They forgot all about being 'on air' and greatly enjoyed the performance. They played their socks off, and afterwards bookings rolled in.

Performing on air gave them a new confidence in themselves and they began to experiment, improvising more freely to develop their own melodic lines and chord changes. Playing the same arrangements over and over for dances can become boring, so it felt good to spice thing up. They worked so hard over the next few weeks that, on one occasion, Jess ended up with a swollen lip and for a time it looked as if she might not be able to go on, but luckily it calmed down sufficiently for her to play. They asked their audience to name their favourites and requests would pour in, then they'd finish with some really hot swing numbers.

'We're a success!' Leah yelled.

We certainly are, Jess thought. If only life could always be this good.

–

Harry considered it to be essential that he try out each of these new girls for himself. Test the merchandise as it were, before selling it to the punters. Not for a moment did it cross his mind that being married required him to be faithful. That wasn't his style, any more than it had been Bernie's. His father had spread his favours wherever it had taken his fancy and no harm had been done by it, not that Harry was aware of. What the little wife didn't know wouldn't hurt her. In any case, a husband was entitled to do as he pleased.

Harry was by no means dissatisfied with his marriage. Leah was a good-looking lass, bonny, and sufficiently voluptuous to stir any man's loins, despite her occasional fussing. He also hoped that she might bring other benefits, such as a bit of brass to the table. Getting a new business going had proved to be far harder than he'd expected. The Yanks were always good spenders and dug deep into their pockets without a care in the world. Our own boys weren't quite so free with their money, as they were less well paid, and more circumspect. A pint or two of good beer came before paying for a tart any time. They preferred to get a bit of 'how's your father' for nothing, if they could.

This latest girl, Honey, as she insisted on being called, although Harry seemed to remember her as Gladys at school, was a bit daft and giggly, but eager enough and willing to learn. He liked them young, around sixteen or seventeen. Honey was twenty-three, only a year or two younger than himself, and therefore a bit long in the tooth for his taste.

However, she was certainly experienced, so that was a bonus.

Once she'd realised that Harry had no time to waste on conversation and the preliminaries, she stroked him in all the right places, bringing him to a pitch of ecstasy that he hadn't experienced since his days as a raw adolescent behind the bike sheds. Blood pounding, and his member throbbing like a mad thing with a life of its own, Harry pushed her roughly back on to the pillows in his room there in the club. He rather thought he'd surprised her with his vigour. There'd been a bored smirk on her face at first, which had swiftly vanished once he got going. She'd soon discovered that he wasn't a man to trifle with, had even cried out at one point when he'd turned her over and done it again. Later, when he let himself into the flat, their little love-nest, as Leah described it, she was waiting for him with a plate of roast pork.

'By heck, that smells good.' He had to hand it to the lass, she could cook as well as the rest of her breed, and she'd done the place up champion. Put up a few pictures, bought a nice new red and beige patterned rug, he noticed. Oh, yes, she knew how to make a man comfortable.

'I've been keeping it warm for you,' she told him, and her smile brought a memory of the fun he'd had with her, making him think of other diversions they could perhaps enjoy before he got down to his dinner.

'I hope that's not all you've been keeping warm, love.' But the delicious aroma of the pork reminded him of a more mundane hunger and, a man of large appetites in every way, he wasted no time in tucking in. There'd be plenty of time later, if he was still in the mood. 'What a good idea of mine to marry a Simmons! You're as good a cook as your dad.'

Leah went pink with pleasure at his praise. 'I've made rhubarb and custard to follow.'

Harry had two helpings. When he'd wiped the last dribble of custard from his chin, he said, 'Speaking of your dad, I were wondering if he'd come round yet, now we've been wed for a while, and were warm for a bob or two.'

'If he's what?' Leah said, giving a little laugh of disbelief. She'd not sat and shared the meal with Harry because there'd been too little meat, and had settled for cheese on toast earlier. Now she began to clear away, happily dreaming of a cosy evening together by the fire. She'd got a smoochy Bing Crosby record on the new gramophone, all ready to play. Harry put out a hand to stop her.

'I mean, is he good for a loan, preferably without interest, naturally. When Dad did a bunk, he left me with a few unpaid bills, nothing serious you understand,' he quickly added, seeing the dismay in her face. 'But it isn't easy to get a business going during wartime, so I wondered if he'd be prepared to cough up a few quid, since we're now family.'

Leah was horrified. She'd known that Harry operated close to the edge, but she'd never for a moment doubted that he was a shrewd businessman, an accomplished wheeler and dealer; or suspected that the club wasn't sound.

'Dad has worries too. Not least getting enough raw materials for the cakes and such like they bake.' She sat down beside him, wanting to help. He was her husband, after all. 'Why don't you ask Jess to hold a dance in the big room? That would make money. The band is very popular now.'

Harry ground his teeth, annoyed that his stupid cousin should be making such a success of her life when his seemed to be falling apart, but he turned this possibility over in his head. Maybe it wasn't such a bad idea, except that he used that room for poker and blackjack. Very popular that was with the Yanks, among others.

The trouble was, he tended to lose the profit as quickly as he made it because he enjoyed a game himself, and he'd had a run of bad luck lately. Nor was it his fault if he'd been forced to borrow money from some shady characters to make ends meet. Everything was so much more expensive than he'd expected. And Harry knew that he didn't want Jess anywhere near his club. 'A dance wouldn't make nowhere near enough brass, not unless she agreed to play for nowt, which I can't see her doing, can you?'

'She might, if we explain how important it is,' but Leah didn't sound too confident, knowing how much Jess disliked Harry, her cousin.

'Best we tap your dad, he's good for a few quid,' Harry stated, swaggering his broad shoulders to remind himself how powerful he was.

'I really don't think so. You know that he and Mother didn't approve of our marriage. They aren't going to take too kindly to being asked to finance your business.'

Harry looked affronted. 'I would have thought they'd be pleased to see their precious little darling well looked after. Her obstinate refusal to squeeze a few quid out of her well-heeled parents irritated him enormously. 'Where's the harm in your dad lending us a few quid? He'd never miss it, a well set-up chap like him. He can afford to do that surely? Like I say, it'd still be in the family.'

'I'm not sure my parents would see it in quite that light. Best we manage on our own, and I have every faith in you Harry.' Leah put her arms about his neck to kiss him on the cheek. Harry shoved her off.

'Well then, if he won't agree to lend us owt, you'll have to borrow it without his permission.'

She frowned. 'I don't understand. How could I do that?'

'By helping yourself to whatever's in that fancy new till he bought, or in that safe he must have tucked away some place. I don't actually care how you do it, or where you find it, but get me some dosh. Right?'

Leah could feel herself start to tremble. An uncomfortable thought was nudging the back of her mind, that this was the real reason he'd married her, in order to get his hands on her father's money. Her family was comfortable but not what anyone could call rich, and surely no one would do such a thing, not in this day and age. It seemed so incredible that Leah gave a little laugh, one that sounded unnatural even to her own ears. 'You surely aren't asking me to steal from my parents?'

'We don't call it stealing, it's just borrowing from the family like. Me and Bert did that all the time. Anyroad, your dad's got that much brass he'll never notice if a bit goes missing.'

'Don't be daft, of course he would.'

'Hey, watch your lip. Why are you calling me daft? Don't you get uppity with me girl. You're my wife now and should do as I say.'

Leah was standing before him, hands on hips, defiance in her blue eyes. 'I'll not steal from my own father, not even for you.'

Before she had time to guess what he was about, let alone take evading action, Harry grasped the back of her neck with his fat, sausage-like fingers and pushed her face down into the remains of his dinner, splattering it all over the new rug she'd bought only the other week.

'When you've cleaned that lot up,' he told her, giving her a little shake to make sure he had her attention, 'You'd do well to count your blessings and remember that you promised to honour and obey. Tomorrow, when you go into work, you'll be dipping your hand into all that lovely loot your pa has stashed away, and sharing it with your beloved husband. Right?'

Without waiting for a reply, he picked up his trilby hat, and strolled out of the door, closing it softly behind him, to show there were no ill feelings.

–

At their next performance, the band was playing at the Empress ballroom in Pendelton. When they'd first started attending dances, there'd been 'No Jiving' notices up everywhere. Now, its popularity was such that jivers simply couldn't be ignored. They needed space and Jess always made a point of playing music especially for them, often a Glenn Miller number such as 'Chattanooga Choo Choo', when they could have the floor entirely to themselves. During the more regular dances, they were expected to keep to one corner. But Jess not only provided jivers with the space and the music they wanted, she also offered prizes for the best couple.

What's more, she did the same for the foxtrot, and all the other dances, which were favourites with the clientele. It was one of the reasons the girls band was so popular, because they were careful to please everybody and managed to create a party atmosphere.

They were booked for a guest spot at the Palais in Bury, invited by their regular musicians, and at the Broadway in Eccles. They also had bookings in Ashton, Levenshulme, the Alhambra Palais and the Savoy Ballroom in Oldham. Dyson's on Devonshire Street was a regular spot for them, usually held on a Tuesday and where the tango was a particular favourite. They were doing well, going up in the world.

Yet despite the band's huge success, Jess wasn't sure if she had the strength to go on. It took every ounce of will power to get herself out of bed each morning, relieved to know that Steve was still away. If and when she found the courage to tell him of her situation was too dreadful to contemplate. Her face felt stiff and unnatural as she attempted to smile at the customers throughout the long day, chatting to them about the weather and the current state of the war, desperate to appear as if everything was perfectly normal. In reality she felt bleak, unable to think of a resolution.

Leah, having watched her with obvious concern, fetched a coffee for them both. 'Can we have a little chat about the state of your depression?'

Jess shook her head. 'We'll maybe talk later.' And she walked away to avoid further questions.

Later, they took a rest break during the interval while a small jazz quartet kept the customers amused. Leah didn't ask her another question, simply sat patiently waiting to hear the reason for her evident gloom. Cora had attempted to offer appropriate consolation with her homespun wisdom and advice. However, Jess couldn't reveal the catastrophic result of that incident to her mother, Lizzie not being interested in anything beyond herself, unless it came out of a bottle. But Jess did feel an urgent need to tell her best friend what she'd suffered. Leah was as close as a sister to her, now that she was one of the family.

To her credit, Leah didn't interrupt as Jess spilled out the sordid tale of being assaulted. When she finally fell silent, still with much left unsaid, lacking the will to reveal full details, Leah put her arms around her and held her close. Her blue eyes were gleaming with anger and tears over the treatment meted out by her uncle. 'No wonder you've been under the weather lately, love. Cry if you wish.'

'I've done that night after night, doubt if I've any tears left.'

'There was me fretting about not getting my parents's approval, but at least I am safely married, if not in their eyes to a suitable man. He can be a bit difficult, but you've had much worse to deal with,' she said, a frown clouding her face. Leah was thinking that although she couldn't pretend things were perfect between herself and Harry, or quite as she'd hoped and expected, it was surely nothing that couldn't be put right, given a little time and love. Jess's problem was the worst imaginable. Rape, by her own uncle! Dear God, what could be worse than that? 'You should have told me this the moment it happened, then I would have stopped complaining about my parent's foolish objections and listened to your problems with great sympathy.'

'I couldn't talk about it then, not even to you.'

'I'm so glad you've told me all this now.' Leah's blue eyes were gentle, then she gathered Jess's two hands firmly between her own. 'So that's why Harry's father, your dreadful Uncle Bernie, was notable by his absence from my wedding? What did Steve say? I should think he'll deeply regret the opportunity to knock his block off.'

Jess cleared her throat. 'Steve is away at the moment, so I haven't told him. Nor do I ever intend to. Whenever I see him again, I'll simply inform him that it's all over between us. We're finished.'

Leah gaped at her in stunned disbelief. 'For heaven's sake, why? You *must* tell him. You can't just walk away without an explanation. That's too cruel. He adores you.'

The pain in Jess's breast was like a giant fist clenching her heart. 'Don't – please. I can't bear it.'

Adele popped her head round the door. 'Two minutes.'

'Right. We're on our way.' Jess at once got to her feet and Leah had to hurry to keep up with her, as she left the dressing room and made her way back to the ballroom.

'You can't just wipe Steve out of your life, as if he's of no account. That is a decision with awesome repercussions. I know you love him, and he loves you. So if you toss him away without telling him what you've suffered, you'll lose him for good. Is that what you want?'

Jess had climbed back on stage and was polishing her trumpet, riffling through sheet music preparatory to starting the second half of the dance. She really had no wish to be lectured about this decision she'd made. Besides, Leah only knew half the story, having made no mention of her 'delicate condition', nor had she any intention of doing so. Not just yet. 'I don't think it matters what I want. I only know that I'm no longer fit to be with him. I couldn't – can't bear to think of being touched by any man ever again.' Tears spilling from her eyes began to roll down her cheeks and she slapped them ruthlessly away. 'Right, girls, we'll start with "Run, Rabbit, Run", through the usual numbers to "Don't Sit Under the Apple Tree".'

Leah's face was gripped with sympathy and an edge of desperation, as she put out a hand to make Jess pause before counting them in. Speaking in a breathless whisper, anxious to make her point, she said, 'I cannot begin to imagine what you're going through, but Steve isn't just any man. I believe he would help you to get over that terrible assault. It's natural for you right now to want to shut him out, but that feeling will pass given time, and you're badly in need of his loving support.'

Jess shook her head. 'I couldn't ask that of him, or anyone. Nor could I let him take the risk when I would be frigid and not a proper wife for him. 'OK, girls, one, two, three...'

Chapter Twenty-Seven

One evening, Jess had her hands deep in a bowl of flour making Yorkshire puddings in the kitchen of the mobile canteen, when she glanced up and was shocked to find Steve leaning on the door jamb, grinning at her.

'I was beginning to think you were avoiding me, now that you're famous. You were never around when I called, and didn't answer my letter.'

Jess covered her lack of composure with as careless a tone as she could manage as she gazed with stunned disbelief at Steve. 'I've just been busy. Anyway, I knew you were working on some special project or other.'

'Is that all you have to say? Not, "Hello Steve. Good to see you, and I've been longing for you day after day"?' He came towards her and Jess quickly went to fetch baking powder to add to the National flour she'd just sieved into a bowl. He frowned slightly. 'I wasn't deliberately neglecting you. It's true that I've been engaged in a big job, as I explained in my note. You did get it, didn't you?'

'Yes, I remember that.'

'I've missed you so much, Jess. I hoped you had missed me. Anyway, I came to say that as from tomorrow I'm all yours, for the next week at least, until I have to go off again. So you can fill me in on all your exciting news and success.'

He looked a little untidy in an ill-matched suit and tie but to Jess he had never looked more handsome, and his smile was so enticing. His hazel eyes twinkled merrily at her, a trilby hat perched beguilingly at the back of his head, and a thatch of unruly red-brown hair falling disarmingly over his forehead. Jess felt an almost unbearable urge to run her fingers through it, smother his beloved face with kisses and tell him how much she loved him. She drew in a deep, calming breath.

'How have I had time to miss you? When I'm not at the tea room, I'm here. When I'm not in either of those places, I'm playing in the band somewhere or other. I've been run off my feet, if you want to know.'

He was about to slide his arms about her waist but Jess sidestepped away, neatly evading his touch as she dashed over to the cupboard to fetch a packet of dried eggs. She simply couldn't have borne it if he'd touched her.

'That much is obvious,' he said, dusting flour from the tip of her nose. 'I must say that it suits you.'

'I did intend to write to you,' Jess said, then wished she could bite back the words, unspoken.

'A billetdoux you mean? Oh yes, please do, I'd really love to get one of those from you, my darling. Why didn't you? There's no need to be shy.' He caught hold of her, pulling her close and nuzzling his mouth against her throat. Forgetting her better judgement, Jess melted against him, growing light-headed with her need to let him kiss her. Yet desperate that sudden desire would yield to her emotion, she pushed him away and turned her agonised gaze away from the hurt that sprang into his eyes.

'What is it, Jess? What's happened? Has someone upset you?'

'No, course not. Like I say, I'm just busy working. Besides, it wouldn't have been an appropriate sort of letter. I needed to tell you, to explain what I feel...' Oh, sweet Jesus, this was far more difficult than she'd ever imagined, even in her worst nightmares. Again she took a deep breath. The only way was simply to come right out with it. 'I think we have to stop seeing each other. It's over.'

The silence following this breathless statement was deep and profound. Jess filled it by adding reconstituted milk to the pudding mix, far too much, then started to beat it hard.

Steve put out a hand to gently stop her. 'Would you mind repeating that, very slowly please?'

Still she didn't look at him. 'As I implied, it's time for us to end our relationship.'

'Why?'

'It doesn't feel right.'

'Pardon?'

'I'm not ready for—'

'Ready for what? Marriage? I don't recall us getting round to discussing such matters, or my asking you. Though I did intend to, sweetheart. Dear lord, you must know that. I thought – believed – we had something strong growing between us. What in hell's name has happened to make you so cold towards me all of a sudden? It's not your girls band, is it? You haven't gone all grand on me?'

'Of course not, don't be silly.'

'Then what is it for God's sake?' When she didn't answer, he gulped in anguish. 'Please talk to me, for pity's sake, Jess.'

'I can't right now. See how busy I am. I'm just explaining that it's over between us. There's nothing more to be said.' And, her hand slightly shaking, she began to pour Yorkshire pudding mixture into sizzling hot pans.

Seeing his face looking pinched and white, and acutely aware of his eyes following her every movement in pained disbelief, Jess turned away, not daring to glance at him. A second or two later she heard him turn on his heel and walk out the door, saying not another word. She felt devastated, as if he'd taken her heart with him.

–

Leah had been edgy all day and now, as her father cashed up and prepared to close the shop for the day, she felt as if she might pass out at any moment, her nerves in such a sorry state. Would he notice that the amount of cash in the till didn't match the written total? Her father glanced up and caught her watching him and she felt her cheeks turn crimson beneath his probing gaze, quite sure he could see the scar of guilt on her soul. What on earth had possessed her to get involved in all of this? Even as she asked herself the question, Leah knew why. Harry's attack was the last thing she'd expected to happen. Now she was afraid he might do something worse were she not to obey his order. She no longer felt in control of her life. Dare she tell Harry that this would be the last time she'd take money from her father, and expect him to apologise for what he demanded?

Her father smiled at her. 'Off home now are you, love? Got something tasty for your man's supper?'

'Yes, I thought I'd make liver and onions tonight.' She could but hope she wouldn't be knocked into it this time.

'With lots of mashed potato to soak up the gravy? Sounds delicious.' Clifford Simmons grinned, considered his daughter thoughtfully for a moment then came over to rest his hands on her shoulders. 'I'm sorry things turned out as they did. Your mother was not keen but...'

'I know it's all right, Dad. I understand.'

'You are happy, aren't you?'

'Of course, never more so.'

'Because if you aren't, if it was all a bad mistake, a bit of rebellion that's gone wrong, you've only to say that and I'd turn heaven and earth round for you, love. You do know that.'

'Thanks, Dad! Don't worry, everything's fine.'

No, it isn't, screamed the voice in her head. But she couldn't tell him that her parents may have been right and she was wrong. But she'd only been married for less than a month and every marriage had its teething problems and could go through sticky patches.

Cliff put his arms about his daughter and gave her a hug. 'Good! I know you want your mother to approve of your choice, and I'm sure Harry Delaney is a grand lad, at heart. Give her time, she'll come round.' He turned back to the till, scooped out a handful of notes, not troubling to count them as he shoved them into his pocket, although later in the evening, when he did the accounts for the day, would he then notice that there were two pound notes missing?

'Drop the sneck on your way out, love. See you tomorrow.' Popping a kiss on her brow, he made his way wearily upstairs, tired after a long day's work and leaving Leah to switch off the lights and let herself out.

Watching him leave, she convinced herself that she would eventually be able to make Harry see the error of his ways. No doubt these were caused by the damage his father had evidently put upon him over the years, as well as the lack of interest from her own parents.

–

Jess was pleased that over the coming weeks they performed well, and she also worked hard at her other jobs too. One evening, she was serving in the mobile canteen when a man walked in, unlike many who visited in that he was not at all halfcut with booze. He was surprisingly quiet, well mannered, and said thank you when she handed him a cup of tea and slice of cake. Thinking he looked familiar, Jess asked if he'd been in before and he freely admitted that he had. 'I'm Doug Morgan, a docker who comes in the canteen now and then. I'm on maintenance work and whenever I get a bit of free time, I often come to listen to you play. I hope you don't mind.'

'Not at all, why should I? Pleased to meet you,' she said, giving him a polite smile before dashing back to the kitchen.

His smile of response was a bit slow in coming, adding an air of seriousness to the oval face with its long, pointed chin. But then he was quite a bit older than herself, no doubt in his early thirties, tall with brown hair slicked down with Brylcreem, long straight nose and eyebrows and pale blue eyes that had a faint look of anguish in them. He came again the next evening, speaking to no one as he silently watched her perform, then said, 'You look a bit tired tonight. Couldn't you sit down for a minute and take a rest?'

'Having finished playing, I'm supposed to get back to work.'

'Aren't you allowed to talk to the customers?'

'Oh yes, but there's a lot to be done so I can't devote too much attention to any one person.'

'I couldn't be that lucky. I've found you're very popular, especially with the men.'

Jess laughed. 'They do like my playing.'

'So do I. You're good at that skill. You also look lovely with that long blonde hair and sweet face. A natural beauty like yours can't be hidden, it shines forth like a beacon of pure light.'

Jess was astounded. She'd never thought of herself as anything other than ordinary and was embarrassed to be complimented in such a manner by a perfect stranger. It left her at a loss for words, unable to think of a sensible thing to say. Though if it had been Steve who'd said such lovely things to her...

'Are you on your own?' she asked, quickly pushing the man she loved out of her head. Oh dear, now this one would think she was being forward and making a play for him. She started to move away but his next words, coming out all in a bluster, gave her pause.

'Sadly yes, my wife and young son died about eighteen months ago and I don't have any family left.'

'Oh, how terrible. I'm so sorry.' Jess assumed they'd been hit by a bomb but didn't like to ask. Who knew what fate had befallen the poor woman and her child? She wondered how he was coping, but it wasn't appropriate to pry too closely into emotions in these difficult times. Yet she couldn't simply walk away from him, not after such a confession. She shyly cleared her throat. 'So, how are you?'

'I miss her. Life isn't much fun any more.'

'Of course! How old was your son?'

'Only eight, and I miss him even more, as we were particularly close. I'm such an ugly old brute I'm not likely to get the chance of another child.'

He gave such a sad smile, Jess felt filled with pity for him. Poor man, to be widowed and lose his only child. Sergeant Ted had impressed upon her how they should always find time to speak to victims, at least for a little while. This evening, she brought them each a cup of what passed for coffee, being the bottled Camp variety, and sat beside him, hoping that a bit of company might cheer him up. He seemed keen to talk about his wife, how she and their son went out one day to buy bread and simply never came home. People all too frequently vanished off the face of the earth during a war. It amazed her that, despite his terrible loss, he could still show an interest in others, herself in particular, gently asking questions. Jess would much rather have shared her troubles with Steve but told herself firmly that he'd been nothing more than a fantasy, and it was easy to talk to a stranger.

She told him a little about her own life, speaking of how desperately she missed her father, not knowing where he was or if he'd survived. She even bitterly related how her mother wasn't capable of looking after her properly because she went out drinking every night, and used to leave her locked in a cellar when the bombs were dropping. But Jess carefully made no mention of Lizzie having once been arrested and imprisoned for shoplifting, and

288

no detail of her other personal problems. Some matters were best kept private. Jess quickly moved on to say how she loved playing the trumpet, to talk of the friends she'd made in the Sally Army and Delaney's All Girls Band and how spending time with them had saved her sanity in this war.

As he was about to leave, the docker asked if he could see her again and Jess experienced a flush of panic. Perhaps she'd been too encouraging, giving the impression that she was available. She shook her head feeling embarrassed, and said how busy she was working at the bakery, as well as here in the mobile canteen.

'Don't you ever get any time off?'

'Of course, but I have friends, as I said, who keep me pretty busy.'

'And no doubt you've got a boyfriend?' he asked, gazing at her with interest.

She had no wish to lead him up the garden path, even if her soft heart was in danger of being won over, which would never do at all, and gave a self-deprecating shrug. 'Sort of.' No need to admit that was all over for an unspeakable reason.

'Ah, so nothing serious! Well, I could take you to the pictures tomorrow, or Saturday. You've made me feel so much better about myself, Jess. I'd really like to get to know you better.'

Oh dear, now she'd lumbered herself with a dilemma. She felt anxious to get the message across that she was not available. 'I'll be too busy working,' she firmly remarked. But as she cleared away the mugs, he kept hanging around as she washed up. Jess could see Harriet glancing curiously in their direction, wondering why one of the customers was in the kitchen area with a tea towel in his hands. Aware that she should insist he leave, Jess took the towel from him and folded it away. 'It's been good chatting with you, but good night. I'll be happy to see you again sometime, whenever you pop in.'

Appearing slightly crestfallen, he said, 'I look forward to that.' And with a polite goodnight, he walked quietly away.

–

'Only two pounds?' Harry had yelled at her that first night Leah handed over what she'd stolen from here father. 'You should do better than this, as I instructed you.'

She'd tried desperately to convince Harry how wrong it was to steal, speaking tenderly and doing her utmost not to upset him. 'I'm not prepared ever to do this again.'

'Oh yes, you bloody will.'

When she'd firmly shook her head, Harry had flung a backhander at her in the form of a clenched fist and knocked her flying. As Leah hit the floor, he'd tipped up the table and sent the remains of his dinner, and all the newly purchased crockery bought as wedding presents by the few friends who had come to their wedding, crashing and smashing around her. Even then he wasn't done with her. He looked as if he was beginning to quite enjoy himself, feeling the power in his own hands that had once resided in his father's. Reaching down, he casually took hold of her arm and dragged her to her feet, then tossed her against the wall where she bounced like a cork before falling to her knees with a whimper.

It came to her then that all Jess had told her about Bernie Delaney must have been true, and his son was every bit as bad. If only she'd listened to Jess's sound advice and believed her, before she'd excitedly agreed to marry this man.

In the days following Leah kept hoping that because of his love for her, Harry would eventually relax and treat her better. Sadly he made no effort to do that. There was a madness in him, a sickness almost, and a part of him that she couldn't reach. She no longer felt herself to be the carefree, adventure loving girl she'd once been. Instead, she felt tired and depressed, jumpy and nervous. Leah weighed every word before she uttered it, was careful not to anger him with a joke when he wasn't in the mood for laughing, or any comment he might construe as criticism. And always made sure that she looked attractive when he came upstairs to the flat, expecting his tea to be ready on the dot of six.

Today, the minute she arrived home from work, Leah dashed around tidying the place up, straightening cushions, wiping every speck of dust away. Harry was oddly fastidious, considering his background and how untidy Cora was. She wanted everything to be lovely, for him, so he would smile and appreciate her efforts to please him. So he would be happy and kind to her.

'Do you like my new dress?' she asked, when he walked through the door an hour later. Leah knew she looked good, with her hair all freshlywashed and shining. She'd even bought a new pink lipstick on Campfield market. Harry himself had provided her with the silk stockings.

He had a glass in his hand, which he didn't set down, even when she put her arms about his neck to give him a kiss. 'Did you get it?' he asked.

'Did I get what?' She drew away, knowing exactly what he was referring to. Leah kept hoping that one of these days he might forget to ask, or think better of this dreadful scheme and agree that she didn't have to steal any more money. So far, she must have taken well over fifty pounds from her father's shop, little by little, and he hadn't even noticed. At least, not a word had been said.

Every day when she arrived at the tea room, she half expected him to angrily confront her with the knowledge of her betrayal, almost wished that he would, so that she could tell Harry the game was up, and then this terrible nightmare would be over at last.

Harry was watching her with eyes as hard as flint, furious that she continued to defy him. There were more days when she brought nothing home, rather than those when she did. At the same time he was savouring the scent of her soft, fair hair, noticing how her breast rose and fell in breathless little gasps. He was keenly aware of the sway of her hips against his crotch when she kissed him. Pulling her roughly towards him, he lifted her skirt and slid his fingers down inside her stocking top, stroking her leg, enjoying how her eyelids fluttered closed as his circling progress homed closer to their target.

'I can make you do owt I want.'

'Oh yes, Harry, you can.' It was always best to agree with him. However much she might loathe herself for it afterwards, it was the safest way.

'And you like that, don't you? Go on, say that you like me to give the orders. Go on, say it!'

'I like you giving me orders, Harry.' A voice inside her head shouted that this wasn't at all true. She hated being used by him. Almost hated him! But he was pushing her down on to the rug, ripping her new dress in his eagerness to remove it, and Leah was deeply afraid he'd beat her again if she resisted him.

Later, when he'd enjoyed her to the full and she'd handed over four crisp white five pound notes, as instructed, Harry decided that all things considered, he was really very pleased with their marriage. Not only did he now have full control of a delightful, obedient little wife, but surely had a hold over his cousin, which he would put into effect any time that he chose.

Chapter Twenty-Eight

One afternoon, the canteen was down by the Brunswick Basin giving the dockers a bit of cheerful sustenance. Approached by Harriet when Jess was on her usual sandwich duties in the kitchen for lunch, she was told her there was someone who wished to see her. Her heart leapt, beating painfully against her breastbone before plunging with dread. But it wasn't Steve, as she'd secretly hoped, despite her sense of loss for him, it was Doug Morgan who stood at the door, cap in hand, shuffling from one booted foot to the other and looking as shy and sheepish as ever.

'Hello Jess, it's me, delighted to see you again.'

She smiled kindly at him. 'Good to see you too.'

'I wondered if you've had a change of heart about that date I once mentioned. If so, I wouldn't mind taking you wherever you wish to go, perhaps a little walk this afternoon, if you are free, and maybe later to the orchestral concert.'

Jess glanced at him filled with a rush of pity. She didn't imagine that he had many friends, being such a quiet and shy man, but he had shown some concern for her, even if she hadn't welcomed his attention. Recalling her sense of depression, she thought she could do with a bit of cheering up and happily agreed that would be lovely.

'It was half day closing at the tea room today and I just popped in here to help with lunch, so why not? I have no other plans.'

Beaming from ear to ear Doug eagerly smiled, offering to wait for her outside until she was ready to go.

Jess became uncomfortably aware of Harriet and Ted's combined gaze, both watching her and listening in to the conversation with open curiosity, clearly wondering why she had accepted this offer and what had gone wrong between her and Steve. Jess made no effort to explain, telling herself that since there was nothing of a romantic nature between herself and Doug Morgan, it was surely perfectly agreeable for her to go out with him.

She enjoyed a short walk with him that afternoon by the River Irwell, but the orchestral concert Doug had promised to take her too that evening, did not start off well. He'd failed to acquire tickets for the Hallé and took her instead to a comic operetta put on by a local amateur group. It wasn't at all to Jess's taste, but she steadfastly sat through an hour and a half of the dullest music imaginable delivered by buxom middle-aged ladies who really shouldn't be attempting to reach those high notes. Just before the interval Jess began to feel slightly queasy and slipped out to the powder room for a cool glass of water. By the time she returned, Doug had bought her a brandy, certain that she was in need of one and looked quite put out when she refused.

'No, I mustn't. I don't drink spirits, thanks all the same.'

'You still look very much below par to me,' he told her. Perhaps you shouldn't have come. Is it something you've eaten, do you reckon?'

'I expect so.'

'Women are so delicate. You really should take better care of yourself.'

'I'm not in the least bit delicate,' she protested, stoutly ignoring the small, chiding voice at the back of her head. 'Anyone can feel a little indisposed, men as well as women. In fact, they often pander to illness far more than a woman does.'

'Oh no, men are bound to be stronger, since they have to earn an honest crust by the sweat of their brow in order to keep their families. It's easier for men to work as they do it so much better. They're more savvy, and once the war is over, women will be able to relax and return to the hearth, where they belong.' He smiled at her as if he had just offered her the key to paradise.

'I really don't see it that way. There's no reason on earth why women shouldn't do exactly the same thing, as they are working hard in this war.' In Jess's opinion Doug had made a bad mistake.

Clearly startled by the firm expression in her brown eyes, he could obviously think of no way to backtrack. Consequently, he dug himself deeper into the pit that yawned before him. 'Men know what's what, do you see? Been out in the world longer, protecting their women-folk. They have the better education, generally speaking, and more intelligence, so they're the ones who must make all the decisions.'

Hadn't she heard very much the same sort of piffle from Harry and Bert. It really wasn't important, yet she couldn't bring herself to let this go unchallenged. 'It's the role of women to go along with the need for their help in today's world, and do it well. I do not agree that men are more intelligent than women.'

He looked as if he was struggling to maintain a degree of politeness to these inflammatory remarks. 'Don't let's quarrel. I didn't mean to upset you, sweetheart. I only wish to please and protect you. Actually, the second act is about to begin and I never meant to spoil the evening for you. Will you forgive me?'

She took a moment to answer. 'Of course, it was simply a difference of opinion. Only please don't call me sweetheart, I don't care for it. All right?'

'Sorry, whatever you say, sweetheart – er, dear lady.'

–

Leah watched, appalled, as her father rolled up the notes and thrust them into his pocket, his face so set with anger it made her shake. 'No, Leah, it's no good. I've paid her what wages she's owed, though she doesn't deserve them, and she's been given her marching orders. There's an end to the matter.'

'But how can you be sure that she's guilty?'

He slammed the till drawer shut, causing it to give a loud, startled ring. 'I never had any problems with money going missing until that girl started working for us. I've told her that I won't employ anyone dishonest, any little madam who thinks she can help herself by dipping her greedy, grubby little fingers into my till.'

Leah knew that the new girl – little more than fifteen and, at this precise moment, running off down Deansgate in floods of tears having been sacked on the spot, dismissed without a reference – was entirely innocent.

In her desperation, Leah went to see Cora for advice, explaining at length about the sorry state of the club, and pouring out all her troubles. 'I know Harry says money's tight and that there are debts, but why ask me to steal from my father in order to provide him with more money?' Surely there must be some other way. He's let out all the rooms, save for a couple he uses for drunken customers who are incapable of getting home. But he says that's not enough. I suggested he ask Jess to hold a dance there to make money, but he won't hear of it.'

Cora scratched her head in puzzlement, the grey strands of wiry hair tightly bound in their usual curling pins, as if in preparation for some future event which never seemed to arrive. Yet she was taking greater pride in herself these days, since her suppers had proved to be such a feature at Jess's dances. Although that didn't quite extend to personal hygiene as there still emanated from her the sour smell of sweat, or, as Cora herself dubbed it, honest toil. 'Our Harry doesn't see things in that light. Your pa has plenty of wealth and he's family, so why shouldn't it be shared round a bit? Anyroad, he's a lost cause is our Harry. I can do nowt. I wouldn't know what to suggest.'

Leah gazed at her, horrified, not quite able to take in that Harry's own mother was apparently going to sit back and do nothing to help. 'Why didn't anyone tell me all this before?'

'Would you have listened? Folk generally don't, once they've made up their minds to do something. I certainly didn't, even though I were warned about Bernie by everyone who knew him. Didn't our Jess say owt?'

'She said Harry was the worst of the lot.'

Cora cackled with laughter, which Leah thought astonishing, considering it was her own son they were talking about. 'Aye, that about sums him up. You'll have to get canny, as we've all learned to do. Pretend you're doing as he says, but actually please yourself. That were generally the answer with our Bernie.'

'And where is he then, your Bernie? I've seen no sign of him for ages,' Leah asked, sighing with exasperation as she realised she was getting absolutely nowhere. Cora didn't seem to appreciate that Harry was a difficult man to refuse, partly because she was coming to fear his temper, and also, to her shame, because she loved him and still hoped that she could change his nasty ways. She hated having to come and beg for help, hated the sour smells in this house, the pile of dirty dishes in the sink. How could Jess tolerate living here? And in the front room, comatose on the horse-hair sofa, was Lizzie, her drunken sot of a mother. What a household!

'The longer he stays away the better,' Cora said, then levering herself out of her chair grabbed the kettle and offered Leah another cuppa, though they'd had two already.

'No thanks, I'd best be on my way. Harry doesn't like me to be late home. You won't say anything about our little chat, will you? Promise?'

'Course I won't, dear. If there's one thing I've learned living in this family all these years, it's to hold me tongue. Mebbe you should too.'

Leah didn't agree and firmly informed Harry when he came in later for his supper, that an innocent young girl had lost her job. 'This can't go on. It must stop now! I'll not steal for you again. *Ever!*'

Harry's jaw tightened with fury, a white line of anger forming about his compressed mouth. 'You'll do as you're told, being my wife. *I'm* in charge, not you.'

'No, you damn well aren't,' she screamed. 'I've told you, I love my dad. God knows why I stole from him in the first place, but now it's over. Got that?' For a brief instant she felt good. Jubilant! Triumphant even. Perhaps if she'd stood up to him before now, things wouldn't have got so bad.

And then he hit her again.

Leah attempted to fend off his blows, getting to her feet every time he knocked her down, determined to defy him. Finally she was forced to remain curled in a tight, protective ball while he gave her a thorough pounding with his big heavy boots. In future, would she have to do exactly as he instructed, steal whatever he told her to, having had all courage knocked out of her.

–

The following Saturday, Doug took Jess to Belle Vue, there being a band concert on and aware how much she enjoyed music. Jess didn't care where they went but was simply thankful that it wasn't a dance. She couldn't imagine being held in anyone's arms but Steve's. Doug wouldn't hear of Jess paying for herself, nor would he tell her how much it cost. 'Women aren't allowed to pay, not by my book. Men should protect women and look after them.' he told her. 'I hope this is the kind of event you approve of.'

'I love listening to music.'

She had plenty of opportunity to tap her feet that afternoon as she listened, enthralled, to ten brass bands and any number of choirs filling the sunny day with the richness of their voices. There were crowds of people watching, marching to the music, clapping and cheering and singing along with them whenever they knew the words. Jess began to feel better, the music soothing her as it always tended to do.

'Didn't you just love that band who played Fascinating Rhythm', and what was that last piece of music played by Rochdale Town Band? It was so marvellous I must tell Ted about it.'

'Who's Ted? Is he your boyfriend?'

Jess giggled. 'No, he's Sergeant Buxton at the mobile canteen. He's given me lessons on the trumpet, for which I'm endlessly grateful.'

They had tea in the Japanese Tea Room and Jess politely thanked Doug for giving her such a wonderful afternoon. 'To think I could have been sitting at home listening to Aunt Cora grumbling about her sciatica, and my mother, Lizzie, no doubt in one of her drunken moods. How blissful to enjoy a whole afternoon away from the Delaney crew. But I mustn't be too late home,' she said, not wanting to run the risk of him thinking this date was anything special.

'Why? Will your mother object and not allow me to take you out again?'

'She doesn't care what I do,' Jess snapped, then felt a beat of guilt over this inappropriate remark. She really must take care, as she had no wish to become involved with this man.

He was regarding her with seriousness. 'You don't sound as if you much care for your family?'

'You could say that,' Jess admitted with a short laugh. 'But that's not strictly true. Cora is a dear friend and her twins a delight. As for the rest, well, let's say there's ample room for improvement, particularly where my uncle is concerned. The longer he stays away, wherever he is, the better.' She then recklessly admitted Bernie's attempt to utilise her charms to attract customers to the club. 'I surely don't look a likely candidate for giving servicemen a good time, isn't that the parlance?'

The expression on Doug's face was one of utter shock. 'My dear girl, you must take care to protect yourself.'

'Don't worry, I've no intention of doing anything so stupid.'

'Do make sure that when he comes back home you keep well away from his evil influence and live somewhere safe.' His homely face brightened, making the thin planes of his cheeks grow pink and his pale, serious eyes appeared almost animated. 'You could stay at my house if you like. I've plenty of room.'

Deeply embarrassed, Jess felt a nudge of alarm. She'd told him too much, all because of his sympathetic manner. Any minute now, she'd be spilling the beans about her possible pregnancy. As ever, she shut that problem out of her mind. 'Enough of this morbid talk, I need a bit of fun. Who doesn't, these days? Let's find a mad game to enjoy.'

'We certainly will.'

They queued for a ride on the Caterpillar, and Jess was startled when the canvas cover came over, plunging them into an eerie green darkness. Out of nowhere he seemed to loom over her. It was then that he stole a kiss, pressing his mouth against hers. Jess felt a tremor of shock and panic reverberate within her, as it had done when her uncle had attacked her, but was compelled to hold her breath before he released her. She was left with a prickling sensation around her mouth, due to the roughness on his chin. Battling with herself not to slap this man, she politely

302

pulled herself free to desperately evade capture. Doug put his arm round her and tried to kiss her again. Pushing him politely away she evaded capture, but they bumped noses and she was the one to apologise.

'Sorry, I'm not very keen on this sort of closeness.'

'Sweet eighteen and never been kissed?'

'Hardly,' she caustically remarked.

His thin face darkened, looking serious. 'Is that because you do indeed have a boyfriend and prefer him to kiss you? Are you still seeing him?'

'No, our relationship is over.' Having fallen in love with Steve and now lost him forever, she could but think how cruel life was for her, wishing she'd not spoken a word about this.

'Ah, I'm glad to hear that. I'm thirty-one, does that bother you?'

'Why should that matter? It's not important. I mean, if you don't mind me being young, why should I object to you being old.' Oh dear!

He gave a hollow sort of laugh and she was mortified by her clumsy impoliteness. She'd meant to insist that there was nothing between them, so why should their age difference be an issue, but somehow it had come out all wrong. Had she offended him? 'I'm so sorry, I simply meant it doesn't matter as we're just friends, not a couple...'

'It's of no consequence,' he said and quietly removed his arm, much to her relief.

–

Jess saw Doug quite often after that and he proved to be a pleasant companion, a kind man doing his utmost to please her. She should be grateful as he'd quite taken her mind off her anguish. At least she assured herself that he had. It seemed an age since she'd seen Steve on that last occasion when she'd told him they should split up, though it was probably only a few weeks.

'You're very good to me. I'm sorry if I'm not quite myself at the moment,' she said one evening as they turned from Bridge Street down Dolefield towards Cumberland Street. They'd been to the Odeon to see Gene Kelly in *For Me and My Gal* and Jess had simply loved the music. She couldn't wait to try out 'After You've Gone' on her trumpet, though she thought 'Oh, You Beautiful Doll' mightn't be so easy to play. She'd even allowed Doug to hold her hand for a short while in an effort to take her mind off Steve. A ploy that hadn't been the success she'd hoped for, as she'd sat there wishing her life wasn't in this dreadful mess.

Time was passing, and she still hadn't resolved her problem.

When she'd first found out about this baby she was carrying, Jess hadn't been able to accept the reality. Now she often felt sick and, try as she might, couldn't seem to get the worry out of her mind as fear struck to the heart of her. What on earth was she going to do? Never in her wildest imaginings had she any wish to be the mother of an illegitimate child. That finger of scorn had always followed Lizzie. Jess had never meant to suffer in the same way, let alone be in a worse situation. She might scold herself for not making practical arrangements, or finding a solution, whatever that might be. She loathed the prospect of giving birth to this child of her uncle. How could she possibly feel happy about that when it had been foisted upon her in such a dreadful way.

Nor was she truly interested in Doug, although felt she should be paying attention to her escort, out of good manners, if nothing else. 'I enjoyed this evening very much. Gene Kelly is a marvellous dancer. I became so engrossed in the film I quite forgot to talk to you, which is unforgivable. You've told me so little about yourself, apart from the fact you lost your wife and child. I mean, have you always worked on the docks?

He looked pleased by her show of interest. 'No, I've moved about a bit: worked in the parcel office on Exchange station, been a coal man, rent collector, and a driver for Burgess's Dairy once over. But I was looking for something with better prospects, so found that job at the docks. I shan't be moving again, even when the war's over. I don't much care for change.'

'What about your parents? I've heard you mention your mother, is she…?'

'She's dead, my father too.'

'Oh, I'm so sorry. I hope, when this war's over, that my dad will come home safe and sound. He's a PoW and I write to him all the time, though I'm not sure if he gets any of my letters, or if he's still alive, having had only one letter from him. I miss him so very much. Being my dad, he's someone to turn to in times of trouble.' A rush of tears filled her eyes and ran, unchecked, down her face. What on earth was wrong with her, blubbing like this?

Doug tut-tutted and smiled warmly at her, then rubbing the sweat from his palms he grasped her small hand between his own and gave it a little pat. Then taking a white handkerchief from his pocket he handed it to her with gentle deference. 'There, there, you don't need your dad, sweetheart – er, dear girl – you've got me. I can guess that you have other family problems, so I'd do anything to make you happy, Jess. I'll take good care of you from now on.'

Chapter Twenty-Nine

Life for Leah wasn't so rosy as she'd hoped, though had she been thinking more clearly she would have recalled that Jess had tried to warn her, right in the beginning. Even Cora had once commented that her lads were 'an acquired taste'.

But she soon learned the truth of that, even between the sheets. Harry was still ready and willing to prove himself the great stud he imagined himself to be, except on the nights he was somewhat the worse for wear, when it was more problematic. Now that he was a married man, he didn't deem it necessary to trouble himself with offering teasing caresses to put her in a receptive mood. His opinion being that, as she was his wife, for heaven's sake why would that matter? It was as if he'd acquired a new toy, which he could pick up and use for his own satisfaction whenever the mood took him. If he wanted 'a bit of the other' as he crudely described the act of love, then he took it, or rather helped himself. Nor were there any more bunches of flowers, no sweet words and soft canoodling.

Leah attempted on one occasion to explain. 'Couldn't you attempt a little more finesse, Harry, then maybe I'd have time to enjoy our lovemaking, assuming it lasted a bit longer?'

'Finesse? What the bleedin' hell are you talking about? Are you suggesting that I'm not capable? Women don't usually say they don't enjoy it. I've never had no complaints before.'

'I didn't mean I don't enjoy it. Of course I do, only—'

'It's all right, girl. I'll not stop where I'm not wanted. There are others more appreciative.' And he stormed off in a sulk, banging the door after him.

Leah ran after him, sobbing that she really didn't mean it, and would he please come back to bed because she loved him. But he didn't pause for a second, eager to get back down to the club where there would be plenty of adoring females, not least an ever-changing parade of barmaids. For the first time, Leah experienced a sense of disquiet. What had she done?

He was well kettled by the time he staggered back upstairs, but not so far gone that he didn't notice how attractive Leah was. He could see the long, slender curve of her thigh beneath the bed covers, the soft mound that was her breast as she lay half on her side, half on her back, deeply asleep and tantalisingly vulnerable. Despite having spent a most pleasant hour with one of the new girls, fresh as a peach and ripe for the picking, just looking at her lying there so inviting made him feel randy again. And she was his wife, dammit. He yanked back the sheets and quickly straddled her. 'Come on love, wake up, let's have a bit of fun, eh?'

'Harry, for heavens's sake, what are you doing? Get off me. I'm half asleep. Give me a minute, for heaven's sake.'

But Harry didn't bother about that. He pulled up her nightie and it didn't take long before he reached a satisfying conclusion. A nice little extra by way of dessert, as you might say. Seconds later he rolled off her and fell into a deep, snoring sleep, spreadeagled across the bed.

Leah snatched up her dressing gown and fled into the tiny kitchen to make herself a calming cup of tea, hoping that she could cry quietly so that he wouldn't hear.

–

Delaney's All Girls Band were next performing at the Ritz. Jess loved playing there, which was always a thrill. Tonight, everyone was in high spirits. They were all singing and laughing, yet underneath there still lingered an echo of sadness, no one certain what the war might still bring. As usual, the place was full of American GIs or Yankee Doodle Dandies, as they were known. It was no wonder that the ballroom had become known as the forty-ninth state. Whitworth Street was chock-a-block with jeeps; with red MP armbands and batons much in evidence, worn by chunky service policemen representing Uncle Sam whose task was to deal with any miscreants who stepped out of line. Not that many did, they were having too good a time, and the MPs were particularly tolerant this evening.

Jess had her own crew intact. They stood up one by one to take their bows as she introduced them. Lulu on saxophone, blond, pageboy-bob swinging suggestively back and forth as she played. Adele with the flashing dark eyes on clarinet, Miss Mona on double bass, still with her trademark blue rinse; and Ena the sexy drummer who vowed to head for a nunnery once the war was over, and temptation had banished from her life. A joke that always brought a good laugh from her pals. Leah was on the piano and last, but by no means least, came Jess Delaney on trumpet.

'Take it away girls. One, two, three…' And the band struck up with 'Don't sit under the apple tree with anyone else but me…'

As well as servicemen – the Brits still out-numbering the Yanks – the place was thronged with excited, giggling girls. Hollywood movies being popular throughout the war, many of them had spent it seeking out their own personal Humphrey Bogart, and those who had succeeded would be heading out west soon.

Jess watched their happy young faces as she played, wondering which of them would be fortunate enough to have their dreams come true. If only her own had.

She made sure that there were plenty of novelty dances to give people the chance to get acquainted, and kissing was an integral part. There were kisses in the 'Progressive Barn Dance', the 'Paul Jones', and even in a Scottish reel where couples were expected to make an arch and kiss their partner before they went through it. People loved it and were shouting out for more. All great fun! And then the lights were lowered for the romantic number of 'Dancing in the Dark'.

What could be more blissful than to have Steve kiss her, were they still a pair. How would she survive without him? He was the only man she could ever love. Wherever she went it was still second nature for her to keep an eye out for a shabbily dressed saxophone player. She only needed to catch a glimpse of a shaggy, red-brown haircut, or a tie askew, for her heart to skip a beat. Not that she'd been fortunate in that respect for some considerable time. Tonight was no exception. Wherever he was, it would be on some important hush-hush operation. Jess knew that were Steve still in the city, he would surely not come to see her ever again, having been dismissed. Oh, but despite her decision to avoid him, how she wished that Steve were here beside her on this lovely evening. It was a feeling she must block out of her mind.

Now, having stepped down from their performance, they took a break and a second band came on. Following their tremendous achievement they were proudly aware of being looked upon as a star attraction. And being well paid. Jess never let on that she would happily have played for nothing, since she loved it so much. Nevertheless it was wonderful to be making more money than she ever had in her life, and still saving hard.

The Ritz ballroom had a two-tier bandstand, one on top of the other, which made the changeover smooth, with scarcely a break in the dancing. Jess was still engrossed with watching the dizzying, spinning steps of the waltzers that, for once, she paid little attention to the band. She could only marvel at the sureness of step, the smooth confidence and expertise of the dancers, all cheered and applauded by an enthusiastic crowd. She could see lovers kissing and cuddling under the guise of innocent dance steps. Watching them dancing cheek to cheek, the memory of being in Steve's arms hit her hard. Jess closed her eyes, her mind obsessed with her loss. She felt a deep ache in her heart when she heard Doug approach her.

'I love dancing, don't you?' she dreamily remarked.

'I don't think a sweet young performer like you should be seen dancing in a place like this. Far too public,' he drily remarked.

She looked startled by this comment. 'Why not? What's wrong with dancing when we take a break?' Jess looked about her at lively couples obviously enjoying themselves as they did a quickstep to 'Little Brown Jug', including Leah with Harry. 'Dancing is perfectly harmless and certainly looks as if everyone here is having fun. It all seems perfectly respectable to me.'

Recognising his mistake, Doug instantly hastened to rectify it. 'If you'd like to dance Jess, I'll be happy to partner you.'

How could she refuse after making such a fuss? 'Well, all right, if you don't mind,' she said. Feeling rather regretful, she allowed him to take her on to the dance floor, striving to appear normal.

When he put his arms about her Jess made sure that she kept a relative distance between them, not at all how she would have danced with Steve. No cheek-to-cheek, hand clenched tight against his heart, let alone thigh pressing against thigh allowed. This was utterly decorous and proper. Even so, it felt embarrassing and entirely wrong! The rough fabric of his suit felt alien to her touch, even the unmistakable smell of tar, rope and possibly the docks emanating from him made her feel strangely nauseous. She could sense his eyes watching her, and desperately searched her mind for something witty or amusing to say, a frothy comment to lighten the heavy atmosphere. She determinedly attempted to enjoy a dance, even with this wrong man. The music changed to 'Now is the Hour' and something in the distinctive tones of a saxophone brought her head up sharply. It was as Doug spun her round in a clumsy manoeuvre, thankfully managing not to tread on her toes, that she saw Steve.

He was playing in the band. She hadn't noticed him until they'd circled the dance floor and come closer to the small stage. Now she could see him so clearly that her heart filled with longing. There was something in the unique way he played, instinctively lifting his head as he brought forth the most magical notes imaginable. Aware of a spurt of tears glittering in her eyes she found herself gazing closely at him, almost as if she'd known he was there all along. He was playing the saxophone and she sensed a wrong note he played as his gaze burned into hers, searing into her soul. She could hardly believe he was here, although she would have known that sound anywhere. Remembering how she'd coldly dismissed him, often still dreaming of this man she loved, now as she regarded him in the flesh, she realised how much she missed him and ached for his touch, having badly underestimated her need.

Oh, why was he here, and he could see that she was in the arms of another man. She felt giddy with misery, trembling in every limb so that she missed a step and would have stumbled had not Doug caught her, taking the opportunity to draw her closer into his arms. She whispered his name – 'Steve. Oh, Steve!' – allowing it to slip over her lips as if by saying it a new life was breathing within her.

'What did you say, sweetheart? Are you tired and in need of a rest?'

Jess agreed that she was and they left the floor. She gladly accepted the lemonade he bought for her. 'It's probably the heat of this room.'

'Perhaps you'd like to go home?'

Jess shook her head. 'No, not yet! We'll take another dance.' A sort of recklessness having come over her, she concentrated on dancing with Doug, telling herself that no matter how difficult, she really mustn't run away. Perhaps it was no bad thing that Steve had seen them together. If she could get through the next ten minutes or so, it might convince him that it was finally over between them and leave her alone. After that, it would surely get easier. Even broken hearts mended eventually, didn't they?

Suddenly Steve was there beside her, having abandoned his saxophone to come looking for her. He was telling a red-faced, angry looking Doug that this was an Excuse-Me and it was his turn now to dance with Jess.

He'd fixed the dance deliberately, Jess guessed. Fortunately, this thought didn't occur to Doug and he graciously, if reluctantly, relinquished her.

They came together with an ease that was heart-breaking. Her hand captured warmly against his chest, his arm about her waist where it seemed to fit perfectly, holding her close so that she could follow every fluid movement of his body, anticipate his next step as every good dancer should. She could feel his warm breath against her cheek, every beat of his heart.

'Is that him, the bloke you've dumped me for?'

'It's not like that at all.'

'Are you saying we can get back together then? If you remember, I do love you.'

She could hardly see him for the shimmer of tears in her eyes. He'd said those precious words she'd so longed to hear. But it was far, far too late. Bernie Delaney had made sure of that. She shook her head in numb misery.

'I can't let you go, Jess.'

'You must.' And suddenly she realised the band was playing 'I'll Be Seeing You'.

Steve pulled her close in his arms and began humming the words softly into her ear.

'"In all the old, familiar places, that my heart and mind embraces… I'll find you in the morning sun and when the night is through, I'll be looking at the moon, but I'll be seeing you."'

Jess could bear no more. She tore herself from his arms, aware of a spurt of tears glittering in her eyes. Not pausing for a second, she ignored his cry urging her to stay, and ran blindly from the room.

–

It was Doug who caught up with her and, restating his belief that she wasn't well, offered to walk her home, insisting it was the gentlemanly thing to do as accidents were rife in the blackout.

Considering she was shivering in anguish over having seen and lost Steve yet again, how could she refuse?

'You're so kind and gentle, Doug,' Jess told him and, wiping her tears away, blew her nose vigorously and tried to smile. 'You make me feel safe. That's why I agreed to go out with you, I suppose. Now, I'll accept your suggestion to take me home.'

Doug tut-tutted and patted her hand, pulled a clean, white handkerchief from his pocket and handed it to her to wipe her eyes. Tucking her arm in his, he gently began to lead her down Oxford Street, then gently asked what had caused her distress. 'I'm delighted to spend time with you. Did that man who was in the band hurt you? Musicians are the lowest of the low, I've always thought.'

'Don't say such things, Doug. I'm a musician too, remember? It wasn't anything Steve did to upset me. I suddenly came over all fuzzy, because of the heat under those lights, not feeling too well as you suspected.' Jess flushed. Her mind was spinning, her heart physically aching, as if someone were squeezing all the life out of it. Oh, why wasn't it Steve who had come to take her home? That was entirely unreasonable of her to expect that, having left him stunned and hurt on the dance floor. And he would, of course, need to go back on stage and play the next number, as if nothing amiss had taken place between them. It had been foolish of her to dance with him, proving to be a dangerous effect upon her heart.

Having accepted Doug's invitation, she felt glad of his company when they came across a few drunken sailors on their way back to their ship after a night on the town. Not that they were in any way violent, only slightly merry, giving her wolf whistles and the like. Jess found them rather amusing but Doug was less inclined to be benevolent towards them.

Taking a grip upon her arm, he said, 'All right lads, leave the little lady alone. She's with me. You see now why you shouldn't be walking about on your own at this time of night,' he gently scolded her when they'd gone. 'You never would if you were my girlfriend.'

Jess struggled to be interested by this comment, or when he told her that he had at last successfully acquired tickets for the Hallé orchestra and would happily take her to hear them play Verdi's 'Requiem' at the King's Hall.

'I'll give that some thought,' she politely commented, then fell into silence.

'You're a very talented and beautiful lady.' He smiled sheepishly at her. 'Actually, we'd be good together, you and me, Jess. I'd give you anything you've ever dreamed of: nice clothes, children, a home of your own that you don't have to share with your hated uncle, or your feckless mother. I'm a simple man but harmless and most caring. My fondness for you has turned into true love, despite you obviously having a problem. I would deem it a privilege and an honour to take you as my wife. I wish to cherish you forever. I could buy you a ring tomorrow for us to become engaged, if you will have me.'

Jess stared at him in stunned disbelief, desperately aware that she'd never had any wish to seek love or passion from this docker, pleasant man though he may be. It was Steve she longed for, despite having just run away from him. But if she couldn't have the man whom she truly loved, and she was pregnant with a baby that was not Steve's, maybe she should admit what her problem was.

'What if I asked you to take on someone else, as well as me?'

'Surely not your entire family?' What had he let himself in for?

'No, a child.'

Doug turned over these surprising words in his brain for several stunned moments. 'I'm not sure I quite understand. I thought you were an only daughter with no brothers and sisters, only cousins.'

'I meant… *my* child.'

'What? I didn't know you had one.'

Jess took a deep breath and told him, as gently and calmly as she could, about her uncle raping her, using the word out loud for the first time, and how she was pregnant as a result. It couldn't have taken more than a few moments but she felt exhausted when she was done, drained of all energy.

A silence stretched endlessly between them.

Doug couldn't deny that he was deeply alarmed and disappointed. He'd wanted her to be pure, chaste as the driven snow. Yet he was afraid to show his feelings for fear of losing her. At length he said: 'I am honoured that you should share this information with me. It can't have been easy for you.'

'N–no, it wasn't easy at all. It was a terrible thing to happen.'

Jess made no mention of her lovemaking with Steve, having put all hope of a life with him out of her mind, as this was not his child. But even though she'd disagreed with Doug's attitude towards women, she'd enjoyed the time she spent with him, and needed someone in her life. She had no wish for her child to be considered illegitimate or called a bastard. But would he accept her conditions?

'In all honesty, the only thing is that I doubt I could be much of a wife to you. Being – assaulted in that way – tends to put me off that sort of thing. To put it bluntly, it would be a marriage in name only. I very much doubt that I could ever – that I would want to have sex with you or – or anyone.'

Doug kept his expression carefully neutral and passive, giving no indication of how much she'd startled him. This was the last thing he'd expected and yet – did it matter? What good had sex ever done for him, and he could easily live without it, if necessary. That ex-boyfriend of hers, Steve, the musician character who she'd danced with, might well be the father of this child, and the tale of being raped by her uncle could be a lie she'd made up to make him feel sorry for her. Doug had no wish to be a father again, particularly to another man's child, but he would never let her down. One word from him and Jess was his for the taking, what he'd dreamed of for so long. He would keep her like a princess in an ivory tower, entirely his. He very gently touched her hand and smiled kindly at her. 'All right, Jess love. I'll gladly agree to that, and look after you and the baby.'

Jess felt deeply moved by the kindness so evident in his gaze, and seeing him as a good man, lonely and sad, who'd experienced the pain of losing a wife and a beloved child, she accepted his offer without the slightest hesitation. This war had destroyed too many lives. Didn't Doug Morgan deserve some compassion, a little loving, just like everyone else? And considering the child that her uncle had saddled her with, didn't she too? If this good man was prepared to take on such a burden, what possible reason could she have for refusing him?

Chapter Thirty

1945

The sun was shining and new life unfurling in the buds on the trees, a beautiful spring day right in the heart of Manchester, outshone only by the delight and happiness on the hundreds of faces that thronged Albert Square, all of them beaming suns in their own right. Wreathed in laughter and smiles, they reflected hearts filled with hope for a new future. 'Manchester Salutes the Allies's declared the hoardings, words emblazoned over a giant V for victory sign.

The war was over at last! Germany had surrendered, the Third Reich was defeated.

Flags of the United Nations were flown, King George VI's broadcast relayed to his loyal subjects. There were flags and bunting everywhere, pictures of Winston Churchill propped up on back yard walls. The streets of Manchester rang with music and laughter, singing and dancing. People danced everywhere, even on top of the air raid shelters, cocking a snook at the hours they'd spent confined in the musty misery within, over so many long years. Bonfires blazed, fireworks exploded and people took rides on gloriously decorated trams just so they could see all the fun.

Later in the day, or certainly by the next morning, reality would show that little had changed. Admittedly the blackout, even the dim-out that had recently replaced it was now over for good. Lights were on again in Manchester, but there were still long queues for food, and even bread. Restrictions continued, though everyone was bored sick with Spam. Even Cora was having trouble finding enough coupons these days to provide the extra fat she needed to make pies for the dances that Jess held each month at some local venue or other.

'Not sure which they like best, my meat and potato pies or your music but you keep playing and I'll keep cooking, love.'

Jess believed that it was the dances and her beloved trumpet which had kept her sane over this last year or more. If it hadn't been for her music, she might well have gone mad. Right now she was playing with all her heart and soul while the women picked up their skirts and danced, finishing with a conga from Albert Square, all along John Dalton Street and down Deansgate, singing at the tops of their voices: 'I'm Looking Over a Four Leaf Clover'.

It was a day to be happy, a day to rejoice and look forward not back; no matter what problems may lie beneath the surface of their superficially contented lives. If nothing had quite turned out as she'd expected, at least she and her friends had survived. They could breathe in the fresh air and freedom, the glorious sunshine of this precious day.

Cora was with them, as she so often was, minding the babies. Leah had a baby girl, who was ten months old, and had given up working at the tea room in order to devote her attention entirely to Susie's welfare, although she still helped out at the club. Much to the surprise of everyone, particularly his wife, even Harry had come to dote upon his daughter, and could often be found dangling her upon his knee. He had even been spotted proudly walking the baby out in her pram on Deansgate, basking in the comments of doting matrons who stopped to admire this delightfully pretty child.

Jess too had given up her job at Doug's insistence, and even the Salvation Army had little need of her now. But she was content to devote her days, at least to her own child, but nothing would prevent her from playing in her precious band.

Despite being a good, kind and caring man, Doug had been a huge disappointment to her, spending as little time as possible with John, or little Johnny as he'd come to be called. Jess sympathised with his lack of interest. Why should he love a child who wasn't his own son?

Jess certainly hadn't expected to love this baby. How could she? A child born out of violence. After being in labour for almost twenty-five hours of seemingly unendurable agony, they'd finally put her child in her arms and she'd felt nothing; had looked down upon him with complete indifference, her heart turned to stone. Family and friends had come to admire him and make comments over who they thought he most resembled. If there was a moment when she'd looked at the baby and imagined that she saw Steve in the round, bright eyed features, and the shaggy brown hair, then she quickly dismissed it as wishful thinking. She knew better.

Even when she'd finally brought him home two weeks later, she could hardly bear to look at him let alone pick him up. Jess would leave him in his cot for hours at a time where he would contentedly sleep, or gurgle to himself. Everyone said what a good, happy baby he was, but feeling she couldn't manage to love her child, as she should, not for the world did she wish him any harm. Jess did her best to care for him, would get up at night without complaint to feed, change and burp him, and walked him out in his pram every afternoon.

Lizzie had come to live with them, as Doug had agreed that she could, but it hadn't worked out quite as Jess had hoped. Any normal mother would have helped with the new baby, but Lizzie was not at all normal. She required too much care herself. At first Jess had hoped that having a grandchild would keep Lizzie off the booze. But due to the club Harry was running, there was no shortage of that commodity and on too many occasions she'd come home to find her mother senseless.

On one, never to be forgotten occasion when little Johnny was just a few months old, Jess had agreed to let her mother hold him, while she pegged out the washing. Lizzie must have wandered off upstairs in search of a quick nip of gin, because Jess suddenly heard a piercing scream and came running in to find that she'd fallen down the stairs. Her heart had very nearly stopped beating, until she realised that Lizzie had thankfully left the baby lying safely in the middle of her bed, having forgotten that she'd taken him up in the first place.

'You could have killed him if you'd fallen with him in your arms. What were you thinking of?' It was then Jess realised how much she really loved her child.

The truth was, Lizzie was beyond common sense of anything that didn't come in the shape of a bottle. Finally,

Doug convinced Lizzie that she should move back in with her sister-in-law; that Jess had enough on her plate looking after a new baby. What a relief that was.

–

Bernie was no more than a distant memory for Cora, one of the many unidentified corpses dug out of the ruins of Manchester's bombed buildings. Cora was not at all troubled by what she'd done. He'd got what he deserved. What she did regret was the effect his dirty interfering had had upon that poor lass's life. Ruined it for her. Cora had attempted to convince her the baby was indeed the child of that musician, Steve Wyman, the love of Jess's life, and giving him up and agreeing to a hasty marriage with Doug would be entirely wrong. Tragically she wouldn't believe that. Cora supposed that it was all too much for the poor lass to bear.

Now, without a moment's hesitation in Cora's opinion, young Johnny was indeed Steve's child. Same red-brown hair, same cheeky expression, and no resemblance at all to any of her own childer, which surely he would have had were he really one of Bernie's by-blows.

Cora believed this marriage of Jess's to be an utter disaster. That man had not a scrap of humanity in him, save for an unhealthy and overriding obsession with her beloved niece. But she held her own counsel, thought of her dearly as one of her own, that poor lass badly needing someone to care for her. There was certainly none forthcoming from her mother.

As if on cue, Lizzie came shuffling into the kitchen. 'Is the kettle on? Is there owt to eat? I'm hungry.'

'Are you ever anything else? If you're not pouring booze down your throat, it's pints of tea. And I rarely see you lift the kettle.'

The two unfriendly women sat in their accustomed stony silence over breakfast, Lizzie nibbling at a slice of bread and marg while enjoying her third cigarette of the day. Cora shared a large pan of porridge with her ten-year-old twins.

'Have you seen Jess lately?' she asked at last.

Lizzie looked blank for a moment, as if she hadn't the first idea who she was talking about.

'Your daughter, Jess, remember her? By heck, you are losing it girl. Do you never think to go round to hers, to see how the poor lass is doing? What sort of mother are you? I can't think why she's always asking after you, why she even cares. When she did have you to stay, you were nowt but a liability to her? Come to think of it, that's all you are to me. Why do I put up with you, eh? You're no flaming use to anyone. Never so much as lift a pot towel.'

'Are you wanting to be rid of me?'

'You could say that. Aye, go on. Sling your hook.'

'And if Bernie comes home, what'll he have to say about you flinging me out into the gutter?'

'He'd probably say that was where you came from in the first place. But he isn't coming home. He's gone for good. I've told you, he's probably got himself another woman somewhere. Who knows? Who cares? I certainly don't.'

Cora had related this fantasy so often that she'd almost come to believe it herself. When in reality he was a heap of old bones in an unmarked grave somewhere. Were he still alive she could have told him that Bert was happily settled with Maisie, married with a little lad of his own. Sandra, at fifteen, was quite the little madam and eyeing up boys as if they'd just come into fashion. And her lovely Tommy would be home soon, for good this time. Except that he'd fallen for a WAAF and would no doubt be tripping down the aisle with her and going off to pastures new pretty soon.

Cora sighed as she rinsed her cup out under the tap to make herself another brew. You only got to keep your children for a short time, then they walked away with scarcely a backward glance. All that agony, all that worrying was supposed to stop then. But Cora was beginning to think that it never would.

'Why don't you ever worry about that lass of yours?' she demanded of Lizzie, who was now busily lighting a fourth cigarette from the stub of the third. 'Can't you see how unhappy she is? Couldn't you help with that lovely little lad she's got? Take an interest at least. Daughters are precious. They should be appreciated.'

Lizzie gazed at Cora out of unfocused eyes. 'When you go down the market, slip in the club and ask your Harry for another bottle of gin, I've run out.'

Cora was still worried about Harry. He never stopped complaining about being hard up and had asked her, of all people, to provide him with money. Cora had to laugh at his cheek. She didn't even get a proper pension, not being able to prove that her husband was dead. She was forced to get by on hand-outs from her sons, but didn't like the way Harry was bullying that pretty wife of his, throwing his brass about like a man with three arms. It would all come to grief, if she was any judge.

'Ask him yourself. I'm not your flippin' slave,' Cora snapped and she tipped all the breakfast dishes into the sink, then went to the bottom of the stairs to shout in her loudest voice, 'If you don't get down here this minute, Sandra, I'll come up to drag you down with the scruff of your neck.'

Jess had done her utmost to follow Cora's wise advice to put the whole sorry tale behind her, but it wasn't easy. Bernie's image did indeed come back to haunt her. Night after night she would see his round, sneering face, feel his big wet slobbering mouth on hers, see the glisten of his greasy hair over his bald head, and she'd wake in a cold sweat. She couldn't pretend she was sorry he was dead, any more than his own wife did. He'd brought little joy into anyone's life, not even to his own sons, who had so easily disposed of his remains.

But if Jess thought too closely about the price she had paid for his interference, she truly would go mad. Not only had he been the reason for Lizzie being sent to jail, Jess would never have lost Steve had it not been for Bernie Delaney. She wished she could agree with Cora that Johnny was Steve's child, but failed to persuade herself to do that, however much she might try.

She picked up the baby and gave him a cuddle, as if to reassure him it wasn't important who his father was, even if to her it most definitely was. Beaming happily, Johnny bobbed his nose against hers in an imitation of the Eskimo kiss she liked to give him, making Jess laugh out loud. How could she ever have not wanted him? She must have been wallowing in self pity, or sick in the head to have deprived him of her love when he'd been born. Where was the point in that? He was the innocent in all of this mess, her child and already a little person in his own right. Whoever his father was she loved him to bits, more than life itself.

'Let's play music and be happy,' Jess told him, and sitting Johnny in his chair, she picked up her trumpet and began to play. He banged his spoon with perfect rhythm, proving he was indeed her child. But it brought tears to her eyes as she was transported back to a time when everything had seemed so straightforward, when she'd dreamed of marrying Steve, and of being the next Ivy Benson. A time when she'd been young, filled with hope for the future, and the joy of loving. If all of those dreams were now gone, she must make the best of what she had left. At least she had her lovely child and her music.

–

Leah really didn't know why she put up with Harry. At first because she still loved him and had hoped that he would calm down. She'd had a passion for him, and out of pride had married him in defiance of her parents. Now she couldn't for shame admit that she'd made a bad mistake. And she was too afraid to leave him, knowing he'd find her and bring her back, there being nowhere safe for her to go. She had once tried packing her bags and going home to her mother. Muriel had taken one look at her daughter standing forlornly on the doorstep, two suitcases at her feet and a brand new baby on her hip, and rolled her eyes in despair.

'So you've had a fall-out with your husband. Didn't I predict that could happen? If you'd listened to me, you could have married Ambrose, who is a splendid man. Well, don't think you can come back home with your tail between your legs. Your father is retiring. Robert is taking over the business and we are moving out to the Fylde coast to enjoy whatever years we have left, without work or worry of any kind.'

Leah had been flabbergasted, unable to believe her ears. 'Are you saying that you won't help and give me a bed for the night, your own daughter and granddaughter?'

'If you must, but only for one night! This marriage was your choice, nothing to do with me. You made your bed, Leah, so lie on it.'

She didn't stay and had never gone back home again. On that occasion she'd ended up at Cora's, trailing round in tears, the baby screaming her head off. Harry had been summoned to his mother's house and been given a thorough talking to, accompanied by a clip around the ear. It had been an almost comical sight to see the round and solid Cora laying into a son. He was so big and brawny he could have flattened her with one hand, had he been of a mind to do so. But with Harry's promises ringing in her ears that he would behave himself in future, Leah had gone home with him, feeling quite optimistic.

She was soon put right on that score.

The minute she'd put Susie down in her cot, Harry had locked the door of the flat and taken off his belt. 'This is for broadcasting our private affairs to all and sundry.' He'd whipped her till her back bled and her blouse was in ribbons on her broken body.

Leah had never risked leaving him again, as he would never let her be free of him.

She'd learned to toe the line and do as she was told to the letter, without thought or argument. Life was easier that way, with less pain and fewer arguments, so she always tried to look on the bright side. She had Susie, after all, who was the world to her, and unlike Doug, Harry had never objected to her playing in the band. Probably because he needed the money she earned from it. No marriage was perfect, and there were times when Harry could be funny and sweet, shower her with presents or take her and Susie out for a special treat, particularly if he'd had a win on the cards. Leah kept telling herself that once he'd got these money problems with the club sorted out, he'd be nice as pie again. She simply had to be patient.

Chapter Thirty-One

Jess and Doug spent most Saturday afternoons in Philips Park. It had become their custom to take little Johnny somewhere special at the weekend, instead of his usual perambulation down by the canal. This was Doug's weekly effort at fatherhood, to prove to neighbours who saw him walk out with his child what a very fine man he was. It was all show, since once out of their sight he would ignore the child completely, almost as if Johnny wasn't even there. Jess accepted this little charade as better than nothing. The afternoon outing was an attempt to show her child a world beyond the muck and grime of the docks, and she believed that the fresh air would do him good.

They sat on the park bench, Doug with his hands on the knees of his best tweed suit, bowler hat set square on his head, lost in a world of his own. A small frown creased his brow revealing no emotion on his unsmiling face. Jess did not interrupt this inner scrutiny of his private thoughts. She had learned that if he wanted to reveal them, then he would do so. If he did not, then nothing she could say would persuade him otherwise.

Jess jiggled the pram and mentally went over the tunes she'd planned for the evening's programme. They were playing at the Ritz, amazing when she remembered how nervous she'd felt when she'd first gone there with Leah right at the start of the war. In truth she was itching for this walk to be over, then she could get over to the ballroom and take the band through a quick rehearsal, leaving little Johnny with Cora, as she always did.

Doug suddenly broke into her thoughts. 'The war now being over, tonight will be the last dance. A good place to finish, at the Ritz.'

'Finish? Last dance? What are you taking about?'

He cleared his throat and sat up a little straighter, his long bony wrists sticking out from the sleeves of his jacket. 'Now that hostilities are over, this dance craze of yours will naturally come to an end, and a good thing too.'

'I beg your pardon? Why should it come to an end?'

'Because there won't be the servicemen around any more, looking to pick up partners. Husbands will be returning home, wives to the fireside, as is only right and proper. So no more dances which, as I say, is a relief. You'll be home every evening from now on, a good thing, as you need to be a proper mother to little Johnny and a good wife to me. It's time for you to hang up your trumpet and put an end to this little hobby of yours.'

Jess was struck dumb for several long seconds before she finally found her voice. '*Little hobby?* I can't believe I'm hearing you say that. *You've* decided I must stop? Don't I have any say in the matter?'

'As your husband, I know what's best for you, my dear? I've worried about you going out and about on your own, and do wish you to be safe.' He rushed on to remind her of when they'd first started walking out together, of how polite and awkward he'd been. 'You must have thought me a right idiot. But then, you were so angry with the world and full of bitterness.'

'True that I was distressed by what had happened to me, and I admit I wasn't in love with you.'

'I accepted that and took you on when nobody else would, despite your being soiled goods. Right now you're definitely in need of peace and relaxation, as do most women after the war, so I hope you will now be a loyal wife.'

Jess winced, feeling a sense of failure and inadequacy. 'I'll do my best,' she said. Then seeing the flare of hurt in his eyes, wished she'd bitten off her tongue. It had become so common for Doug to seek these reassurances, how easy it was to offend him.

He gave her hand a little pat, just as if she had suffered a tantrum. 'Not convinced you should work there tonight. The town will be rowdy and full of drunks, following the VE Day celebrations. You must send your apologies.'

Jess looked at him in disbelief. 'What are you saying? I can't simply not turn up, as I'm the band leader. What about the other girls? How could they manage without me?'

'They'll manage if they must. Nobody is indispensable, dear. You'd best stay home.' He always addressed her in this way, having stopped using the word "sweetheart", which was what she had been to Steve, never to Doug.

'Sorry, but why would I?'

He looked at her then with the faintest hint of disapproval in his steady gaze. 'Because I wish you to.'

The moment they arrived back home, he went to put on the kettle for their afternoon tea while Jess dashed upstairs. In ten minutes flat she was washed and changed, picked up Johnny and collected the baby's overnight bag, then was flying downstairs and out of the house before Doug had chance to come from the kitchen to check what had caused the front door to bang so loudly.

They next day, Doug firmly scolded her for her disobedience, treating her like a recalcitrant child. 'I'm disappointed in you, Jess. I thought I'd made it clear that you were not to attend.'

Jess listened to him with a weary sigh. 'If you mean because last night I attended the Ritz, you are wrong. It was a brilliant occasion, absolutely wonderful. If you'd been there, you'd have seen for yourself what a great success Delaney's All Girls Band was, and you would have been proud of me.' The bubbles of excitement she'd experienced the night before, as heady as champagne, had been wonderful. Streamers had been thrown across the ballroom, people had sung 'Auld Lang Syne' with tears of happiness in their eyes. They'd clung to each other and sobbed for those they had lost who would never return to know this glorious peace. All Doug did was to remain aloof, criticise and deprive her of the one thing that brought her happiness. She frequently told herself that he was a good man and a caring husband, if not the best of fathers. But by allowing him to provide the respectability she'd always craved for herself and her child, she'd condemned them both to a sterile existence. Jess realised that it had been a bad mistake to marry him.

He leaned closer and placed his mouth upon hers, his hand creeping beneath the shelter of her coat to cup her breast and gave it a little squeeze. Jess shivered, imagining another pair of lips and dear face. Sometimes she ached for Steve so much it was like a knife twisting in her heart.

Revelling his score of victory by kissing her, Doug said, 'Your baby is two years old, Jess. I've been very patient, allowing you time to recover from your anguish. No one can say otherwise. Perhaps now you'll become more willing to relax and accept me.'

This sounded ominously like a threat.

–

Cora called in on Jess one Tuesday morning when she went down the market. 'How you fettling, chuck? How's my little man?' Johnny jumped up and down in a lively way, grinning and chortling happily to see her. She picked up the infant to give him a cuddle, 'By heck, you're a real champion. Look at that smile, fair warms the cockles of your heart, doesn't it?'

Jess laughingly agreed that he could charm the birds out of the trees with that rapturous smile of his. He was a remarkably cheerful child. Nothing seemed to trouble him, and he'd readily smile at anyone. No wonder everybody loved him. Everyone, that is, except Doug.

As the two women walked around Campfield Market, glad to be out of a blustering wind, it felt like stepping into another world filled with interesting aromas from the mounds of fruit and veg, cuts of pink pork meat and red polony sausages on display. Cora bought a little wooden toy train for Johnny, and Jess scolded her for not being able to afford such treats, now she'd no regular income coming in.

'Nay, my lads slip me a bit when they can. Our Bert's very generous and even Tommy sends me something now and then, though he's saving up to be wed, so that's tailing off now. Our Harry's been a bit tight lately. Has Leah said owt about him?'

Jess shook her head, frowning slightly. 'She says very little, has become much quieter these last few months, not at all the bubbly personality I used to know. I do worry about her. Do you think they're having problems, her and Harry?'

Cora sucked in her breath. Did Jess suspect what was going on behind closed doors, Leah having got herself mixed up with the Delaneys? Or maybe she liked to think that everything was hunky-dory for her friend. 'I don't reckon their trade's too bright. It'll get worse now the Yanks are going back home.'

'I suppose so.'

'You're doing well though, with that band.' Cora cast her a sideways glance, chiding the familiar worry at the back of her head, knowing it did no good to poke her nose in to Harry's business. Except, happen for once, she should give it a try. That wife of his looked thin as a drink of water, and somebody should do something before she slipped through a crack in the pavement. 'It's none of my business and I don't like to pry, but I suppose you do pay Leah something for playing in the band.'

Jess had been choosing a few rosy apples for Johnny as a treat, now she paused, surprised by this question. 'Of course I do. We all earn good money from the band. It's an equal partnership.'

'Then what d'you reckon she does with her money? She doesn't improve the clothes on her back, though that kiddy doesn't go short of owt.'

'Harry dotes on her, I think he's always buying her presents. But you're right, Leah gets very little for herself these days. I wonder why? Perhaps, like me, she's saving it for a rainy day.'

'If it rains much more on that lass, she'll flaming drown.'

Jess abruptly stopped walking and turned to frown at Cora. 'What do you know that I don't? Come on, get it off your chest.'

Cora stared at her in wide-eyed innocence. 'What would I know?'

'Quite a lot, I should imagine.'

'Well, I'm saying nowt.'

'Yes you are. We're going into old Ma Greenwood's café here. I shall buy you pie and peas and you're going to tell me all you know about Harry and Leah.'

Having tied Johnny to a chair, his bib neatly in place with a dish of peas before him, Cora's plump, homely face creased with such concern that for the first time she looked like an old woman. 'Can't you see how thin and scraggy she's gone lately. I reckon Harry beats the hell out of that poor lass.'

Jess went deathly pale at this dreadful news. Why had she not guessed what was going on? Like father, like son. Somehow, she felt as if she had personally let Leah down by not being there to protect her. 'Oh, my God, I thought her problem was just running around after her new baby.'

Cora dolefully shook her head. 'She's always bleating on about money. Same as our Harry is. He says Bernie left them with debts. I'm not sure whether that's true or not, but I were wondering, what with you doing so nicely with that band of yours, whether you couldn't lend him a bob or two.'

'You want me to give Harry money?'

'I said a loan, for your friend's sake. It'll happen get them out of whatever hole they're in, and it might persuade him to stop taking it out on that lass, stop him bullying her into nicking from her dad.'

Her appetite vanished, Jess put down her knife and fork. 'Oh Cora, not that as well.'

'Afraid so! She told me not to say anything and I haven't, but she badly needs help. Clifford Simmons gave one lass the sack over theft, innocent though the poor girl was, and Leah had to be more careful after that. But Harry won't allow her to stop. Once he's got the flaming bit between his teeth, there's no budging him.'

'I'll definitely help Leah, not him. I won't lend him a single penny, not while I live and breathe. I know he's your lad, Cora, but so help me, he's more his father's son than yours. He's Bernie all over again, come back to haunt me.'

A comment that proved to be more prophetic than she could ever have imagined!

The very next time the band played, Jess took the opportunity to speak to Leah, asking her how she was, remarking on how thin she'd become and would a bit more money help?

'It went down like a barrage balloon,' Jess told Cora afterwards. 'Wouldn't hear of a loan, or even a rise in her pay, insisting she was fine, thank you very much, and what gossip had I been listening to?'

Cora groaned. 'I hope you didn't say it came from me.'

'Of course I didn't.' The two women chewed the problem over, but in the end decided that they could do nothing more at present, except keep a close watch on events.

Harry was a worried man. He'd taken risks to get where he was, as had his father before him: nicking booze, running an illegal card school, using girls for what he thought they did best. Another was getting involved with Jimmy Doyle, generally known as Little Jimmy since he was the brother of Big Pat, the female all-in wrestler. He was a small, stocky man with gentle Irish eyes, but despite his diminutive size, he was not a man to cross. Not least because if he ever did find himself in a spot of bother, he called Big Pat in to help.

Harry hadn't given this association too much consideration in the past, simply because taking risks was par for the course, certainly to a Delaney. Then a couple of unexpected visitors to his establishment one day in early June, were to change his mind on that score.

Setting up the club had strained Harry's powers of imagination, and the gaming school had been one step too far. Bernie had done the renovations but equipping it all, putting in those chandeliers which gave the place taste, however brash, had been Harry's idea. When Bernie's money had run out Harry had borrowed a few quid from Jimmy, who'd shown interest in the project from the start. Thus it hadn't been his father who'd run up the debts, as he'd claimed, but Harry himself and he'd been aware that one day Jimmy Doyle would call in for more payment. So when two of Jimmy's sidekicks turned up at his door, Harry was studiously polite to them, ever circumspect when it came to saving his own skin, giving them a free chaser with the beers they ordered.

'It's good to see you appreciate what Mr Doyle has done for you,' said one.

Harry hastened to assure them just how grateful he was.

'Were you considering showing this gratitude in a concrete way, any time soon?' asked the other, an altogether nastier piece of goods in Harry's opinion, with that twisted leer and a cast in one eye.

'Indeed, I shall be making another substantial repayment by the end of next week.' Harry knew that he hadn't a hope in hell of doing any such thing, not unless his luck changed. He'd always believed that the owner of a card school was the one who made all the profit, but he'd discovered to his cost that wasn't the case at all. By the time he'd paid staff, barmen, cleaners, a couple of heavies to watch the punters didn't cheat him, there was precious little left over for his own pocket. He got his cut from the girls and the tenants he found to occupy the other rooms above the club, but that barely covered the cost of maintaining this establishment, which was huge. It was all very worrying.

'Next Saturday, first thing,' he said, reassuring himself as much as them, and pouring second whiskies all round.

'This Friday would be better.'

Harry swallowed carefully, still smiling. 'This Friday it is then.'

If I don't do something quick I'll be a goner by Saturday week, he thought. Maybe it was time to call in a few debts.

–

Jess took to calling round to see Leah more often than previously, trying on several occasions to persuade her friend to confide in her. So far all efforts had been fruitless, Leah remaining steadfastly silent about her troubles.

She insisted that all was generally well with her marriage, nothing she couldn't cope with.

These visits hadn't gone down too well with Harry who started complaining Jess was like a constant bad smell around the place. Then one afternoon while she was waiting for her friend to call, it was Harry who came up the stairs to the flat, glass in hand as usual, sprawled in his chair and, quite out of the blue asked point blank how much she was making in the band.

Jess was caught unawares. 'I think that's my business, not yours.'

'As a matter of fact, it's mine too, since my wife is playing in it.'

'Leah gets her fair share, as we all do. She would be the first to tell you that.'

'Let's put it this way,' Harry said with what might pass for a smile. 'It isn't enough. We need more, and you owe it to us.'

Cautiously not mentioning how she'd offered Leah a rise and a loan, which she'd refused to accept, Jess said, 'I owe you nothing. I assume you are doing well, and perhaps don't appreciate how loyal Leah is to you.'

'You haven't changed a bit. Still the same lippy cow you ever were.' He carefully set down his half drunk beer and came to stand threateningly close, leaning over her with his hands resting on each arm of the chair where she sat, effectively trapping her within it. 'You in fact owe me a lot. Had it not been for your provoking my dad, Mam would never have needed to lay him out cold, then me and Bert wouldn't have had to bury our father in that bomb site. Have you any idea how that makes a chap feel? It's not very nice, I can tell you that for nowt.'

Jess felt as if all sounds and images were coming from some great distance, and she was floating above it, drifting backwards into the realm of nightmares. 'I – I'm not sure I understand what you're saying.'

'Aye, you understand well enough. When our Mam clocked him one, she finished old Bernie off for good. Happen it were a hefty rolling pin, or else he had a thin skull. Either way, because of you, she's a murderess. Do you hear? Our mam could be hanged for knocking off her old man, so don't try saying that you owe me *nowt.*' He pushed his big face up close to hers, spittle forming at the corners of his mouth. 'You must get me some hard cash, or happen it'll all have to come out in the open. Only the way *I'll* tell the story, it'll be *you* doing the time, not our mam. And you have a son to think of, remember. What would happen to him if you were incarcerated, as your mam once was? Got that, chuck? Loud and clear?'

Jess knew she was trembling with shock and went sick at the thought. Filled with silent horror, she watched him wipe the froth from a mouth twisted into a sneer, looking more than ever like his father. 'You wouldn't want owt to happen to our lovely Cora, now do you, even though she killed my dad. Happen I'm not too bothered either way which of you cops it, so long as you pay up. Preferably in cash.'

Chapter Thirty-Two

Jess thought this was a nightmare from which she might never wake. She felt quite unable to fully grasp that Cora had killed Bernie. Dear lord, what a mess! So that was why they hadn't seen hide nor hair of him in all this time. Harry had said that they'd buried him in some bomb site. He'd clearly never been found or identified.

Worried as she was over how to deal with the matter, she couldn't let it lie. 'Is it true?' she asked Cora.

Barely pausing in the rolling of pastry for yet another pie, she calmly replied, 'Whatever Bernie got, he had it coming to him. Not fit to lick your boots, the nasty bugger.'

Jess sat staring at her aunt, dazed. She couldn't help wondering if the rolling pin she was using now for the pastry, was the self-same implement she'd used on him. 'Cora, tell me straight. Did you really do for him with that rolling pin?'

'Happen I'm stronger than I look. But like I say, he asked for it, great bully that he was. He'd no right to interfere with you in that way, no matter how drunk he were, or how far he managed to go — you know what I mean. I had to save you, lass, what else could I do?'

'Oh Cora, what can I say?'

'You could say good riddance to bad rubbish. I do, everyday.' By the determined set of her several chins, she clearly meant it. 'Put this behind you. You've got a new life now, not the one you intended to have, but there's not a blind bit of good in moping. What can't be cured must be endured.' As if this settled the matter, she rolled up the pastry lid onto the wooden pin and spread it neatly over the pie dish before trimming away the excess pastry with a very sharp knife.

Jess next put a suggestion to Harry, one she'd given careful thought to over a number of days. She chose late afternoon when the club was closed, knowing he'd be there polishing the glasses and counting his winnings.

As soon as he saw her through the glass of the door he eagerly went to let her in, even offered her a small sherry on the assumption she'd brought him the money.

'I knew you'd come round, that you'd see the sense in my request since you, of all people, wouldn't want to risk incarceration, let alone being hanged for something you didn't do.' He smirked at her, well pleased with himself.

Jess took the seat he offered at a small table and Harry sat opposite, quaffing beer in a self-satisfied way while she sipped quietly at her sherry. Eventually, Jess said, 'How would it be if I bought the place off you?'

He put down his glass. 'What did you say?'

'If you're not managing to make a go of this club, I'll buy it off you, take it off your hands. We'll agree a fair price. Get it independently valued with everything above board. I'll settle your debts, get whoever's putting pressure on you off your back once and for all, and you'll have enough left over to start again somewhere else.'

That way, Jess hoped, if he was free of debt and fear he might behave better towards his long-suffering wife. She could think of no other way to help her dearest friend, since Leah refused to admit there was even a problem.

Harry was looking at her as if she'd grown two heads, had gone mad or something. His eyes were dilated with shock, probably because he'd never imagined she was quite so well placed. His next words confirmed that. 'By heck, you like to throw your brass about. So you have made more money out of that band than Leah?'

'No, I told you, we took fair shares but I've saved mine whereas her earnings have been wasted by you. So, what do you say? It's a fair offer.'

'And what would you do with a club?' he sneered.

'I'd smarten it up and run dances here. Turn it into a decent place to visit instead of the dive it currently is. I'd have nothing to do with the kind of low-life you get involved with.' Jess dropped an envelope on the table. It lay between them like a gauntlet; a challenge. 'That's a down payment, to show good faith. It will no doubt take some time to get the legal wheels moving, so that'll help pacify whoever's pressing you for payment.'

Jess was no fool. She understood her cousin too well for that. He'd kept quiet all these years about his father's fate so that if he were ever in a tight spot he could use it to his advantage. Besides which, she'd had a quiet word with Bert and got herself filled in on the details.

Harry picked up the packet and weighed it in his hands. 'It's not enough.'

'It's all you're getting, for now. Get the place valued. Speak to your solicitor, if you can find one prepared to work for you, and you'll get the balance when the legal work goes through, and I may need to take a loan from the bank. In the meantime…' And here she leaned across the small table that divided them to look him directly in the eye. 'If I hear of you laying another finger on Leah, the deal's off, and Jimmy Doyle and his squaddies can have you for dinner. Got that?'

Whereupon, she got to her feet and walked calmly from the room, leaving Harry shouting and yelling after her that she couldn't bossily talk to him like that.

'I just did.'

–

Leah, quietly weeping into her handkerchief, wrapped her arms about her dear friend as the two girls sat on a cold stonewall.

'Life is so unfair. We came all through the war unscathed, only to ruin our lives with a stupid decision. You to give up Steve who adored you, all because of that dreadful attack by Bernie, and me to marry Bernie's equally dreadful son. What a mess we made of our lives.'

'We weren't to know,' Jess said at last. 'I did what I thought was for the best. I honestly believed that I could never be a proper wife to Steve. And I didn't want him to take me on out of pity.'

'I know, love. And I was potty about handsome Harry. Couldn't keep my hands off him. You at least married a gentleman, which is more than can be said for your nasty cousin.'

'Oh Leah, you don't know the half of it. How was I to know that Doug would take no interest in little Johnny? What can I do about that?'

Leah looked at her sadly, and gently stroked her arm. 'He's Steve's son, isn't he? Go on, you can say it because, deep down, you must now recognise he obviously is. Doug certainly does. That's the real reason why he loathes the poor little mite. I could have told you it was you he wanted, not a replacement son. But then you weren't in the mood to listen to common sense? Neither was I, far too determined to marry Harry Delaney, allowing no one to talk me out of it. Not my mother, Dad or Robert, who all did their best to make me see what I was letting myself in for. I wouldn't even listen to you, my best friend. Is it any wonder that it's all gone horribly wrong?'

'Do you realise, Leah, the Delaneys have ruined both our lives.'

'It would seem so.' Leah's eyes, which she'd only just mopped dry, filled again with a rush of tears.

Jess agreed, finding a role of tears sliding over her own cheeks. There was a small silence while both girls absorbed this fact and wept together.

'Is Harry very mean to you?'

'Serves me right if he is.'

'Serves us both right. No, we mustn't say such a thing. It isn't our fault at all. We can't have Harry treat you so badly. We must do something to stop him. I've tried to help by offering to buy the club off him and settle his debts that way.'

'Huh! He'd never agree to that. He loves to be in control.'

'Then tell me what else I can do?'

'What would you suggest? Give him a good talking to? Cora's tried that already and got nowhere with it.'

'You could leave him.'

'Where could I go, and how could I stop him from dragging me back and punishing me for showing him up? He might not love me but he needs me around, and he adores Susie. He'd never let me take her from him. I'd have to go right away where he couldn't ever find me, then I'd lose you, the band, and probably my mind.' Leah's tone was bleak and they clung together, weeping all the more, for they seemed to be utterly powerless.

'At least we have the pleasure of our girls's band,' Jess softly said. 'And we've received a new offer.'

'Thank goodness for that.'

–

To Doug's utter surprise and dismay, Jess announced that the band was going on tour. She hadn't even asked his permission.

'Will this be the last one?' he sourly asked, as she scooped cereal into little Johnny's mouth at breakfast.

Jess sighed. 'Of course not! Don't attempt to take my music away from me, please.'

But he persisted, asking what problems she could possibly have? 'You are my *wife*, for goodness's sake, and I am responsible for taking care of you.'

She simply looked up at him and laughed.

'Oh Doug, you're such an old fuddy-duddy. This is the end of the war, for goodness's sake, and a wife is entitled to make her own choice in life. Now do stop fussing. Cora will look after Johnny, as usual. She has to take Sam and Seb to the dentist this morning so she won't be back till around dinner time. But since you're on late shift, you can mind him for a few hours, then take him round to her later, as we've got to catch the ten-thirty bus as the first gig is in Birmingham, so we've a long journey ahead.'

'What! Why on earth are you travelling so far?'

To Jess, it felt irritable that she had to ask her husband to do this small task for her, as he never volunteered to help with Johnny. She gave a sigh.

'Why not? After Birmingham, over the next week or two we'll go on to Leicester, Wolverhampton, Rhyl, then back up to Preston. Ena has made the bookings and we're all thrilled to bits. Our first real tour. So exciting! But don't worry, we'll be back here in Manchester this Thursday and, as I say, Cora will take care of Johnny.'

'Thursday?' He firmly insisted that simply wasn't possible, that she must stay home and behave as a good wife should.

She listened patiently to his outburst, then patted his cheek and reminded him not to forget to wear his scarf when he went off to work, as the mornings were turning quite nippy. Having packed all the necessary belongings for her child, she gave him a kiss and a hug, then within minutes, she was gone.

Left alone in the kitchen with this child, the one he'd had to accept as part of the bargain in order to get Jess to be his wife, Doug glared at the boy, sitting there in sublime ignorance, grinning good naturedly as he happily banged a spoon on his high chair. This in fact was definitely *not* his responsibility. He'd expected her to have it adopted, as she'd admitted she might before the creature was born. But then she'd changed her mind and insisted on keeping it.

Why had Jess risked being constantly reminded of that unspeakable assault by keeping this child? Respectably, a marriage in name only was what he'd agreed upon. He'd certainly had no wish to venture into intimacy with a woman sullied and despoiled by her own uncle. It had suited him perfectly, but he could now be changing his mind. It had suited her even more, but she was too obsessed with playing music, and not a good wife. It was one thing to play for the Salvation Army, quite another to make an exhibition of herself in front of all those men. And she was paramount about providing herself with independence.

He really wasn't having that.

In no time at all, Doug had Johnny dressed in his coat and strapped in to his perambulator, then took him round to Cumberland Street. As Jess had predicted there was no sign of Cora. The kitchen was empty save for Lizzie, who sat with her skinny legs dangling over the arm of her battered old chair, smoking one of her endless cigarettes. He could tell by the glazed look in her eyes that she'd had a few drinks, even if he hadn't noticed the bottle poking out from under the cushion beside her. The room, as ever, was suffocatingly hot with a fire half way up the chimney and an all-pervading sour smell of boiled cabbage and human sweat. Doug wheeled the pram in, parked it beside her and said in a loud voice, as if addressing an idiot.

'I've fetched the child, as arranged. Cora knows all about it. I've got one or two jobs to do before I go off to work, so I'll leave him with you, all right?'

Minutes later he was out in the street, a free man. He'd no intention of being ruled by Jess, much as he relished her lovely face, the way she moved and the softness of her breasts, whenever he found the opportunity to touch her.

The tour was going well. They were playing in ballrooms where the great Joe Loss himself had played, plus other illustrious names such as Oscar Rabin and Jack Parnell. Jess idolised famous band leaders such as Benny Goodman, Tommy Dorsey and Ivy Benson, hoping to follow in their successful footsteps. Ena had already got them a substantial booking in the Isle of Man for the summer, and another in Brighton over Christmas, which wouldn't please Doug one bit, but was so exciting. Jess couldn't understand why he was being so difficult, yet was determined not to let him get her down. The war was over and this was a new beginning for them all. Who knew what they might achieve?

All the girls were equally thrilled with their success, looking forward to their first tour with eager anticipation. They didn't mind if the digs were a bit seedy, if ration books and points were still the order of the day. There was a great optimism in the air and even Miss Mona, thumping out the rhythm on her double bass with gusto would often cry, 'Today Manchester. Tomorrow, the world.'

They played well, then stepped down for the next band. Jess could hardly believe it when she again heard the play of a saxophone, and saw that it was Steve. He fortunately didn't see her, being huddled in the shadows with Adele, Lulu and the other girls. She could slip away and hide in the dressing room until it was time for them to go on again, except that she couldn't bring herself to do that. With memories of the last dance they'd ever had together ringing in her head, Jess turned on her heels and fled.

Outside, she drew in great gulps of clear night air, desperate to block out the potent images tormenting her brain. How could she find the courage to go back inside, trying to decide in agony whether she could ever face him, let alone speak of her reality. It was some moments later that she heard Steve's voice.

'Jess? Is that you?'

She stared at him in shocked disbelief. His face looked tired, drawn and sad and yet his eyes were alight, as if he couldn't quite believe he was seeing her. 'I never knew your band would be playing tonight, till you got up on that stage and played like an angel. If it's possible, Jess, you're even better at that task than you were. And you're still playing my trumpet. I felt so proud. But when you dashed out, were you running away from me yet again?'

She could find no answer, nor even her own voice. Just hearing Steve speak her name and finding him here filled her with desire. How she longed to reach out and touch him. Yet it was not appropriate for her to do that, seeing him again was almost more than she could bear.

He took another tentative step towards her, said her name again, barely more than a whisper this time but it was enough. 'Oh, I've missed you so much, Jess. God, you'll never know how much.' And taking her in his arms he kissed her with a passion she could not resist. How was that possible when she'd only ever loved Steve? It was the most wonderful moment in her life.

Stroking her cheek, he said, 'Don't leave me ever again! Seeing you run off, darling, I slipped offstage longing to find you, and was given details of your problem from Leah. Despite what that damned uncle of yours did to you, according to Cora he didn't successfully rape you because she hit him, and put an end to his dreadful assault, thank the lord. So this child you have is apparently mine, not his. I love you so much I'm thrilled to learn this fact, remembering when and why we happily made love.'

Overwhelmed by what he was saying, Jess no longer felt any guilt or shame, only joy and a beautiful, burgeoning happiness. Being madly in love, it must be the most natural thing in the world for them to be together, even though to Jess it seemed like a miracle. Why had she ever imagined that Bernie's assault could come between them, or that it would make her less of a woman? She must have been mad and certainly not thinking clearly. Or else Steve's great love for her had cured her of the horrors of that night. She didn't care a jot about Doug, and so wished she hadn't married him. All that mattered was that she was now in Steve's arms, and the joy that he was telling her he still loved her.

Only ever having loved this man, when their performances were finally over, she went with him to his hotel room and laid beside him in his bed. Jess felt as if this was the most natural thing in the world for them to be together, even though it seemed like a miracle.

At first, each afraid of making a mistake, they'd been content to simply gaze at each other, quite unable to stop smiling, so delighted to be together. Growing bolder, they'd blissfully begun to explore these newly awakened emotions, which grew ever more powerful and intense. They felt no guilt, no shame. They belonged together, always had and always would. Yes, they'd both cried a little over being so long separated, driven apart by events, but as they became more relaxed their emotions sated, it had simply become blissful to relish their desire and love for each other. Their night of lovemaking was wonderful, tender and slightly hesitant. Jess could feel only joy and a beautiful, burgeoning happiness.

Steve's single bed proved to be quite inadequate, and covers and pillows were tossed aside, or slid of their own accord to the floor. Jess fell asleep in Steve's arms and when he accidentally rolled off the narrow bed, waking up with a bump, the young lovers laughed till the tears rolled down their cheeks. Their senses stirred, they couldn't resist kissing and making love all over again, till finally they fell into a deep sleep of fulfilled contentment, arms and legs entwined about each other, clinging on tight.

Only Leah knew where to find her, having been quietly informed by Jess that she meant to spend the night with Steve at his digs, so it was her old friend who woke her from this blissful reunion with a heavy hammering on the door early in the morning. As Steve staggered from the bed to fling it open, she stood framed within it, fighting for breath and quite unable to speak. Then Jess could hardly believe it when Leah said that Johnny had been taken to hospital, fighting for his life.

Chapter Thirty-Three

Jess feared she would never forgive herself for deserting her beloved child. How could she selfishly consider her music to be important? She didn't deserve to be forgiven, or to have been blessed with him. How could she have been so stupid as to trust Doug, when she knew only too well how little he cared about her precious son? Were her baby to die what reason would she have to go on living?

'Will he be all right? Will he live?' Jess asked the well meaning nurse for the hundredth time that night, as she came to report on little Johnny's progress. 'Tell me he's going to survive.'

'We're doing our best to make sure of that, Mrs Morgan.'

'Do remember how delicate he is, he's only a young boy. Please, take good care of him.'

'We will, dear, don't fret. But you must keep calm. The doctors can do a great deal these days, with burns. That's one good thing that has come about after this terrible war.'

Jess felt sick at the thought of her tiny baby suffering what so many of those poor pilots had. She prayed for her child, the doctor and all the nurses; prayed as she had never prayed before. She bargained with God, sobbed and pleaded, promising to be a much better wife and mother in future, if he would please save her son. All she could do was hope Johnny would be spared.

And then she heard the full, unexpurgated story of the accident and her distress turned to anger. She could feel the rage boiling up inside her like a furnace about to explode. She heard how Doug had left the boy with a drunken Lizzie and, growing quickly bored with the lack of attention, little Johnny had leaned closer to the old Lancashire range where the stock pan sat simmering on the metal hob before the fire. Cora boiled the goodness from bones in there, and added vegetables from time to time. Perhaps fascinated by the steam as it rose from the boiling water, he'd made a grab for the handle and the pan and its contents fell all over himself.

The doctors had told her the little boy was fairly fortunate, that it could have been much worse. But his poor little feet, his hands and arms, were badly scalded and would need expert treatment, perhaps skin grafts eventually. He was being given expert care, put on plenty of fluids, but Jess had been told that the shock alone could badly affect him.

'How could you have been so unmindful of his well-being to leave him with Lizzie?' she roared at Doug. 'Don't you know well enough what a feckless, useless drunkard she is? She can't even look after herself properly, let alone a child. How could you be so stupid?'

For once Doug looked ashenfaced, as if the accident had shocked him to the core and left him shaken and stunned. Then in a stubborn way he compressed his mouth into a thin, hard line, as if he resented this accusation. 'If you'd been at home where you belong, there wouldn't have been a problem.'

'You only needed to mind him till dinner time. Was that too much to ask? Why couldn't you at least do that for me?'

Doug turned away and folded his arms, offering no apology, apparently unwilling to accept the blame. Even in the depths of despair, Jess felt guilt rage through her yet again for not taking her child earlier to Cora. Steve had wanted to come with her when they'd first been told the news, but she'd said that it wouldn't be right for him and Doug to meet. It would be like putting a match to tinder. Jess had been utterly distraught, not even certain what she was going to find when she and Leah got to the hospital, yet believed that allowing these two men to meet was more than she could cope with.

–

Jess felt such resentment towards her stupid mother who had blighted her life. She could clearly remember the cold dampness of the cellar, the fear of being buried alive. And as if ruining her own young life wasn't bad enough, Lizzie had now damaged that of her beloved son. Unable to help herself while they sat in the waiting room, she railed at her mother, as if a lifetime of complaints bubbled to the surface.

'What kind of useless mother are you that you can't take care of your own grandchild? I expect you were drunk, as usual. Don't you ever think of anyone or anything besides yourself? So help me, I'll swing for you one day, I swear it. When have you ever been anything but a useless—'

Leah grasped Jess's hands to pull her away from Lizzie, fearful of what the two might do to each other. She'd never seen her friend so distressed, oblivious to the tears coursing down her face, and to anyone else's feelings but her own, all because of the terrible fear growing inside her friend that she might lose her son. Leah spoke to her in a calm, gentle voice, 'Sit down, Jess love. Relax. This isn't the moment to be casting blame. Let's wait till we hear what the doctors have to say, shall we? I'll fetch you a nice cup of tea.'

And so they waited. All night long: Jess, Doug, Leah, Cora, and even Sandra, who'd loved her little cousin to bits, she said, choking back tears.

Lizzie had been the one to call for help from the neighbours, although it had taken Ma Pickles's son, Josh, to run and phone for an ambulance, Lizzie herself far too inebriated to cope. Ma Pickles had not accompanied them to the hospital as she'd been left to wait in for Cora, and later had stayed on to care for Sam and Seb. For the first time in her life, Cora gave no thought to her own children, nor did she attempt to solve the problem by providing food for everyone. This was all quite beyond her. She sat in silent contemplation, eyes deep and fathomless, holding tight to Jess's hand.

Lizzie had sat in silence for hours, her eyes wide and blank, but then for no apparent reason began whimpering like an injured kitten, a sound which gradually increased in volume as the night wore on. She grew ever more restless, probably more in need of a drink, till finally she launched into a full-throated wail.

'Can't you shut her up?' Doug asked Jess, clearly embarrassed by his mother-in-law's wild behaviour. He gave the impression that he'd never wanted either the child or this woman, stating he'd be damned if he'd put up with any more disruption to his calm and quiet life. 'What good are we all doing, sitting about here? Get your coat on, Jess. It's time we went home.'

'No! You go, I'm staying. My child needs me and I don't need you, or my drunken mother!'

Lizzie swivelled about and screamed at Jess, lashing out at her with her fingernails. 'You're the devil's spawn. Get out of my sight! I don't want you either! Bane of my life you are. Go, go, go!'

A plump little nurse came hurrying along the corridor like a steam train to inform them in furiously hushed tones how, if they didn't keep Lizzie quiet and make her behave, they would all have to leave. She pointed out what a huge favour the hospital was doing allowing them to stay, all due to the kind heart of the doctor.

In the end, far from being able to shut her up, Lizzie's wails grew to fever pitch, and she began wandering down the corridor, frantically knocking and scrabbling at doors, even opening them, as if seeking someone, though no one could be sure what or who that was. Each of them attempted to coax her back with bribes of tea and biscuits, all to no avail. After barely two seconds she would jump to her feet and go off again, wailing like the proverbial banshee and growing ever more demented. She didn't seem to understand where she was, or why she had come here.

Fighting off Jess's frantic attempt to lead her once more back to her seat, she began shrieking and screaming. 'Where's Bernie? I need him. Fetch him for me.'

'We've lost him, as you damn well know. But I'm his wife, not you,' Cora said. 'By heck, you've lost all sense.'

The nurse agreed and Lizzie was gently rounded up like a stray cat and taken away to some nether region of the hospital, where she would receive the care she needed.

'By which they mean knock-out drops of the non-alcoholic variety,' said Cora, drily. 'Happen we can all get a bit of peace now.'

By morning, Johnny was showing definite signs of improvement, but it was carefully explained to Jess that the burns would take time to heal and there was always the risk of infection. It would be some weeks before he fully recovered but was now out of danger.

'Thank God for that.'

Several other friends called in that day, including the girls from the band, and Harriet and Sergeant Ted on their way home from the mission. They all in turn offered what comfort they could, would pace the floor with Jess for a while, or simply hold her close in a silent hug. Then finally left her in peace and Jess was allowed to visit her child for a short time, before being packed off back to the waiting room where she would sit, feeling numb, as if she'd slipped from reality into another world.

When ordered to go home for a rest that evening, she found Steve waiting for her outside the hospital. He held her close and gave her a warm, loving hug, saying that he'd spoken to Cora. 'She has confirmed that little Johnny is my son!'

Jess gave a weak smile, aware that keeping her baby a secret from him had been entirely the wrong decision, and now mere trivia in the face of their child's dangerous condition. 'I was never sure of what Bernie did to me, and assumed Johnny was the consequence of his assault. But he has grown to look so much like you, Steve, with red-brown hair and hazel green eyes so I do now believe that he is your son.'

'Then for God's sake Jess, I desperately want to be with you to see him tomorrow.'

'That could be a little inappropriate. I'll let you know the moment he shows the sign of recovery. Be patient, my love, please.'

—

When Leah reached home in the late morning, Harry was waiting for her.

'Have you been seeing a fancy man? Is that where you've been this last day and night?'

'Not at all! I've been with Jess at the hospital.' She began to tell him about little Johnny's accident, but he wasn't listening. He carried on shouting and roaring at her and Leah turned from him in disgust. Worn out and tired from the long bus journey, traumatised by the long night of waiting and drained from helping Jess cope with the guarded optimism of the hospital, all she wanted to do was drop into bed and sleep.

Harry followed her into the bedroom, still yelling. 'I heard all about that Steve character having it off with Jess.'

Leah was surprised. 'How did you hear?'

'It's common knowledge. The gossip is all over the pub. Cheap little tart. Is that what you get up to on these gigs? Shaming us all.' He'd been furious that Jess had turned the tables on him by insisting she only give him money in return for ownership of the club. Why wasn't she respectful of him like other folk? It didn't make sense. How dare the trollop defy him? True, the down-payment, as she termed it, had allowed him to fend off

Jimmy for a bit but he couldn't go on in this fashion. He was going to have to accept her terms, or go under. The electricity board were threatening to cut off the electric and the phone had already been disconnected. How could a chap do business with such problems on his hands? And Jimmy would be back tomorrow, demanding the rest of his dosh.

To add insult to injury, his wife had turned up late and hadn't even been paid for that tour away from home. Some tale about Jess not having had time to deal with that. All excuses, in Harry's opinion. God knows what the little tarts got up to. He was having none of it.

'What kind of a mother are you?' he shouted, pleased when Leah cowered away from him, recognising that he still held the power. Perhaps now was the moment to reinforce that fact. Harry hadn't allowed her to take baby Susie on tour with her, insisting that he could look after his daughter very well himself in the club. Not that he was terribly good at that, but there were always plenty of women around to help. Now he made it clear that if she transgressed, she'd never see her child again.

Leah began to tremble, the thought of losing Susie didn't bear thinking about. That must never happen. She attempted a reassuring smile, usually the best way to placate him when he was in one of his bad moods, since he hated tears.

'Don't be silly, of course I haven't been seeing anyone. Why would I want to have a fancy man when I've got you and little Susie. I wouldn't take the risk of losing her, you can be sure of that, Harry.'

Sometimes it didn't seem to matter what she did or said: whether she pleaded, teased or begged, he seemed to be beyond reason, his course of action as unstoppable as an express train. So it was on this occasion. He punched her with his fist right in the stomach; a favourite spot since no one could see the bruises, then pushed her face down on the bed, ripped off her clothes and drove into her with the kind of unremitting force that had nothing at all do with love.

'That'll teach you not to make a cuckold of me.'

'But I didn't…!'

'Shut your mouth. That's what you'll get again if you ever do.'

Apparently satisfied that he'd brought her to heel and properly subdued her, he stormed out of the flat, and it wasn't hard to guess where he was going.

–

So this was married life. Little more than two years into it, and the mere prospect of spending the rest of her life with this brute, was driving Leah to the brink of insanity. Lying weeping on the bed, nursing the latest in a long line of sores and bruises, she wondered what on earth she'd ever seen in him? What had happened to the handsome, teasing, flirtatious man she'd married? Where was the love, the care, the cheerful banter, the excitement and fun they'd once enjoyed together? It had all gone, or else had never existed in the first place and he'd tricked her, been playing a game till he had her in his thrall, able to do with her what he wished, including turning her into a thief.

Leah had known for quite a while about his empire of tarts who came and went with dizzying regularity in the club below. She'd gone looking for him one night and found him in bed with a young girl who still looked as if she should be in school. At first she'd been upset, screamed and railed, feeling betrayed and degraded at sharing her husband with a prostitute. 'Don't think you can come to me, after you've slept with such creatures,' she'd shrieked at him, but Harry had only laughed.

'Why would it matter? They don't object to you.'

'I'm your *wife*! I deserve better.'

'You should be thankful for what you get. I'm considered quite a catch round here. Anyroad, don't worry, love, I'll not see you go short.' And he'd slammed her up against the wall, ripped open her blouse, pushed up her skirt to take her there and then on the top landing, in full view of the silly little whore.

'Whoops, spare my blushes,' the girl had said, and gone off giggling.

Leah had ceased to care what he did after that. At least while Harry was tasting their favours, he was leaving her alone.

All Harry thought about now – perhaps all he'd ever cared about – was the club, apart from himself, that is. And all he talked about was how he could get more money. Leah knew that cash dribbled through his fingers like water. Now that lights were allowed once again, he left them on all the time and ran up huge electricity bills. He gave the tenants too much time to pay their rents because they were often his only customers in the bar, and he needed them around. And the illegal card school met less frequently these days, now that so many of the GIs were returning home. They'd never been particularly troubled about rules and regulations during the war, perfectly willing to take a risk for the sake of a bit of fun to liven those difficult times. Other servicemen had joined in for the same reason, along with more nefarious characters, the kind Harry would have been wiser not to have in the club at all.

Now men were going home to their families, trying to take up life where they'd left off six years earlier, or start new ones. They were busy finding themselves jobs, opening businesses, thrilled by the prospect of peace and filled with hope for the future. This left Harry with the dross, not only making less profit but also with the kind of customer who didn't like to wait to get paid, if money was due to them. Leah knew that her husband was finding himself in a tight corner, with gambling and liquor bills to pay and not enough money coming in. This made him a loose canon, and who knew what he might do next?

Chapter Thirty-Four

Jess sat by her son's bedside for hours on end day after day, frequently defying the nurses whenever they tried to shoo her out and send her home.

'Rules are rules. They have to be kept,' the stern, plump nurse would say. 'We don't want little Johnny to get an infection, now do we? Visiting is two o'clock until three each day, not a minute more. Now you must go home, Mrs Morgan, and get some rest yourself.'

In Jess's opinion she no longer had a home to go to. Her one, all-consuming desire was for Johnny to get well again. What would happen after that, she didn't know, and really didn't care. And so she went to Cora, pacing her floor, paying no attention to the comings and goings of children in the little house, refusing to eat, growing thinner by the day in her anguish, till finally, alerted by Cora to her plight, Steve came for her and took charge.

'You're wasting away, Jess. What good will you be then to Johnny? Come with me, love. Let me take care of you.' And, with deep and loving thankfulness, she did.

It was six weeks before the baby was allowed home, by which time Jess's marriage was over. She'd left Doug, given up all pretence of their being a happy couple, and had moved in with Steve. If this was wrong, then so be it. To Jess's way of thinking, they belonged together and who better to care for the pair of them, than Johnny's own father. To see this father and son together at last, filled her with an indescribable joy. How on earth she could have believed that this precious boy was anyone else's but Steve's was beyond belief. How very foolish she'd been. Just seeing them together confirmed that Cora had been right all along. Johnny was clearly Steve's son, same hair, same smile, even the tilt of his head. And it was wonderful to see them taking such delight in each other.

'Forget the past,' Steve told her. 'We can put all those mistakes behind us and begin again.'

'What about Doug? We're still married, don't forget.'

'I love you. We're together. That's all that really counts.'

And best of all, Johnny was on the mend, the end of the poor little boy's misery was at last in sight. His scars would take a little time to heal but he was strong, straight and firm, and it was all too evident that he was eager to walk. He was constantly trying to pull himself up by the table leg or a chair arm.

Jess remained consumed by guilt and lost interest in everything else, including her precious band. Bernie and Doug had tried, for different reasons, to stop her playing her trumpet, now her son's accident had destroyed all hope in her. She locked it away and declared that she would never pick it up again. 'No more music. If I hadn't put the needs of the band before those of my own child, then he wouldn't be in the condition he's in now.'

Everyone: Cora, Leah, Steve, and all the girls in the band, insisted that this was nonsense, that she was not to blame, and had brought Johnny with her whenever possible. But she refused to listen. From now on she meant to be a full-time mother. If there was to be a new beginning, she wanted it to be as perfect as possible. She longed to be free to marry Steve. Besides, though she hadn't told him yet, she suspected she was again pregnant.

She went to see Doug and began by apologising for the unhappiness she had caused him. 'I should never have agreed to marry you in the first place when I was in love with Steve and was clearly going to bear his child. I'm so sorry. My only excuse is that at the time I believed Johnny was Bernie's. I can see now that wasn't the case, as he didn't manage to fully rape me, thanks to Cora. It's Steve that Johnny resembles, not Bernie, who's thankfully vanished,' she added, giving no details of what had truly happened to her uncle. 'Steve and I, having found each other again, we wish to marry and be a proper family, so I'm asking you to release me, and give me my freedom.'

Doug looked at her for a long moment, then smiled and said, 'I forgive you for blaming me, Jess. I appreciate that you were upset so there's no need for you to apologise. I won't bear you any grudge for this silly little fling you've had with that dreadful musician. You're still my wife and, so far as I'm concerned, always will be, so there's absolutely no necessity for you to consider leaving. You, and – little Johnny – are welcome to stay. This is your rightful home, after all. Now, what are you making me for my tea, dear?'

Jess stared at him, aghast. 'You haven't heard a word I've said, have you? You can't even say my child's name without stumbling over it.' Giving him a dismissive look she walked out the door. Divorce or no divorce, she'd no intention of ever coming back.

–

It was one night just before midnight that Leah dragged herself out of bed and went to make herself a mug of hot milk. Harry was either out gambling, or sleeping with one of his girls, as usual. She never asked what he was up to or where he'd been, as she really had no wish to know, let alone irritate him by asking for details. The flat felt empty and silent, deeply depressing. She went and checked on baby Susie, fast asleep on her stomach in her crib. Leah's heart softened with love for her child. If only there were some way of getting free of Harry Delaney, making an escape to a place where he'd never find her.

The trouble was, she didn't have any money, which galled her somewhat as she'd earned plenty from the band but had been forced to hand over every penny to her greedy husband. A thought struck her. There was no safe, so perhaps he'd hid it somewhere. Surely he didn't gamble it all away. If she could find enough money tucked away some place, she'd take Susie and run. They could go to Liverpool and catch the ferry to Ireland. Somewhere far away from Harry Delaney, where he would never think to look. No matter what the cost, she couldn't go on like this any longer. She'd had enough.

Leah began searching drawers, tugging them out and riffling through them at reckless speed, frequently glancing over her shoulder, afraid that he might return at any moment and catch her in the act of plundering his belongings. She went through every pocket of his suits, even climbed up to examine the top of the wardrobe, but could find nothing. As she stood on the stool looking around the bedroom from this unusual angle, she noticed one of the floorboards under the bed. It was a slightly different colour from all the rest and not quite so neatly fitted.

Quickly, she jumped down, tossed aside a pegged rug which partially obscured it and tried to prise it up with her fingernails. It took a kitchen knife and finally a screw driver, before she managed to lift up the board. Beneath it she found a box hidden in the dusty depths, quite small and square. Pulling open the lid, Leah stared in surprise and horror at the contents. A cameo brooch and a pretty blue necklace, which she instantly recognised as jewellery her aunt had given her as a present on her return from a holiday in Madeira. These precious items had been stolen during that long ago air raid. It was then that she heard the door bang.

'What the bleedin' hell do you think you're doing?'

When Harry knocked her flying this time, she was quite unable to get up, and darkness filled her.

Harry was quite certain that he'd killed her. And if he had, he'd ruined everything. There was no way that Jess would give in to his demands, not if he'd done for her best friend. In which case he'd be forced to hand over the club, else how would he settle his debts with Jimmy? He couldn't even use this flaming jewellery to get him out of trouble. He'd already been offered a derisory sum for the brooch and the necklace was glass, a worthless trinket, its only value pure sentiment. He looked down at the inert body of his wife with open contempt.

'Hardly worth dying for, you stupid cow.'

It was then that it finally sank in that paying off his debts was the least of his worries. Harry really had no wish to feel the hangman's rope about his neck. In the circumstances, he did the only logical thing. He ran.

Chapter Thirty-Five

1947

The lights were turned down low. Outside, snow was softly falling in what was proving to be the coldest winter on record, but here in a warm, cosy room on Deansgate, Delaney's All Girls Band were playing a medley of their most requested numbers. They'd begun, as always, with 'Don't Sit Under The Apple Tree', wandered down memory lane through all the old wartime hits such as 'Wish Me Luck' and 'Bye Bye Blackbird', then rip-roared their way through several more old favourites including 'Pennsylvania 65000' and 'Chattanooga Choo Choo'. The customers were now jiving to 'In The Mood' as the girls put all their hearts and souls into the number.

As always on the nights when he wasn't on stage himself in some dance hall or other, Steve was seated at the back with his arm about Jess.

'They're good, these girls in your band, nearly playing as well as you used to.' She'd kept to the vow she'd made and not touched her trumpet since the day Johnny had been scalded. Steve, along with the other band members, friends and family, had tried every way they could think of to persuade her to play. He was trying again now.

'Think of the waste. What would Mr Yoffey have to say about you neglecting such a God-given talent?' They both still remembered with great affection the old man who had sadly ended his days in the Isle-of-Man Alien's camp, but at least had lived a long and happy life and been instrumental in bringing them together.

Jess remained adamant. 'Talented or not, there's no reason why I should play, considering the damage it caused.'

Steve patiently reminded her that their son was not only fully recovered but a lively youngster who never sat still for a minute, tearing around the place as if to make up for all those sedentary, painful weeks he'd spent in hospital. His new young sister, Caroline, clearly adored him and was desperately trying to catch up.

'Yes, but look at what it did to Lizzie, spending all those months incarcerated in a mental institution where they fed her pills and potions, gave her cold baths and goodness knows what electrotherapy treatment. It doesn't bear thinking of. No wonder she went off her head, raving like a maniac or slumped in depression. The poor woman didn't know where she was, or why she was there, feeling locked up again, having served time in jail. Hadn't she suffered enough?'

'It probably saved her life, Jess. She'd have died of alcohol poisoning otherwise. You know she would.'

'Oh, you're probably right, but it took forever.'

Steve gave up the argument, as he usually did, and called out for the girls to play his all time favourite, 'I'll Be Seeing You'. 'That was the night I first told you that I loved you, and you responded by running away and marrying another man.'

372

Jess had never again gone cap in hand to beg Doug for a divorce. She'd sent letters, both from herself personally and via her solicitor. All had been ignored. In the end, she'd given up the campaign and settled for what she had. She and Steve had been considered to be quite a Bohemian couple, both musicians with two children, happily living together as a family and running what was quickly developing into one of Manchester's favourite night-spots, though still unwed.

Then one day Steve had informed her that he'd succeeded in persuading Doug to face reality and free her, and going down on his knee, he'd said, 'Please darling, will you marry me? I love you so much I'm thrilled to remember when and why we happily first made love, and the beautiful children we have.'

'Oh, yes please.'

Wrapping herself in his arms to accept more kisses, her heart pounded with desire. At last she'd become his wife, which filled her with joy and a beautiful, burgeoning happiness. Thankfully, she no longer felt any guilt or shame, and Steve's love for her had cured her of the horrors of Bernie's assault. They belonged together, always had and always would.

Deep down Jess appreciated how fortunate she was, but poor Leah had suffered two broken ribs and a broken cheekbone, spending weeks in hospital and needing two operations before they were certain she'd ever be able to see or move again. Jess had sworn never to speak to her cousin Harry again, were she ever to come across him.

The word was that, like his father before him, he'd done a runner and vanished. Only Cora, Bert and Jess knew the truth that Bernie hadn't run anywhere. Harry Delaney hadn't been sighted in Deansgate Village from that day to this. Legend had it that he never did pay his debts, that Jimmy and his brigade of ex-squaddies were still keeping an eye open for him, just in case he ever ventured back on their territory. Jess and Steve had paid them off, moved into the flat and taken over the club. They sacked the prostitutes, completely refurbished the place and due to much hard work and endeavour, it was now thriving.

Leah, having made a good recovery from her dreadful injuries, occupied two of the best rooms above the club, together with her daughter, Susie. Lizzie occupied one as a bedsit. A shadow of her former self, rumour had it that she never touched a drop of the hard stuff these days. Didn't dare, for fear Jess would turn her out in the street. Although they were said to be largely reconciled, Lizzie wasn't taking any chances.

Cora remained contentedly in Cumberland Street with her twins and Sandra, now quite a young woman who was causing her mother endless bother. Young Tommy was back in the fold after the war, with his new wife happily expecting their first child. Cora could hardly wait for a new addition to the Delaney flock, always willing to mind Jess or Leah's children for an hour or two, and was a frequent visitor to her son Bert's house where his wife, Maisie, had recently delivered her third son. Cora was in seventh heaven. The Delaneys, she thought, were going from strength to strength.

Tonight, Jess was shocked when she saw Lizzie leap to her feet, while Cora looked frantically across at Jess, to see if she'd noticed who her mother was staring at.

Putting one hand on Steve's shoulder for support, Jess said, 'I don't believe it. Dad, is that you?' She moved slowly forward, her face chalkwhite, as if she were seeing a ghost.

The man in the door turned when he heard the sound of her voice, and a smile lit him, crinkling his eyes in that old familiar way she loved so much, though the face was one in which the bones stood out sharply, ravaged by starvation and the result of an incarceration neither his wife, nor his loving daughter could ever fully understand.

'Jess love, how are you?' Jake wrapped his arms about her, blessing the angels who had guarded him all these years, just so he could return and see his lovely daughter again. Tears flowed but neither suffered any embarrassment, or paid any heed to the sighs and warm whispers of their audience. They clung to each other, laughed and wept, then stood back and marvelled.

'I can't believe it's really you.'

'It is me for sure, love! And you look a right little cracker. Always knew you'd turn out that way. Eeh, hello Lizzie lass, you're looking... well.' Only Jess noticed the pause and look of shock in his eyes.

Lizzie herself appeared utterly stunned by the return of her husband, and almost as worn out by time as he was, if for a very different reason. But Jake's attention was back with his daughter who was now introducing him excitedly to Steve, telling him of her children asleep upstairs with their nanny, then asked how he'd managed to find her. Jake was laughing at this deluge of information.

'I found you because this club of yours bears my name. And I understood that this was your band, so why aren't you up there playing in it?'

Jess looked at him in wonder for another half minute, vaguely aware of Steve's voice softly remarking, 'Good question. Why aren't you up there, Jess?'

And suddenly Jess knew that she must play for Steve and her dad, who had first taught her the beauty and magic of music. Her fingers were itching to touch the valves, her lips poised to coax liquid gold from her precious instrument. But where had she put it that long time ago?

'Oh dear, where's my trumpet?'

'Whose trumpet?'

'All right, *your* trumpet. Where is it? Please may I borrow it one more time.'

'With pleasure,' Steve grinned, bringing it out from behind his back and handing it to her, rather like a magician pulling a rabbit from a hat.

Jess couldn't help but laugh, before kissing him with beloved thanks. 'You've had it waiting every time the girls went on stage, haven't you?'

'I certainly have. Hoping for the day you saw sense and finally erased your panic.'

Jess took her rightful place on stage.

'This is for my dad,' she told her attentive audience. 'He's been away a long time, like many of you here tonight he's been kept from these shores against his will, being a PoW. Now he's safely back home, having travelled across an ocean to hear me play. I might be a bit rusty but if I can remember which button to press on this thing, I'll give it a go.' She sent a radiant smile to these two men in her life, and then lifted the trumpet to her lips and began to play: 'I'll be seeing you, in all the old familiar places...'

There wasn't a dry eye in the house as they listened and applauded her. Jess had been reborn.

A Salford Saga

Ruby McBride
The Favourite Child
The Castlefield Collector
Dancing on Deansgate